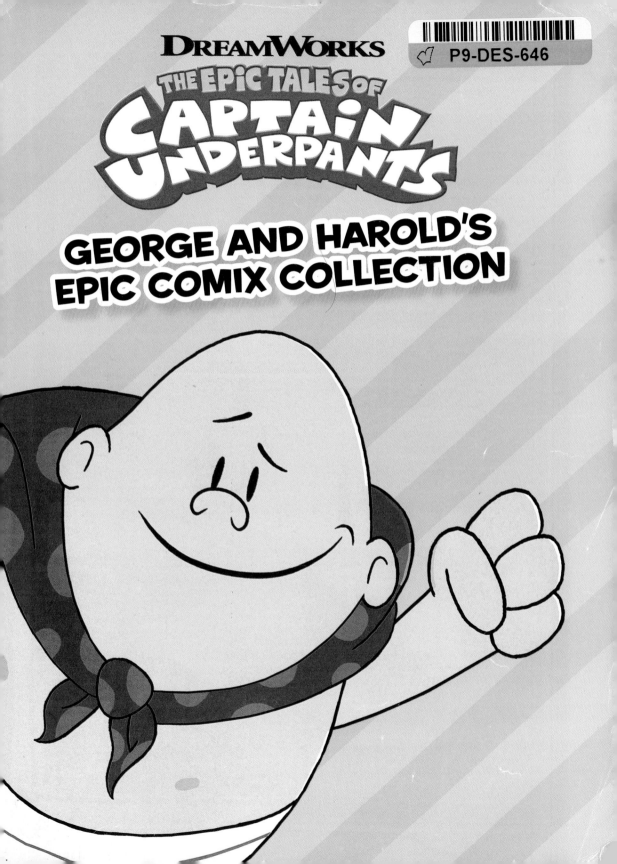

THE EPIC TALES OF CAPTAIN UNDERPANTS

DREAMWORKS

GEORGE AND HAROLD'S EPIC COMIX COLLECTION

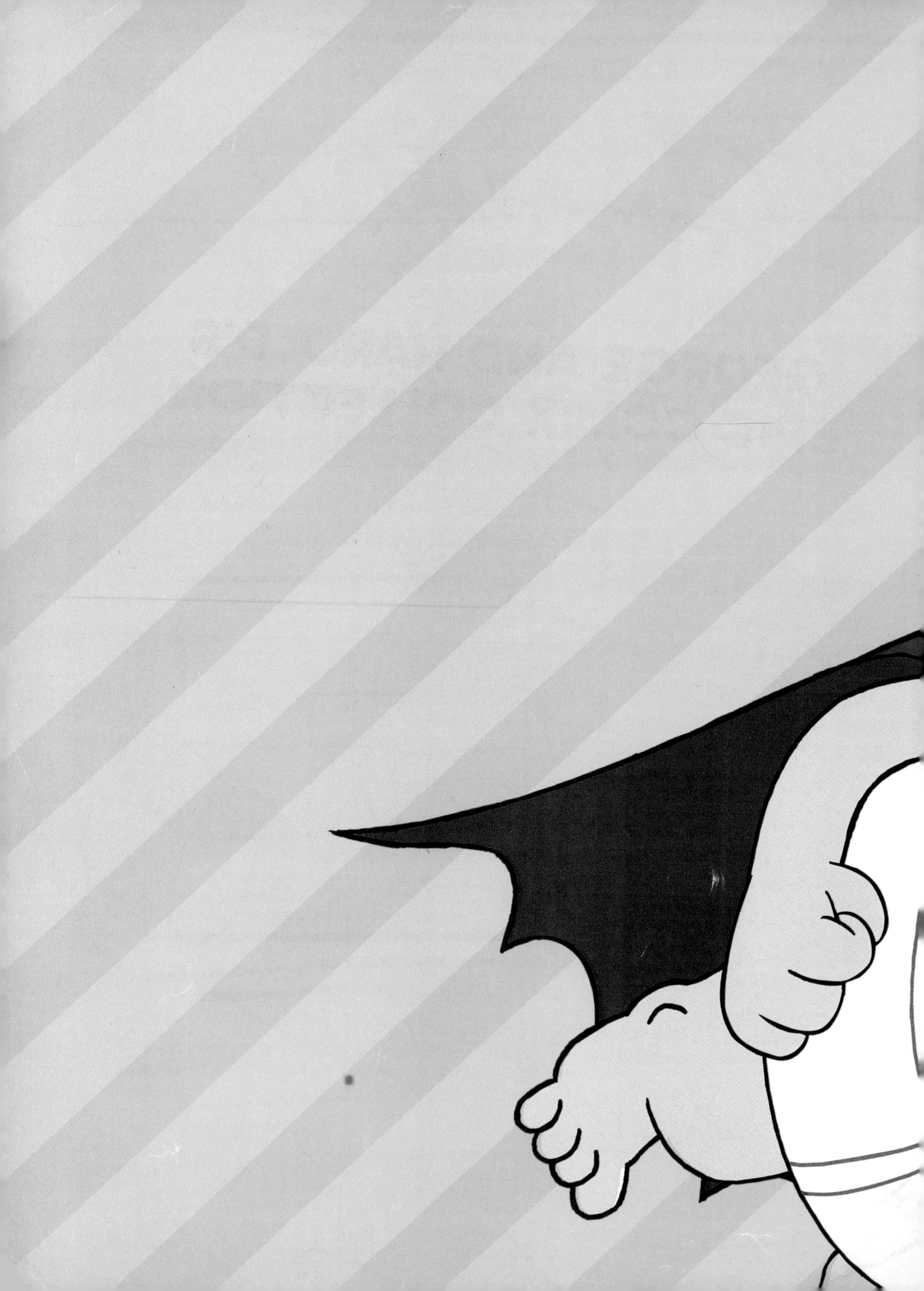

DREAMWORKS

THE EPIC TALES OF CAPTAIN UNDERPANTS

GEORGE AND HAROLD'S EPIC COMIX COLLECTION

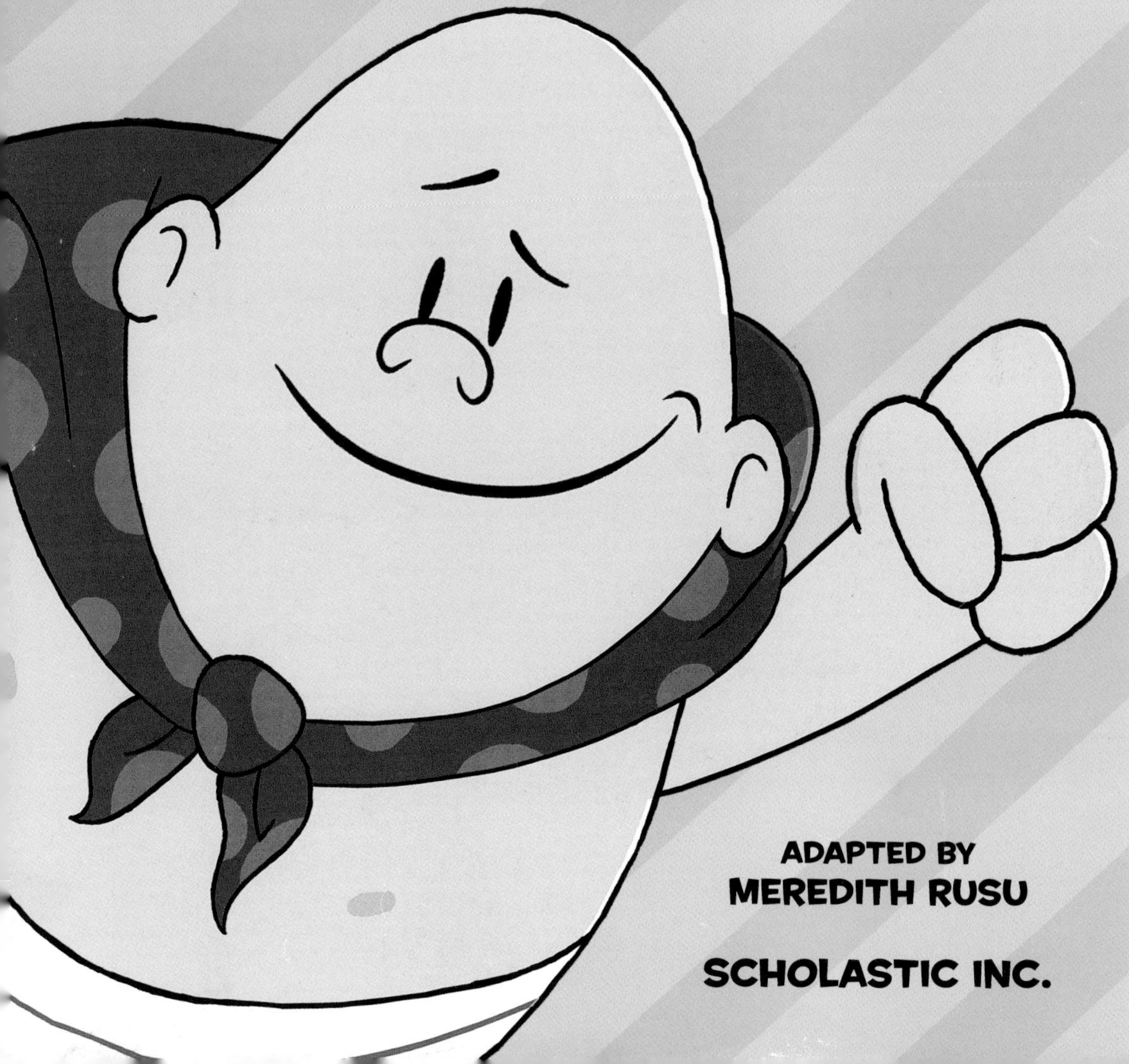

ADAPTED BY
MEREDITH RUSU

SCHOLASTIC INC.

All rights reserved. Published by Scholastic Inc., *Publishers since 1920*. SCHOLASTIC and associated logos are trademarks and/or registered trademarks of Scholastic Inc. CAPTAIN UNDERPANTS, TREE HOUSE COMIX, and related designs are trademarks and/or registered trademarks of Dav Pilkey.

The publisher does not have any control over and does not assume any responsibility for author or third-party websites or their content.

Photos ©: 28-29 background and throughout: vectorplus/Shutterstock.

ISBN 978-1-338-26246-9

10 9 8 7 6 5 4   21 22 23

Printed in the U.S.A.   40

First printing 2019

Book design by Mercedes Padró

CONTENTS

Tree House Comix, Inc. Presents:
The Most Epic Captain Underpants Comics of All Time

THIS IS GEORGE BEARD AND HAROLD HUTCHINS. GEORGE IS THE KID ON THE LEFT WITH THE FLAT TOP AND TIE. HAROLD IS THE ONE ON THE RIGHT WITH THE BAD HAIRCUT. REMEMBER THAT NOW.

GEORGE AND HAROLD MAKE COMIC BOOKS. AND THEIR FAVORITE SUPERHERO IS CAPTAIN UNDERPANTS—*TRA-LA-LAAAAA!* WHAT NO ONE REALIZES (BECAUSE IT'S A SECRET) IS THAT WHENEVER GEORGE AND HAROLD SNAP THEIR FINGERS, THEIR MEAN SCHOOL PRINCIPAL, MR. KRUPP, TURNS *INTO* CAPTAIN UNDERPANTS—FOR REAL! AND THE COMIC BOOK ADVENTURES THEY DRAW KIND OF, SORT OF, COME TO LIFE, TOO!

GEORGE AND HAROLD HAVE CREATED HUNDREDS OF CAPTAIN UNDERPANTS COMIC BOOKS. *THIS* IS A COLLECTION OF SOME OF THEIR ABSOLUTE FAVORITES—THE ONES WITH THE BIGGEST BADDIES, THE NASTIEST NAYSAYERS, AND THE FEISTIEST FART MONSTERS! (THAT'S A REAL THING. IT'S AS SMELLY AS IT SOUNDS.)

BUT DON'T TAKE GEORGE AND HAROLD'S WORD FOR IT—TURN THE PAGE TO START READING THE MOST **EPIC** COMIC COLLECTION EVER, AND SEE FOR YOURSELF!

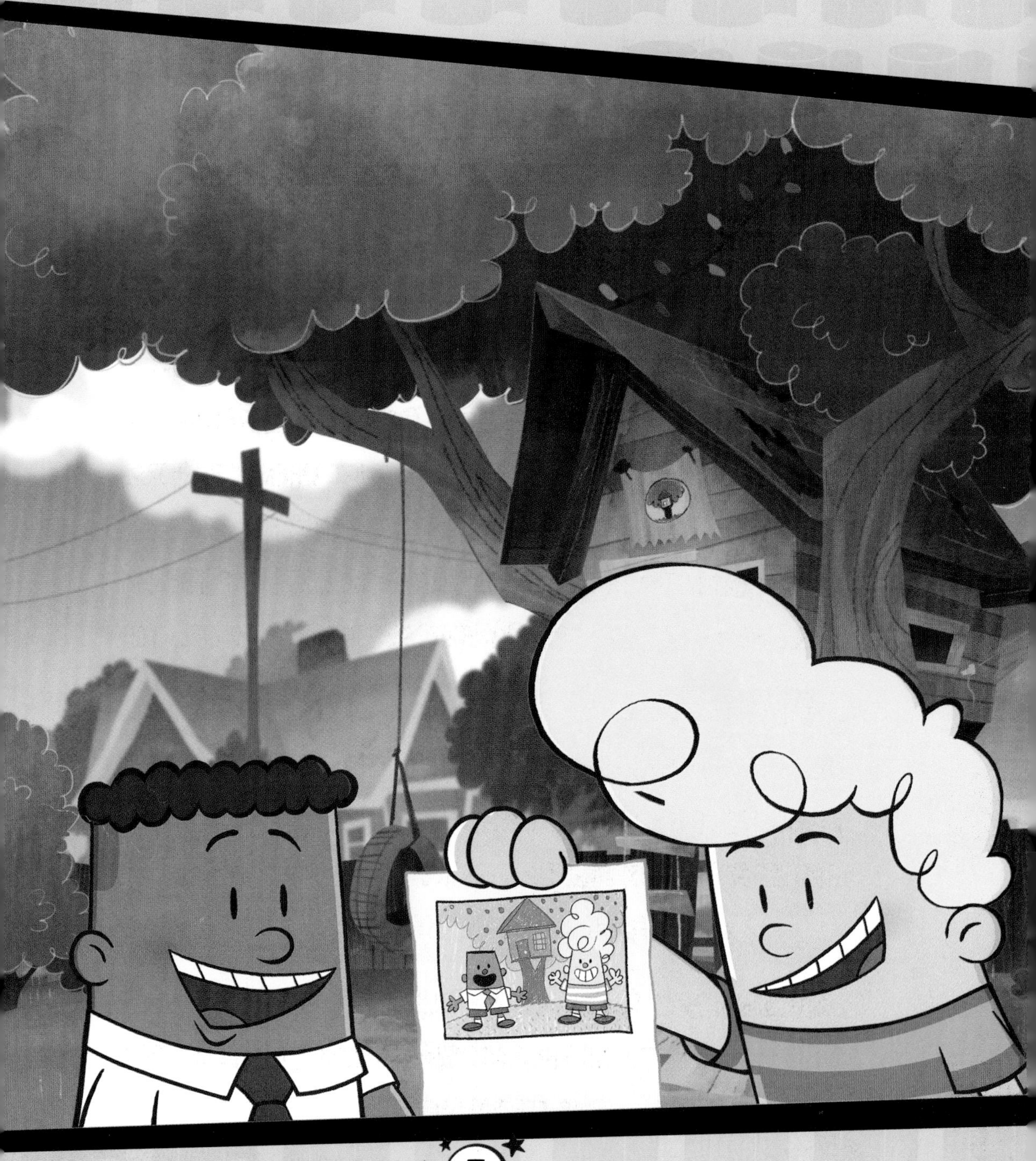

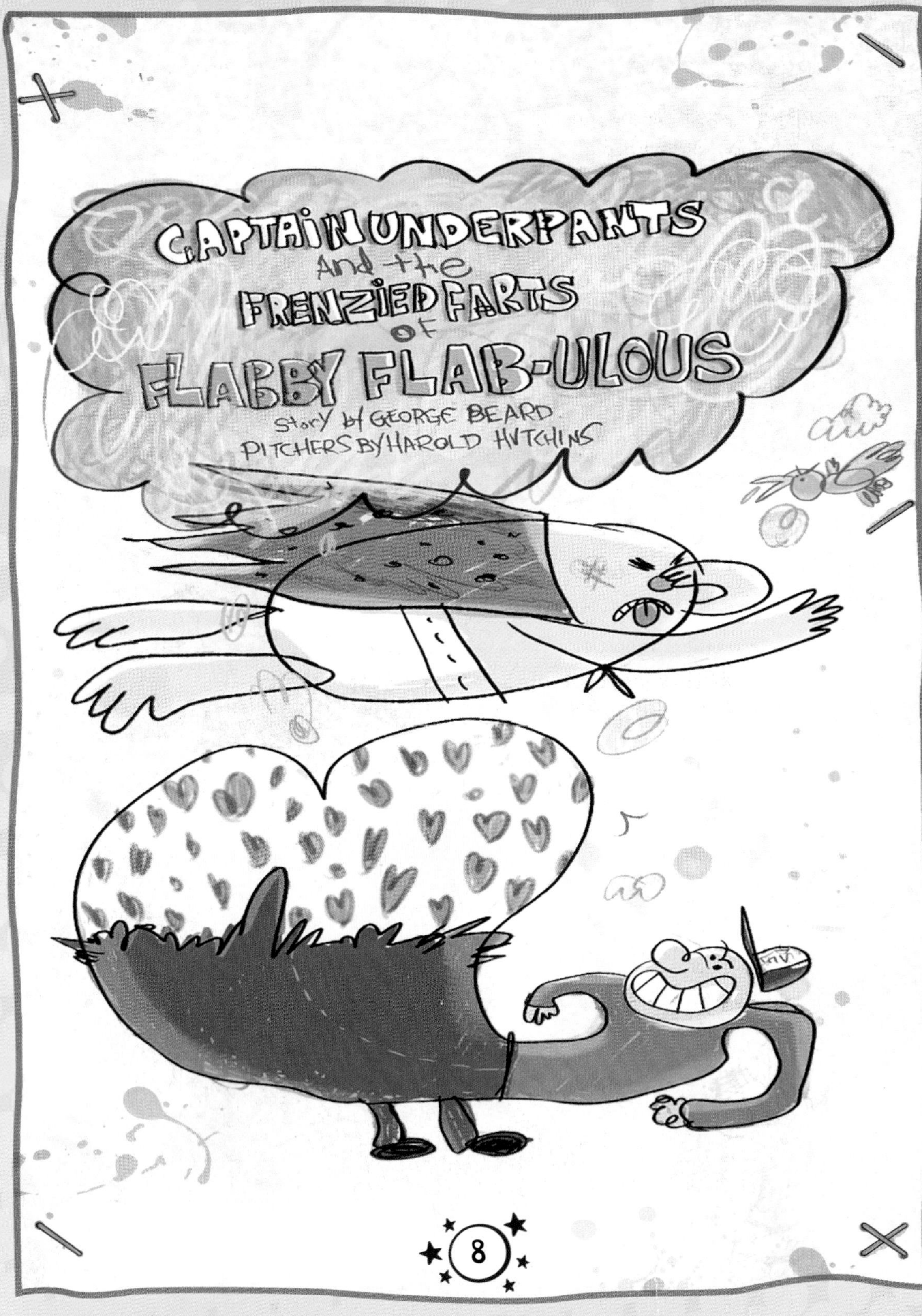
CAPTAIN UNDERPANTS
and the
FRENZIED FARTS
of
FLABBY FLAB-ULOUS
Story by GEORGE BEARD
PITCHERS BY HAROLD HUTCHINS

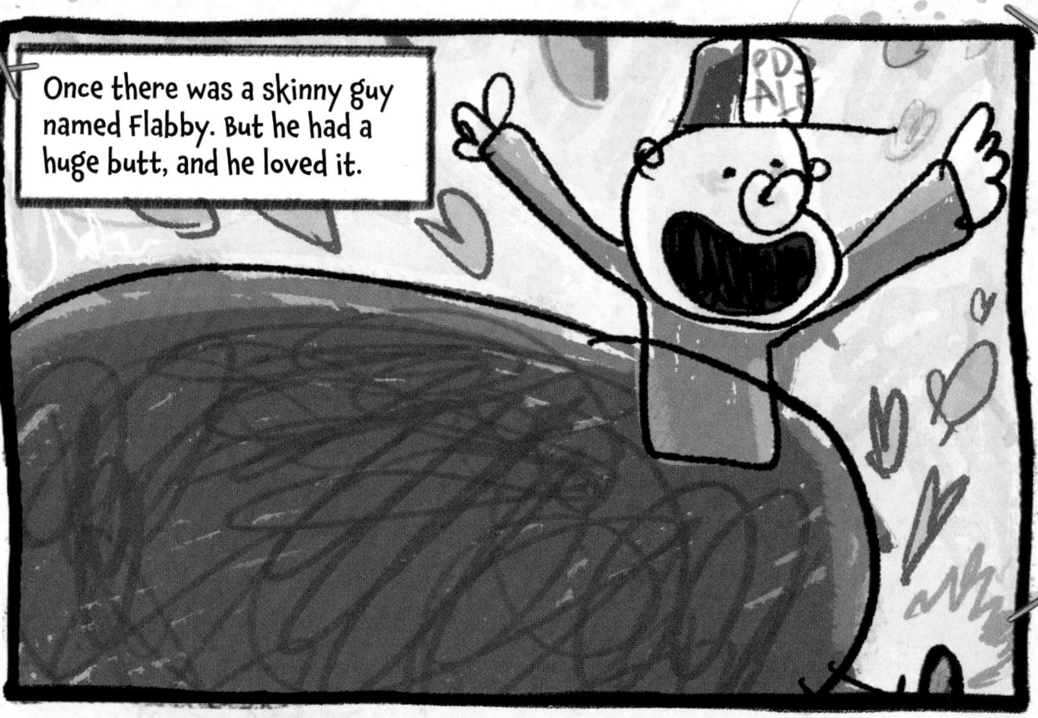
Once there was a skinny guy named Flabby. But he had a huge butt, and he loved it.

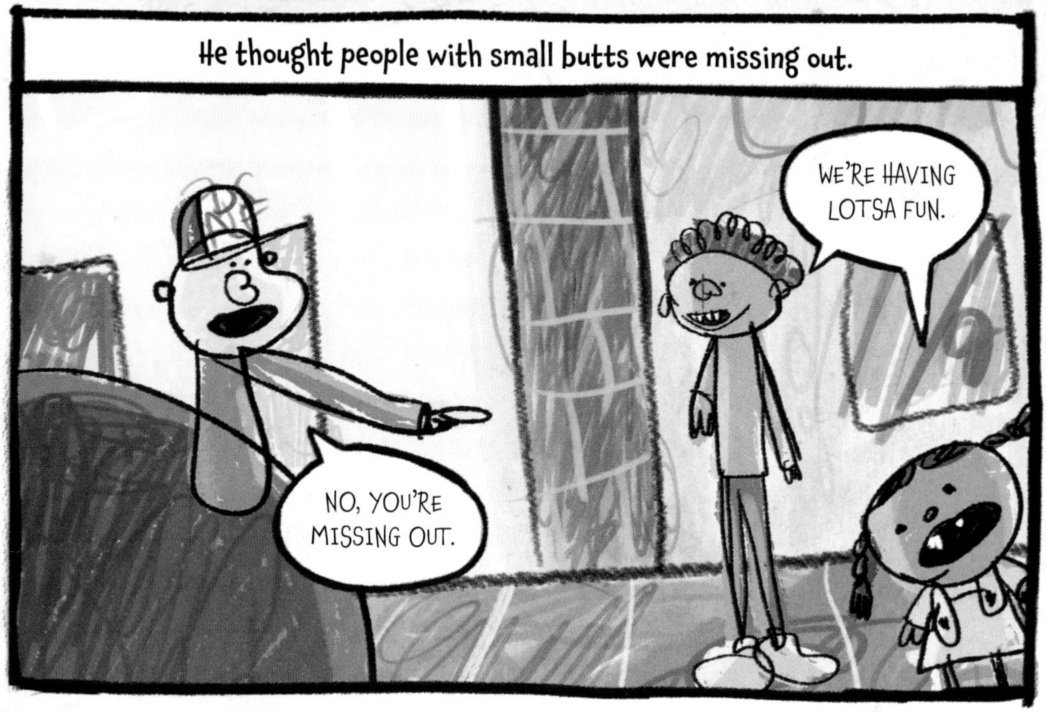
He thought people with small butts were missing out.
WE'RE HAVING LOTSA FUN.
NO, YOU'RE MISSING OUT.

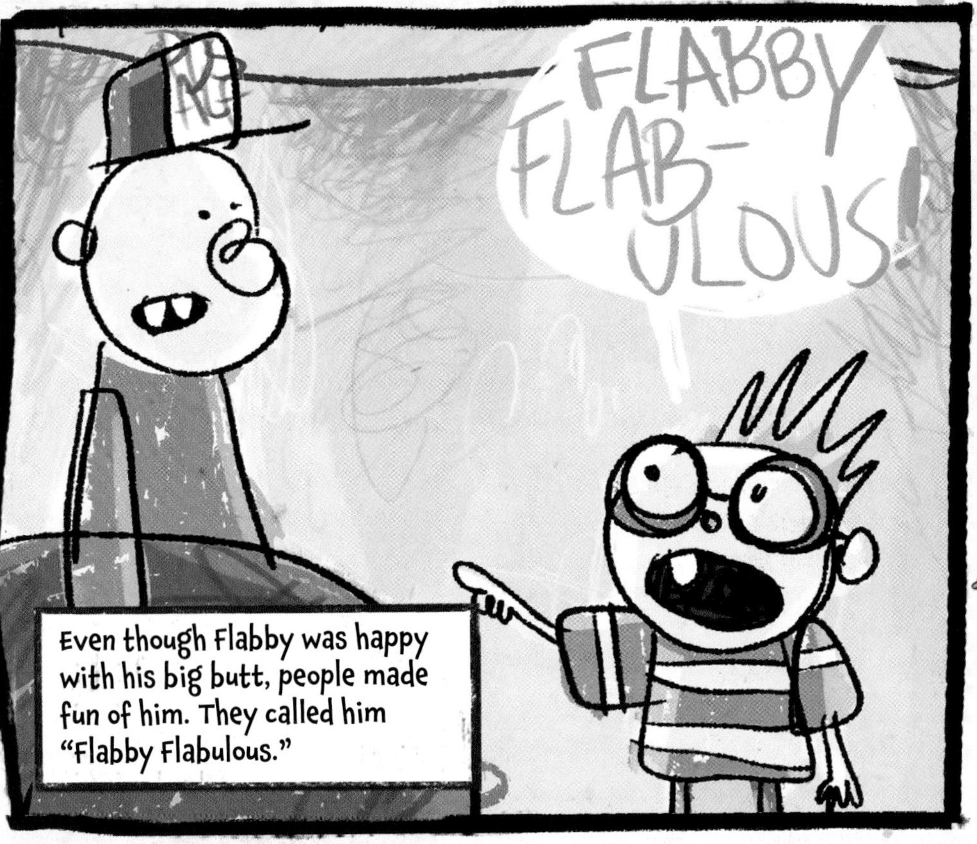
FLABBY FLAB-ULOUS!
Even though Flabby was happy with his big butt, people made fun of him. They called him "Flabby Flabulous."

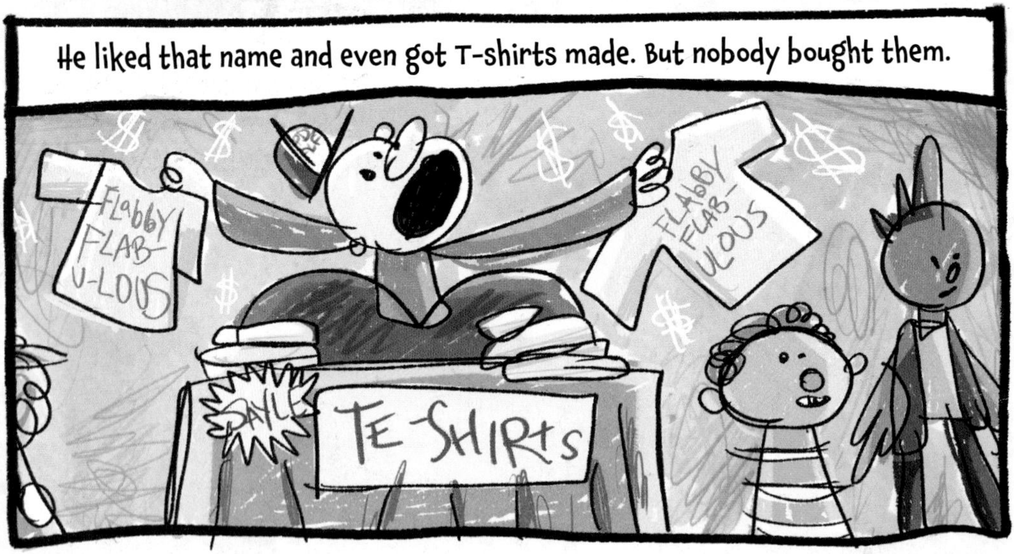
He liked that name and even got T-shirts made. But nobody bought them.
Flabby FLAB-U-LOUS
FLABBY FLAB-ULOUS
TE-SHIRts

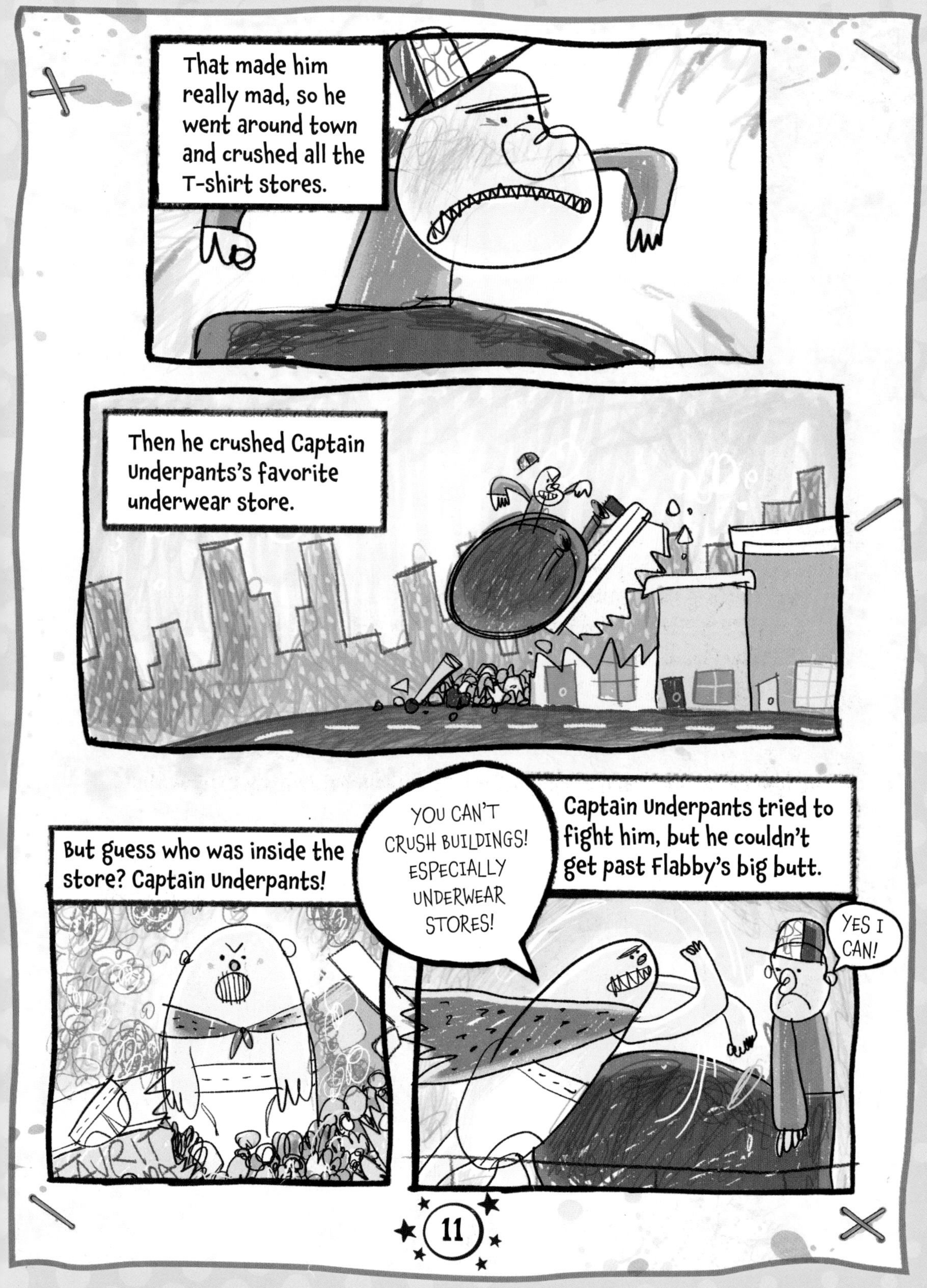
That made him really mad, so he went around town and crushed all the T-shirt stores.
Then he crushed Captain Underpants's favorite underwear store.
But guess who was inside the store? Captain Underpants!
YOU CAN'T CRUSH BUILDINGS! ESPECIALLY UNDERWEAR STORES!
Captain Underpants tried to fight him, but he couldn't get past Flabby's big butt.
YES I CAN!

I KNOW WHAT TO DO! I'LL USE MY WEDGIE POWER!

Captain Underpants pulled an extra pair of underwear from his utility waistband.

But he needed to look for something bigger to give Flabby Flabulous a wedgie.

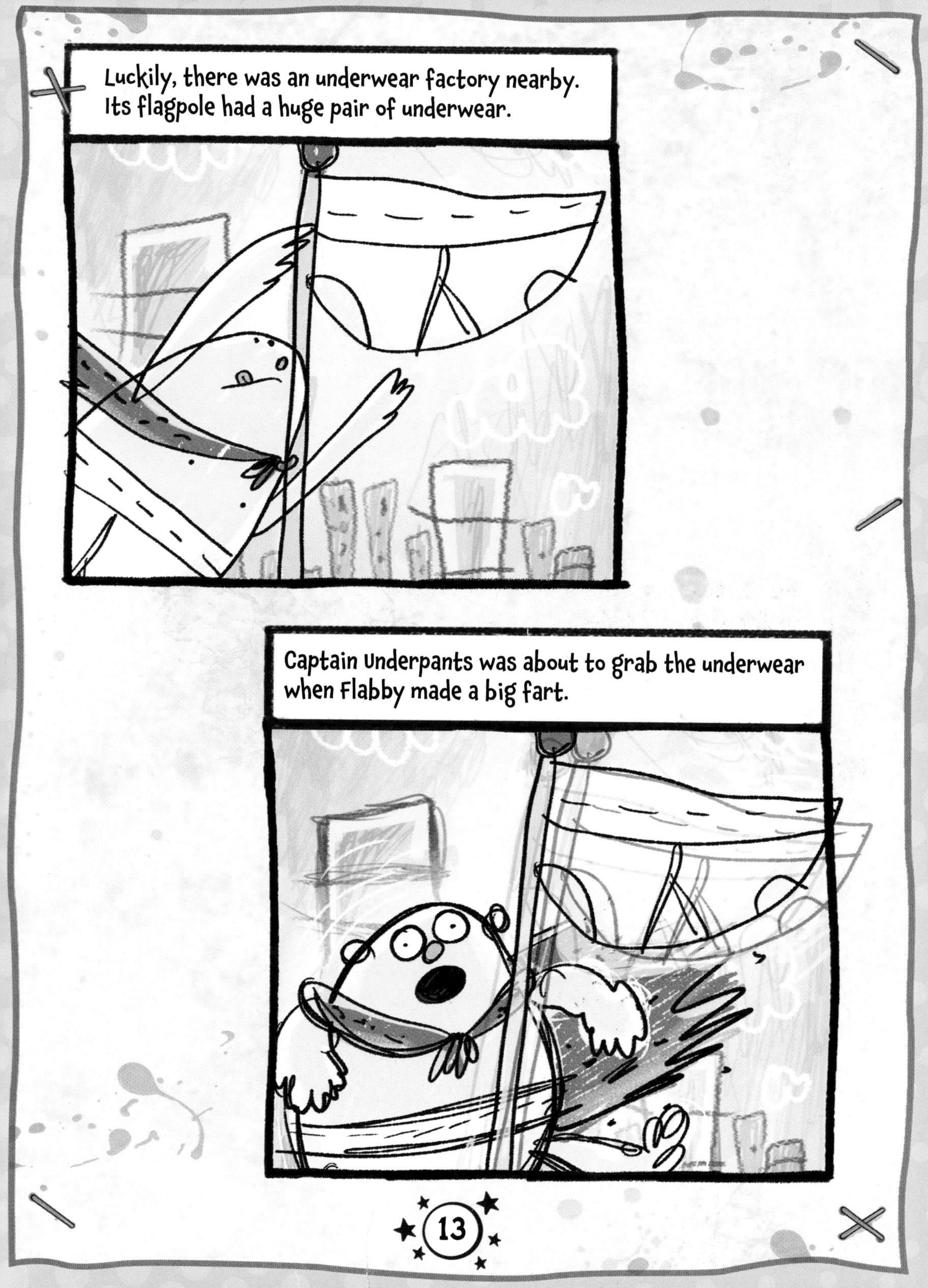
Luckily, there was an underwear factory nearby. Its flagpole had a huge pair of underwear.
Captain Underpants was about to grab the underwear when Flabby made a big fart.

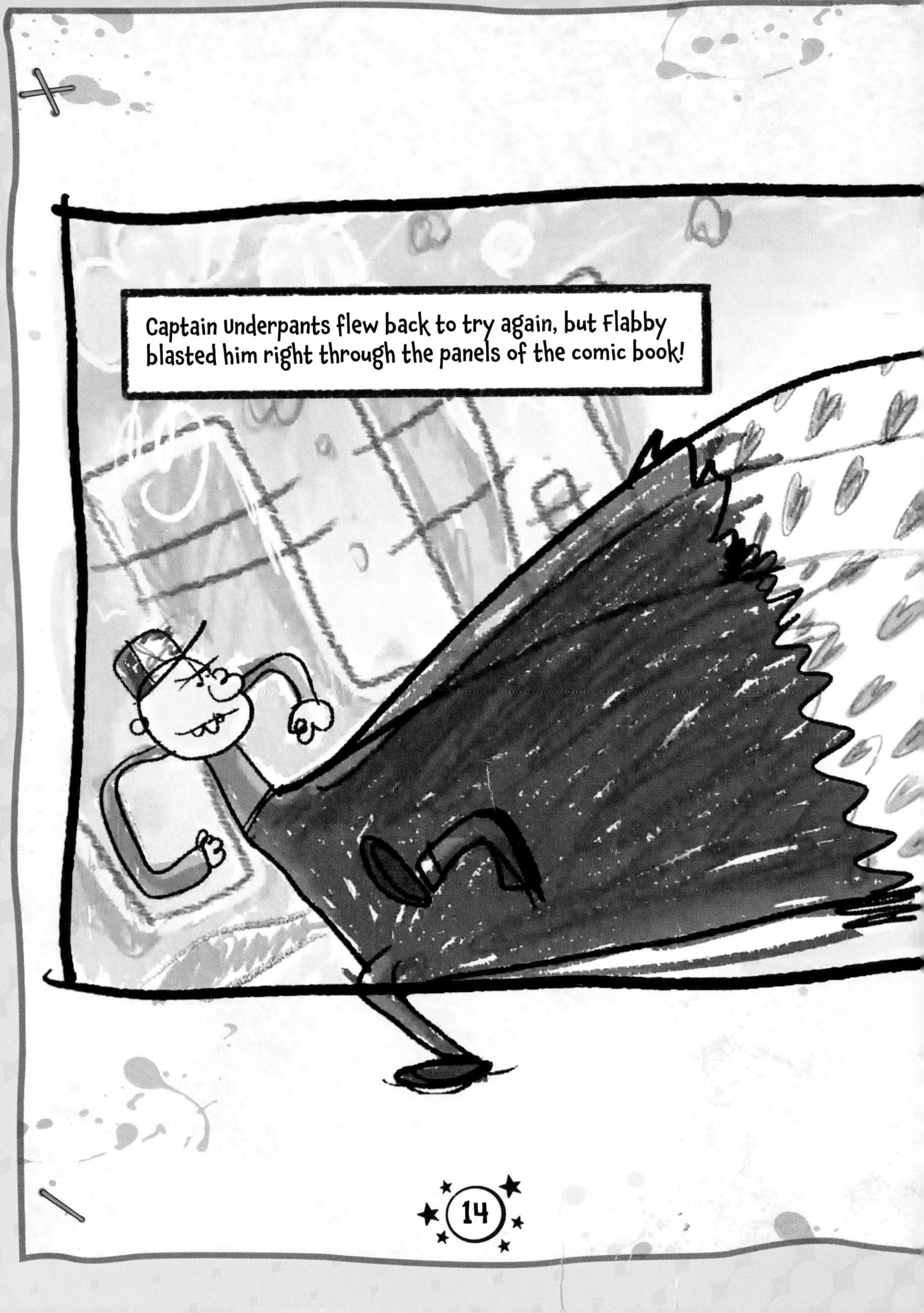
Captain Underpants flew back to try again, but Flabby blasted him right through the panels of the comic book!

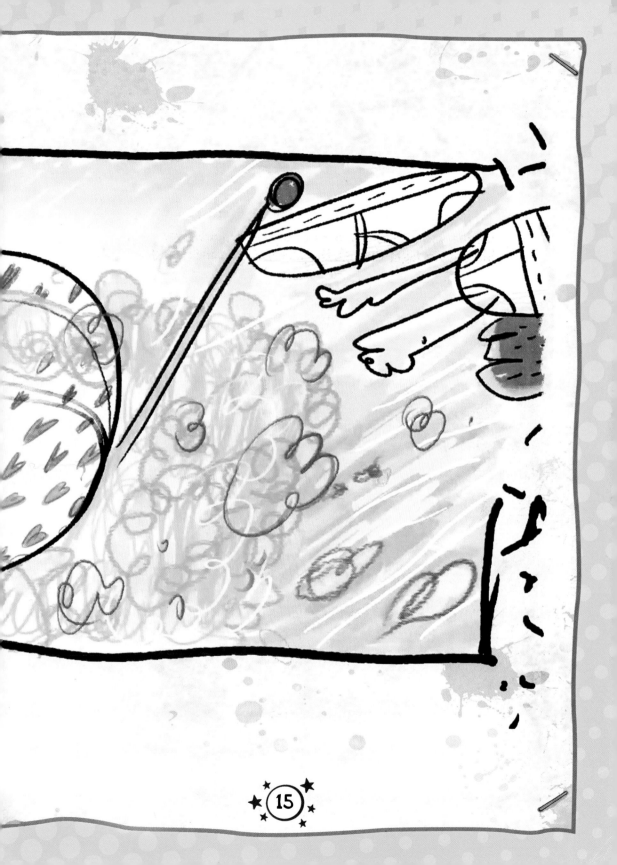

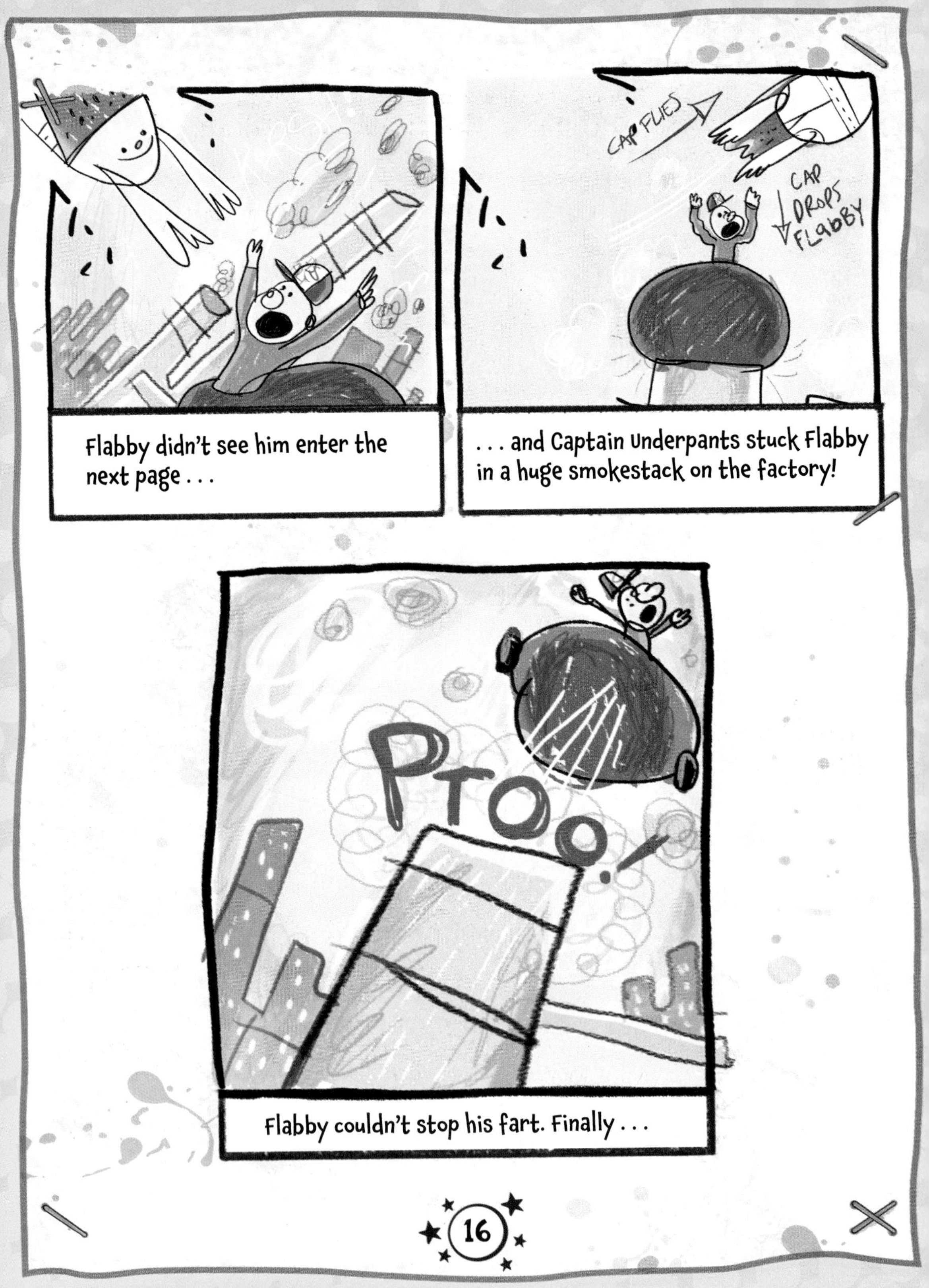
Flabby didn't see him enter the next page . . .
CAP FLIES
CAP DROPS FLABBY
. . . and Captain Underpants stuck Flabby in a huge smokestack on the factory!
PTOO!
Flabby couldn't stop his fart. Finally . . .

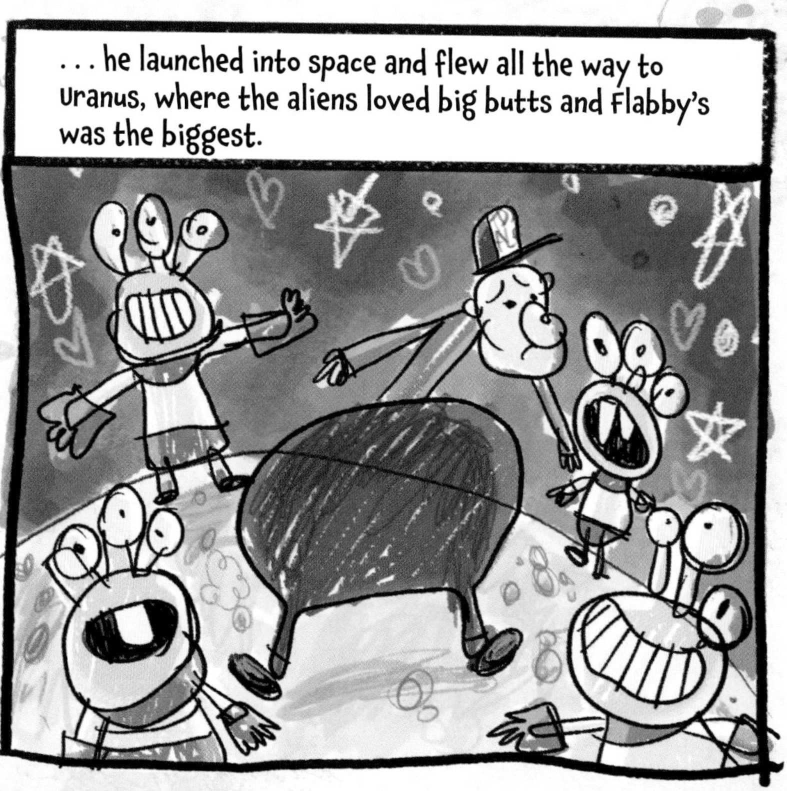
. . . he launched into space and flew all the way to Uranus, where the aliens loved big butts and Flabby's was the biggest.

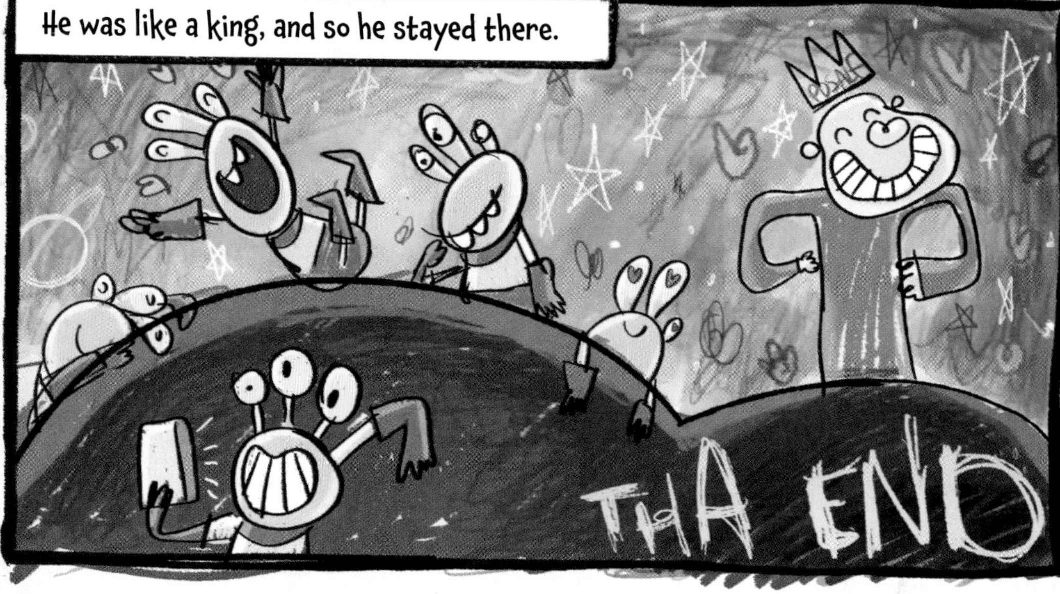
He was like a king, and so he stayed there.
THA END

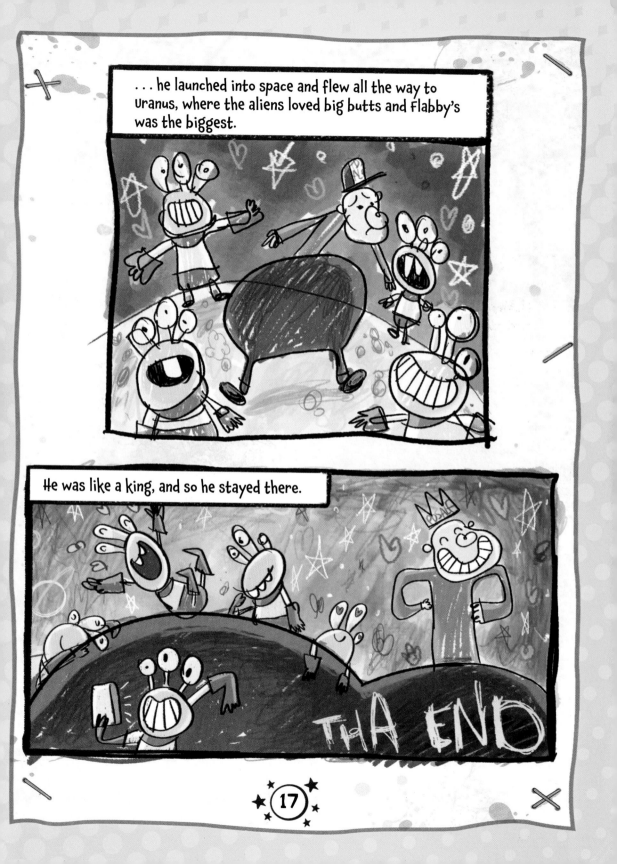

CAPTAIN UNDERPANTS AND George + Harold the HEROIC HAMMERING of the HOMEWORK-HEADED HORROR!

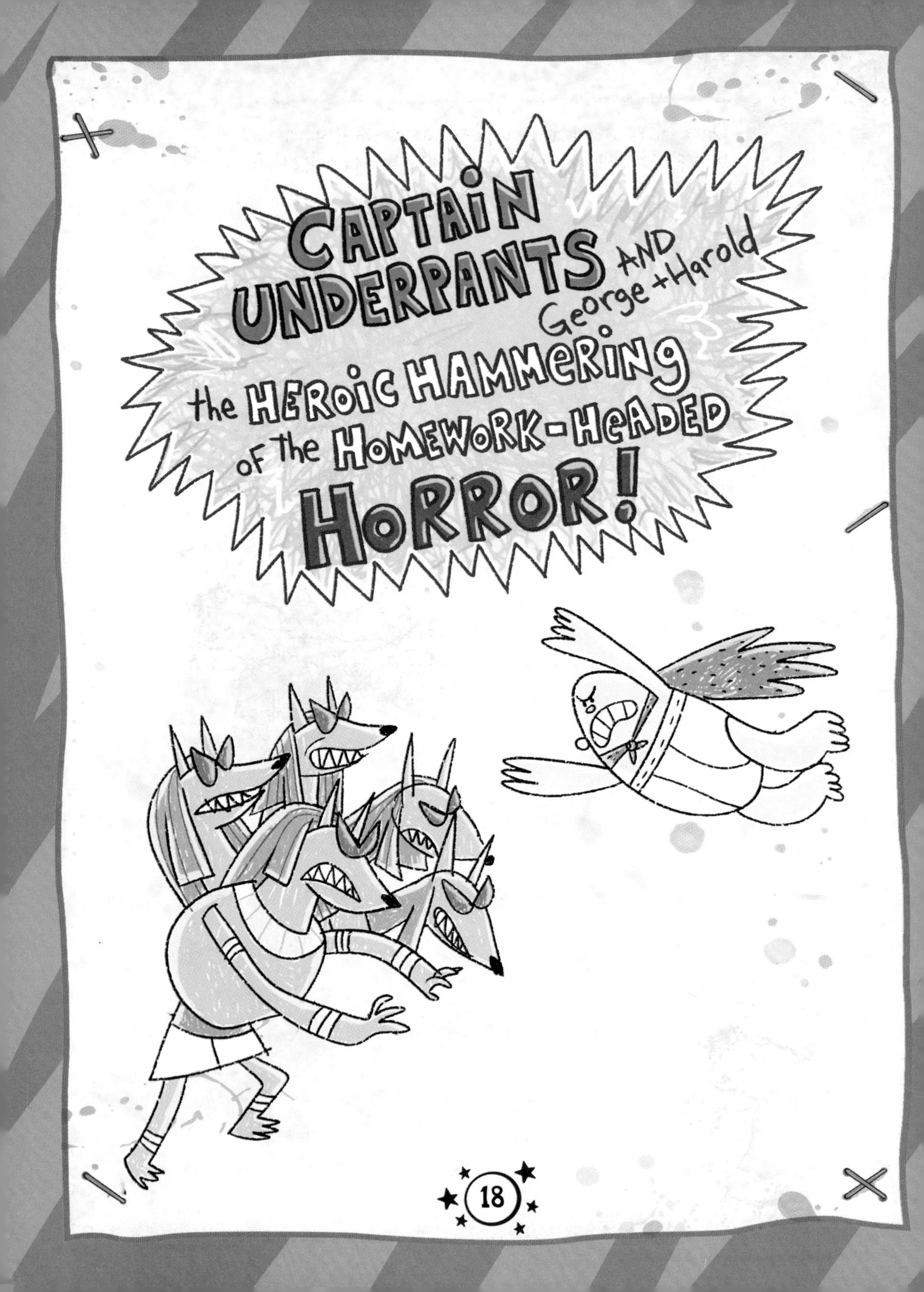

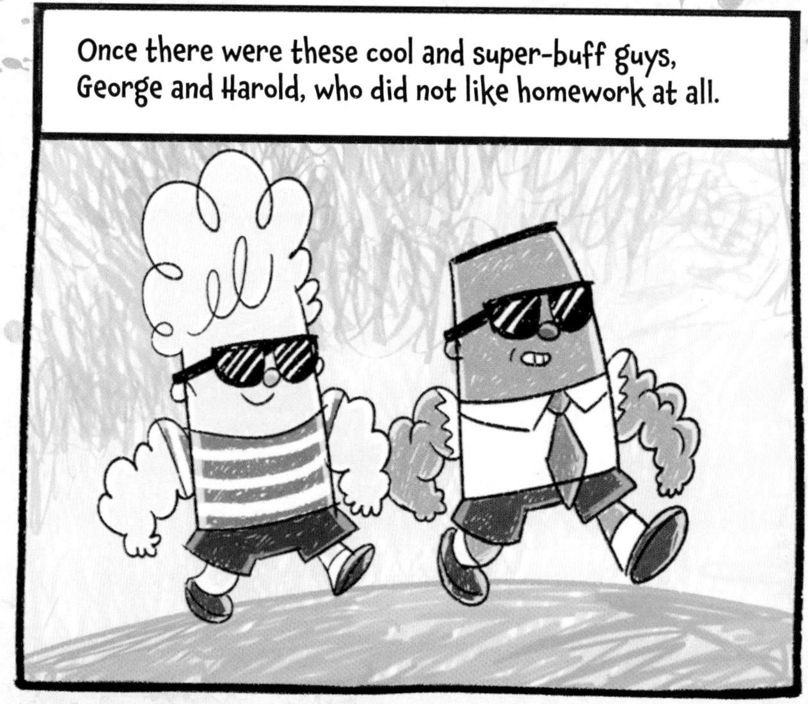
Once there were these cool and super-buff guys, George and Harold, who did not like homework at all.

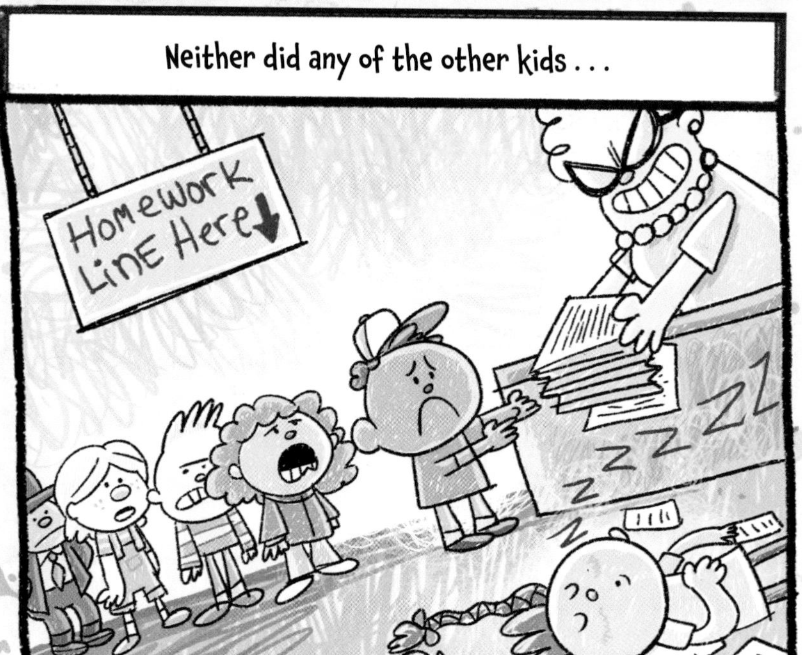
Neither did any of the other kids . . .
Homework Line Here
Z Z Z Z
Z

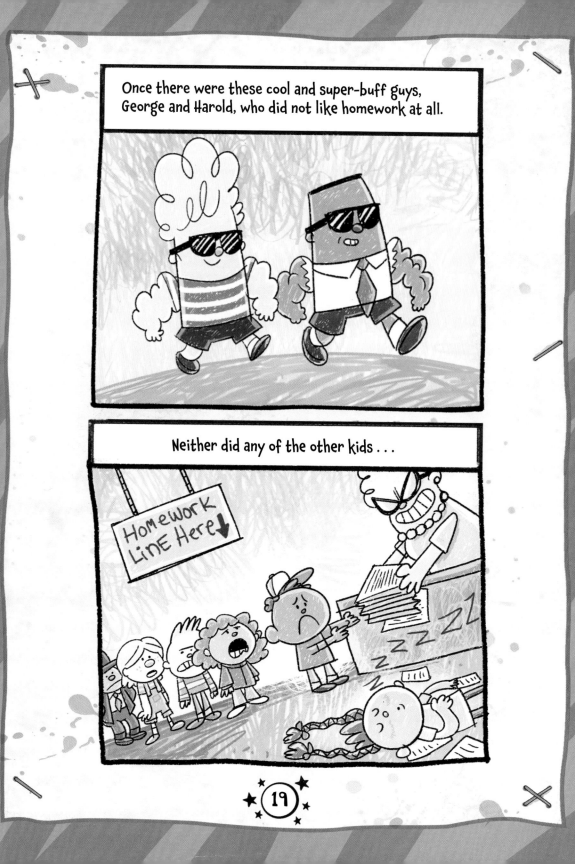

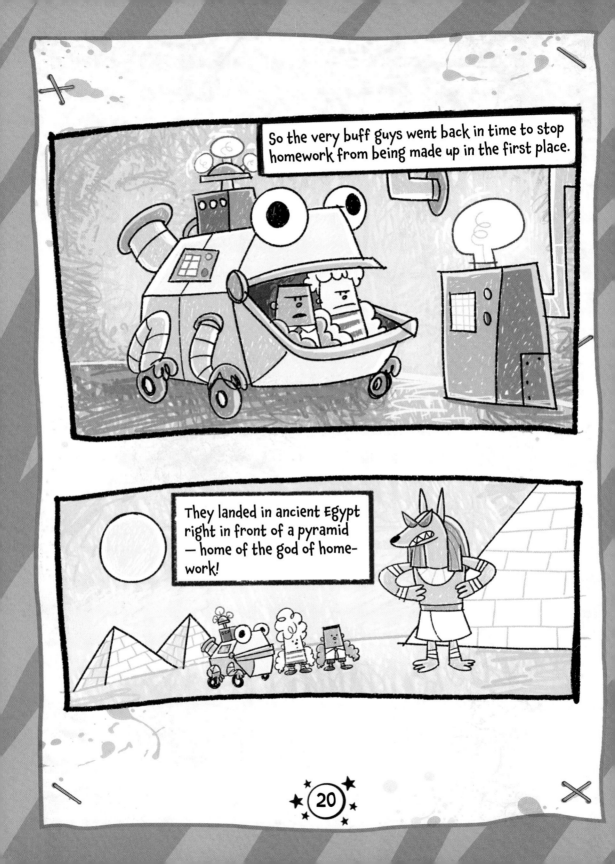

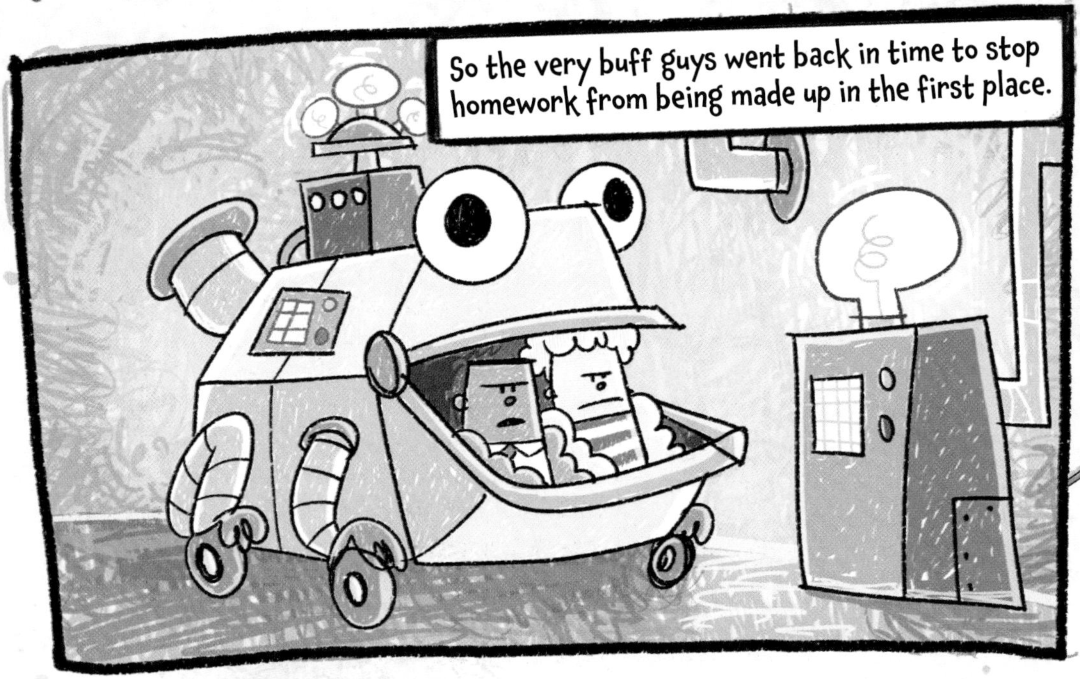
So the very buff guys went back in time to stop homework from being made up in the first place.

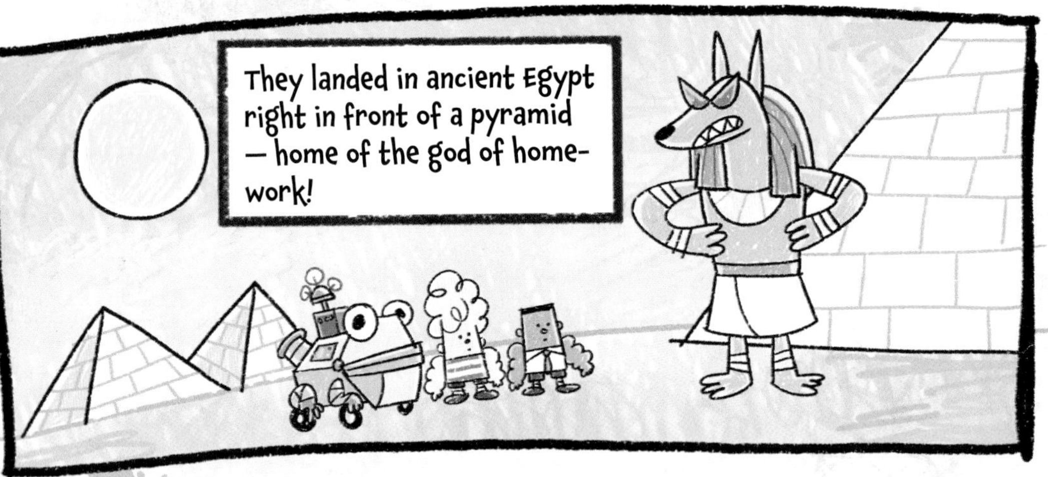
They landed in ancient Egypt right in front of a pyramid — home of the god of home-work!

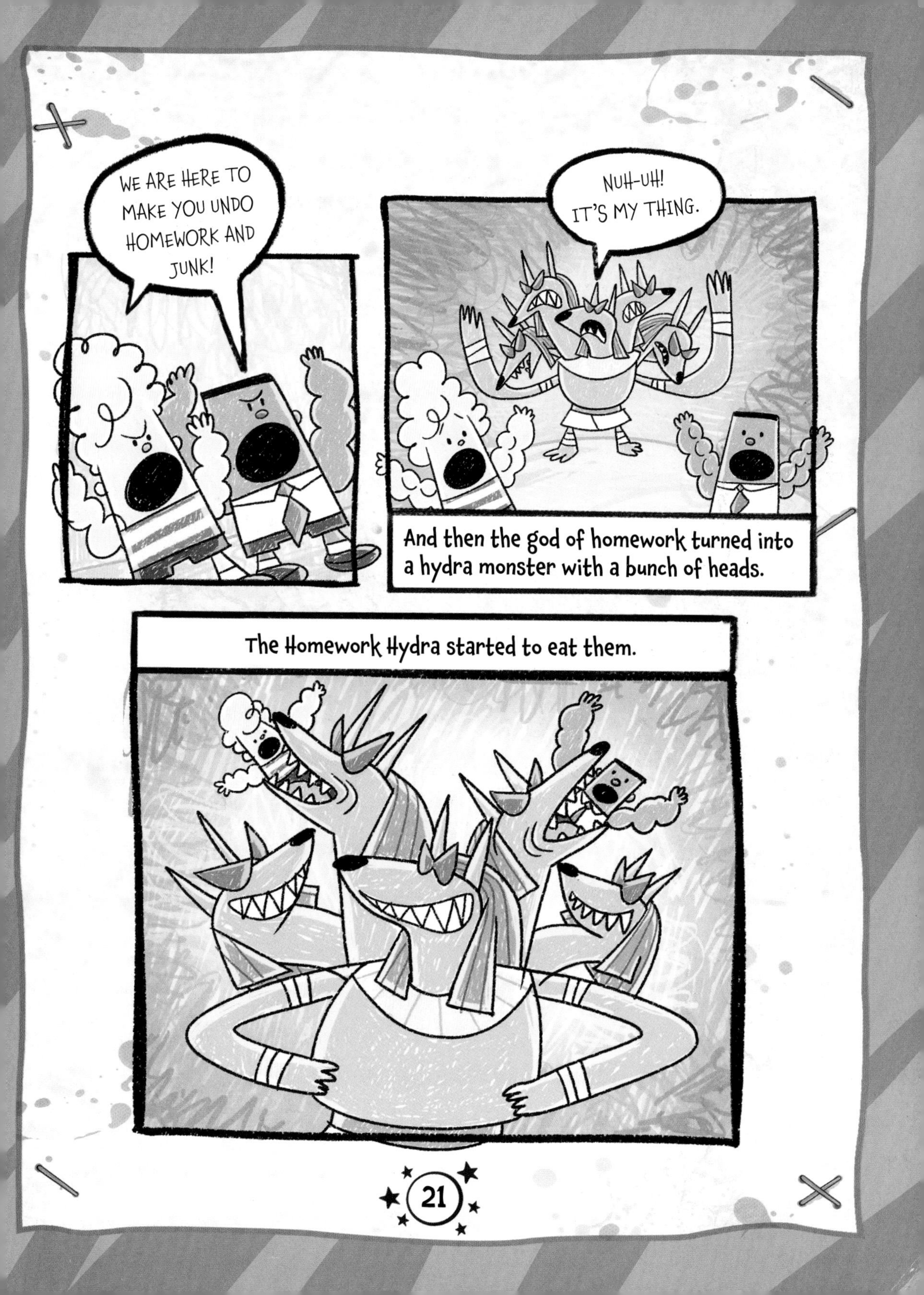
WE ARE HERE TO MAKE YOU UNDO HOMEWORK AND JUNK!
NUH-UH! IT'S MY THING.
And then the god of homework turned into a hydra monster with a bunch of heads.
The Homework Hydra started to eat them.

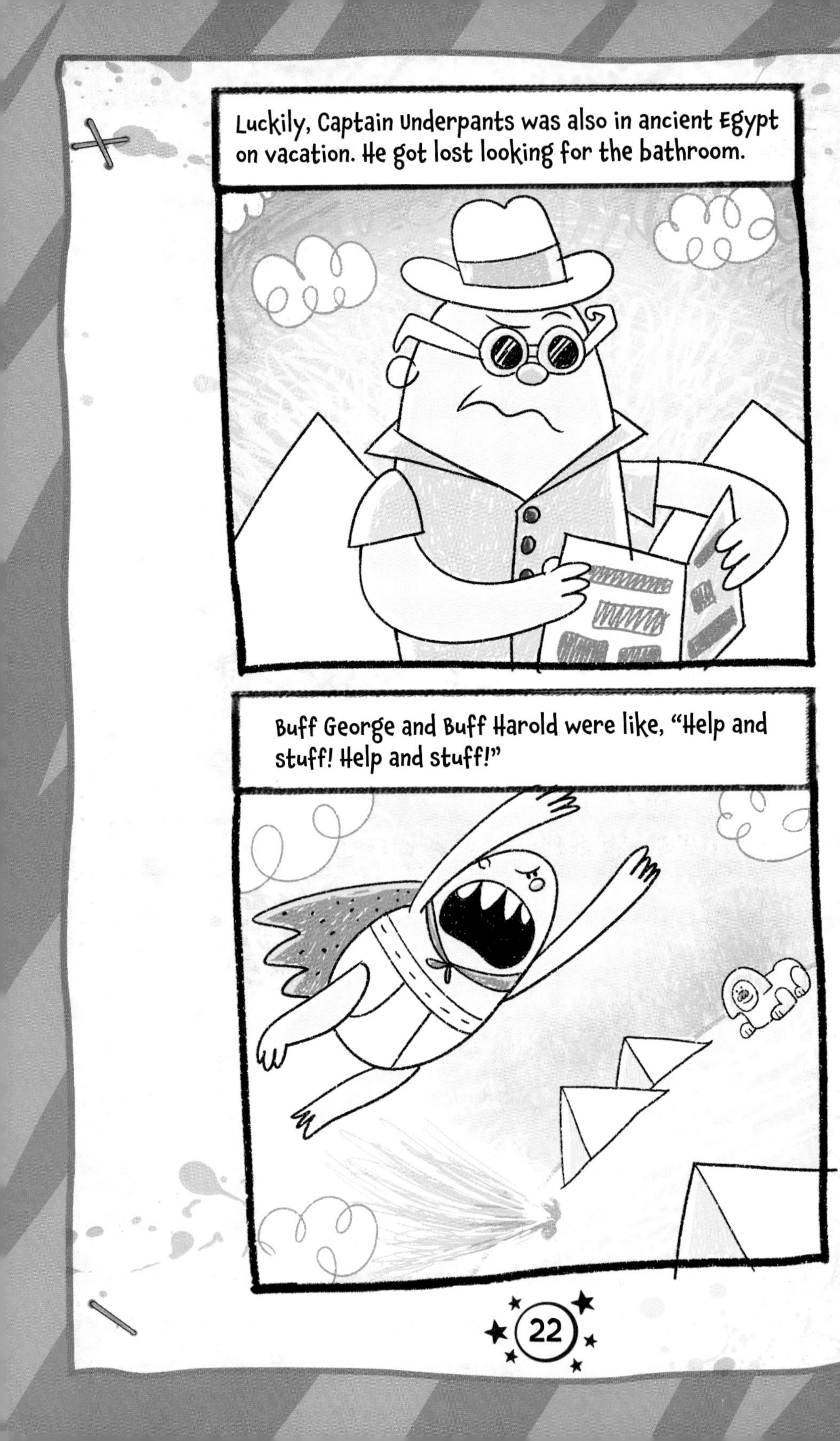
Luckily, Captain Underpants was also in ancient Egypt on vacation. He got lost looking for the bathroom.
Buff George and Buff Harold were like, "Help and stuff! Help and stuff!"

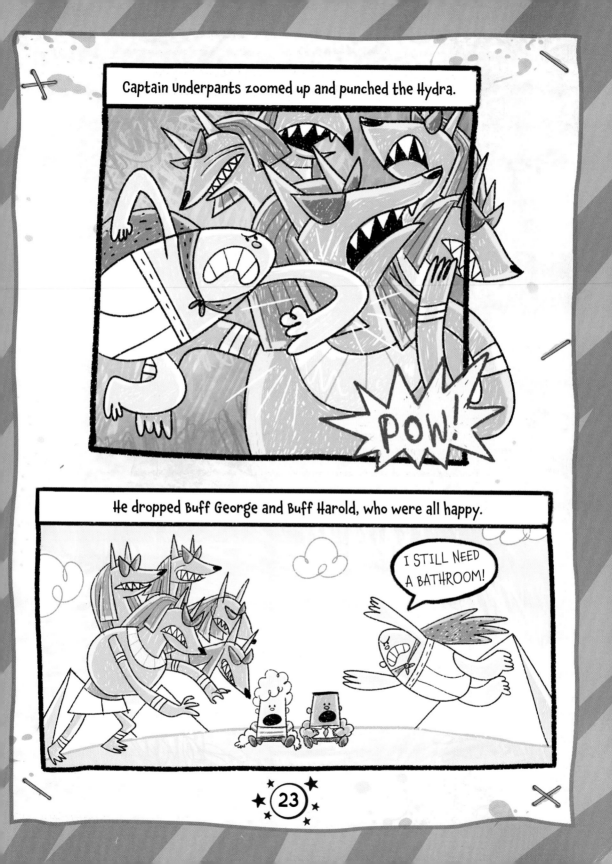

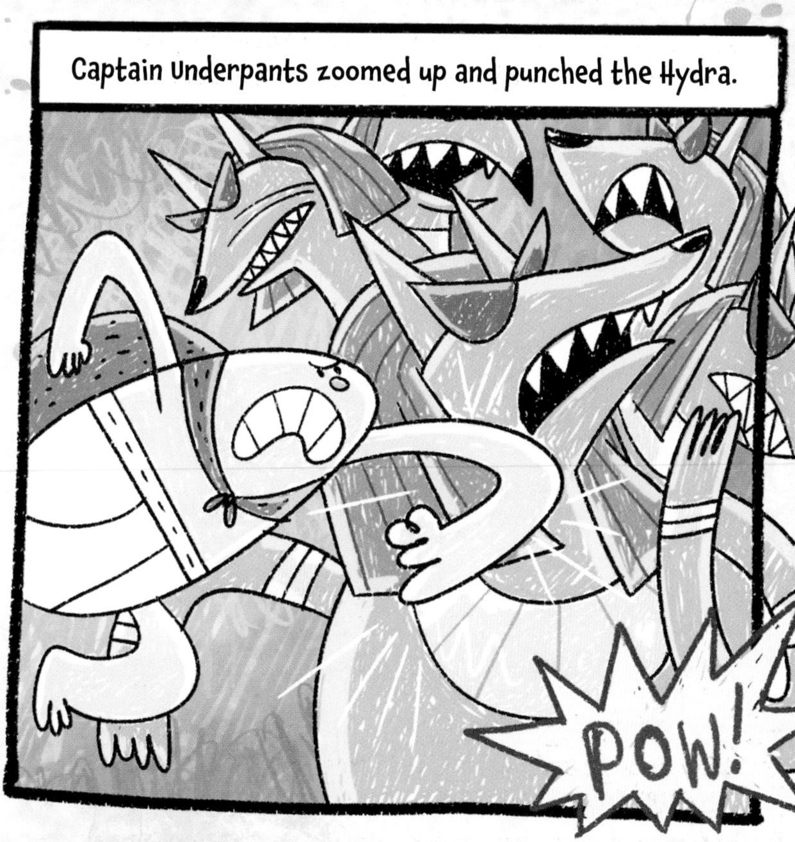
Captain Underpants zoomed up and punched the Hydra.
POW!

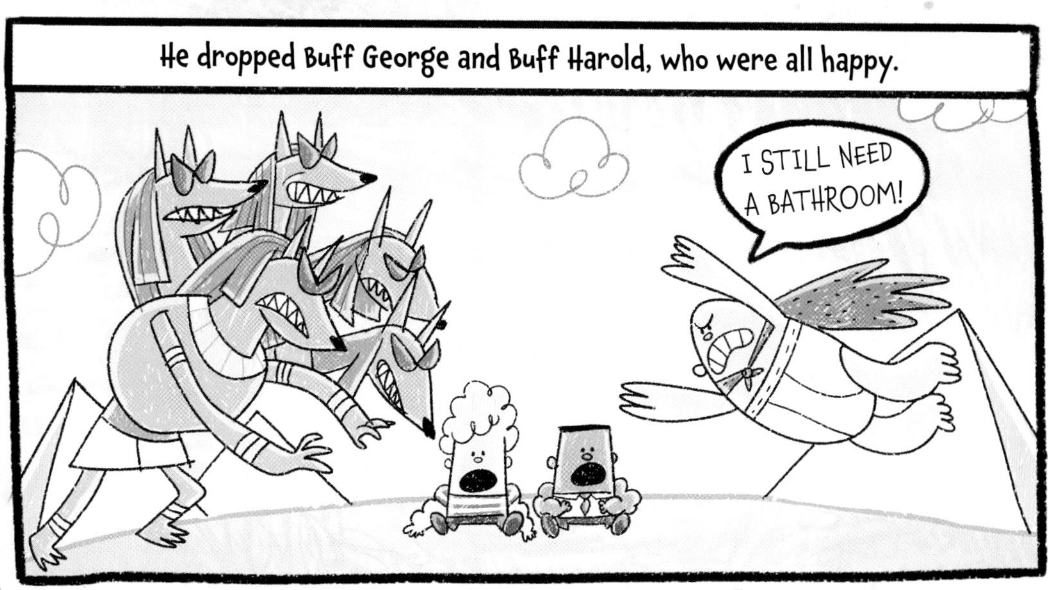
He dropped Buff George and Buff Harold, who were all happy.
I STILL NEED A BATHROOM!

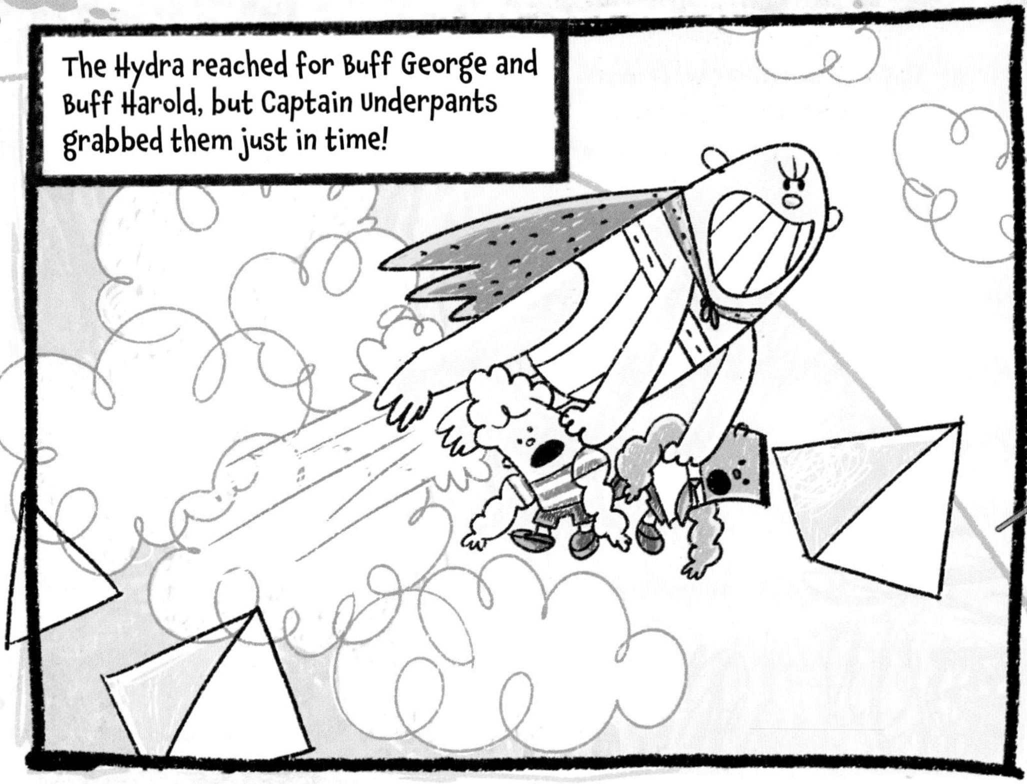
The Hydra reached for Buff George and Buff Harold, but Captain Underpants grabbed them just in time!

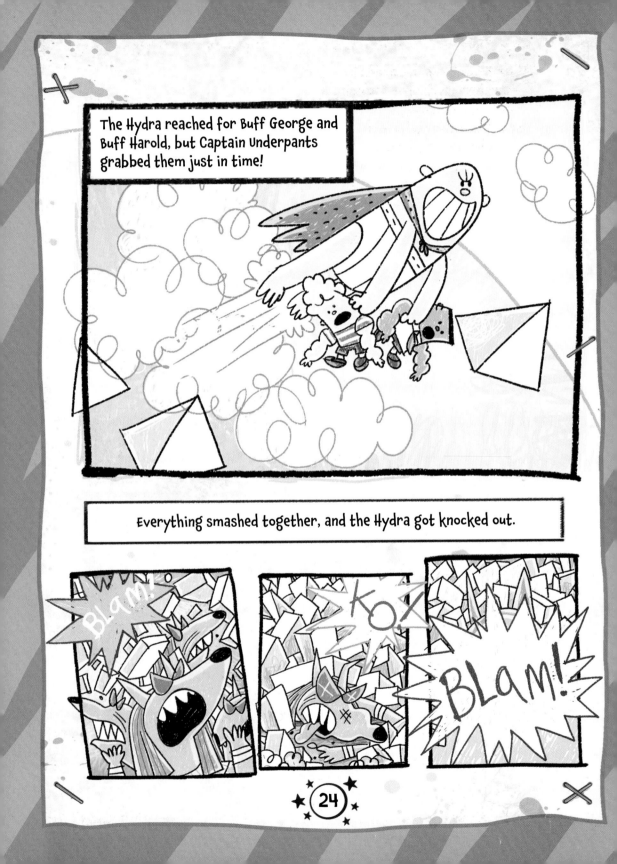

Everything smashed together, and the Hydra got knocked out.

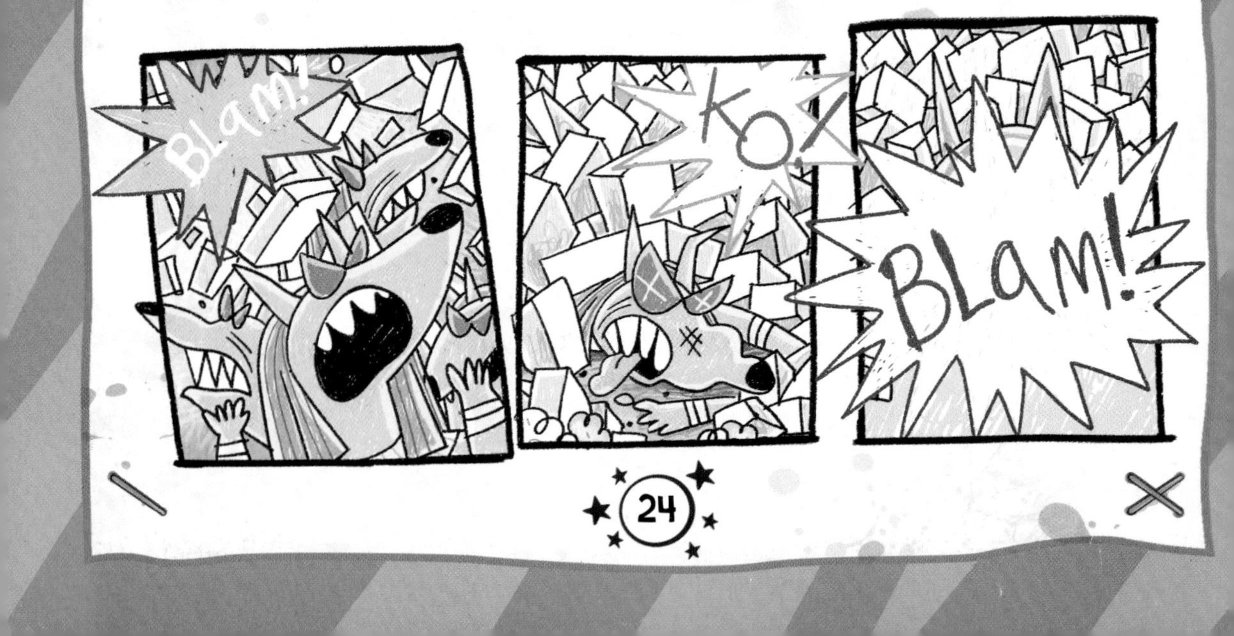
BLAM!
KO!
BLAM!

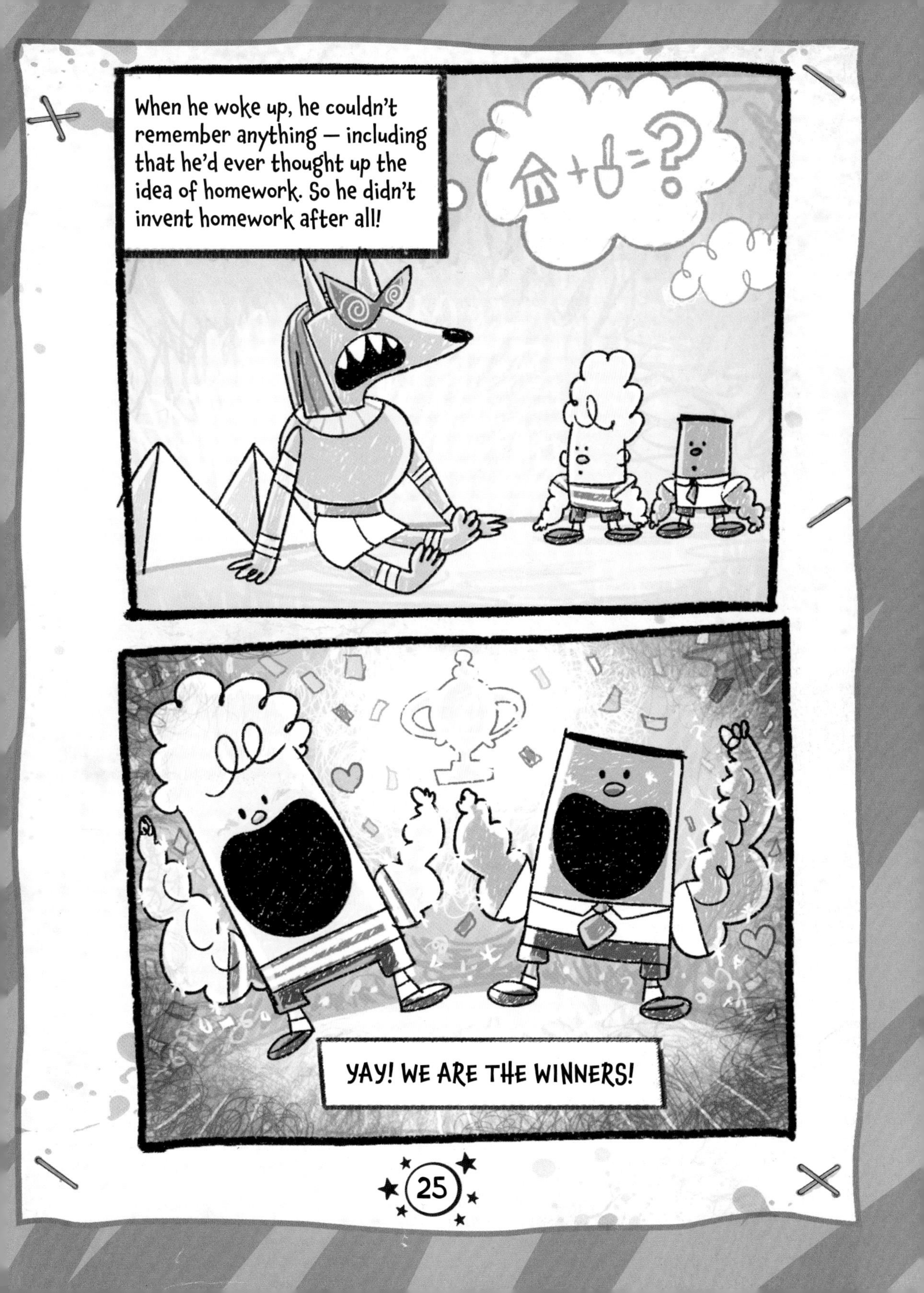
When he woke up, he couldn't remember anything — including that he'd ever thought up the idea of homework. So he didn't invent homework after all!
YAY! WE ARE THE WINNERS!

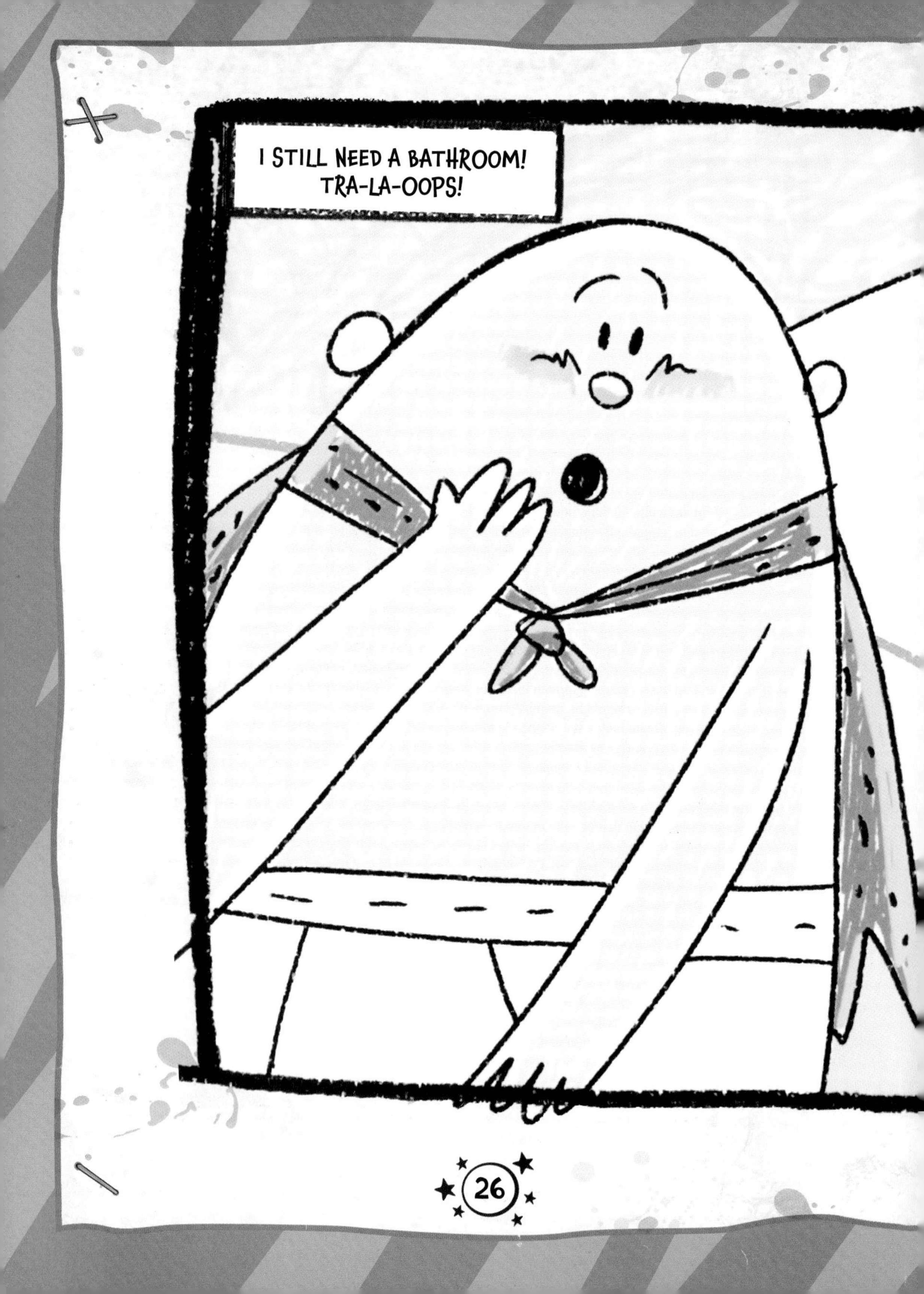
I STILL NEED A BATHROOM!
TRA-LA-OOPS!

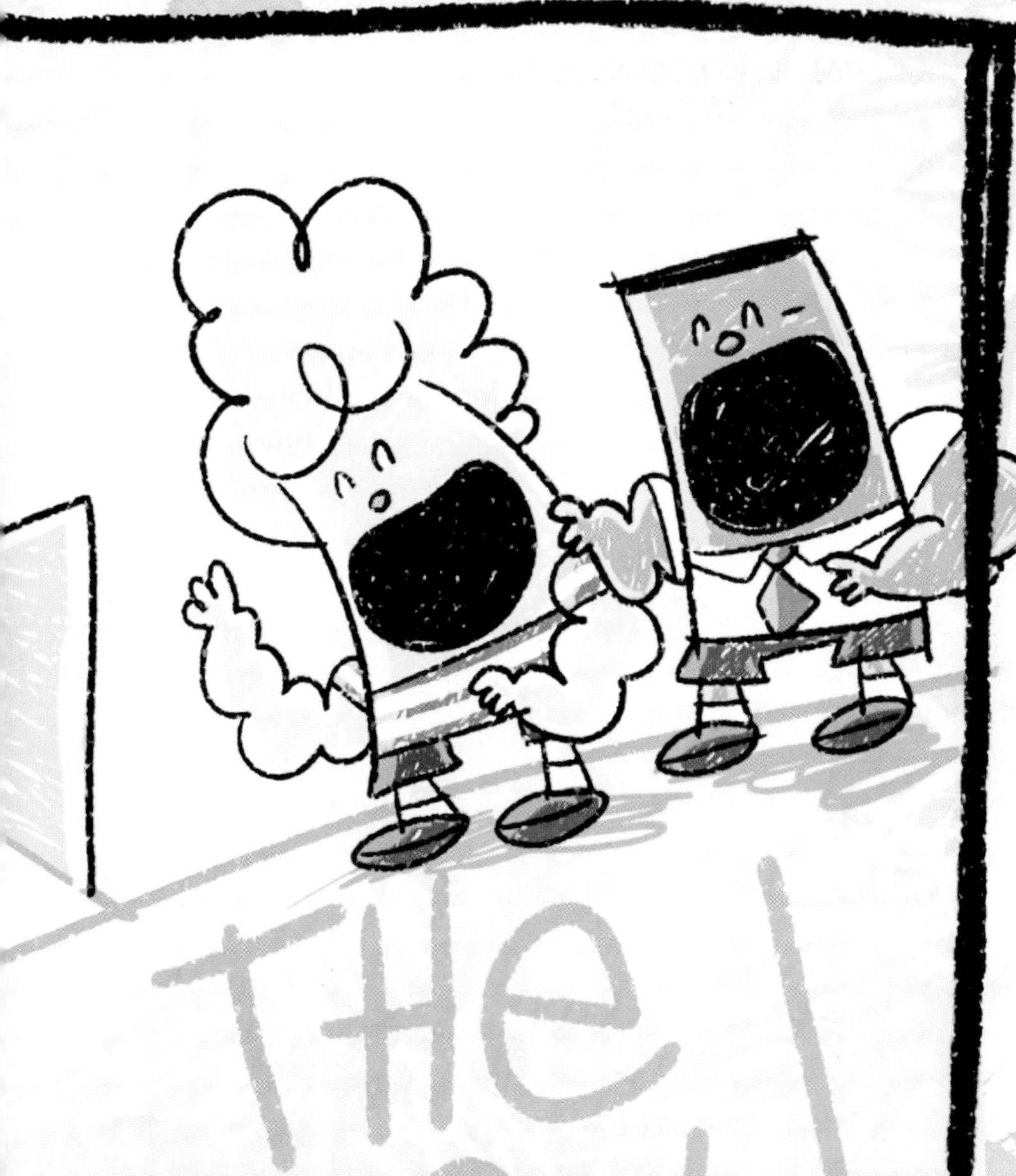
THE END

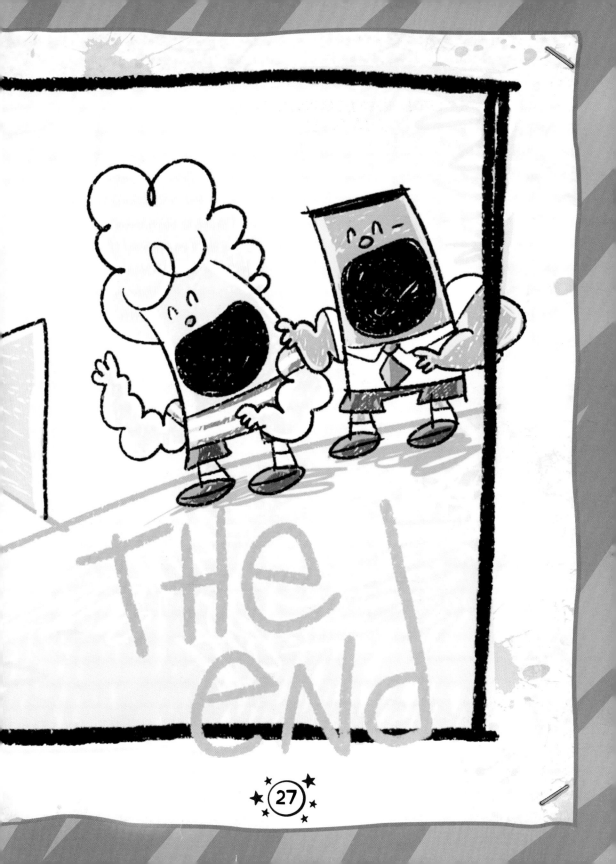

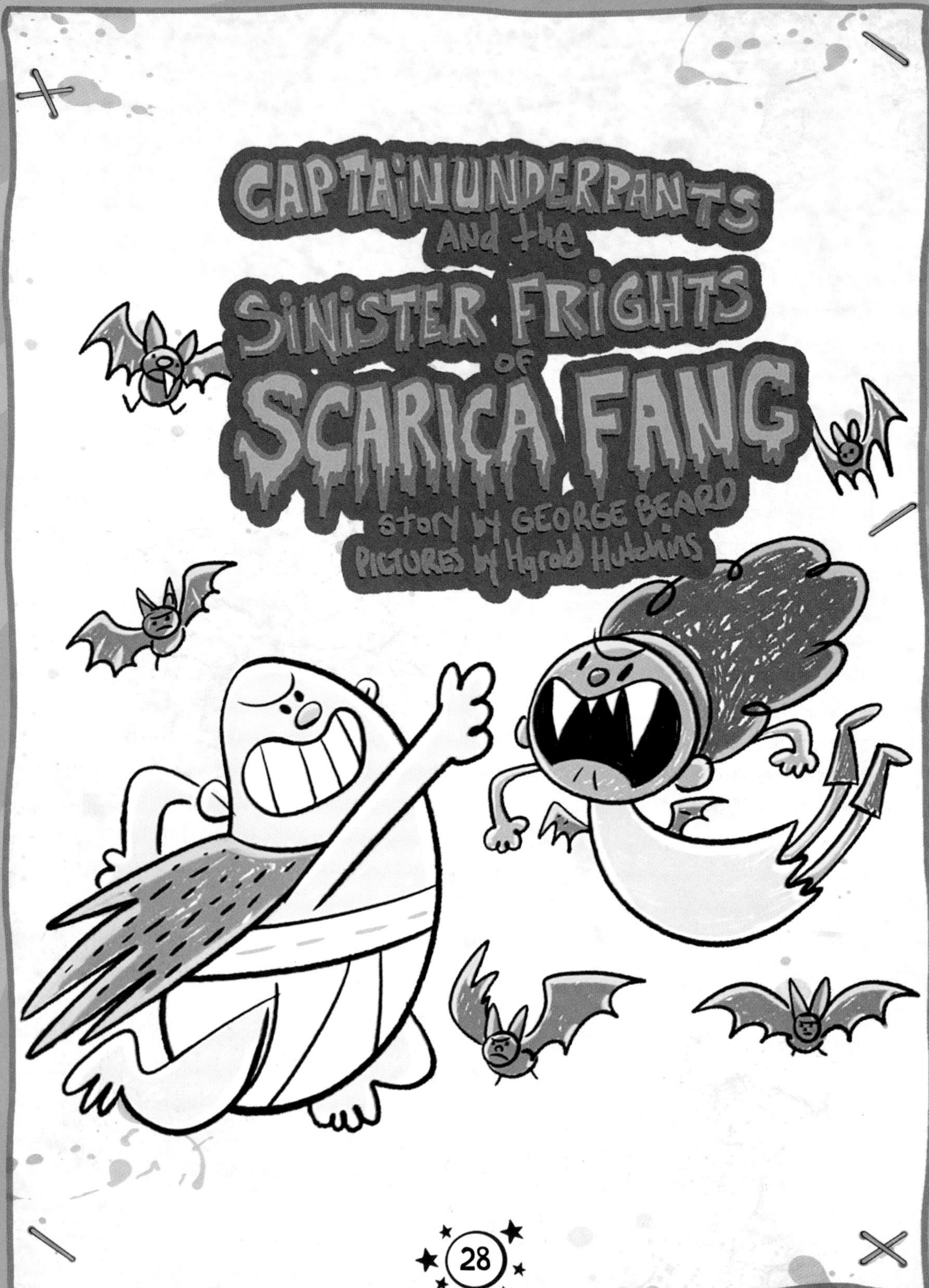
CAPTAIN UNDERPANTS
AND the
SINISTER FRIGHTS
OF
SCARICA FANG
story by GEORGE BEARD
PICTURES by Harold Hutchins

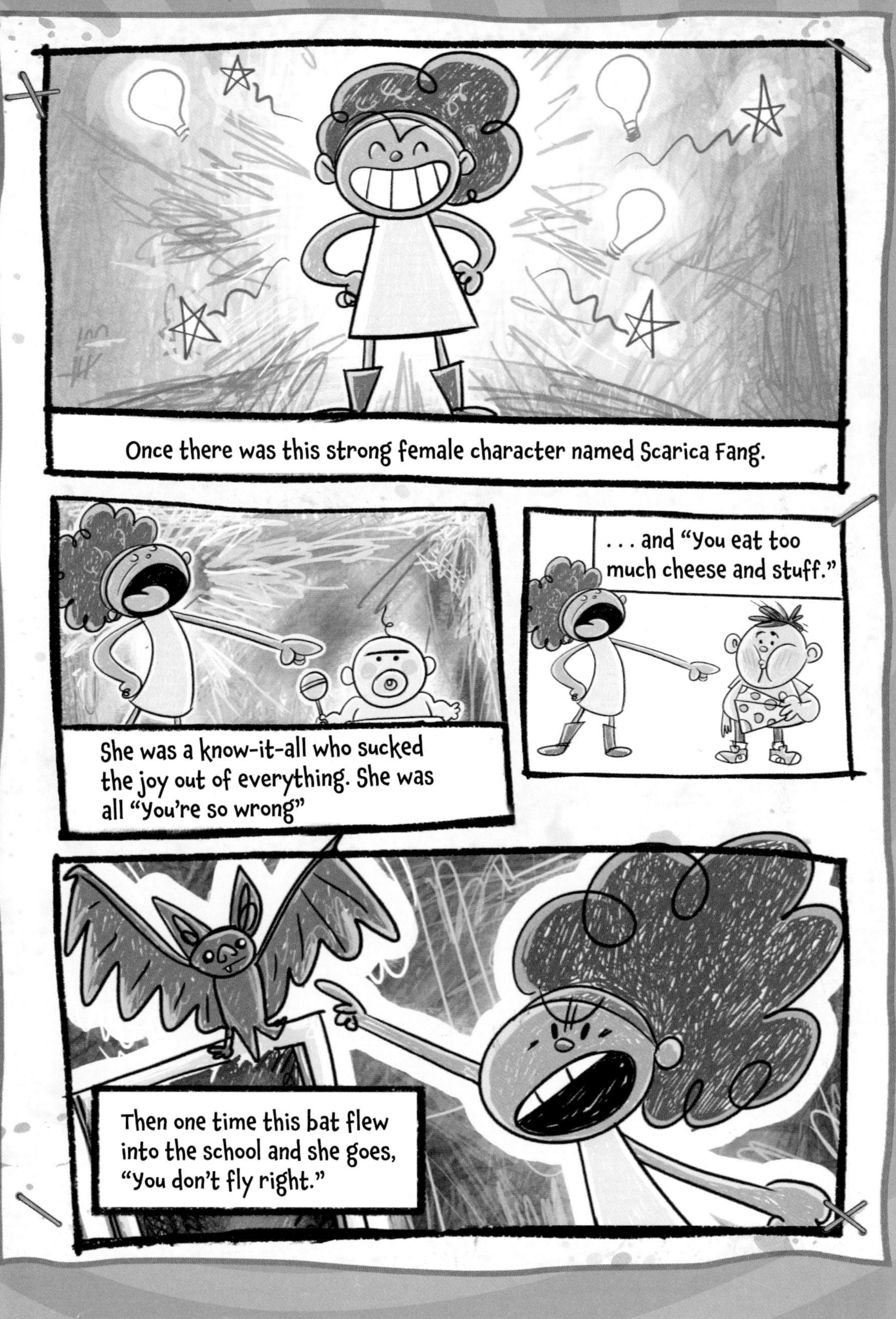
Once there was this strong female character named Scarica Fang.
She was a know-it-all who sucked the joy out of everything. She was all "You're so wrong"
. . . and "You eat too much cheese and stuff."
Then one time this bat flew into the school and she goes, "You don't fly right."

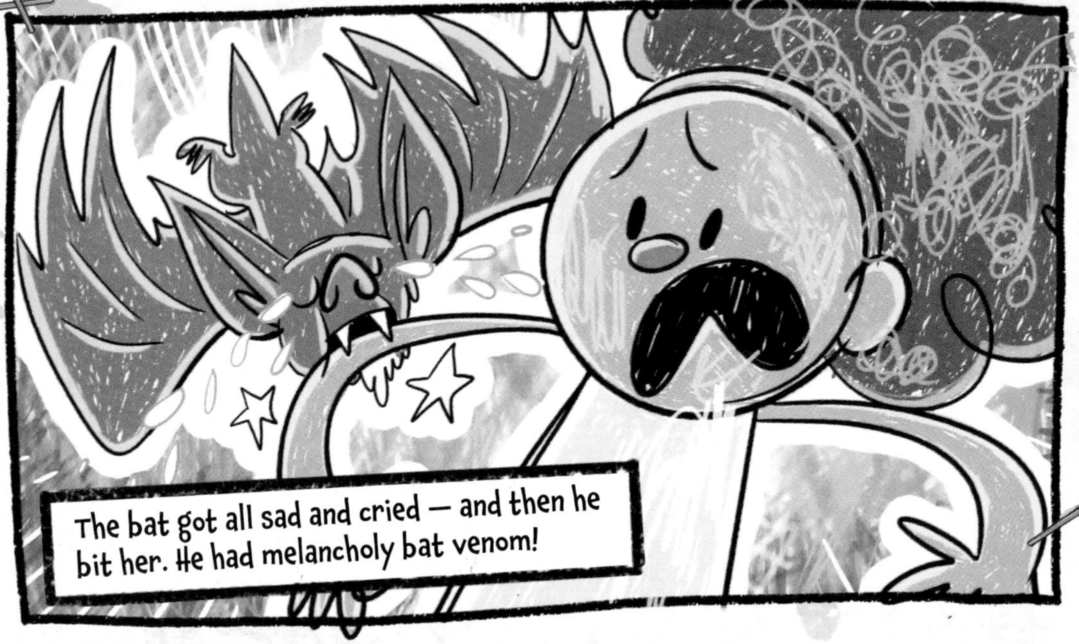
The bat got all sad and cried — and then he bit her. He had melancholy bat venom!

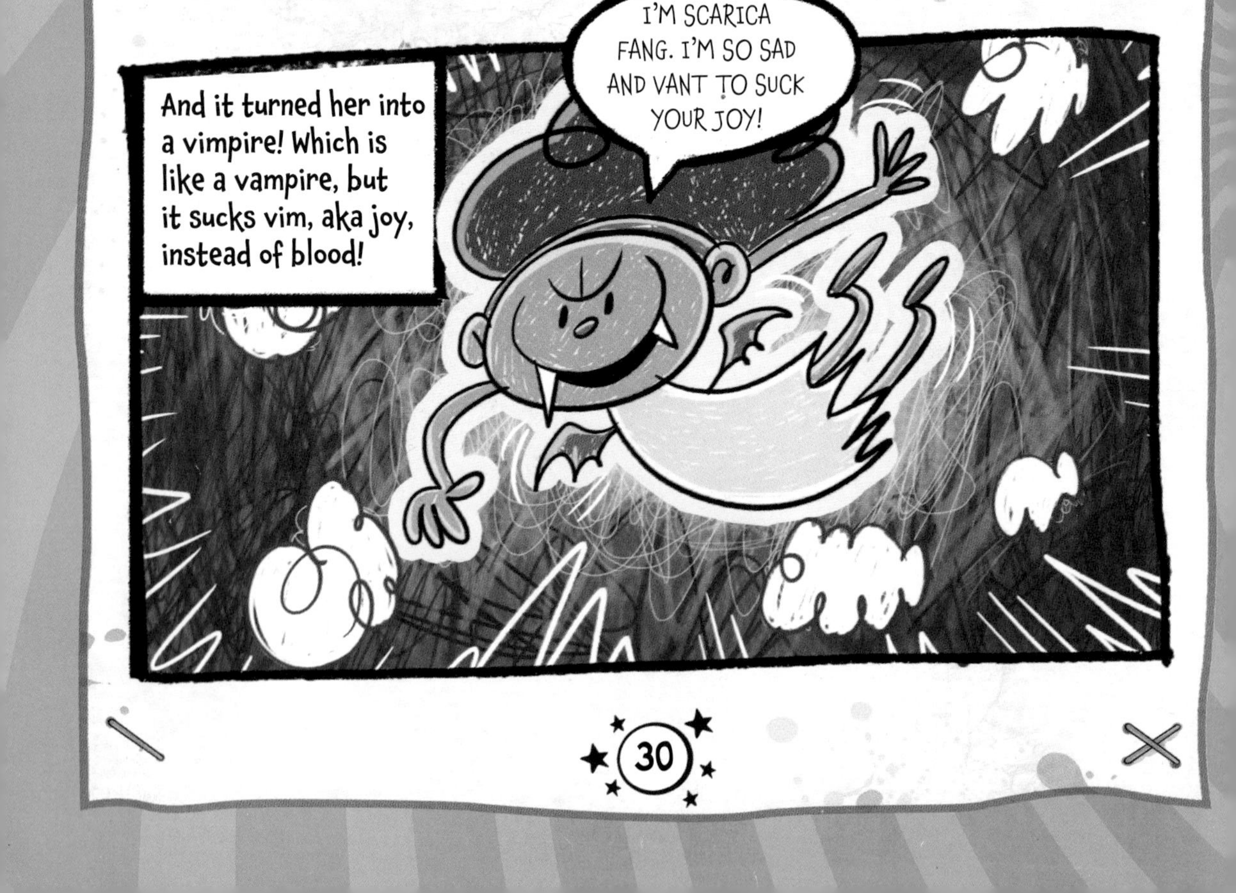
And it turned her into a vimpire! Which is like a vampire, but it sucks vim, aka joy, instead of blood!
I'M SCARICA FANG. I'M SO SAD AND VANT TO SUCK YOUR JOY!

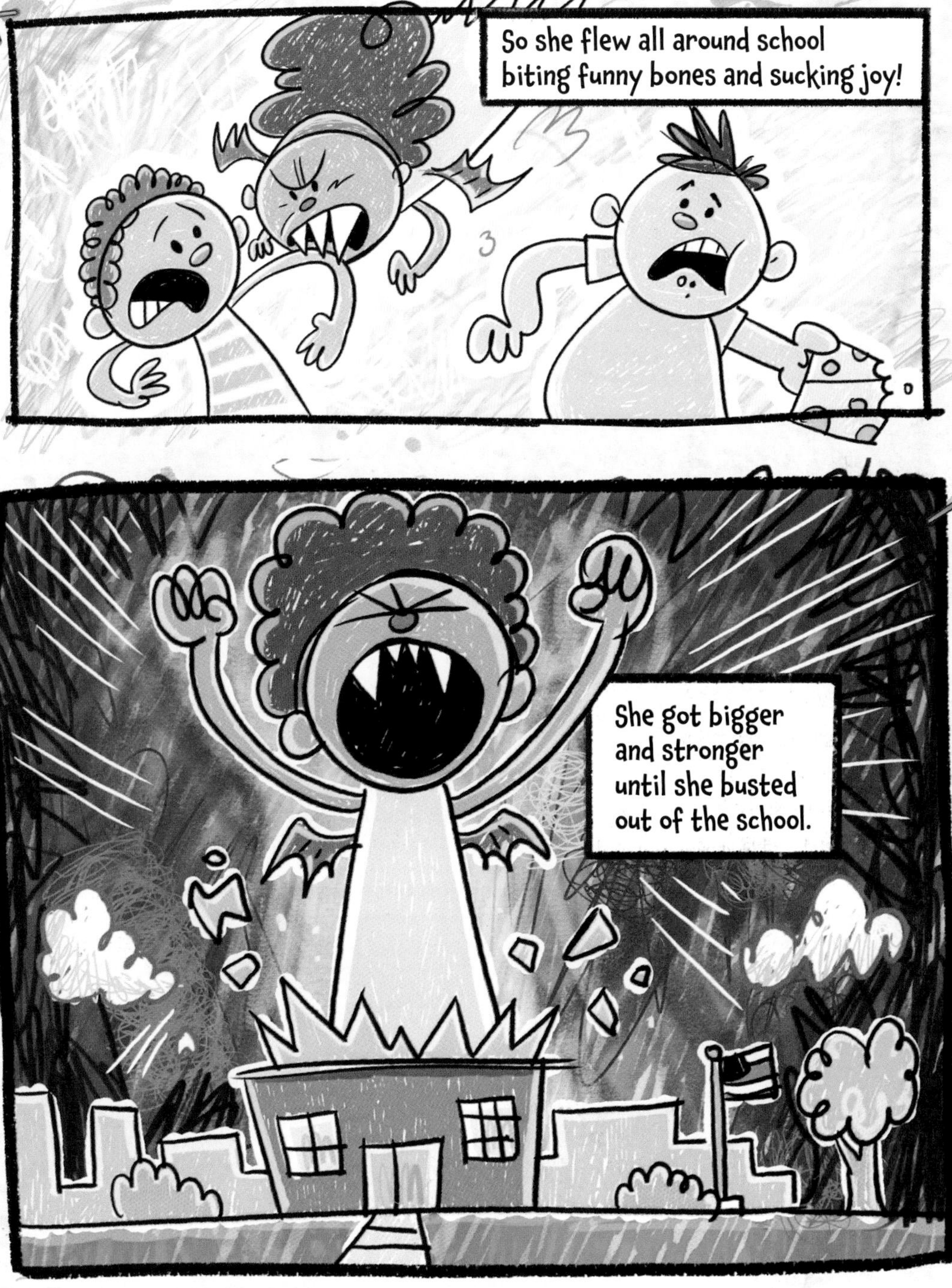
So she flew all around school biting funny bones and sucking joy!
She got bigger and stronger until she busted out of the school.

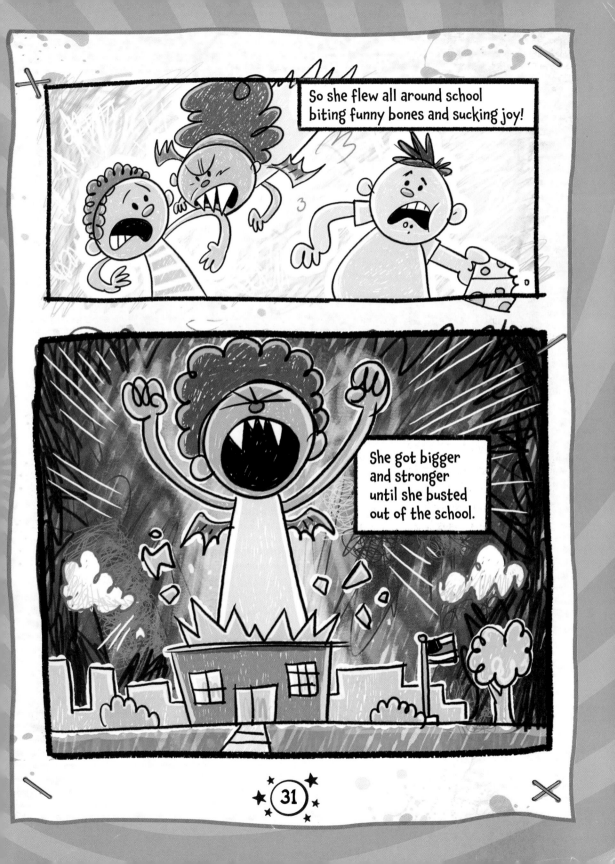

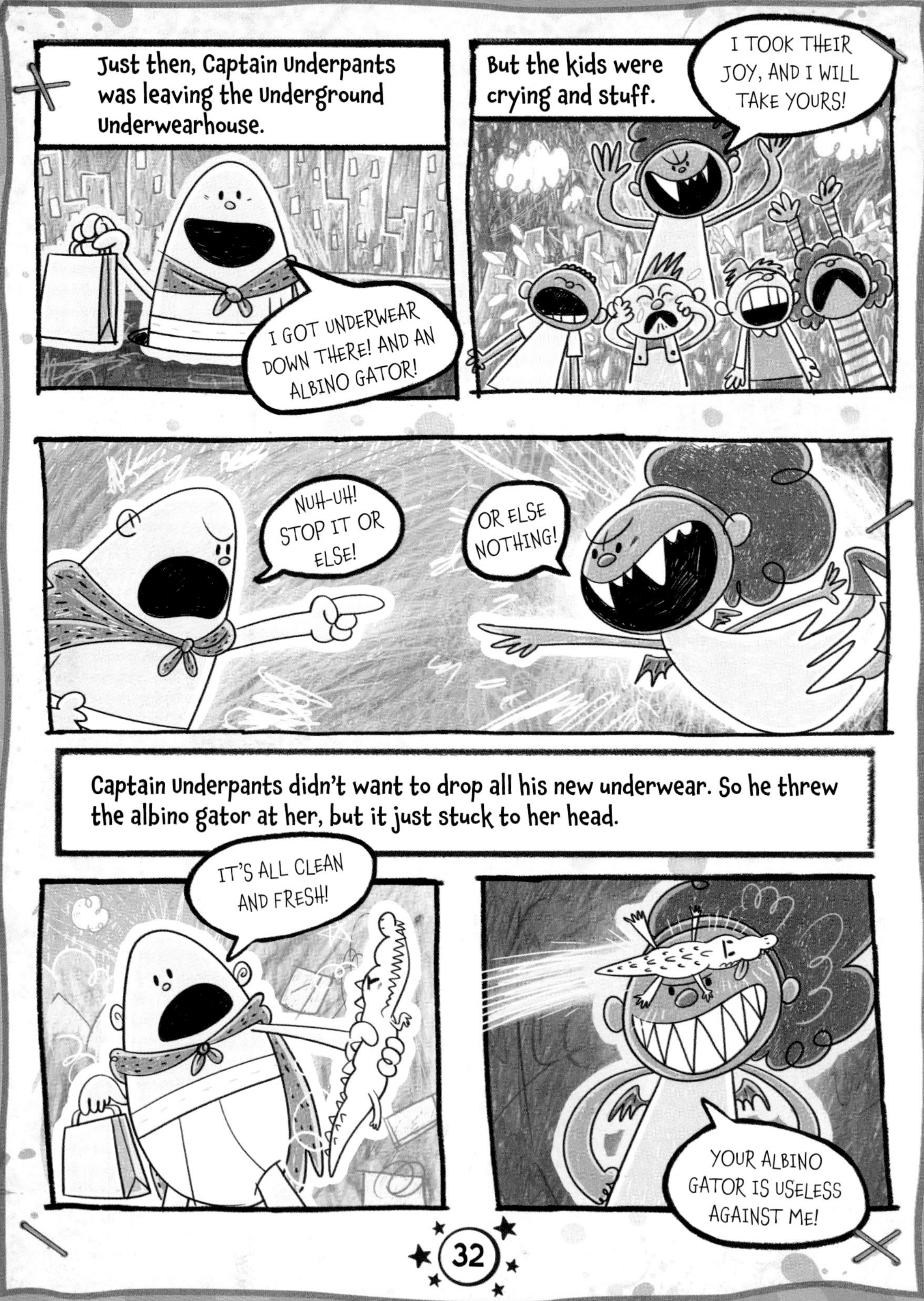
Just then, Captain Underpants was leaving the Underground Underwearhouse.
I GOT UNDERWEAR DOWN THERE! AND AN ALBINO GATOR!
But the kids were crying and stuff.
I TOOK THEIR JOY, AND I WILL TAKE YOURS!
NUH-UH! STOP IT OR ELSE!
OR ELSE NOTHING!
Captain Underpants didn't want to drop all his new underwear. So he threw the albino gator at her, but it just stuck to her head.
IT'S ALL CLEAN AND FRESH!
YOUR ALBINO GATOR IS USELESS AGAINST ME!

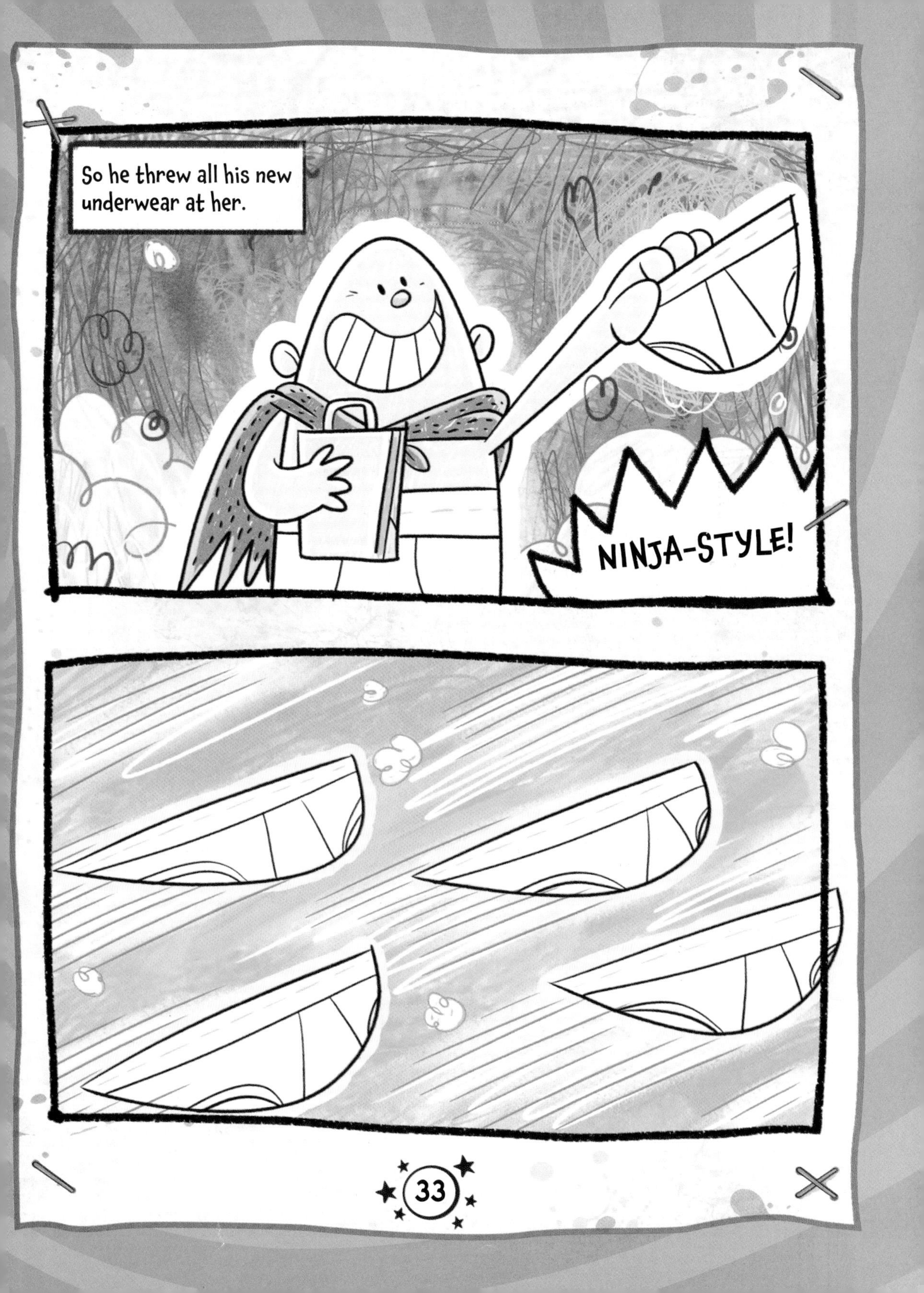
So he threw all his new underwear at her.
NINJA-STYLE!

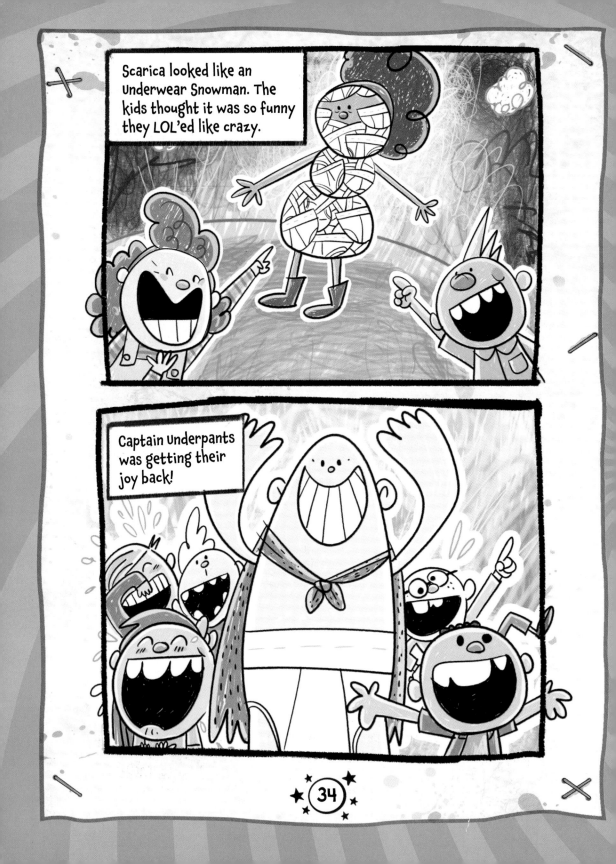

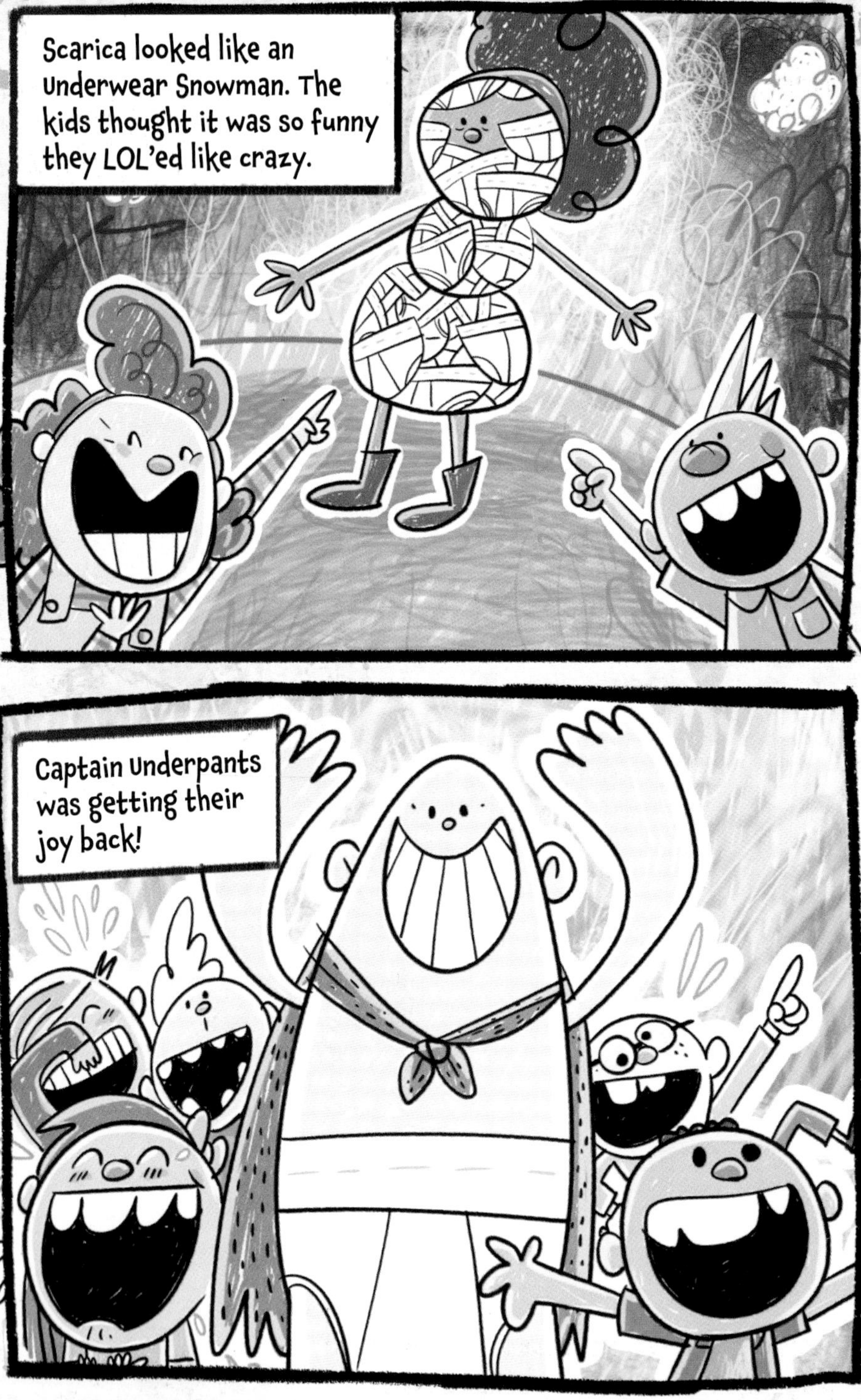
Scarica looked like an Underwear Snowman. The kids thought it was so funny they LOL'ed like crazy.
Captain Underpants was getting their joy back!

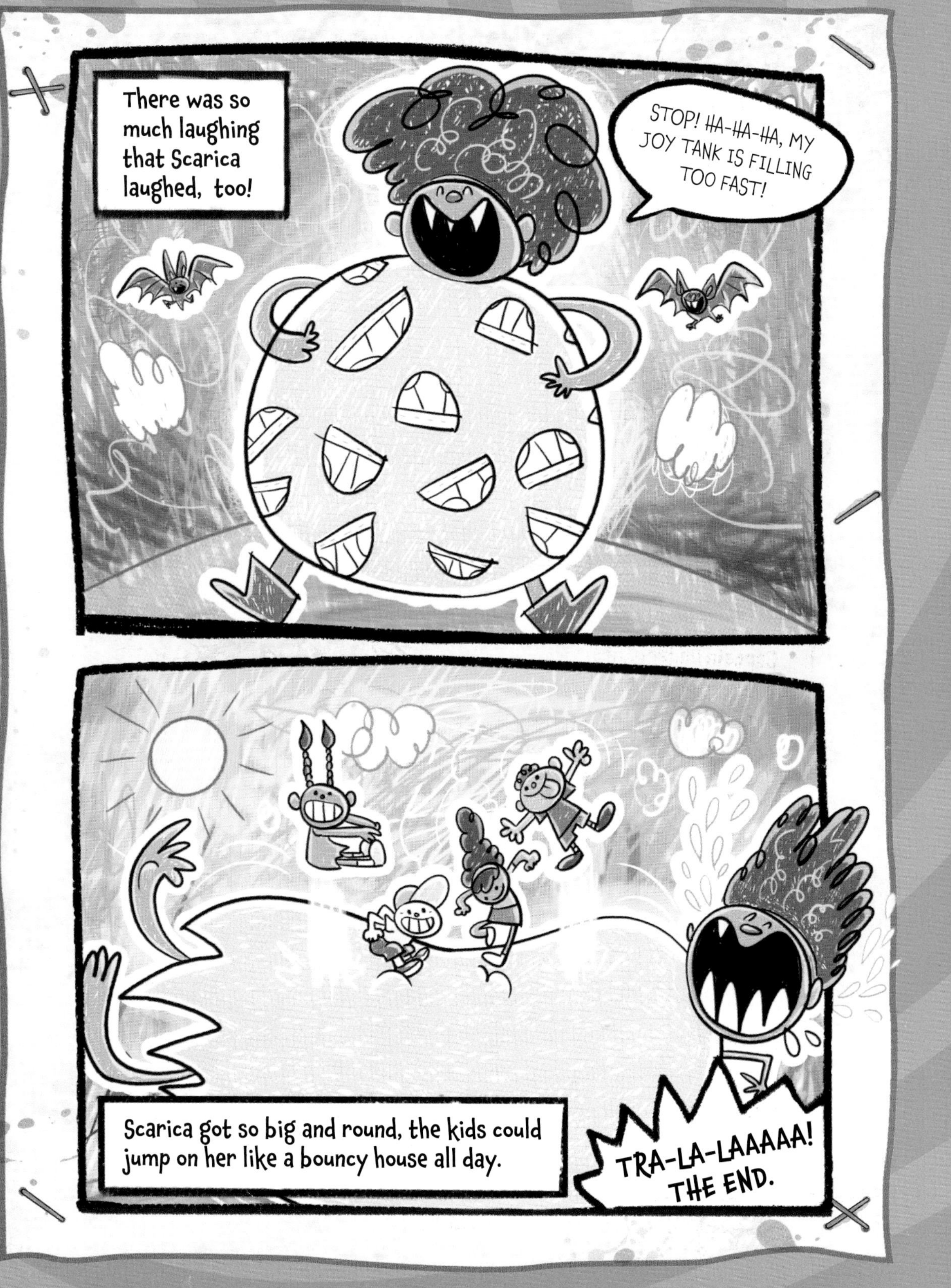

There was so much laughing that Scarica laughed, too!
STOP! HA-HA-HA, MY JOY TANK IS FILLING TOO FAST!
Scarica got so big and round, the kids could jump on her like a bouncy house all day.
TRA-LA-LAAAAA! THE END.

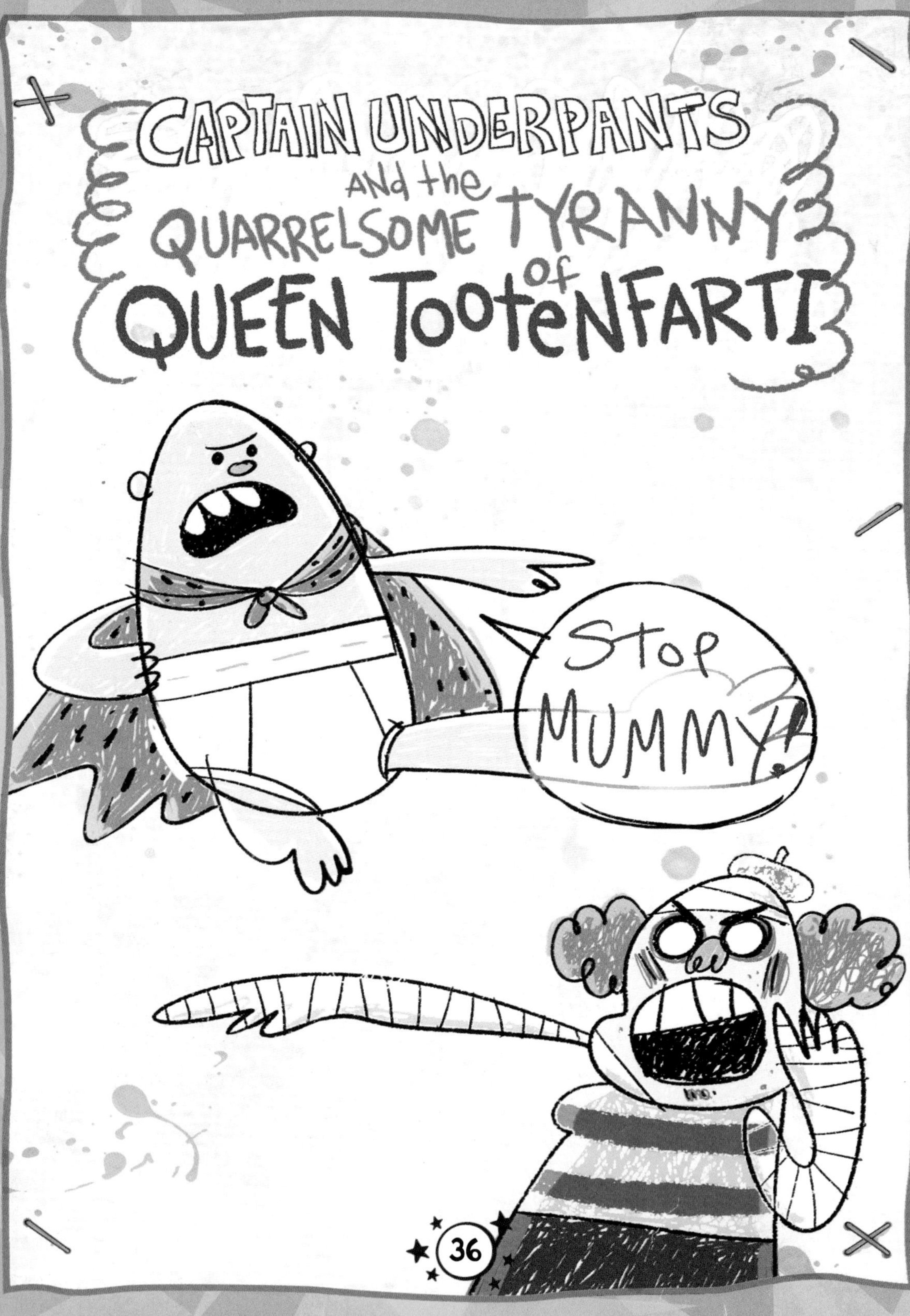
CAPTAIN UNDERPANTS
and the
QUARRELSOME TYRANNY
of
QUEEN TOOTENFARTI
STOP MUMMY!

Once there was this annoying French teacher who was awful and really loved French stuff and made all the kids talk French.

One day she took the kids on a field trip in a bus and stuff.

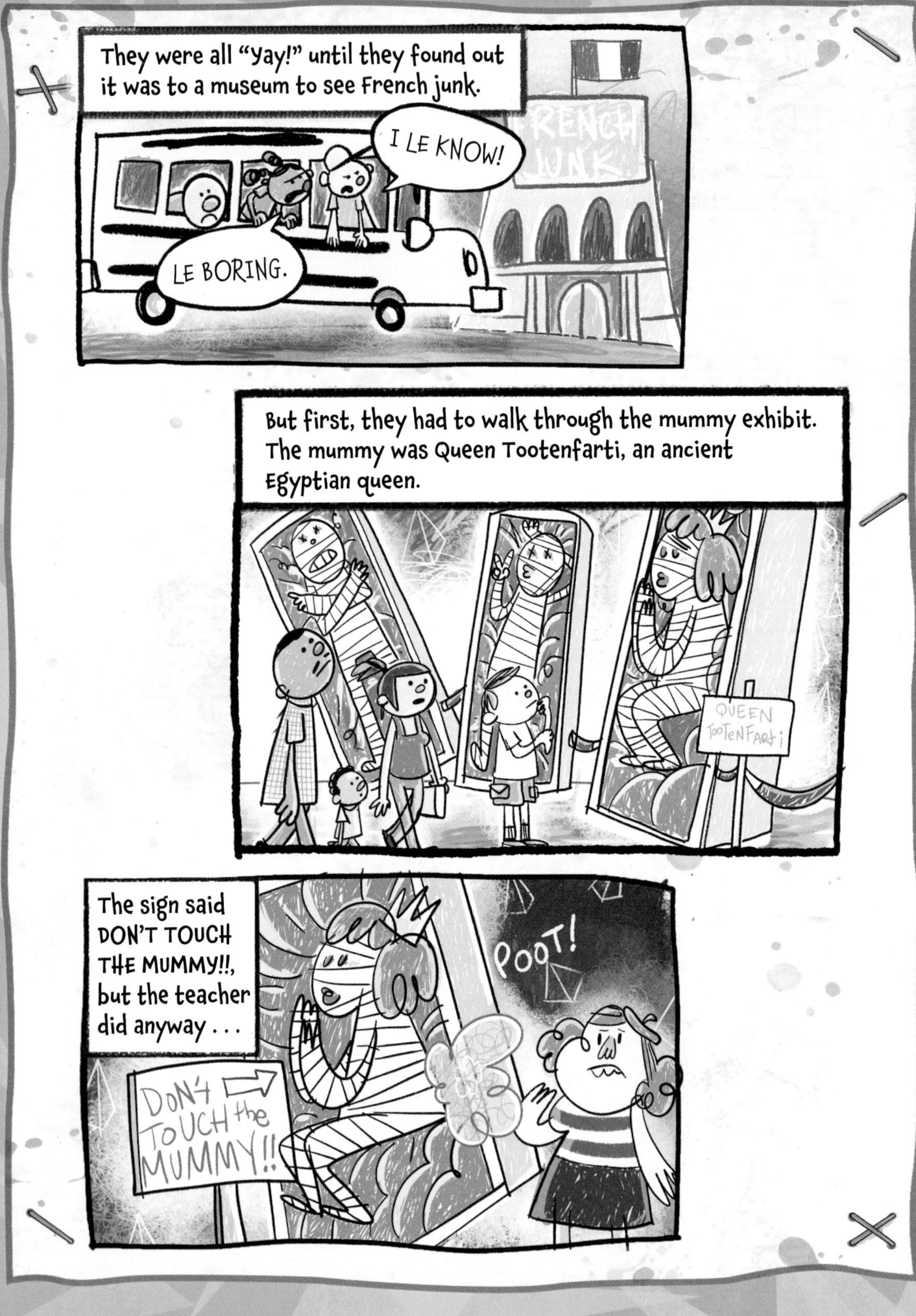
They were all "yay!" until they found out it was to a museum to see French junk.
FRENCH JUNK
I LE KNOW!
LE BORING.
But first, they had to walk through the mummy exhibit. The mummy was Queen Tootenfarti, an ancient Egyptian queen.
QUEEN TOOTENFARTi
The sign said DON'T TOUCH THE MUMMY!!, but the teacher did anyway . . .
POOT!
DON'T TOUCH the MUMMY!!

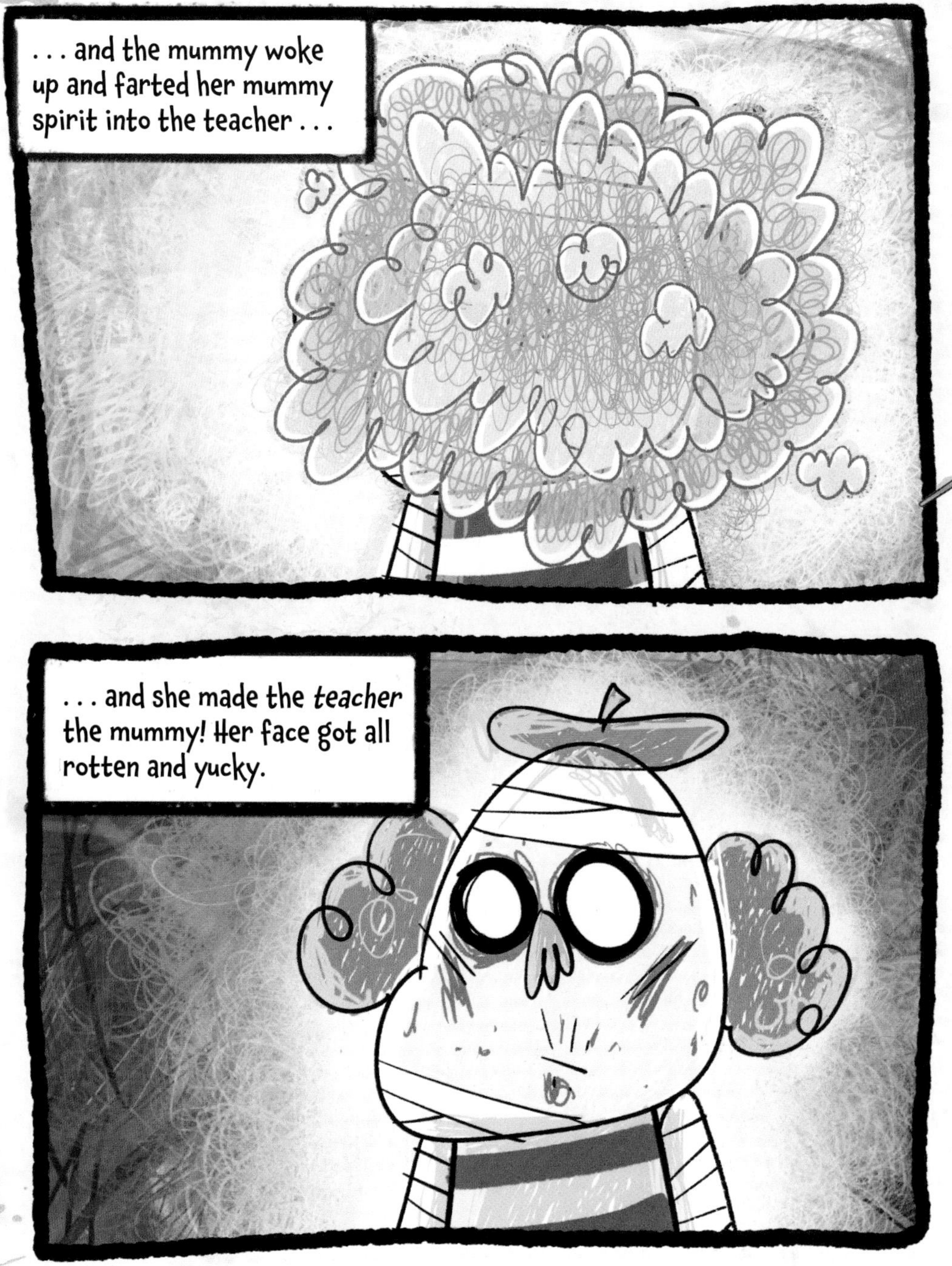
. . . and the mummy woke up and farted her mummy spirit into the teacher . . .
. . . and she made the *teacher* the mummy! Her face got all rotten and yucky.

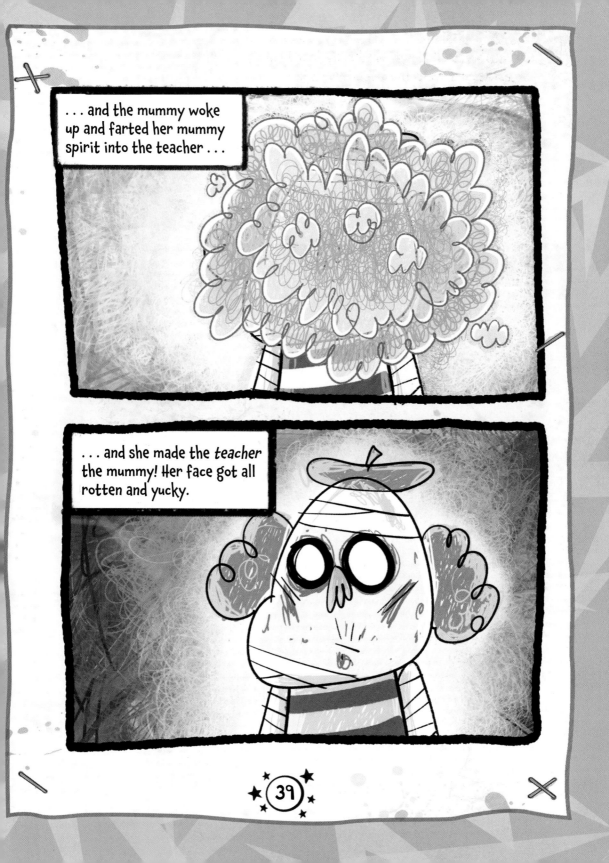

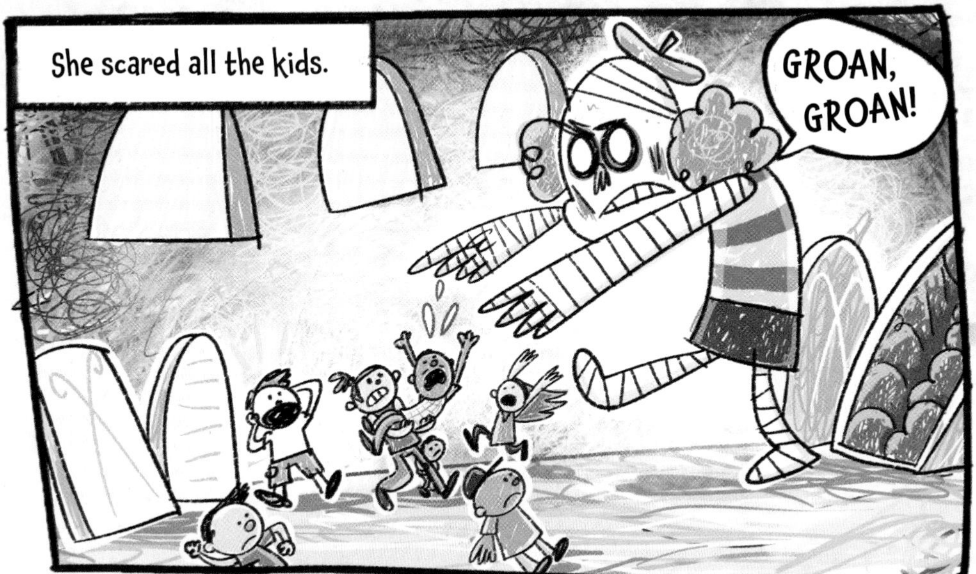
She scared all the kids.
GROAN, GROAN!

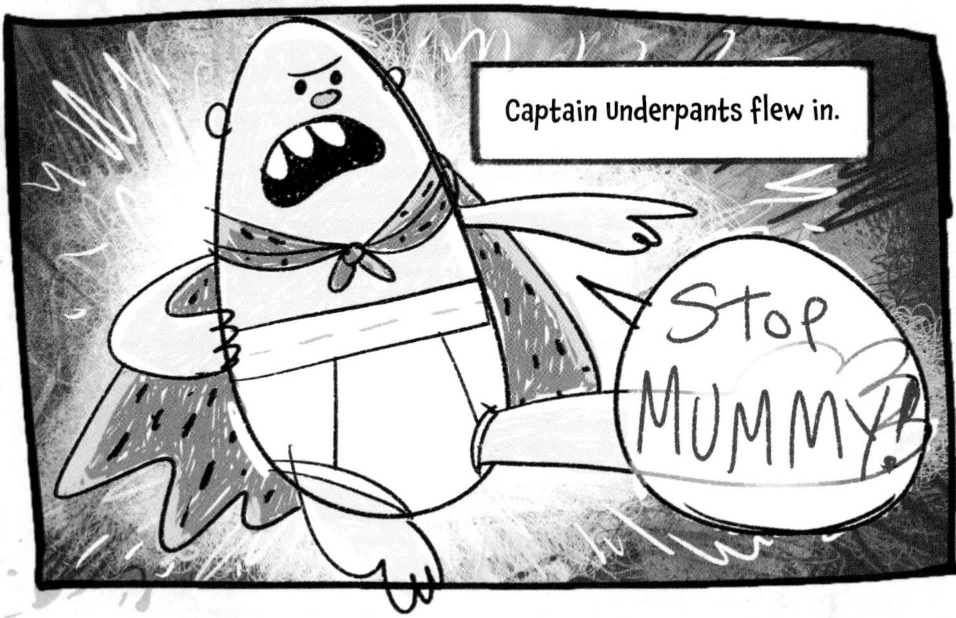
Captain Underpants flew in.
Stop MUMMY!

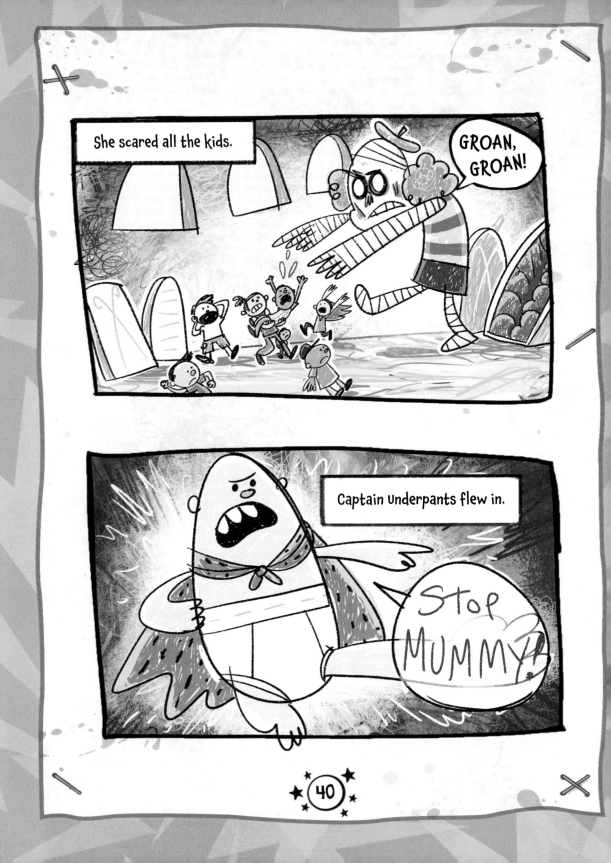

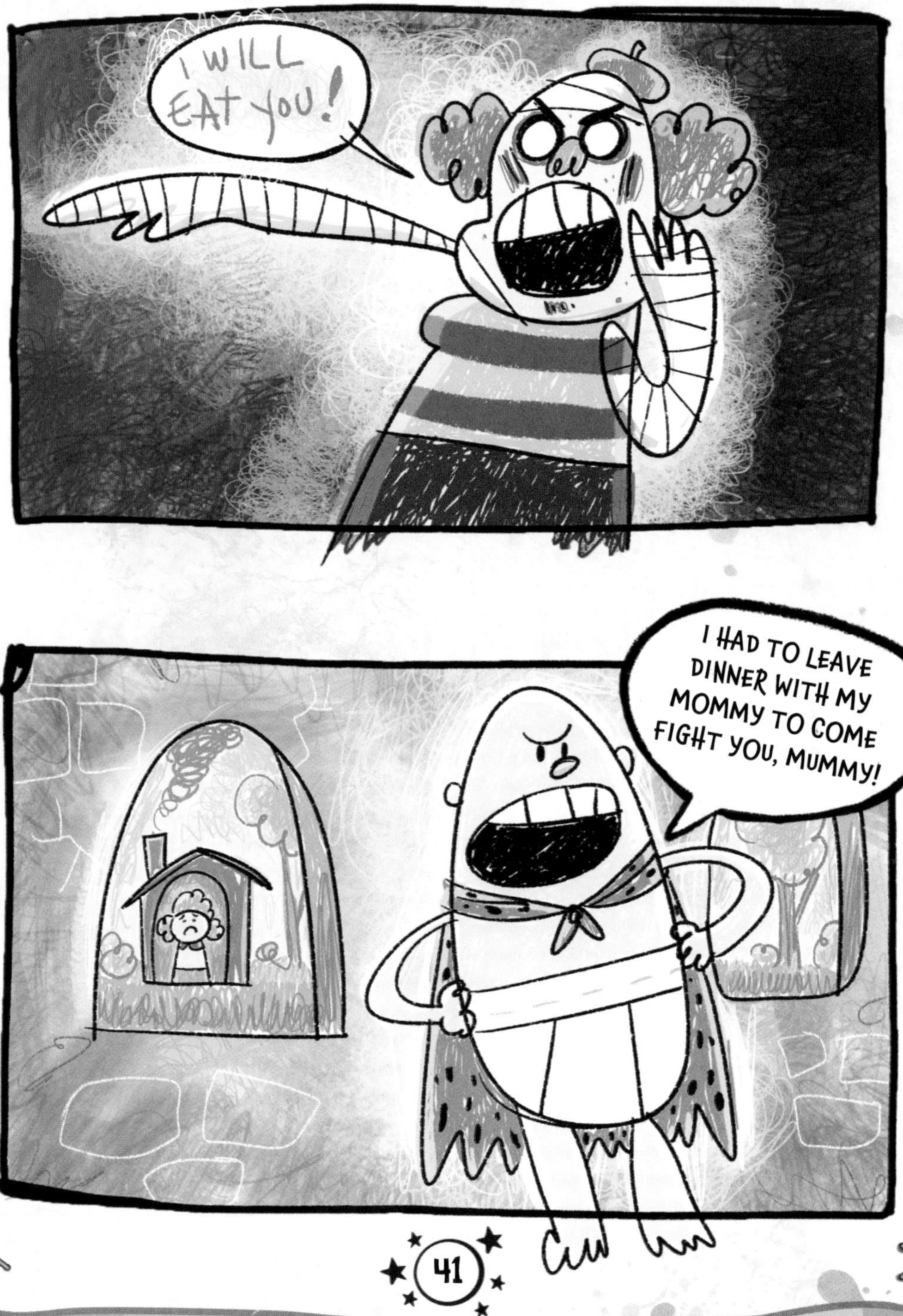
I WILL EAT YOU!
I HAD TO LEAVE DINNER WITH MY MOMMY TO COME FIGHT YOU, MUMMY!

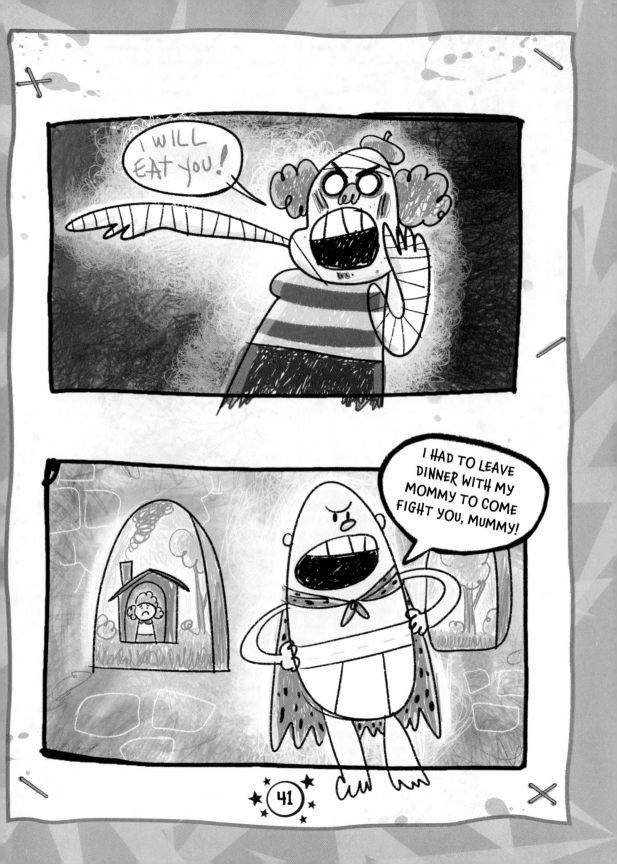

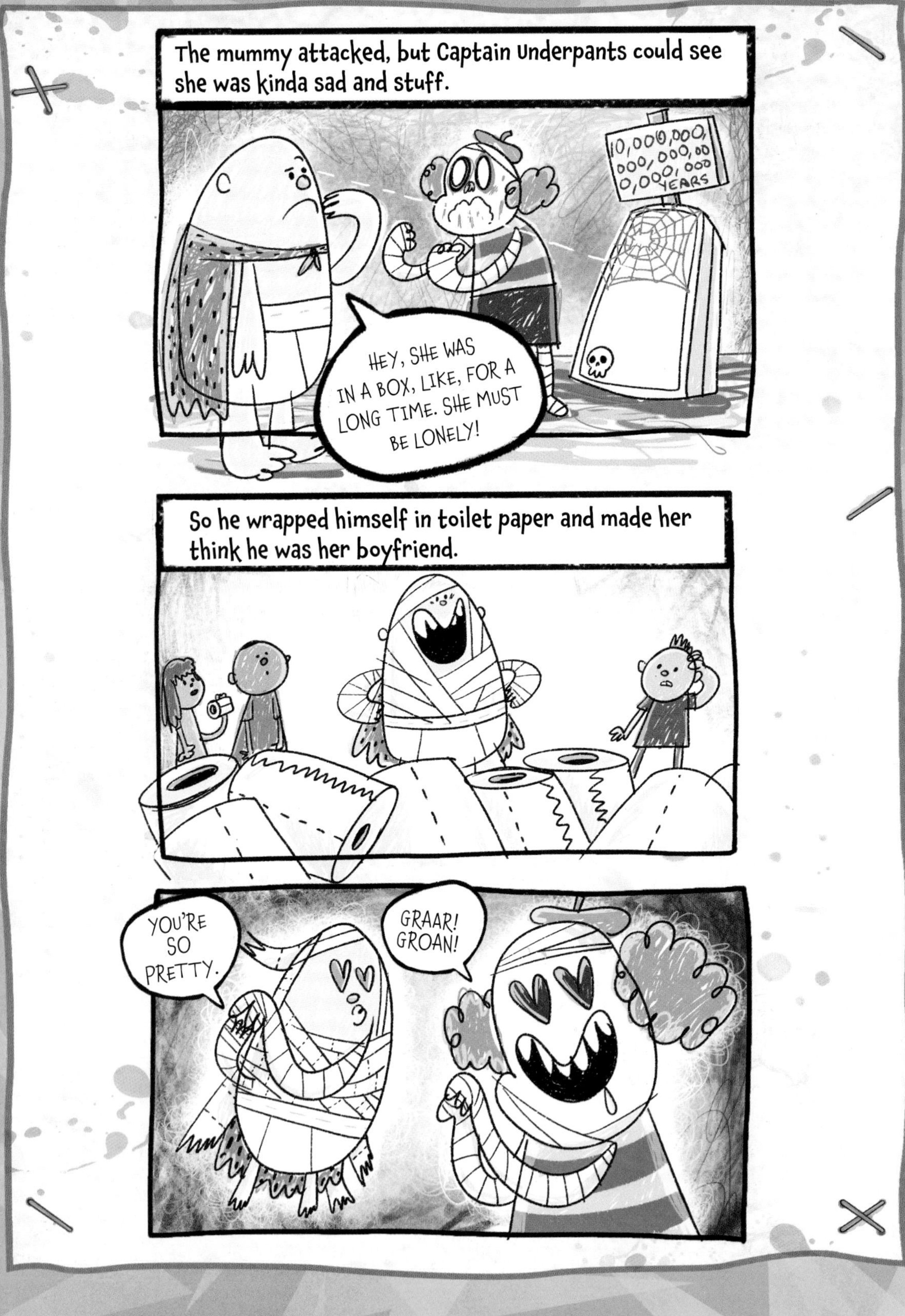
The mummy attacked, but Captain Underpants could see she was kinda sad and stuff.
10,000,000,000,000,000,000,000,000 YEARS
HEY, SHE WAS IN A BOX, LIKE, FOR A LONG TIME. SHE MUST BE LONELY!
So he wrapped himself in toilet paper and made her think he was her boyfriend.
YOU'RE SO PRETTY.
GRAAR! GROAN!

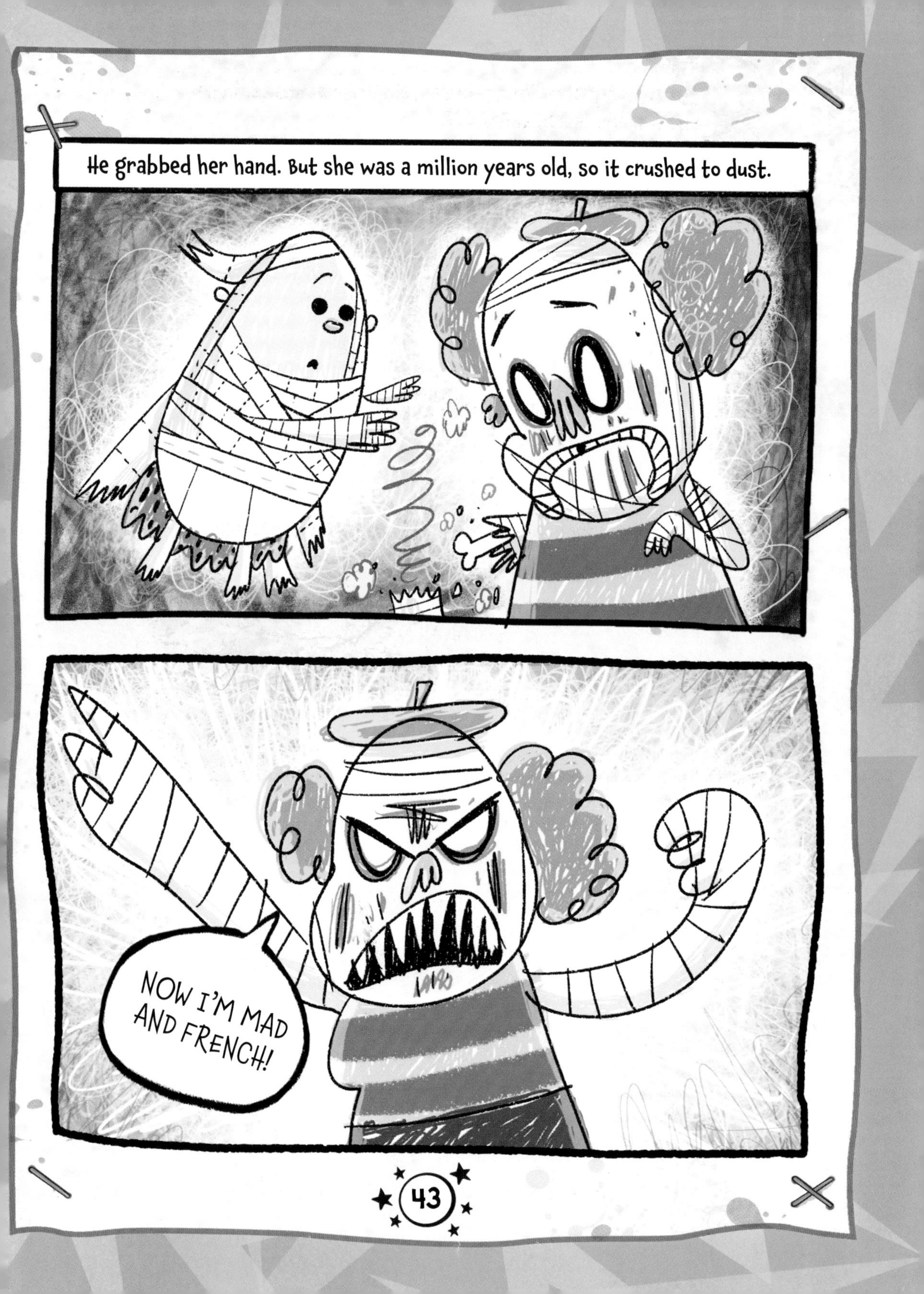
He grabbed her hand. But she was a million years old, so it crushed to dust.
NOW I'M MAD AND FRENCH!

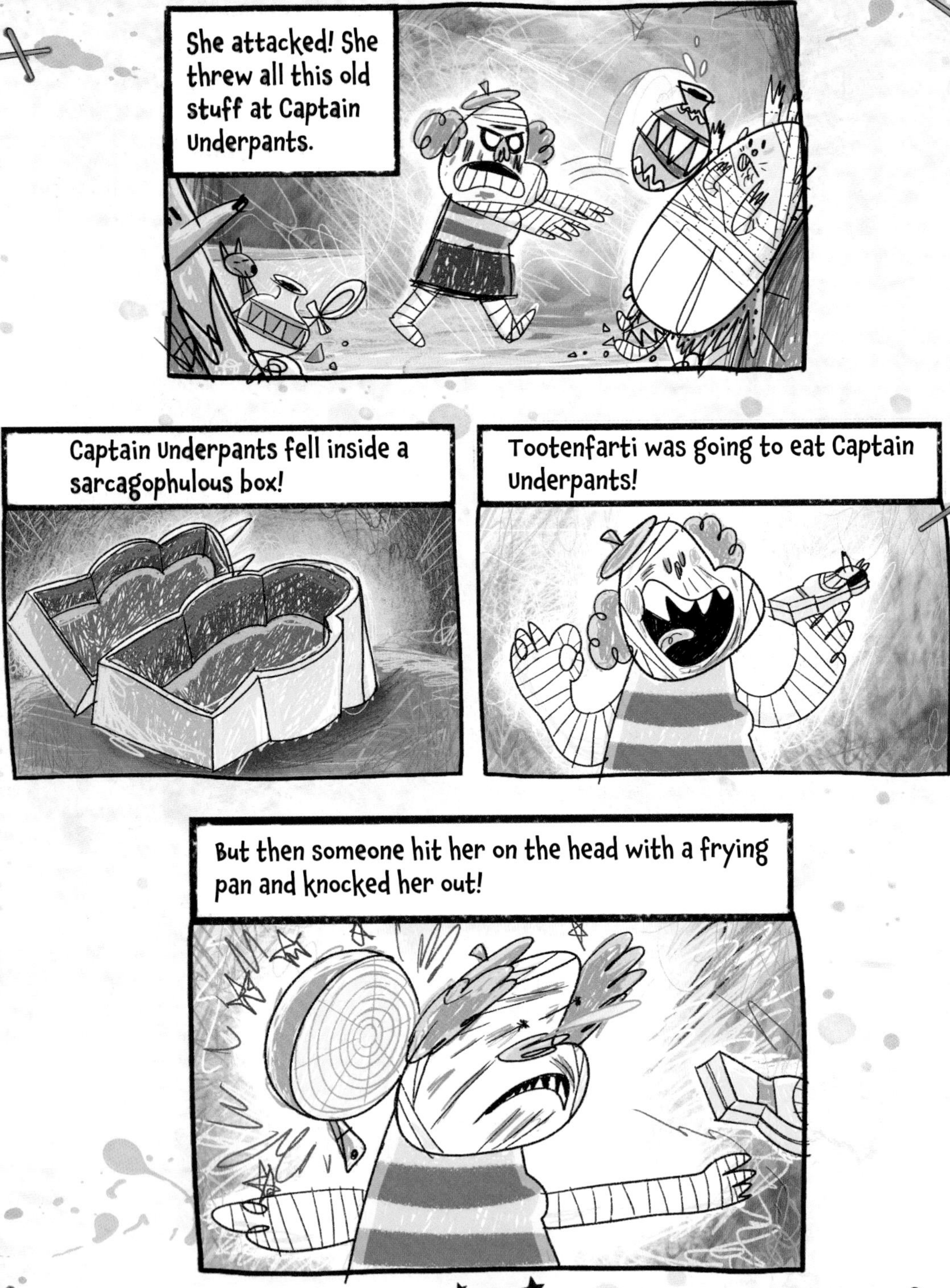
She attacked! She threw all this old stuff at Captain Underpants.
Captain Underpants fell inside a sarcagophulous box!
Tootenfarti was going to eat Captain Underpants!
But then someone hit her on the head with a frying pan and knocked her out!

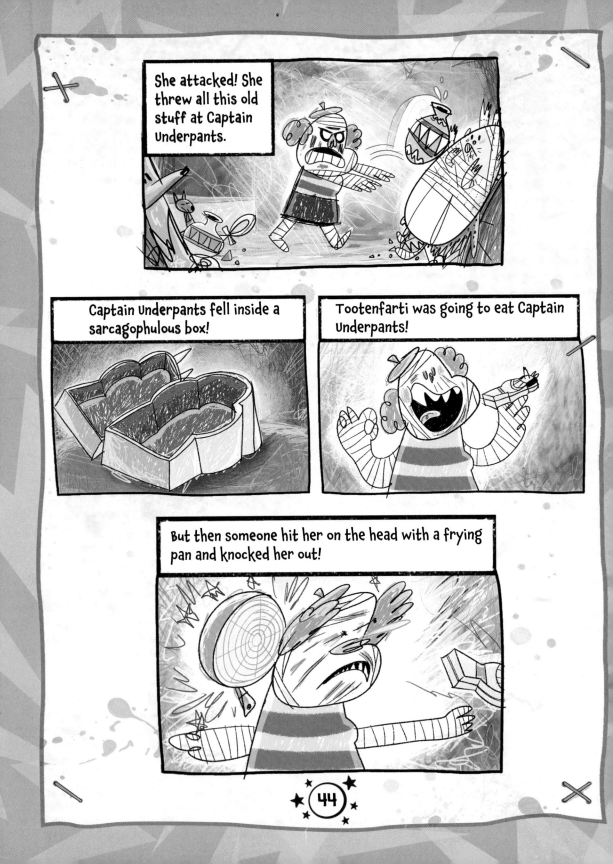

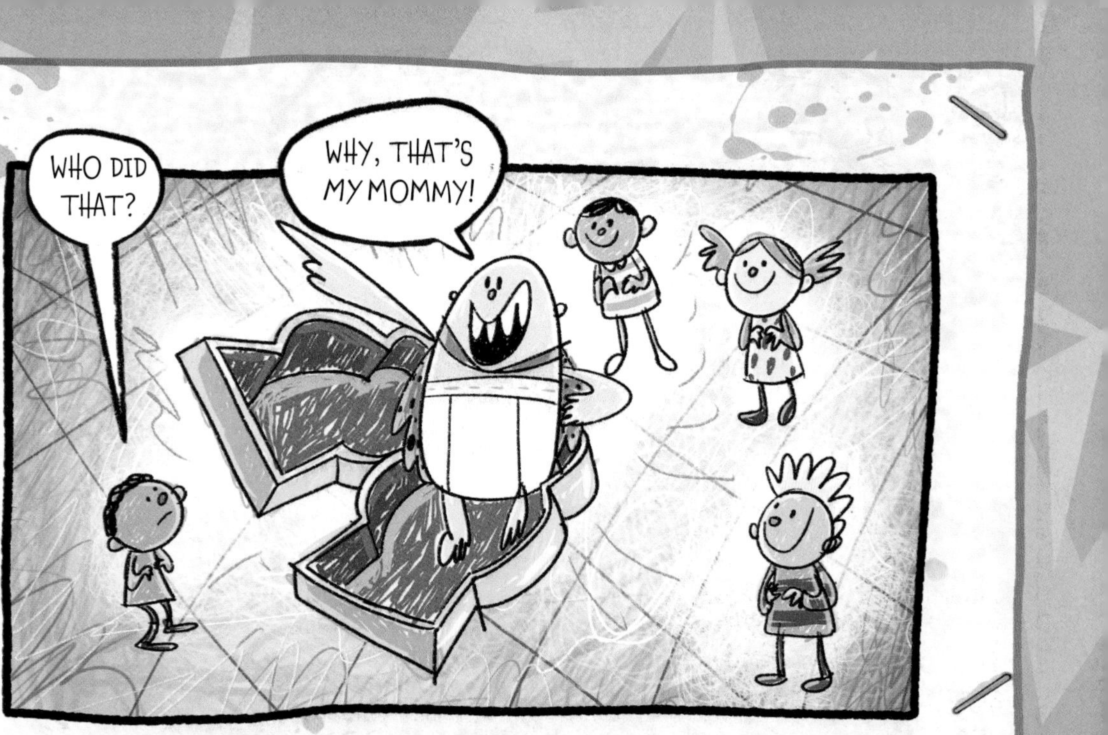
WHO DID THAT?
WHY, THAT'S MY MOMMY!

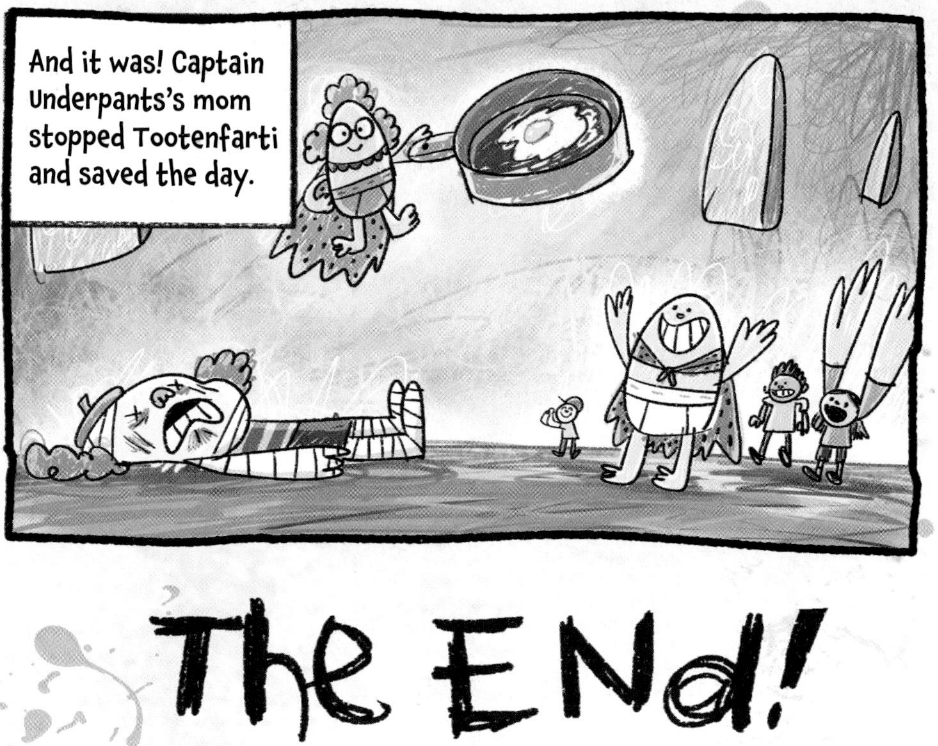
And it was! Captain Underpants's mom stopped Tootenfarti and saved the day.

The End!

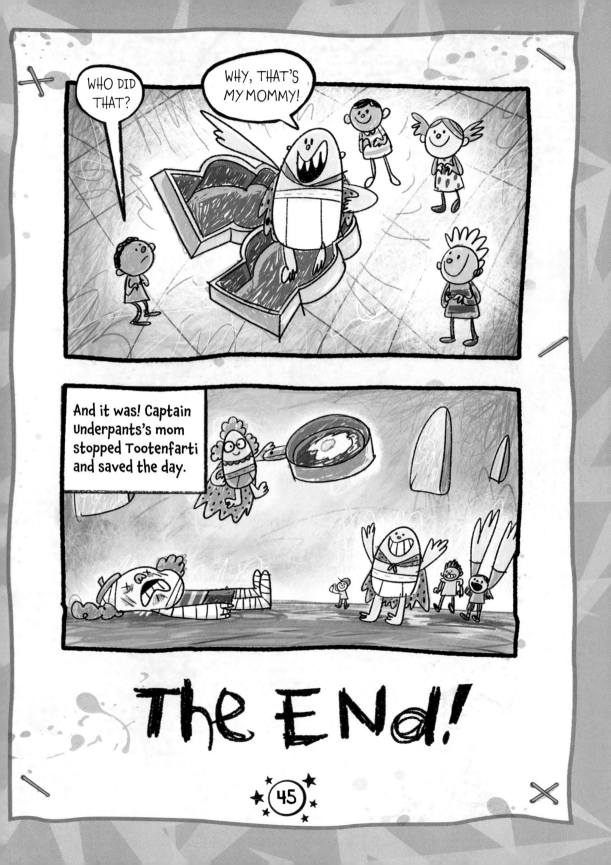

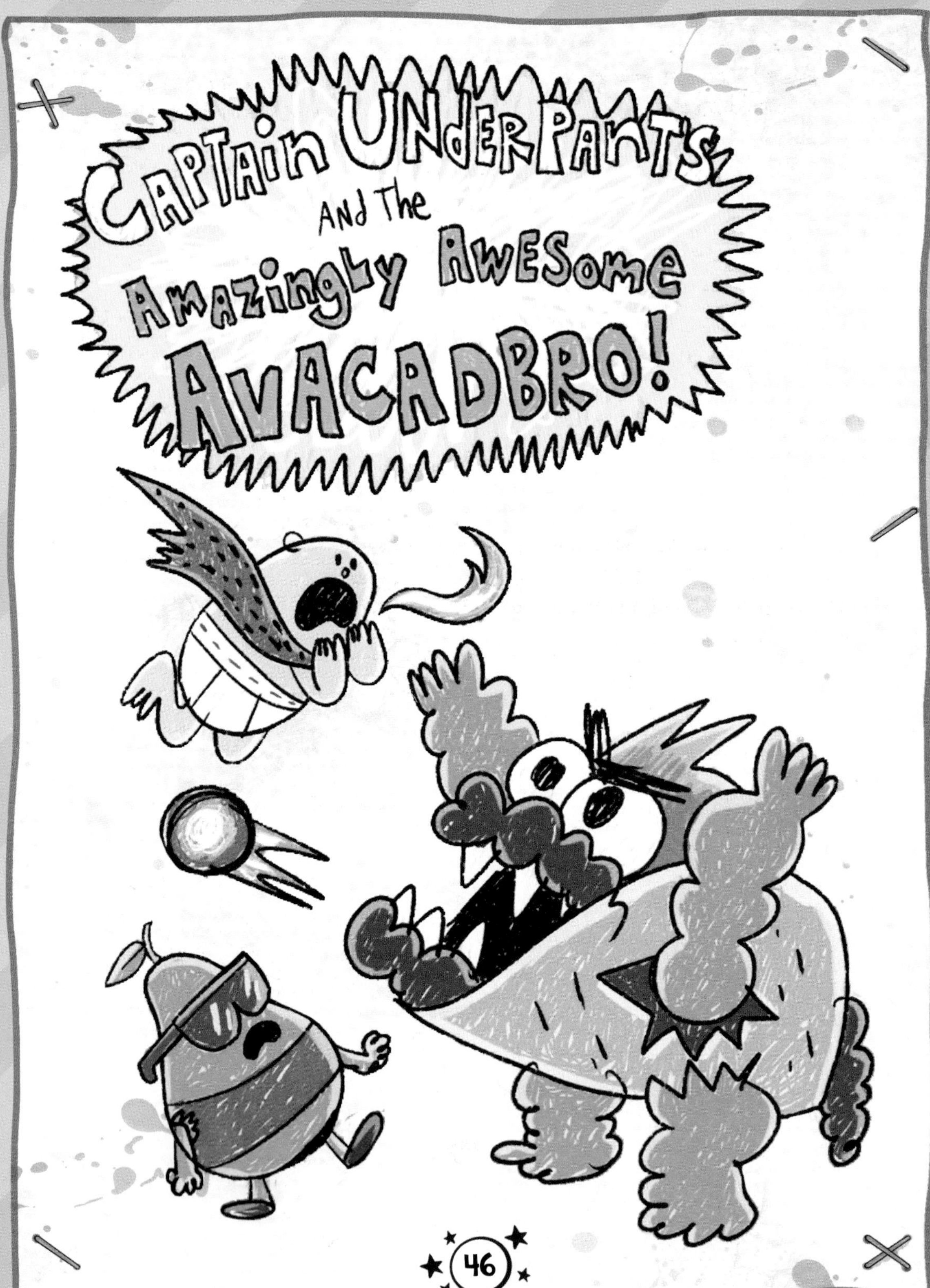
Captain Underpants
and the
Amazingly Awesome
Avacadbro!

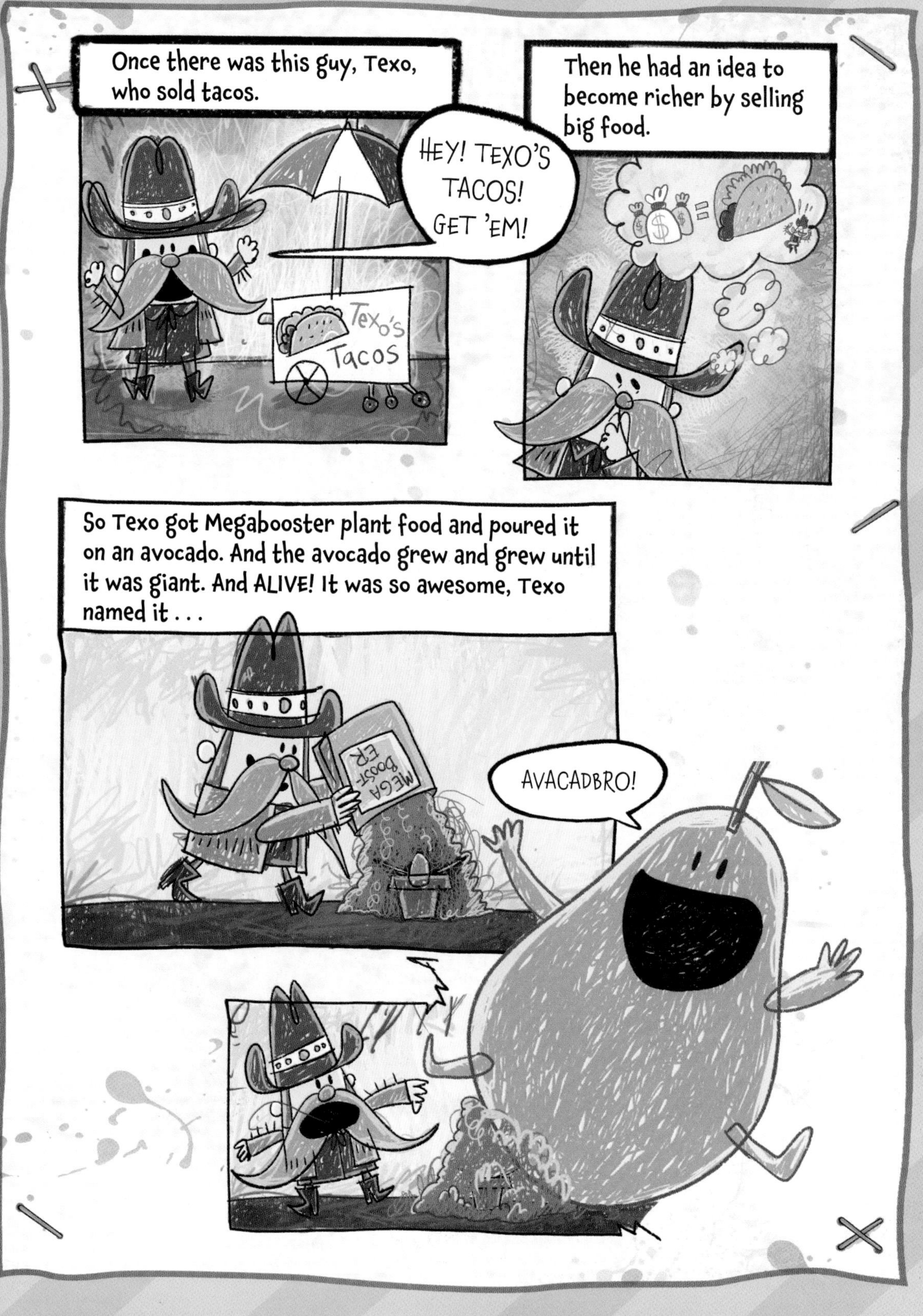
Once there was this guy, Texo, who sold tacos.
HEY! TEXO'S TACOS! GET 'EM!
Texo's Tacos
Then he had an idea to become richer by selling big food.
So Texo got Megabooster plant food and poured it on an avocado. And the avocado grew and grew until it was giant. And ALIVE! It was so awesome, Texo named it . . .
MEGA BOOST-ER
AVACADBRO!

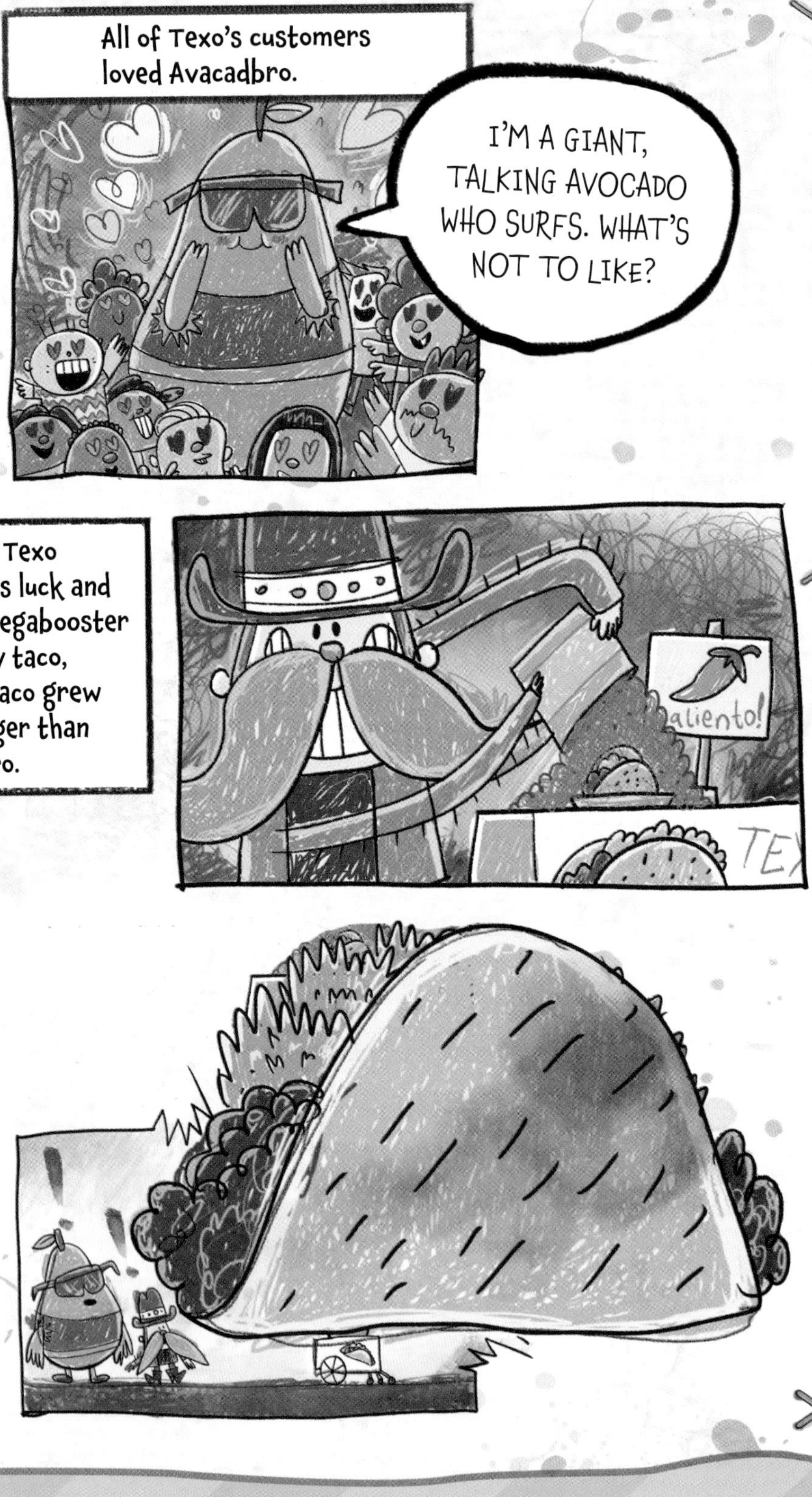
All of Texo's customers loved Avacadbro.
I'M A GIANT, TALKING AVOCADO WHO SURFS. WHAT'S NOT TO LIKE?
But then, Texo pushed his luck and poured Megabooster on a spicy taco, and the taco grew even bigger than Avacadbro.

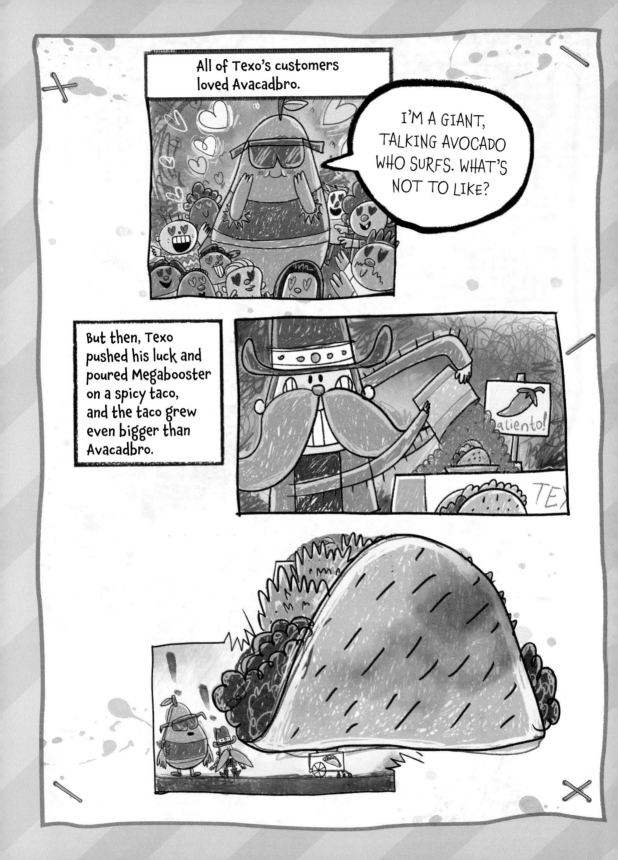

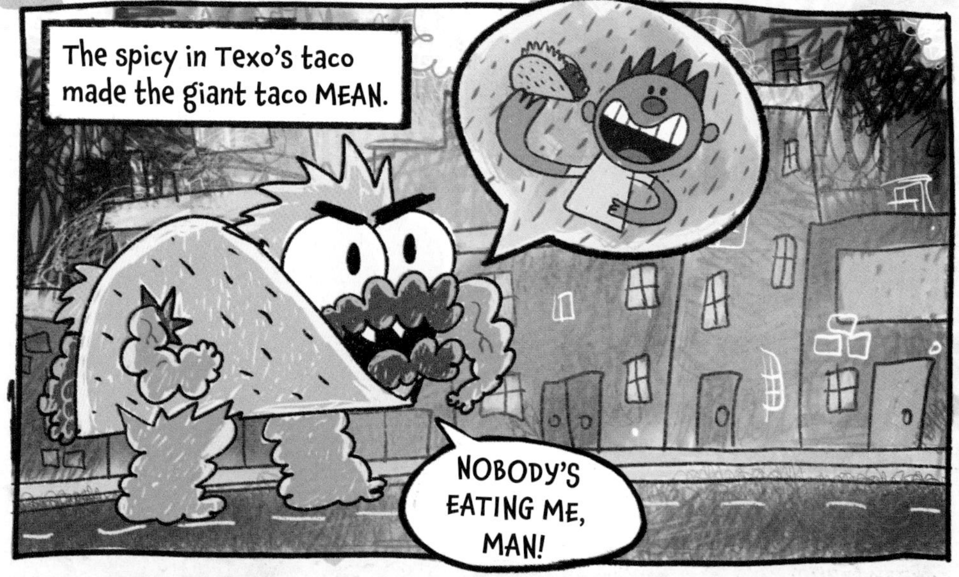
The spicy in Texo's taco made the giant taco MEAN.
NOBODY'S EATING ME, MAN!

It crushed buses! And shot fireballs at the mayor's pants, just as the mayor was about to give a medal to who?

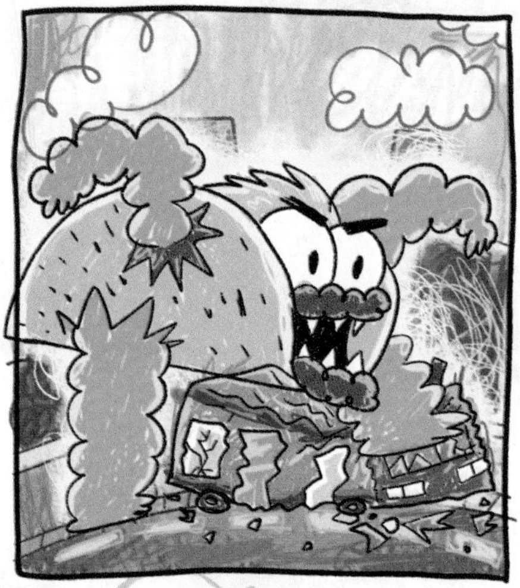

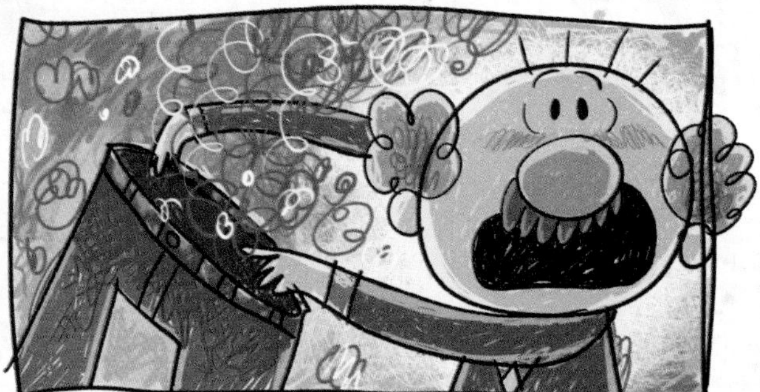

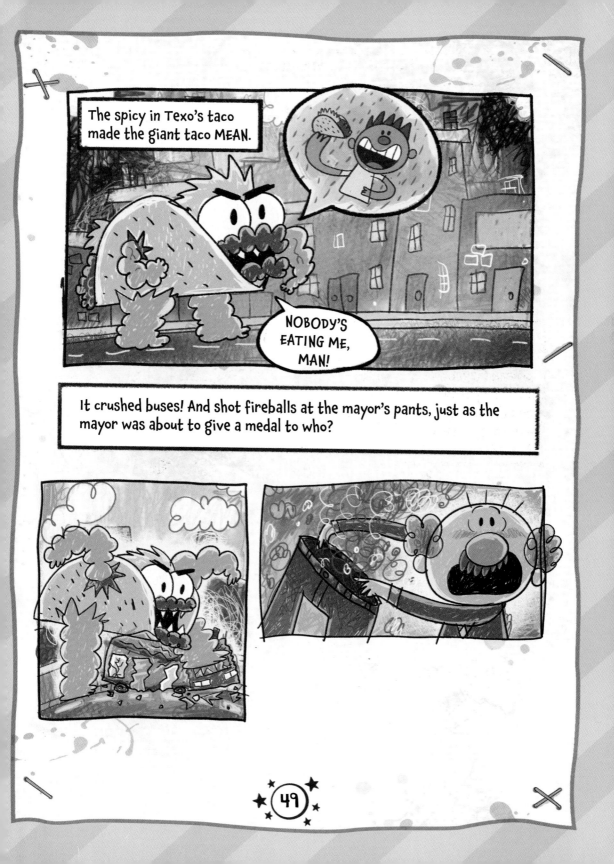

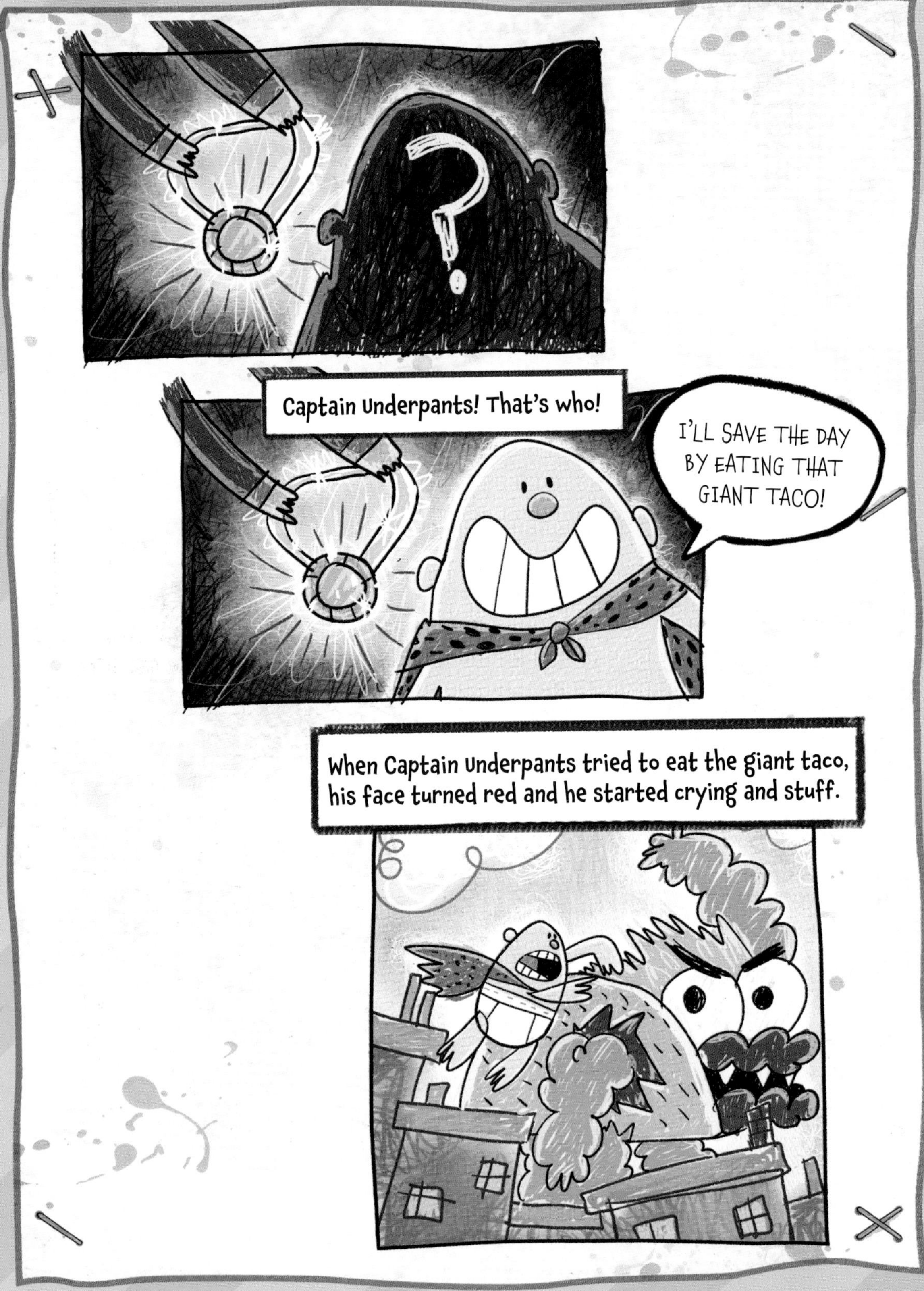
Captain Underpants! That's who!
I'LL SAVE THE DAY BY EATING THAT GIANT TACO!
When Captain Underpants tried to eat the giant taco, his face turned red and he started crying and stuff.

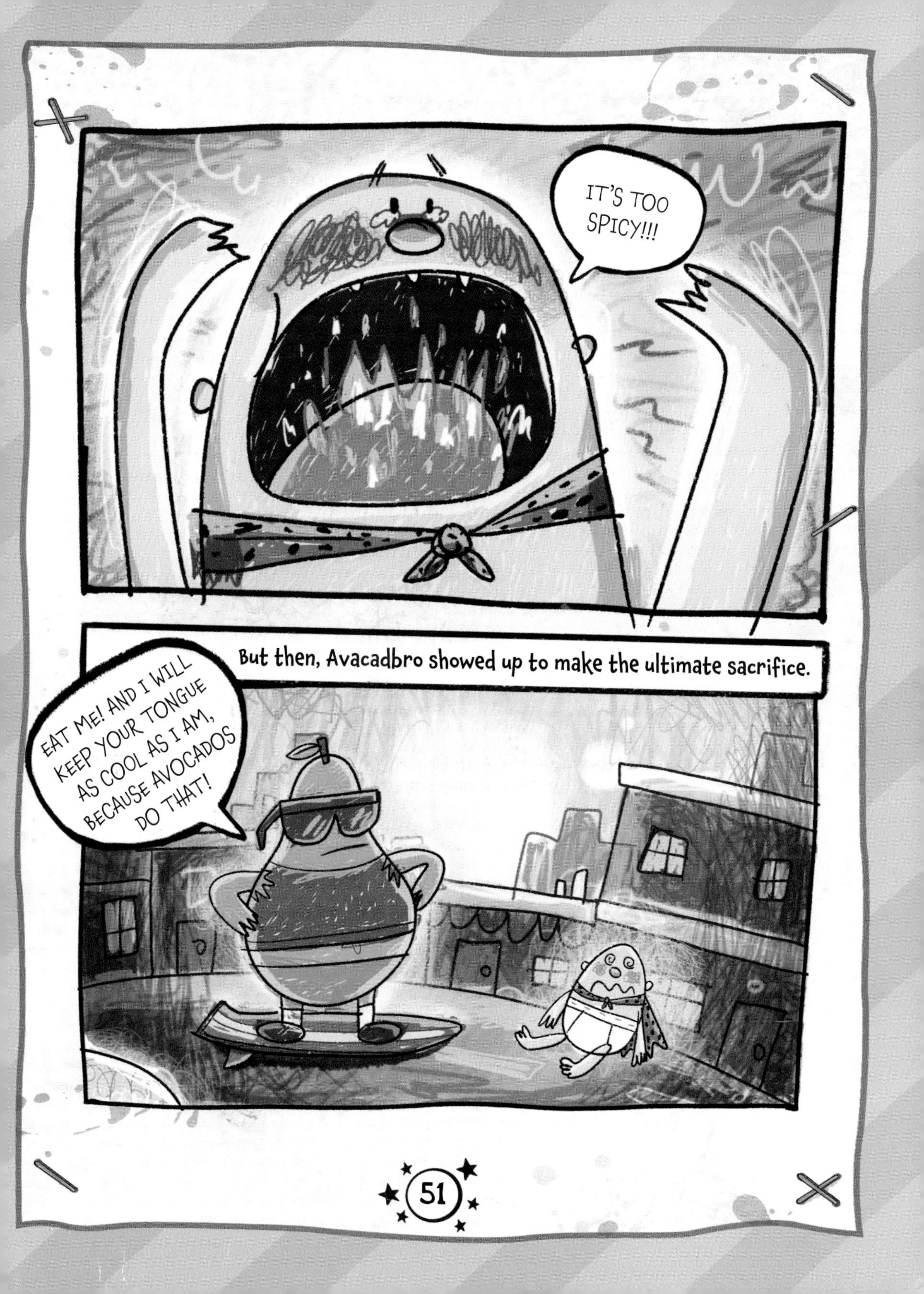
IT'S TOO SPICY!!!
But then, Avacadbro showed up to make the ultimate sacrifice.
EAT ME! AND I WILL KEEP YOUR TONGUE AS COOL AS I AM, BECAUSE AVOCADOS DO THAT!

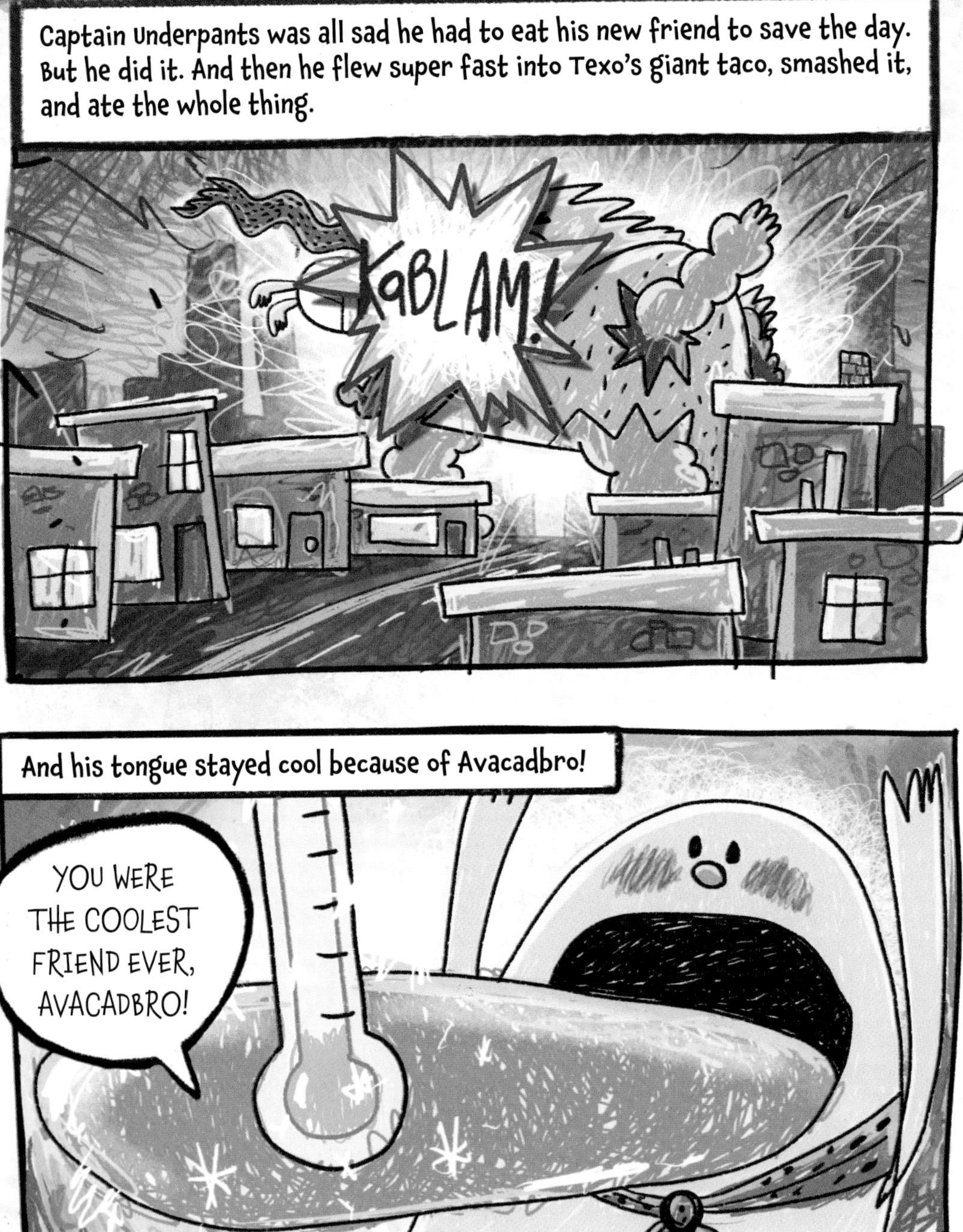
Captain Underpants was all sad he had to eat his new friend to save the day. But he did it. And then he flew super fast into Texo's giant taco, smashed it, and ate the whole thing.
KABLAM!
And his tongue stayed cool because of Avacadbro!
YOU WERE THE COOLEST FRIEND EVER, AVACADBRO!

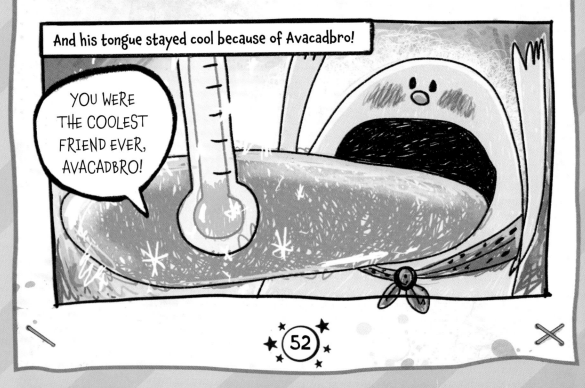

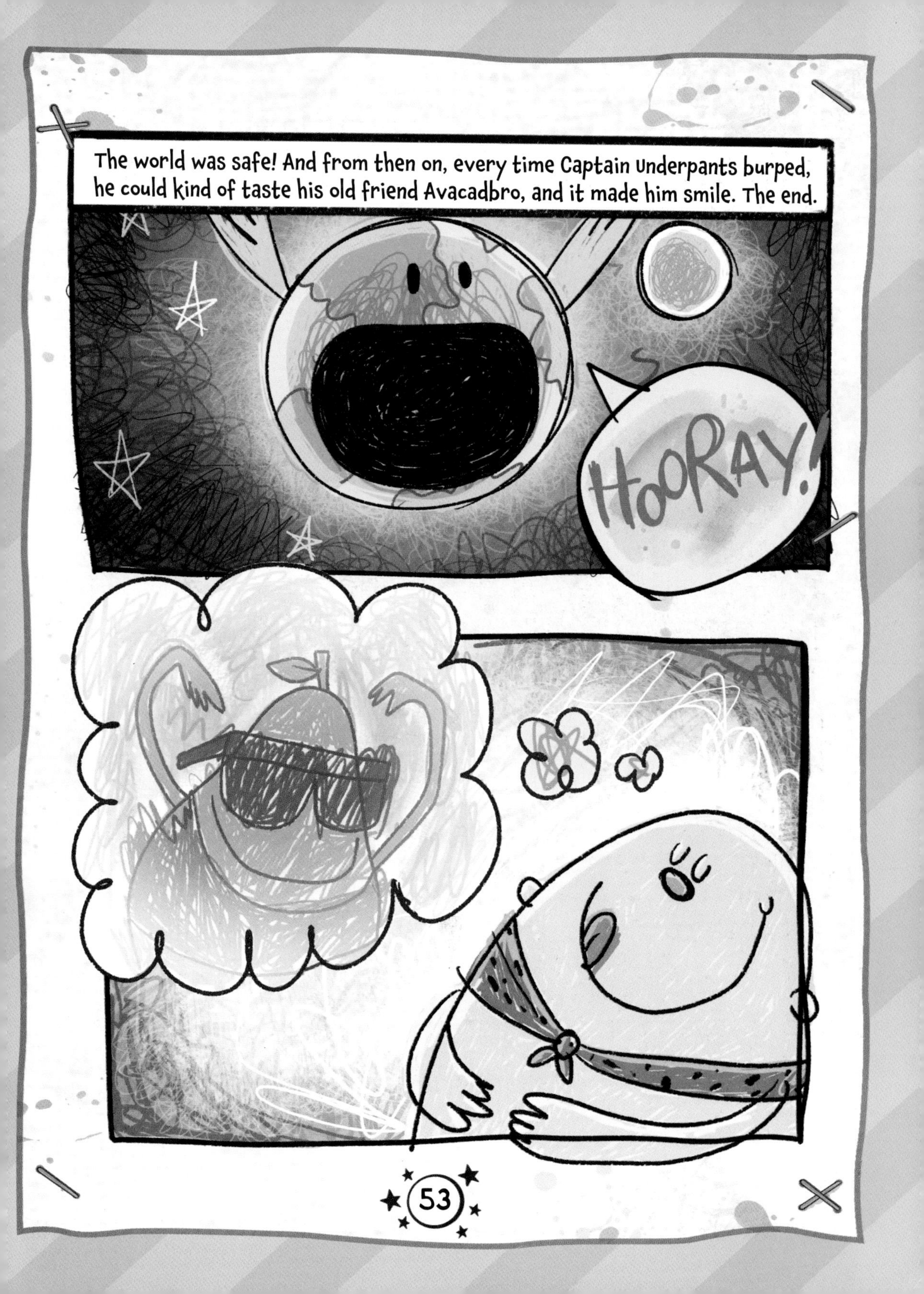
The world was safe! And from then on, every time Captain Underpants burped, he could kind of taste his old friend Avacadbro, and it made him smile. The end.
HOORAY!

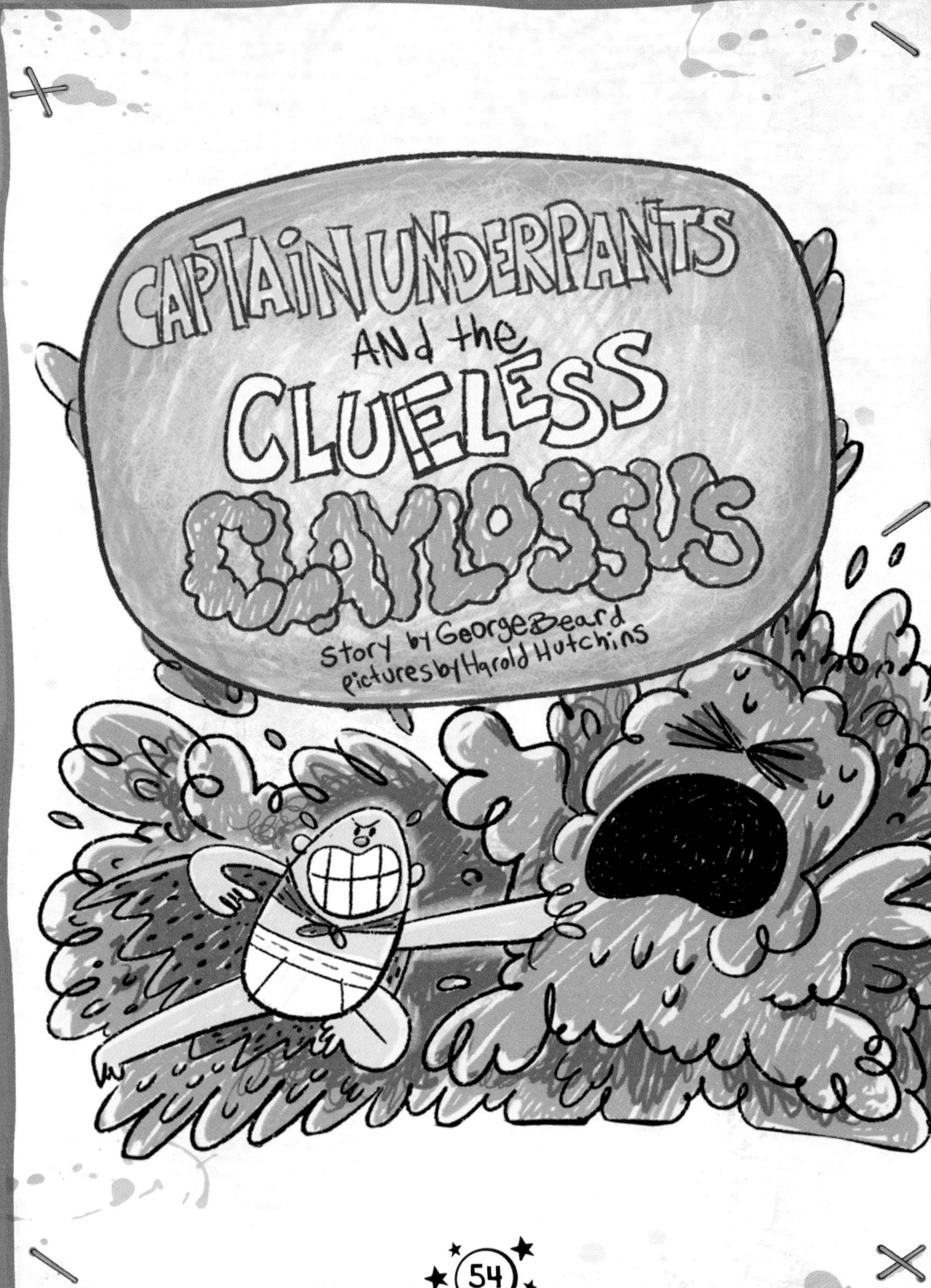
CAPTAIN UNDERPANTS
AND the
CLUELESS
CLAYLOSSUS
story by George Beard
pictures by Harold Hutchins

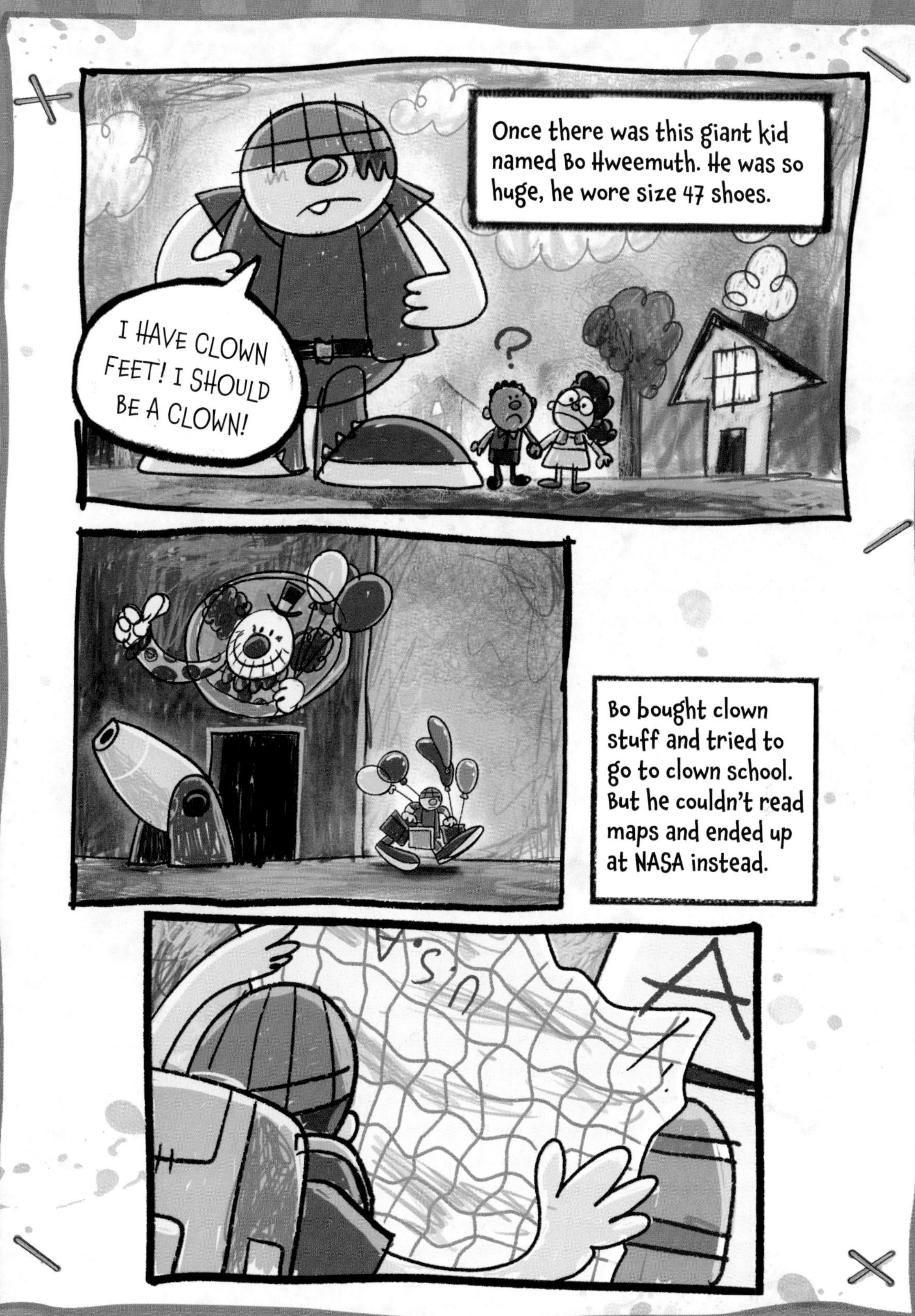
Once there was this giant kid named Bo Hweemuth. He was so huge, he wore size 47 shoes.
I HAVE CLOWN FEET! I SHOULD BE A CLOWN!
?
Bo bought clown stuff and tried to go to clown school. But he couldn't read maps and ended up at NASA instead.
U.S.A.
A

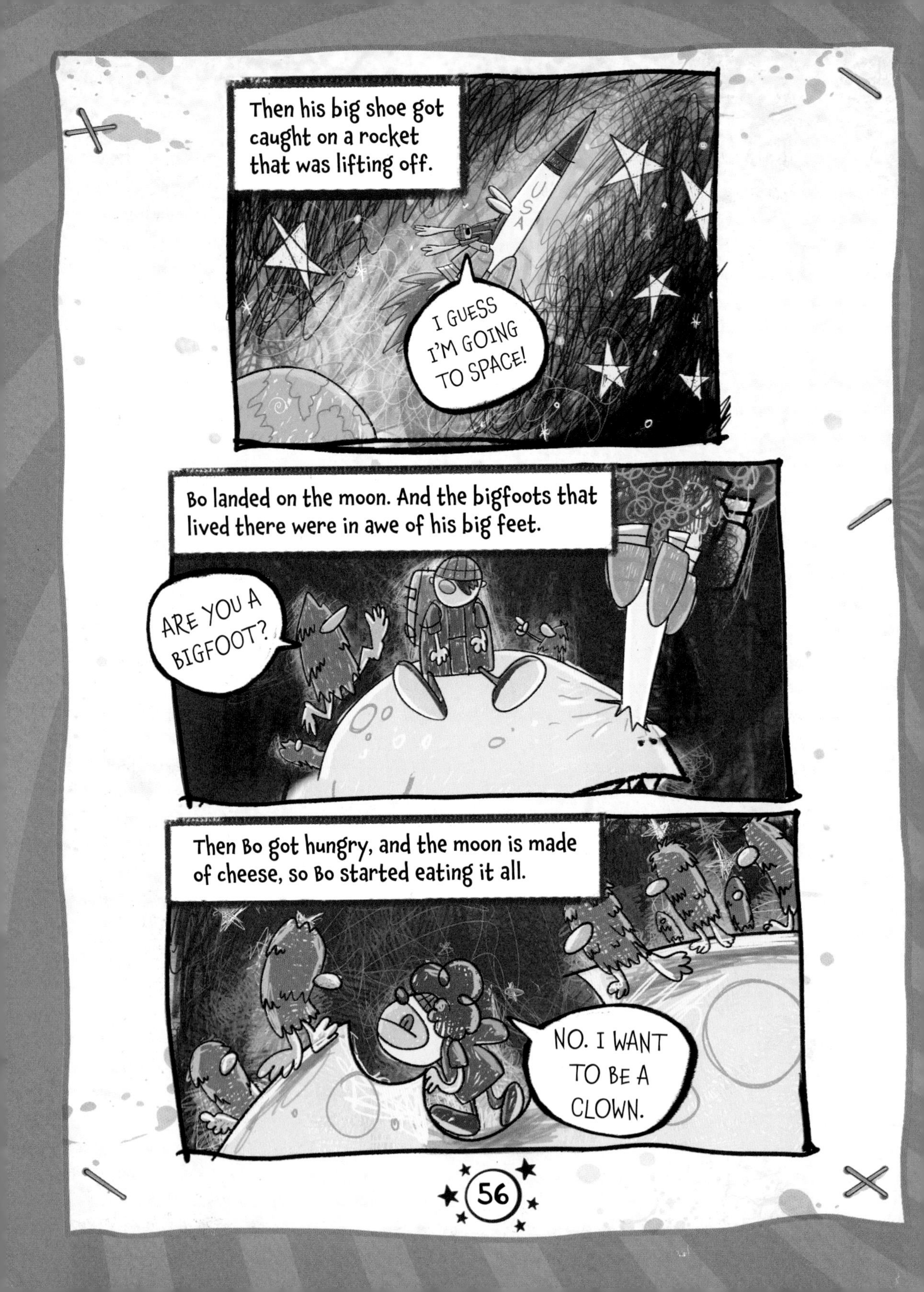
Then his big shoe got caught on a rocket that was lifting off.
USA
I GUESS I'M GOING TO SPACE!
Bo landed on the moon. And the bigfoots that lived there were in awe of his big feet.
ARE YOU A BIGFOOT?
Then Bo got hungry, and the moon is made of cheese, so Bo started eating it all.
NO. I WANT TO BE A CLOWN.

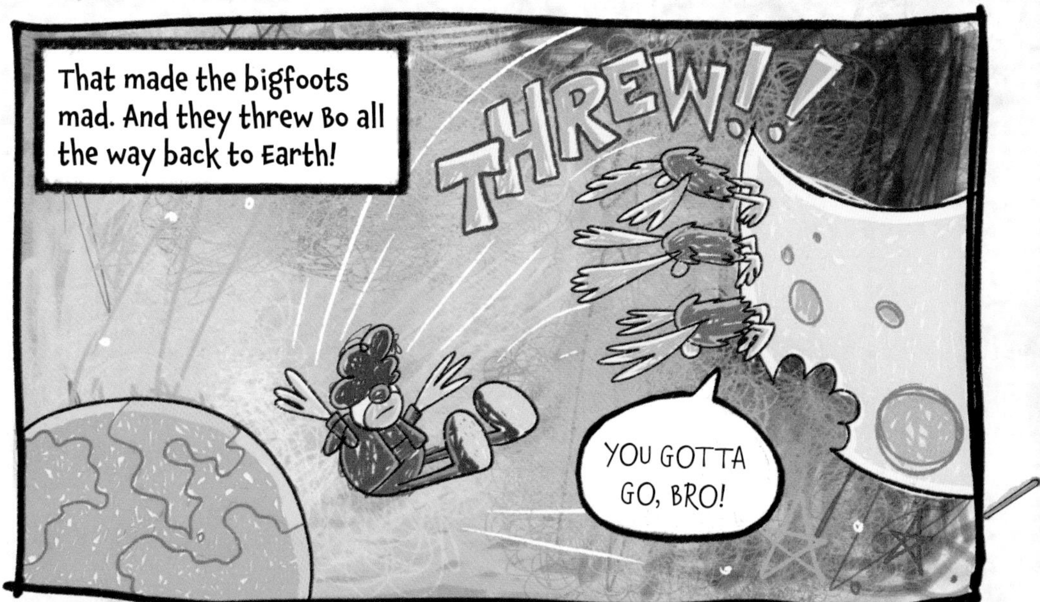
That made the bigfoots mad. And they threw Bo all the way back to Earth!
THREW!!
YOU GOTTA GO, BRO!

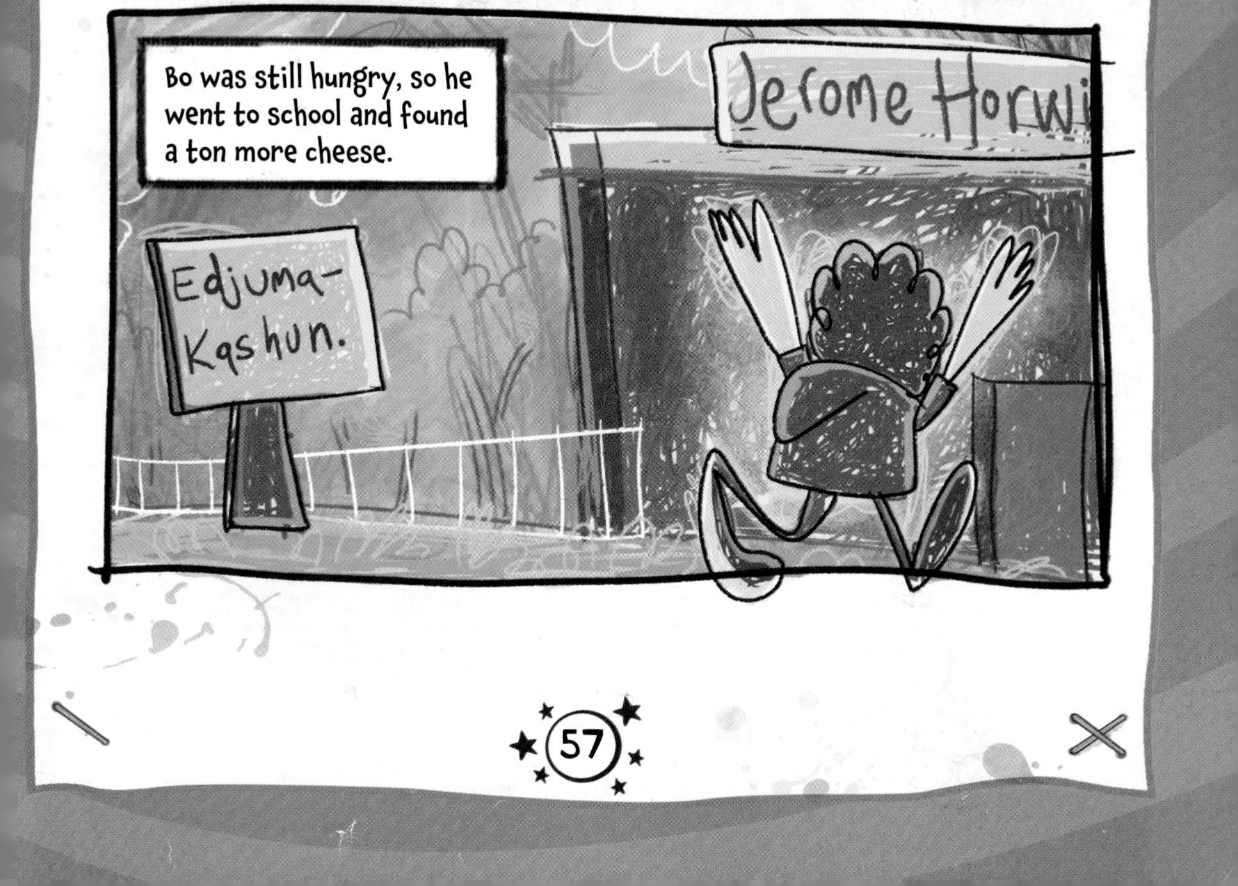
Bo was still hungry, so he went to school and found a ton more cheese.
Jerome Horwi
Edjuma-Kashun.

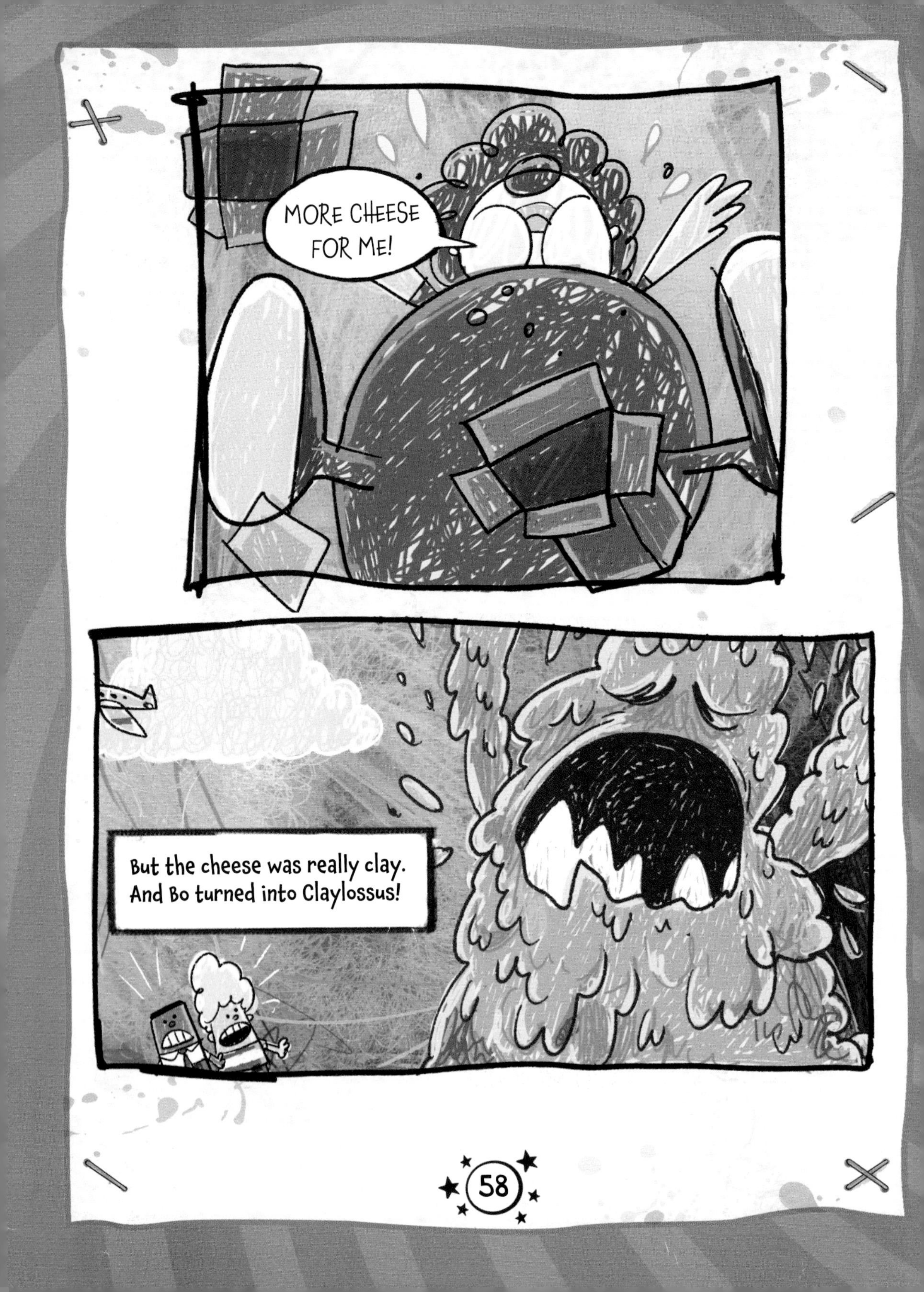
MORE CHEESE FOR ME!
But the cheese was really clay.
And Bo turned into Claylossus!

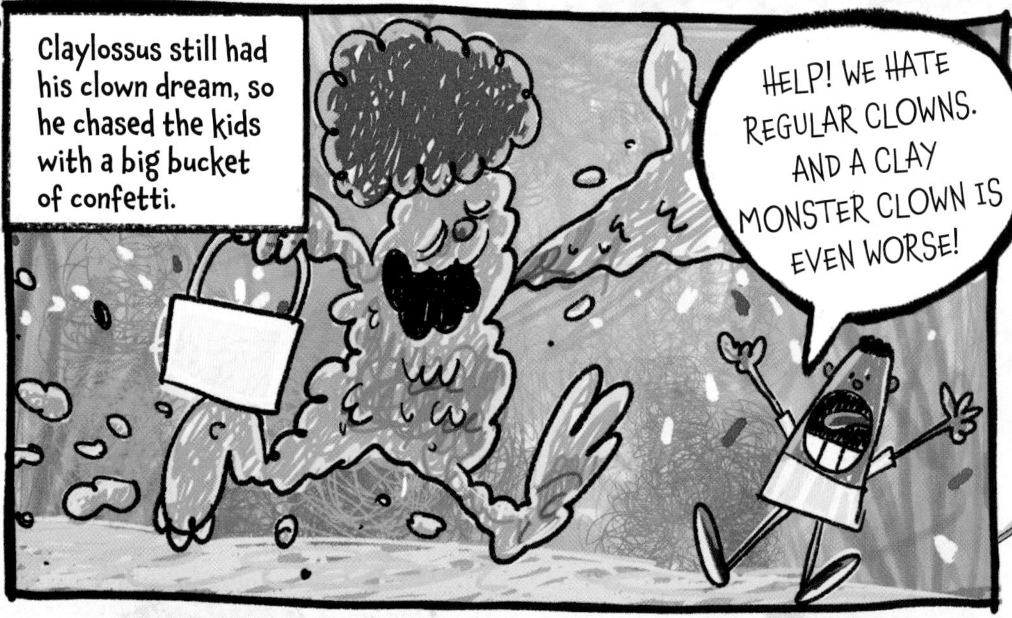
Claylossus still had his clown dream, so he chased the kids with a big bucket of confetti.
HELP! WE HATE REGULAR CLOWNS. AND A CLAY MONSTER CLOWN IS EVEN WORSE!

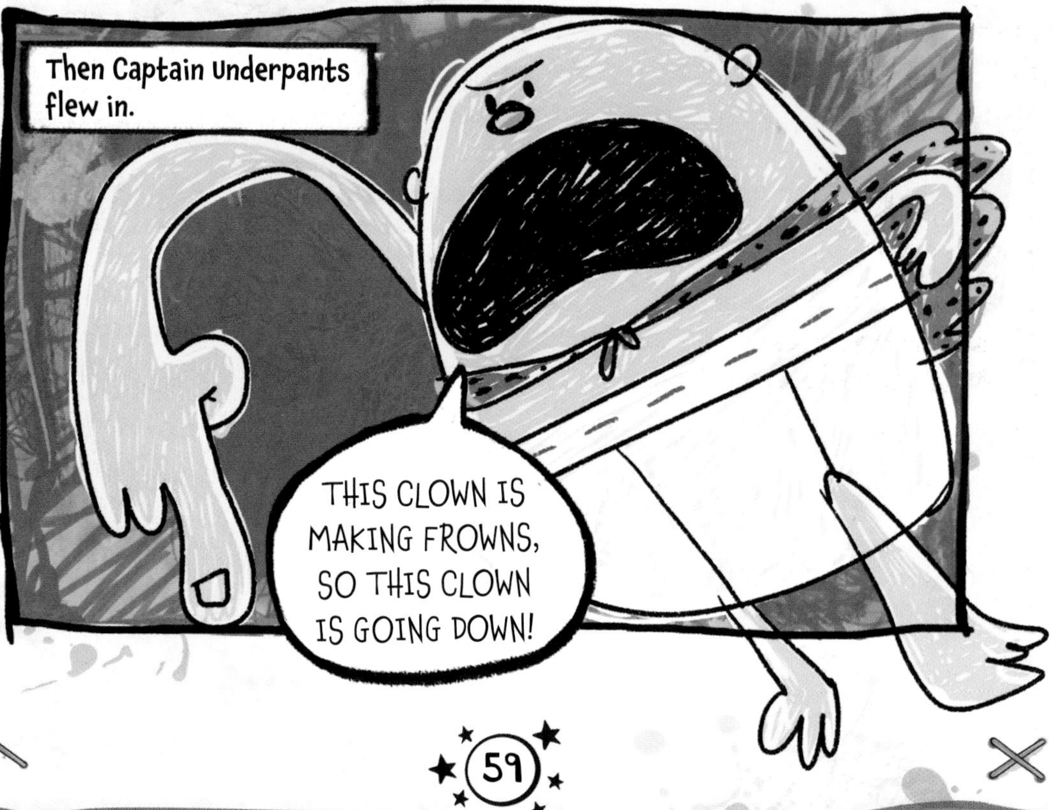
Then Captain Underpants flew in.
THIS CLOWN IS MAKING FROWNS, SO THIS CLOWN IS GOING DOWN!

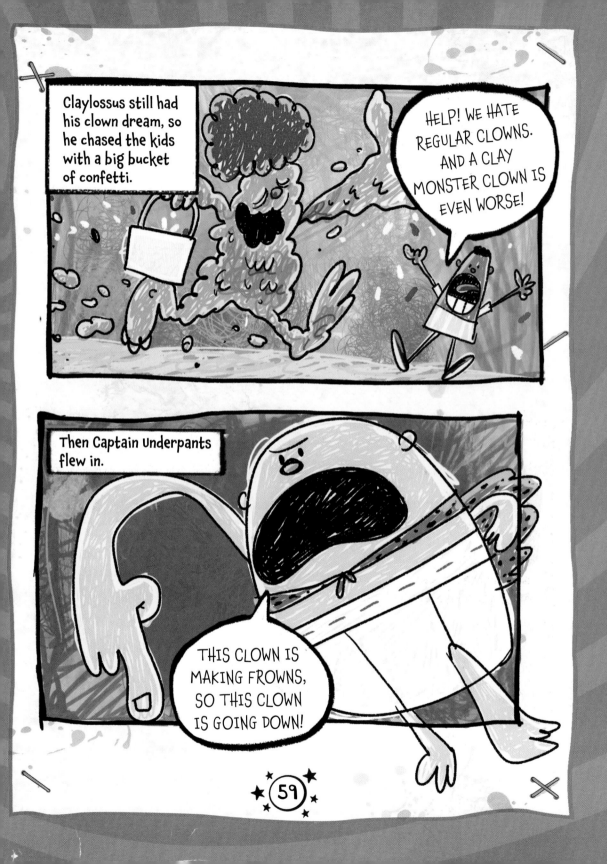

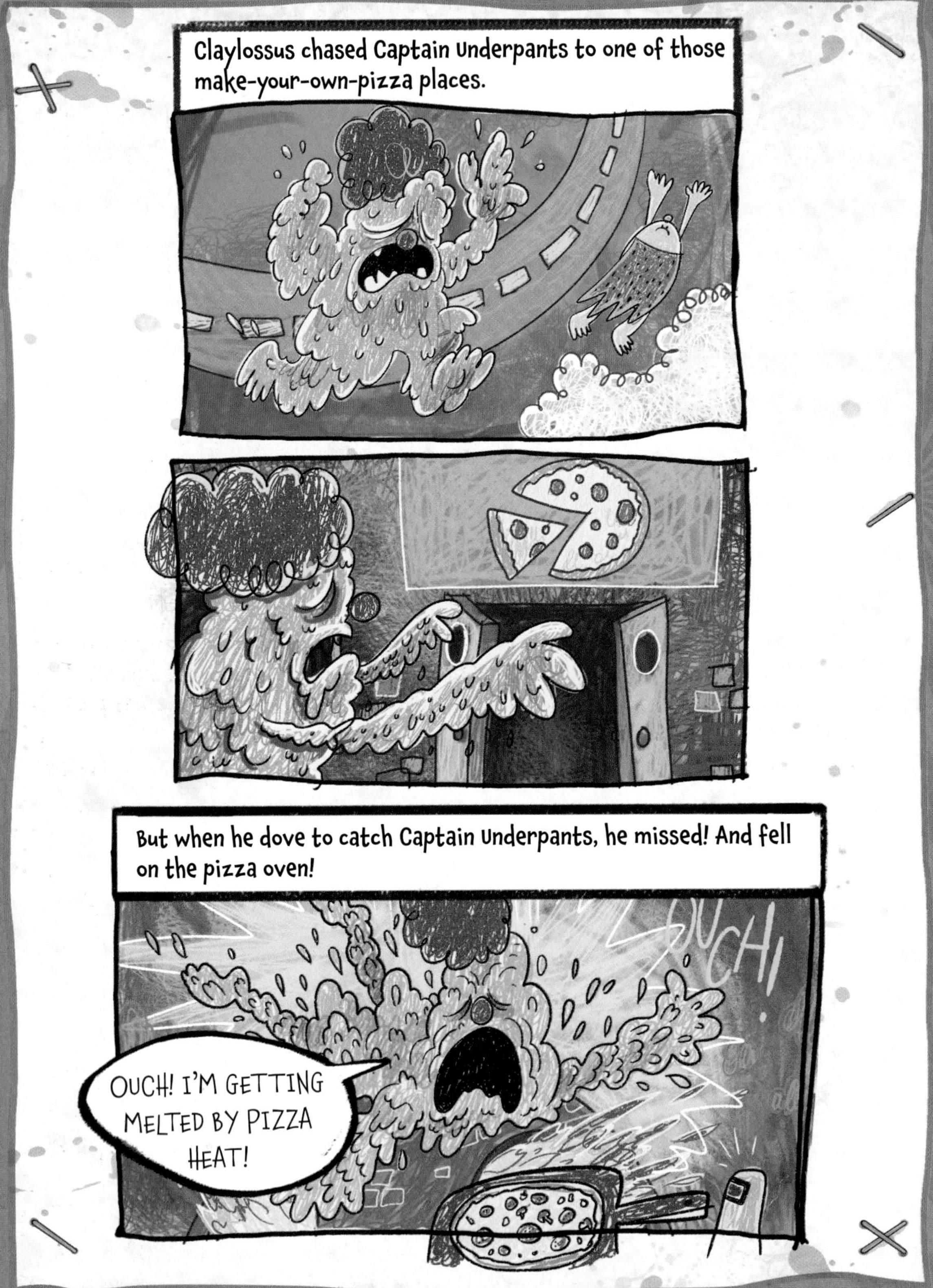
Claylossus chased Captain Underpants to one of those make-your-own-pizza places.
But when he dove to catch Captain Underpants, he missed! And fell on the pizza oven!
OUCH!
OUCH! I'M GETTING MELTED BY PIZZA HEAT!

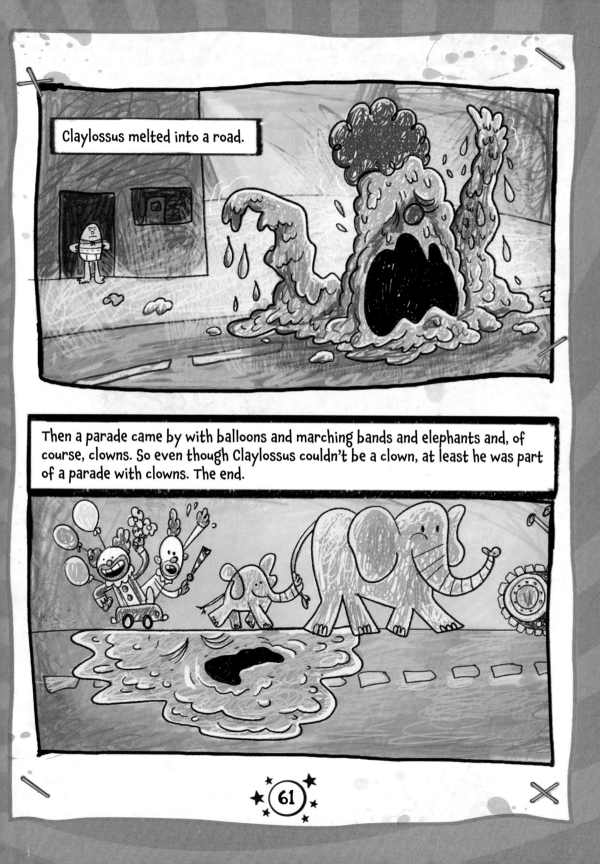

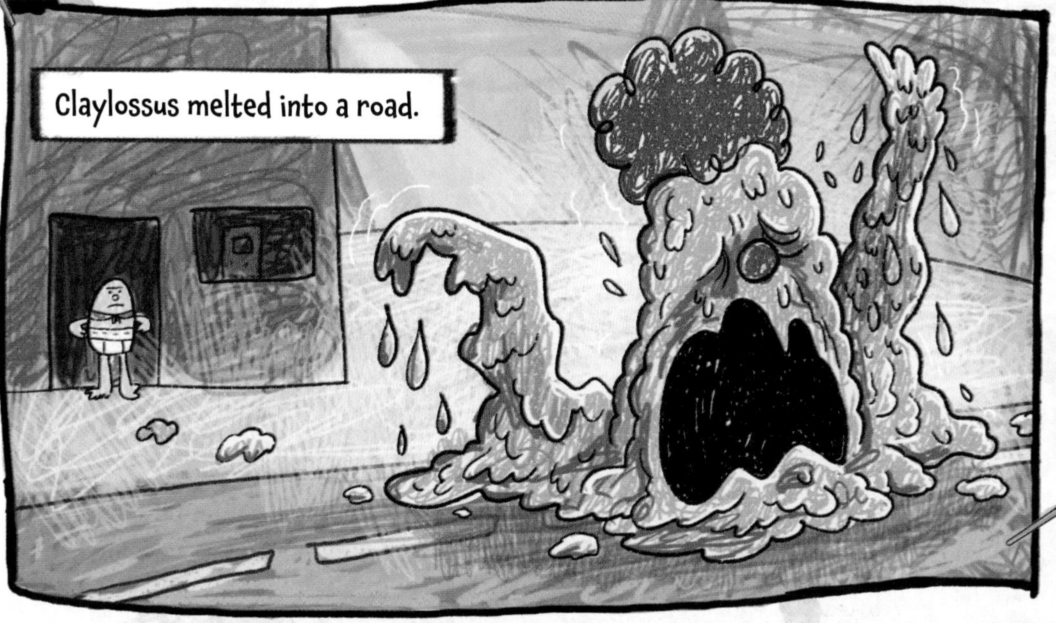
Claylossus melted into a road.

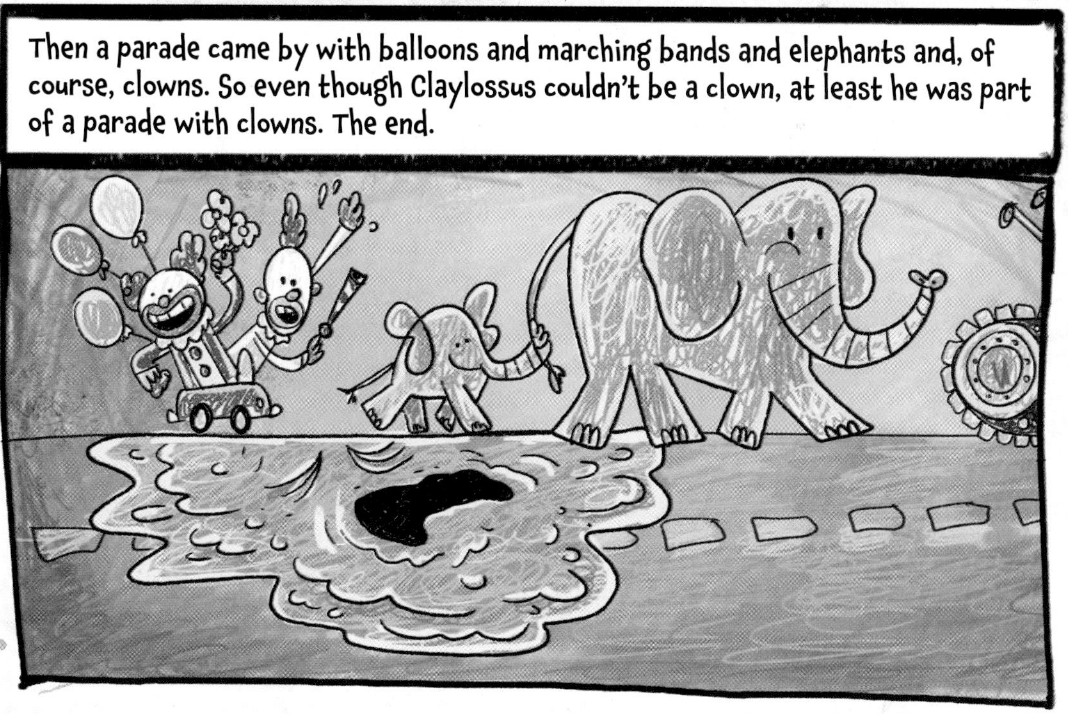
Then a parade came by with balloons and marching bands and elephants and, of course, clowns. So even though Claylossus couldn't be a clown, at least he was part of a parade with clowns. The end.

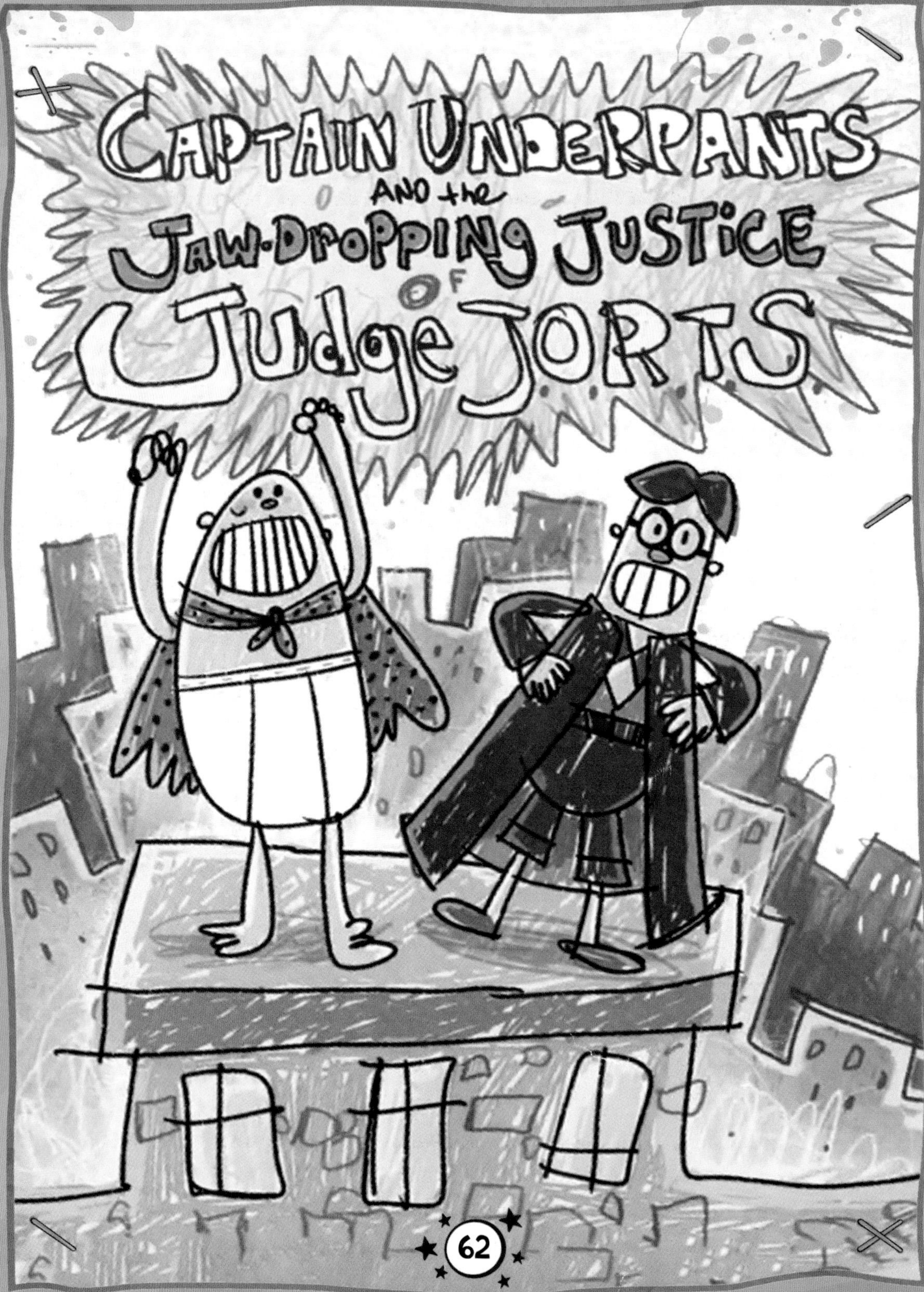
CAPTAIN UNDERPANTS
AND the
JAW-DROPPING JUSTICE
OF
Judge JORTS

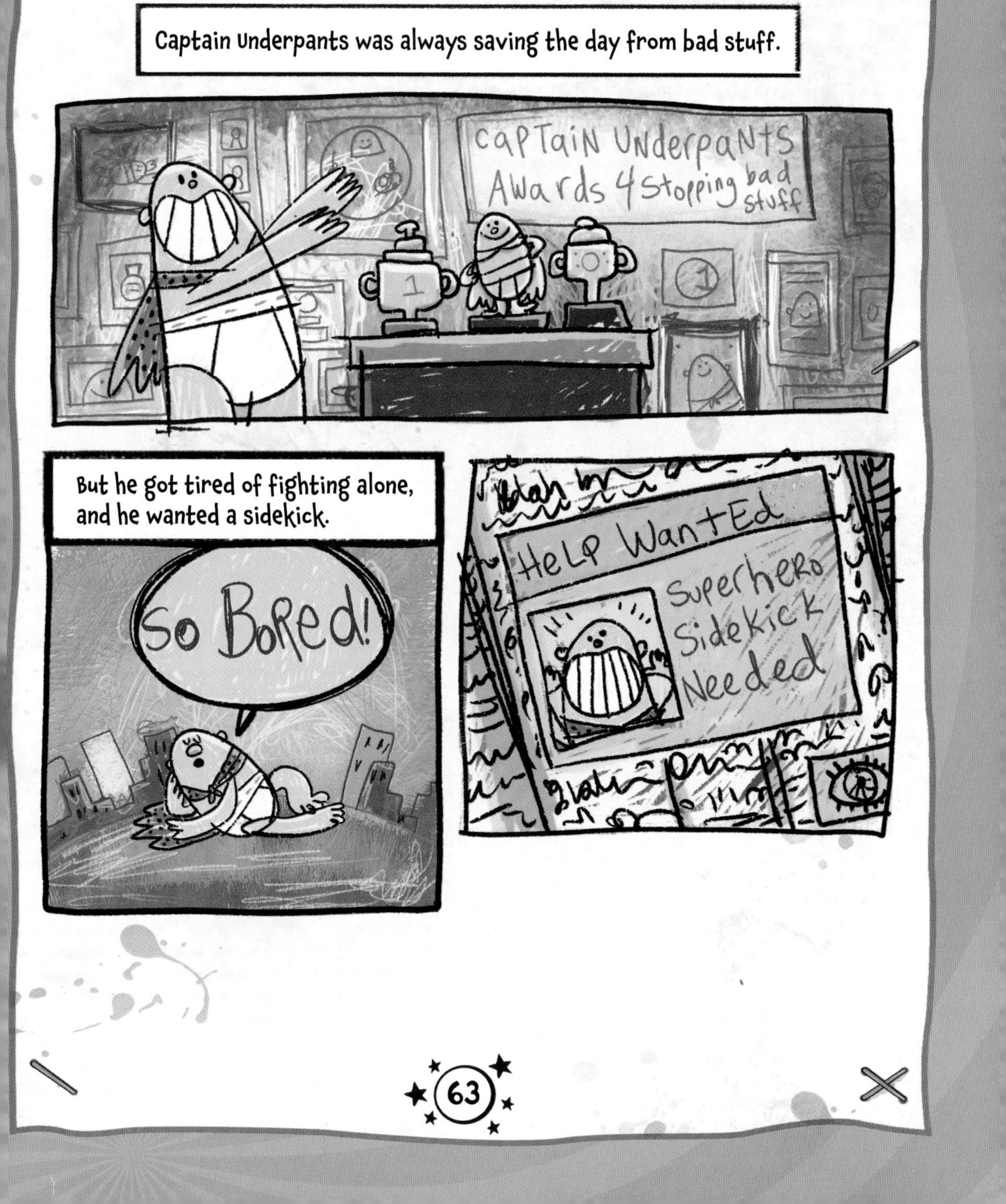
Captain Underpants was always saving the day from bad stuff.
Captain Underpants Awards 4 Stopping bad stuff
But he got tired of fighting alone, and he wanted a sidekick.
So Bored!
Help Wanted
Superhero Sidekick Needed

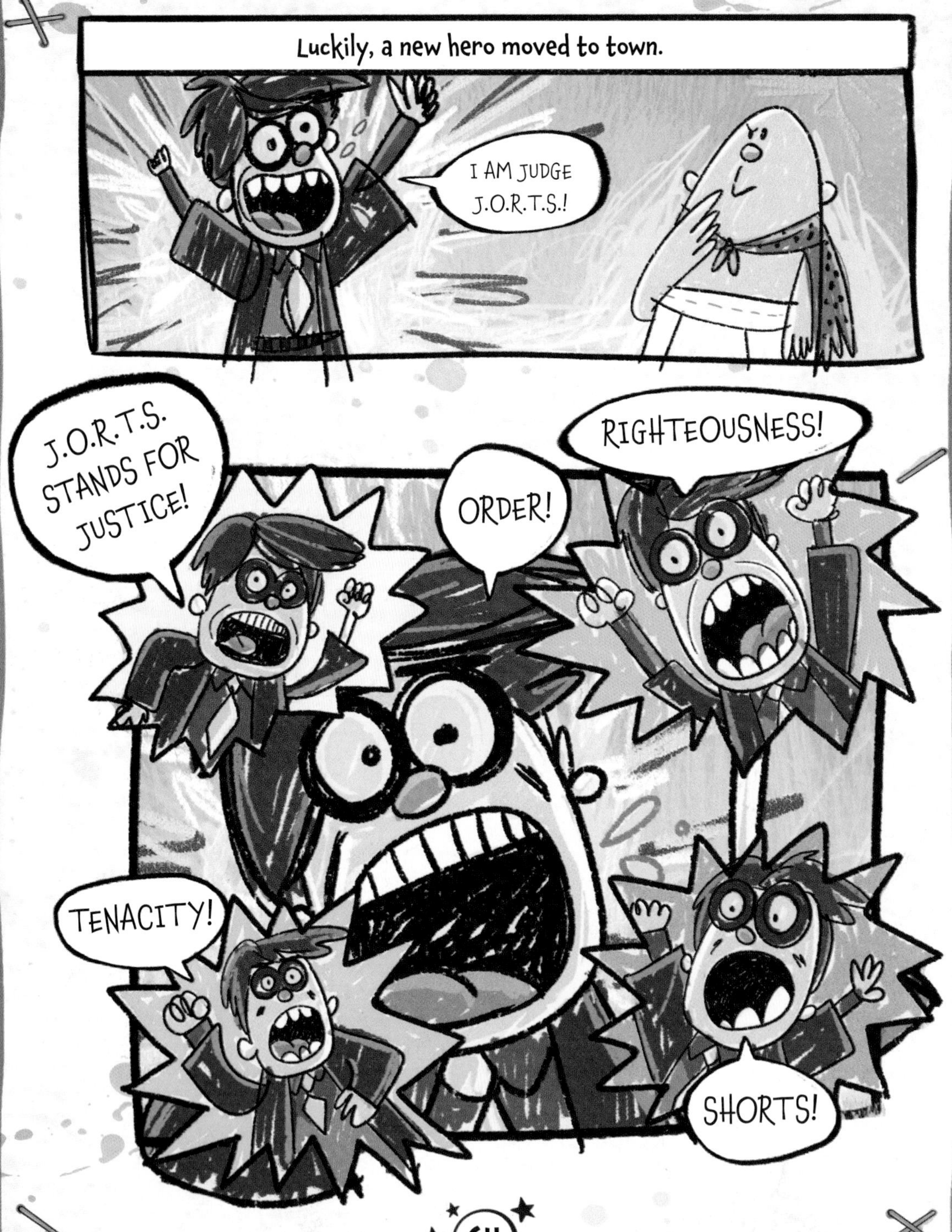
Luckily, a new hero moved to town.
I AM JUDGE J.O.R.T.S.!
J.O.R.T.S. STANDS FOR JUSTICE!
ORDER!
RIGHTEOUSNESS!
TENACITY!
SHORTS!

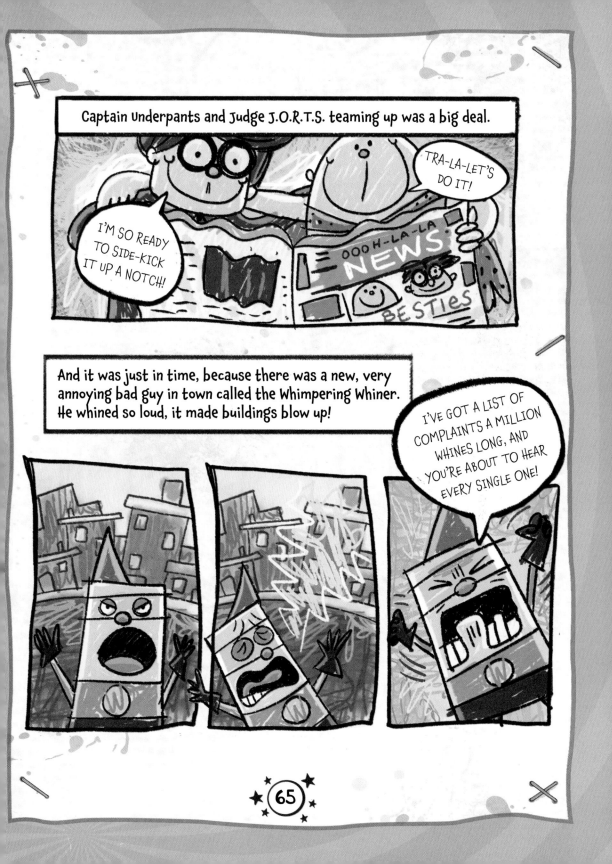

Captain Underpants and Judge J.O.R.T.S. teaming up was a big deal.

I'M SO READY TO SIDE-KICK IT UP A NOTCH!

TRA-LA-LET'S DO IT!

OOOH-LA-LA NEWS

BESTIES

And it was just in time, because there was a new, very annoying bad guy in town called the Whimpering Whiner. He whined so loud, it made buildings blow up!

I'VE GOT A LIST OF COMPLAINTS A MILLION WHINES LONG, AND YOU'RE ABOUT TO HEAR EVERY SINGLE ONE!

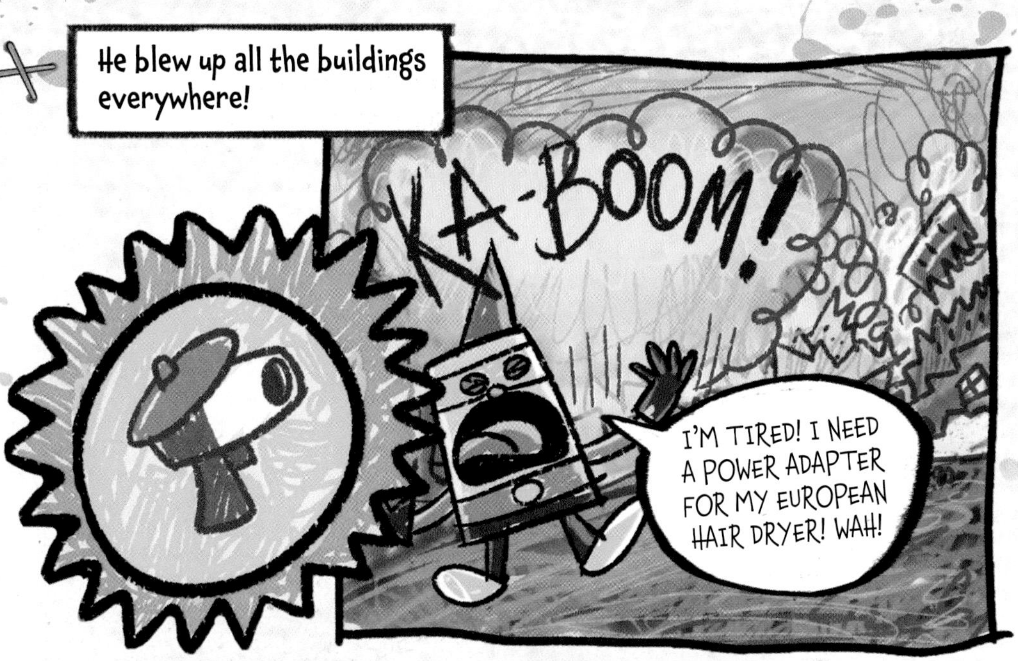
He blew up all the buildings everywhere!
KA-BOOM!
I'M TIRED! I NEED A POWER ADAPTER FOR MY EUROPEAN HAIR DRYER! WAH!

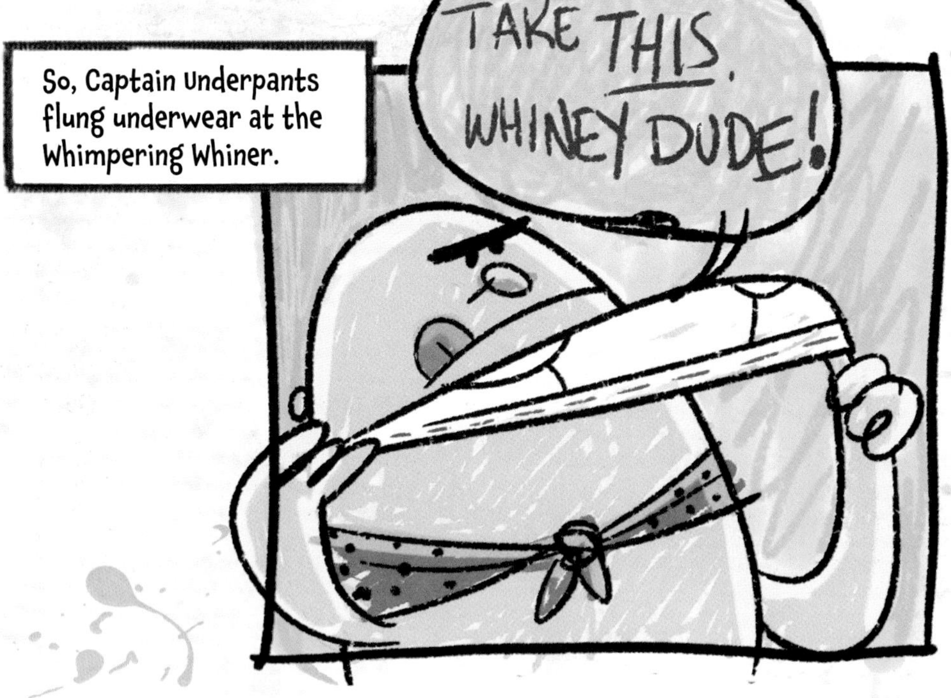
So, Captain Underpants flung underwear at the Whimpering Whiner.
TAKE THIS, WHINEY DUDE!

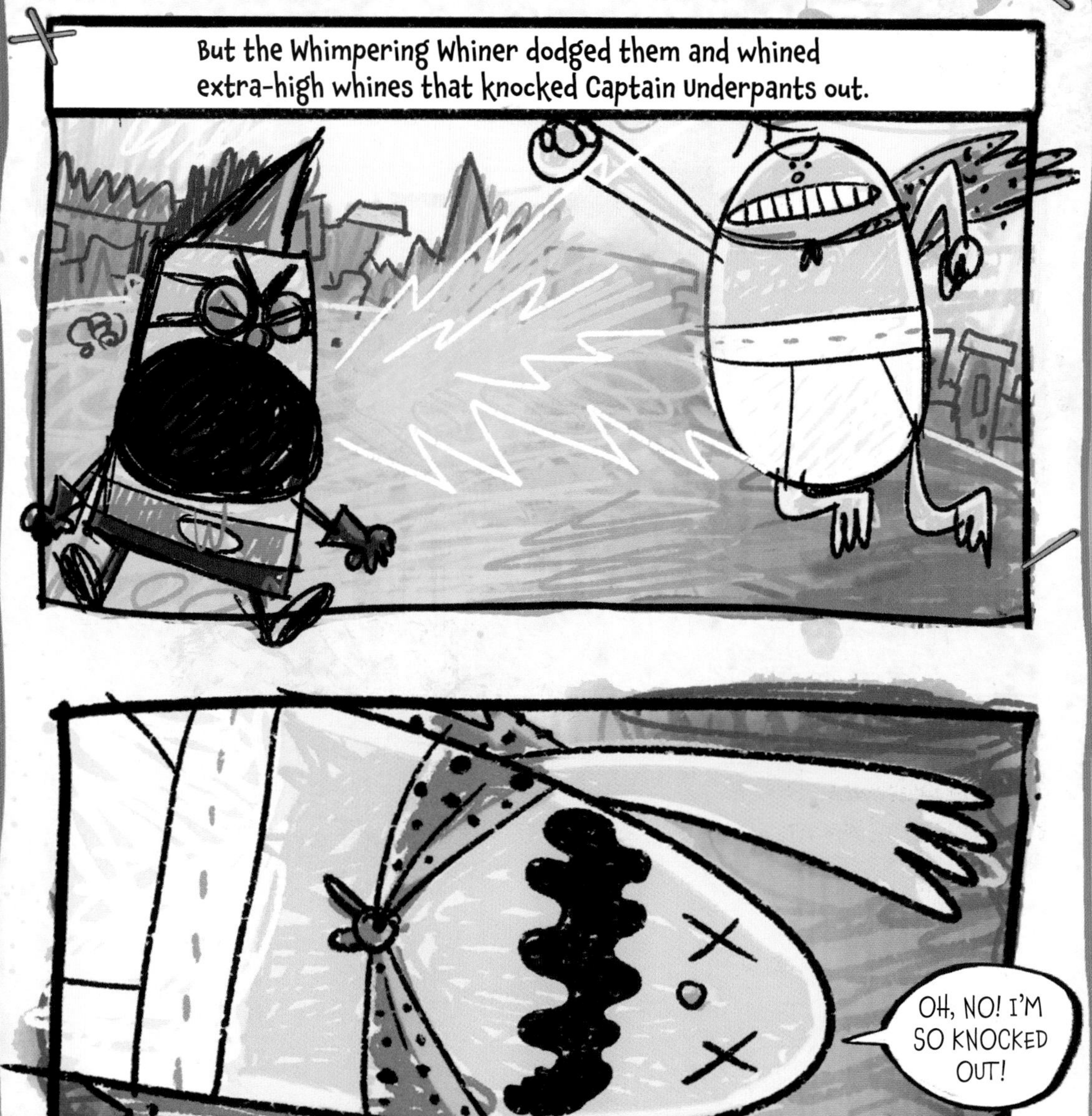
But the Whimpering Whiner dodged them and whined extra-high whines that knocked Captain Underpants out.
OH, NO! I'M SO KNOCKED OUT!

So, Judge J.O.R.T.S. had to save the day. Luckily, he was as smart as he was handsome and strong.

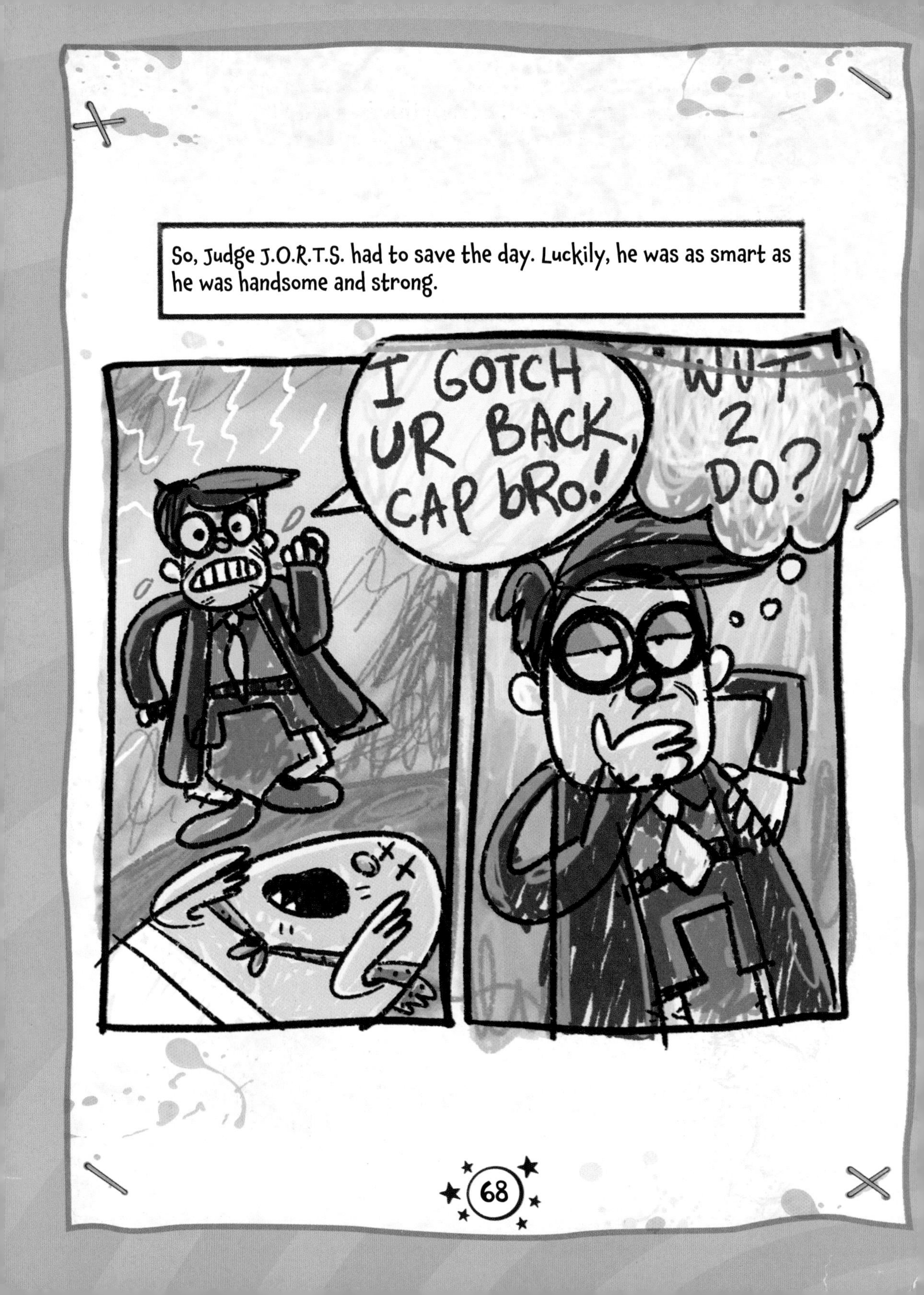
I GOTCH UR BACK, CAP bRo!
WUT 2 DO?

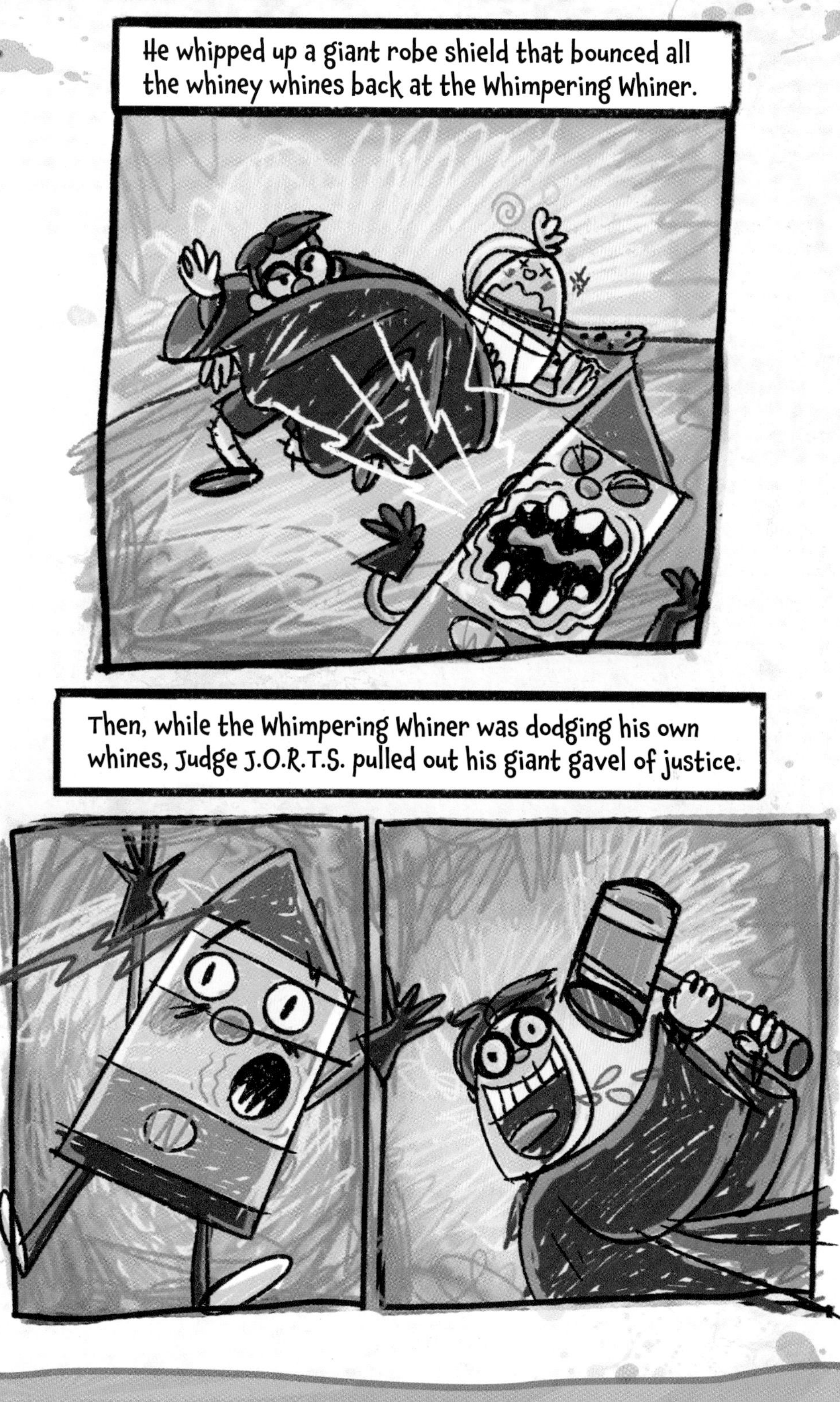
He whipped up a giant robe shield that bounced all the whiney whines back at the Whimpering Whiner.
Then, while the Whimpering Whiner was dodging his own whines, Judge J.O.R.T.S. pulled out his giant gavel of justice.

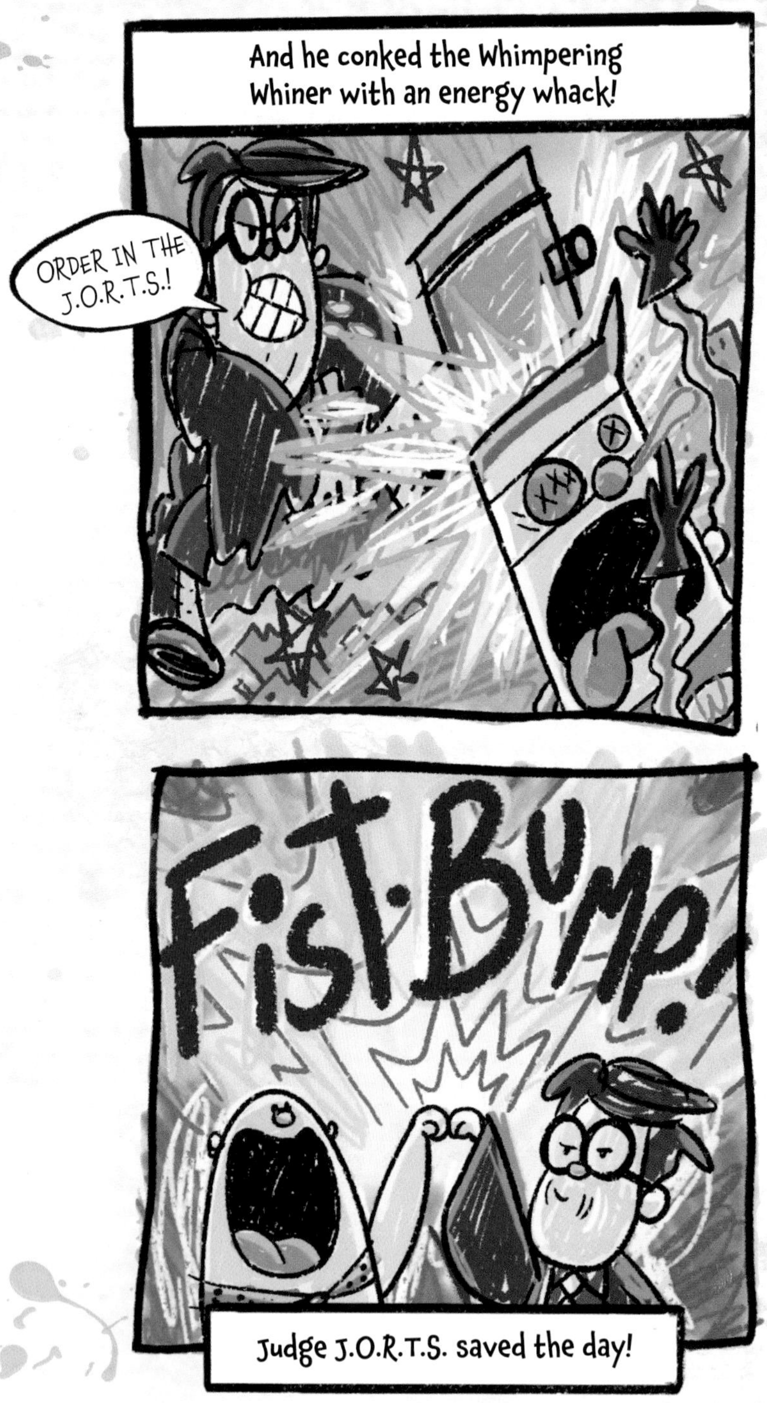
And he conked the Whimpering Whiner with an energy whack!
ORDER IN THE J.O.R.T.S.!
FIST BUMP!
Judge J.O.R.T.S. saved the day!

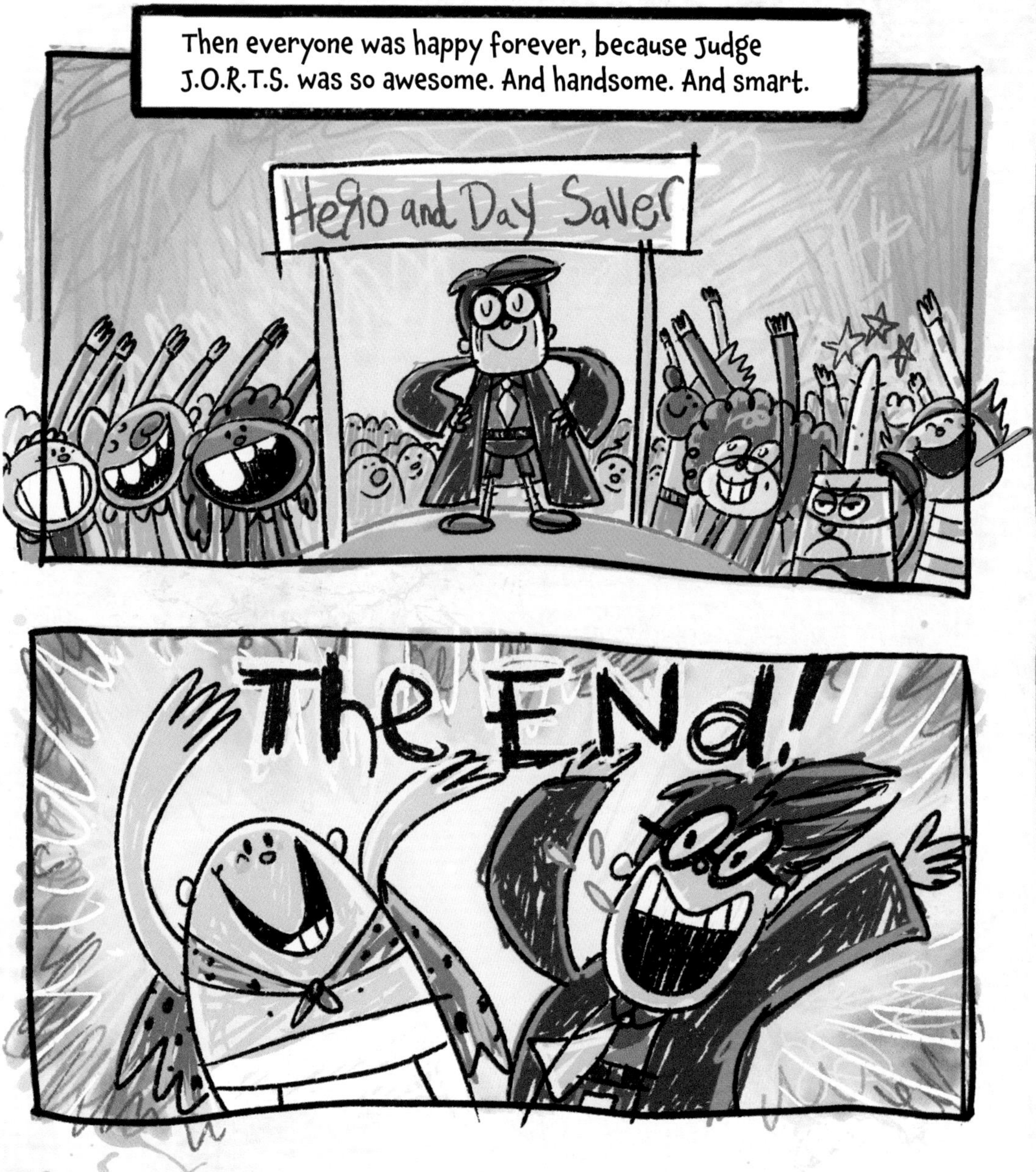
Then everyone was happy forever, because Judge J.O.R.T.S. was so awesome. And handsome. And smart.
Hero and Day Saver
The End!

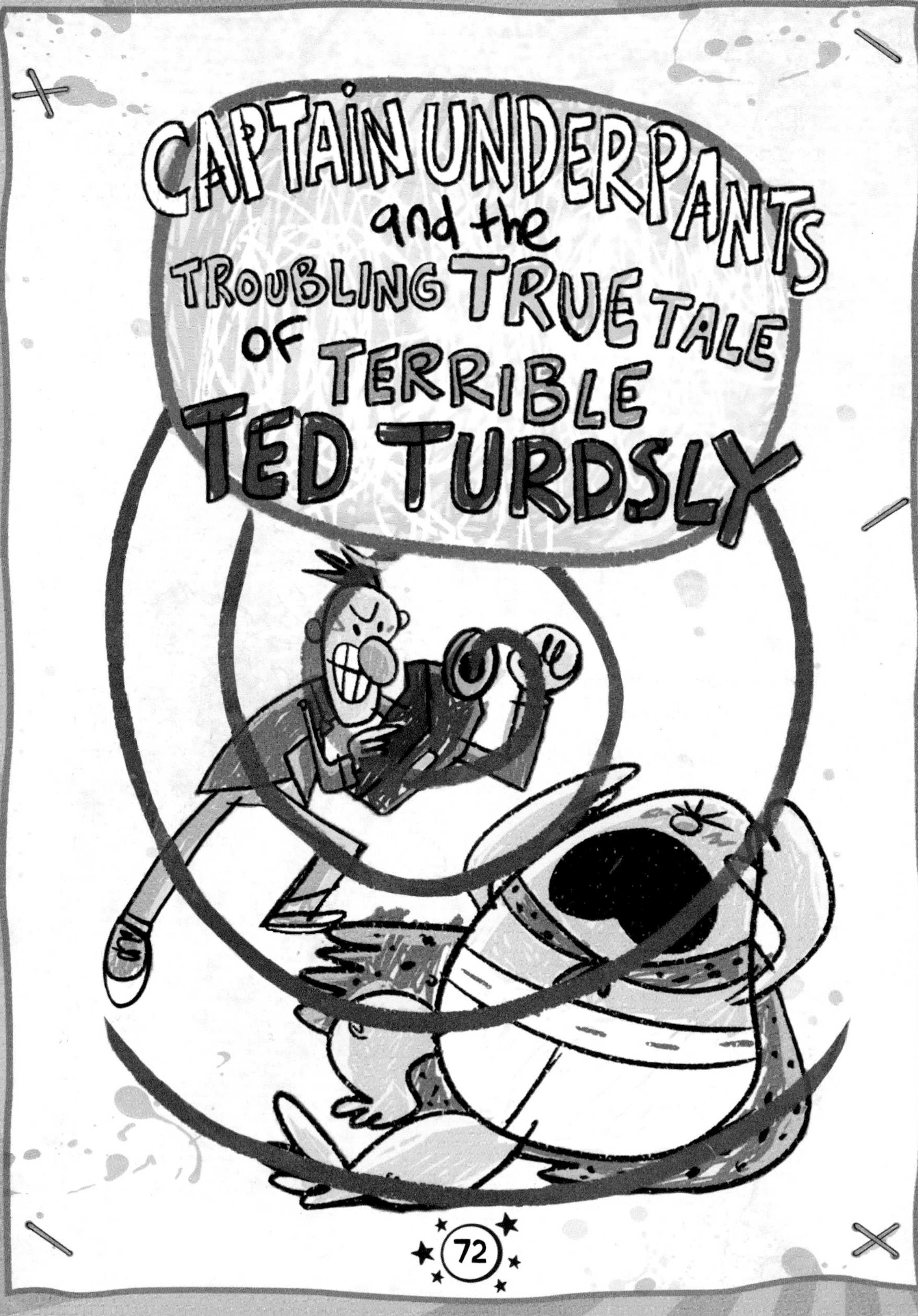
CAPTAIN UNDERPANTS
and the
TROUBLING TRUE TALE
OF TERRIBLE
TED TURDSLY

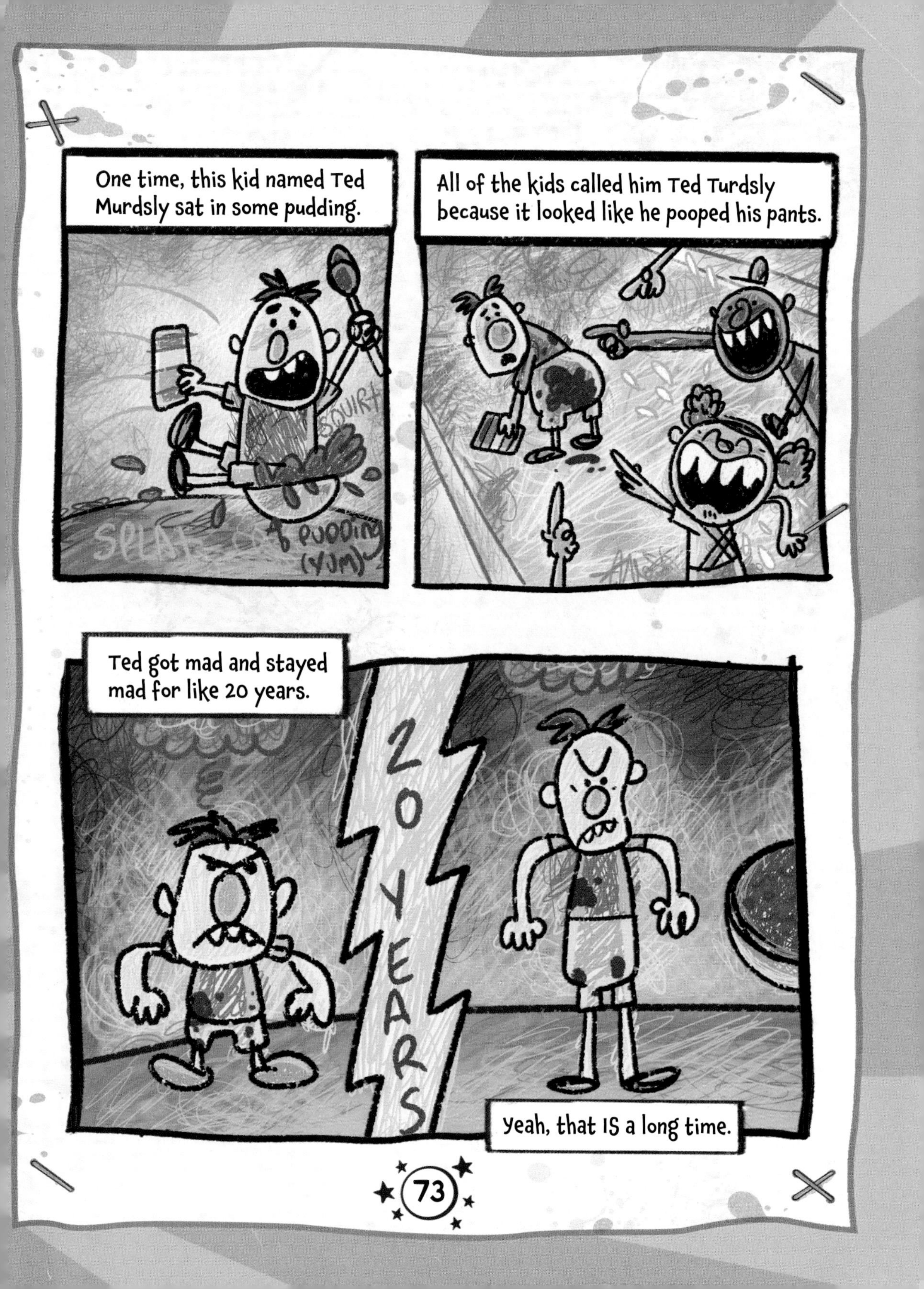
One time, this kid named Ted Murdsly sat in some pudding.
SQUIRT
SPLAT
PUDDING (YUM)
All of the kids called him Ted Turdsly because it looked like he pooped his pants.
Ted got mad and stayed mad for like 20 years.
20 YEARS
Yeah, that IS a long time.

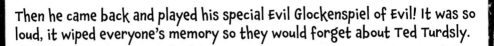

Then he came back and played his special Evil Glockenspiel of Evil! It was so loud, it wiped everyone's memory so they would forget about Ted Turdsly.

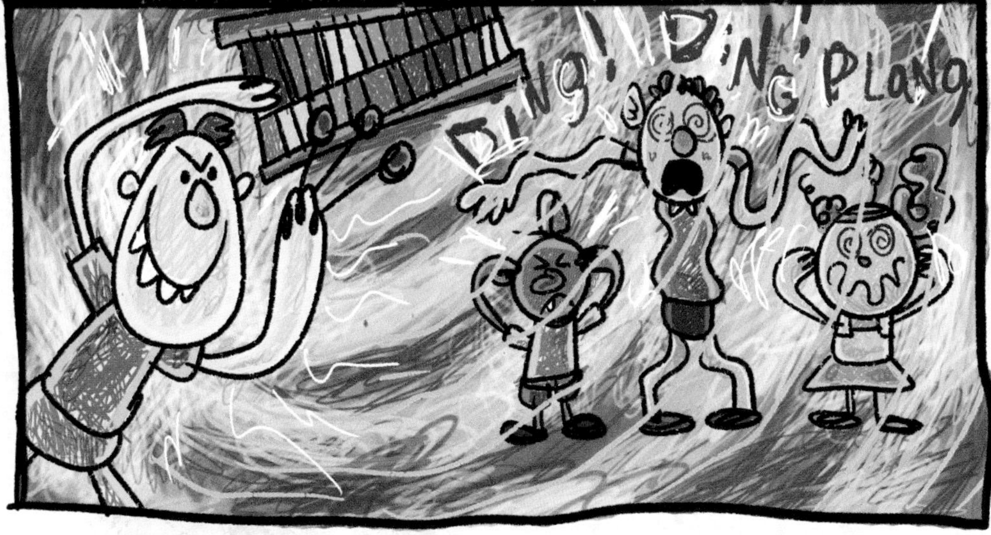
DING!
PLANG

Then he made himself the principal and told everyone that he was cool, like a champion jet-skier trophy winner.

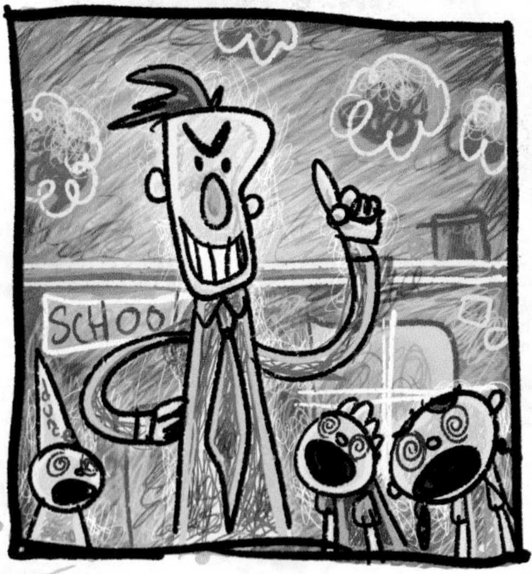
SCHOO

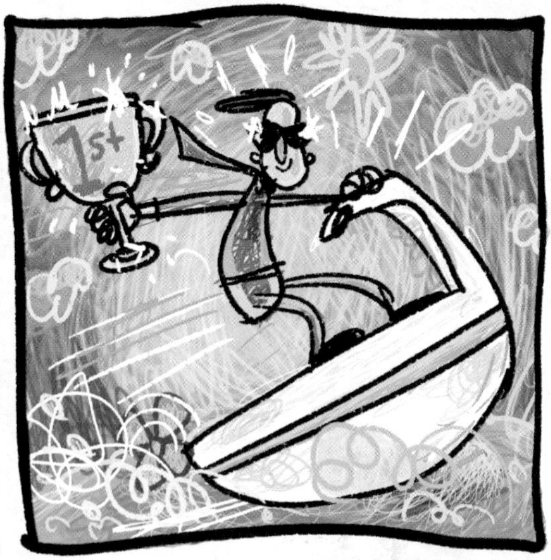
1st

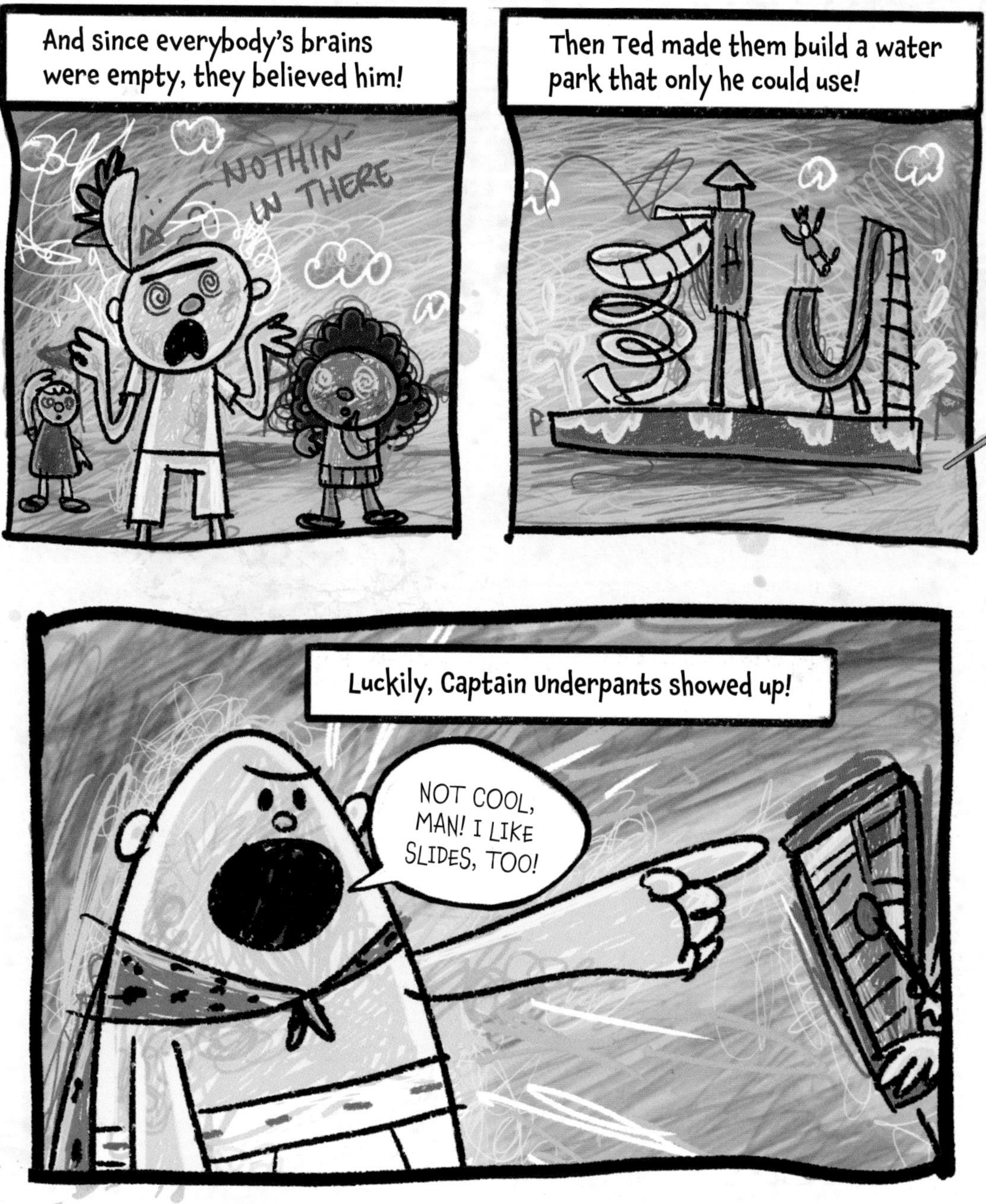
And since everybody's brains were empty, they believed him!
NOTHIN' IN THERE
Then Ted made them build a water park that only he could use!
Luckily, Captain Underpants showed up!
NOT COOL, MAN! I LIKE SLIDES, TOO!

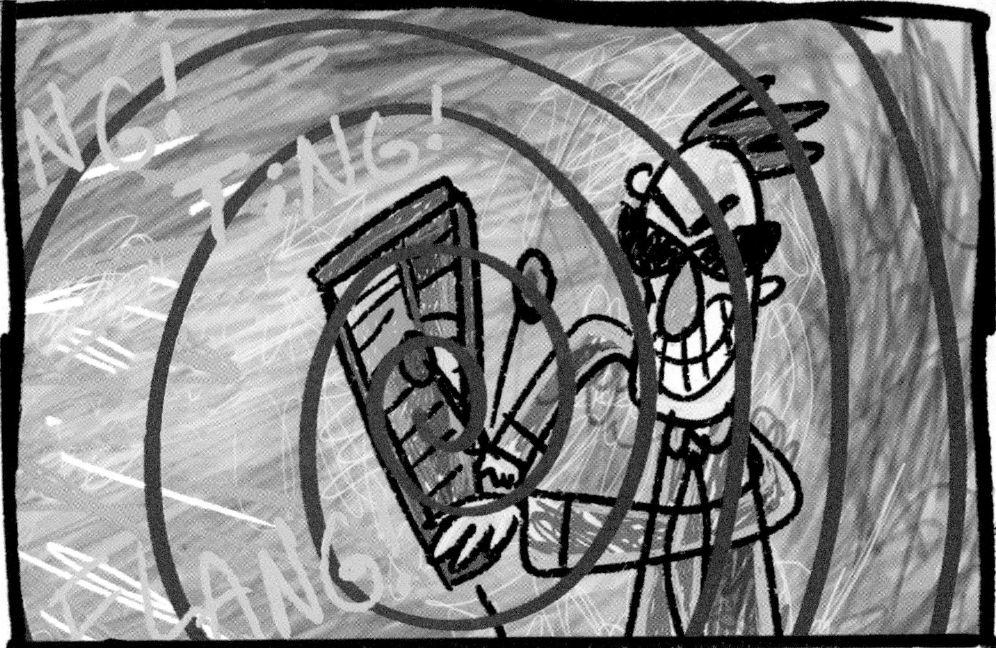
TiNG!

Ted played his Evil Glockenspiel of Evil so loud it wiped Captain Underpants's memory and made him forget he had powers!

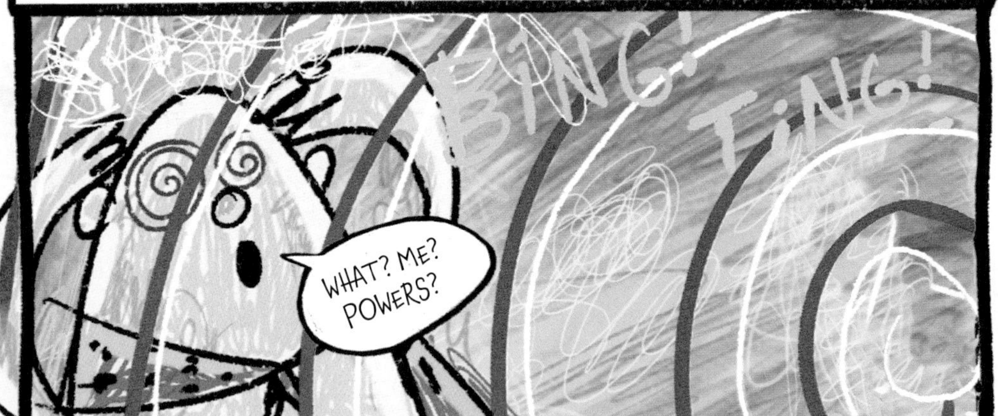
BiNG!
TiNG!
WHAT? ME? POWERS?

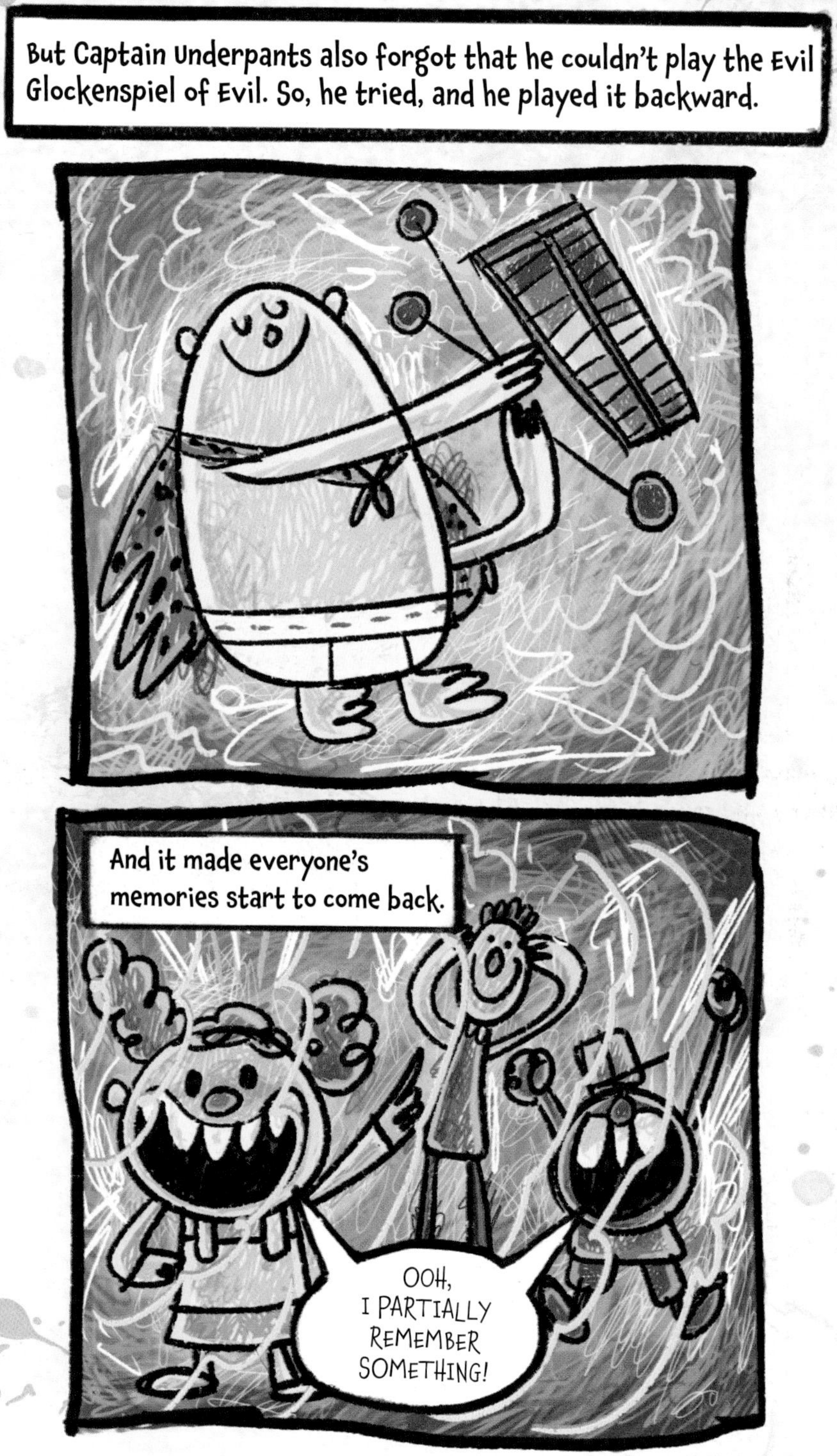
But Captain Underpants also forgot that he couldn't play the Evil Glockenspiel of Evil. So, he tried, and he played it backward.
And it made everyone's memories start to come back.
OOH, I PARTIALLY REMEMBER SOMETHING!

Then Captain Underpants put Ted in undie-cuffs and he muffled the mind-erasing Evil Glockenspiel of Evil forever with underwear.

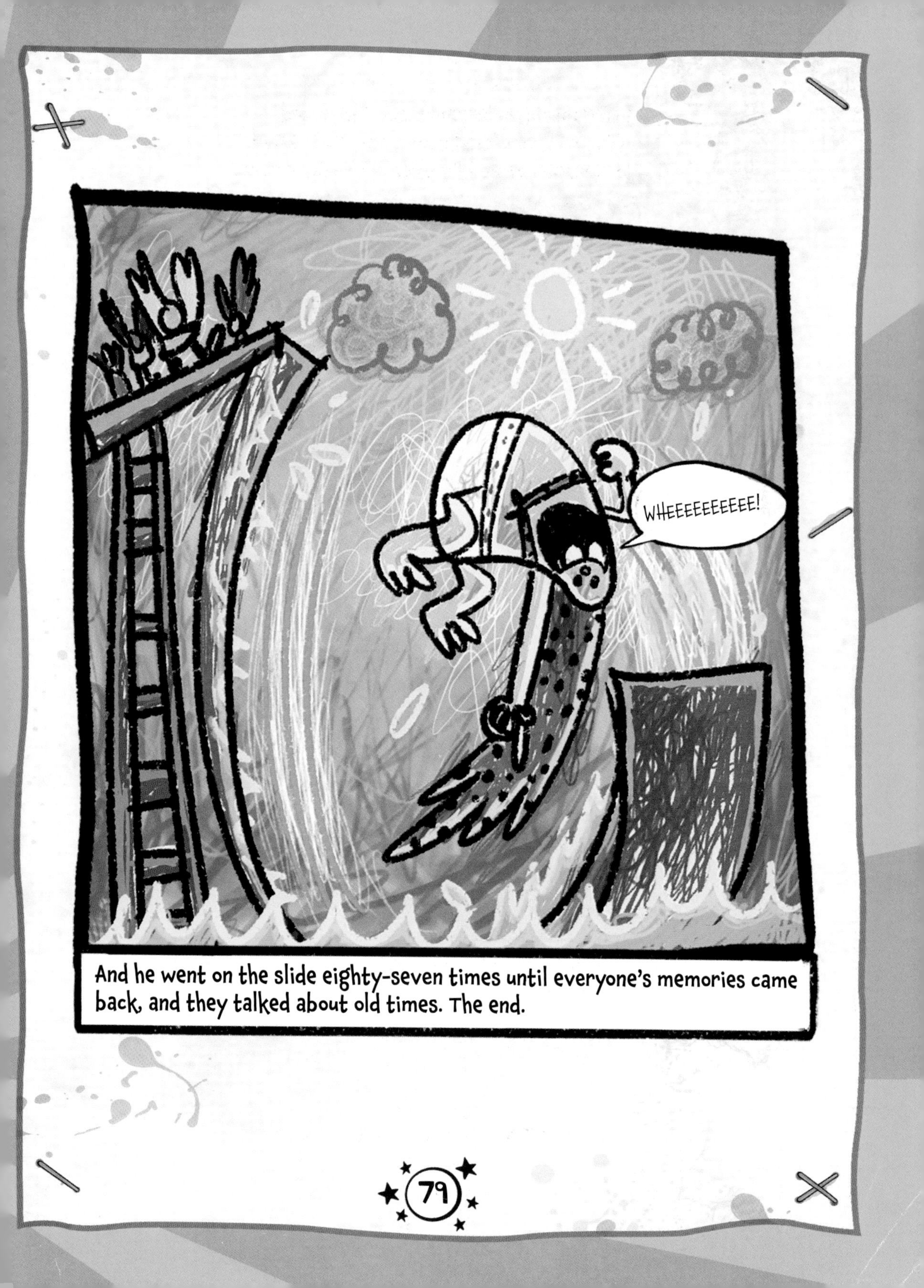
WHEEEEEEEEEE!
And he went on the slide eighty-seven times until everyone's memories came back, and they talked about old times. The end.

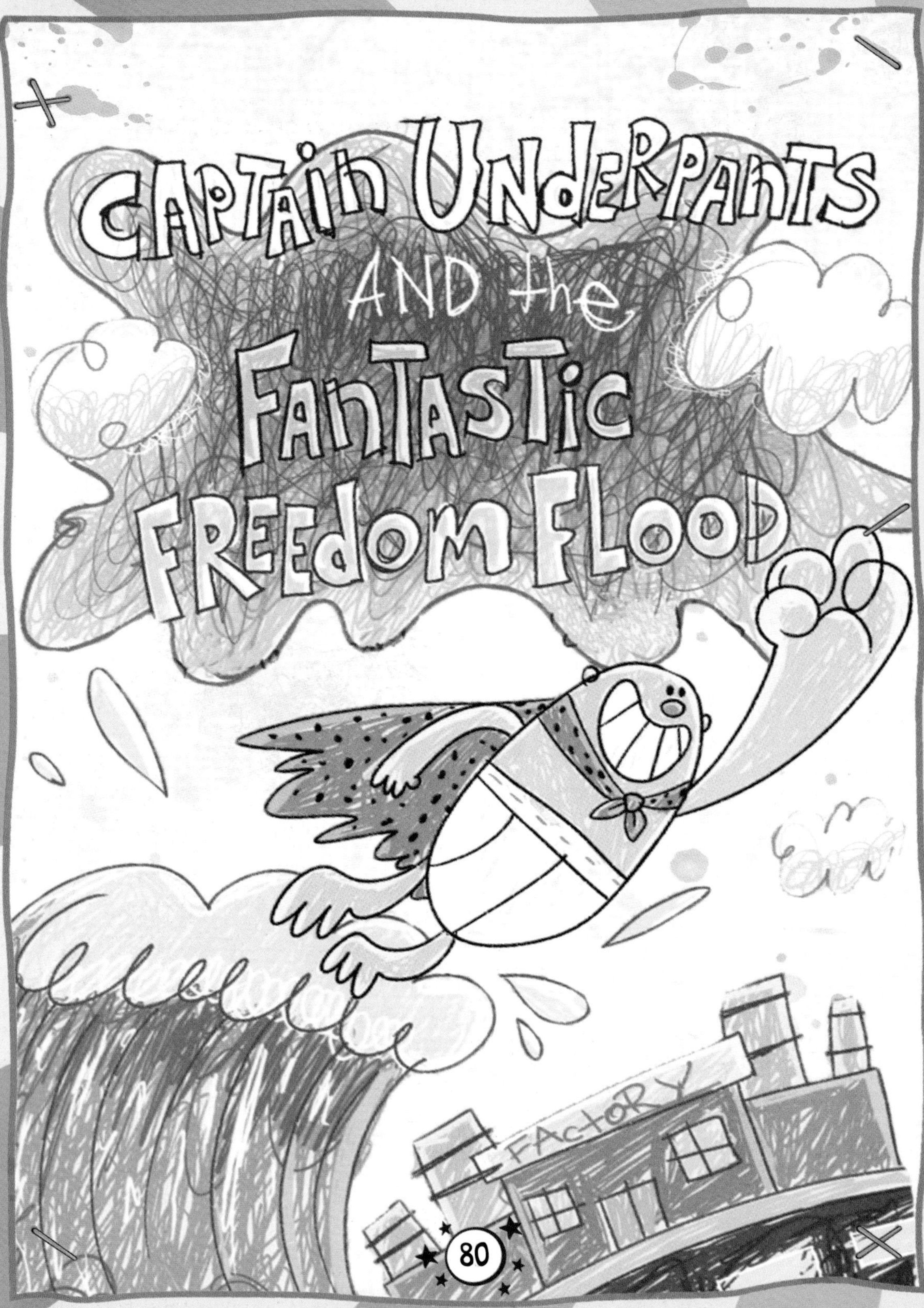
CAPTAIN UNDERPANTS
AND the
FANTASTIC
FREEDOM FLOOD
FACTORY
FACTORY

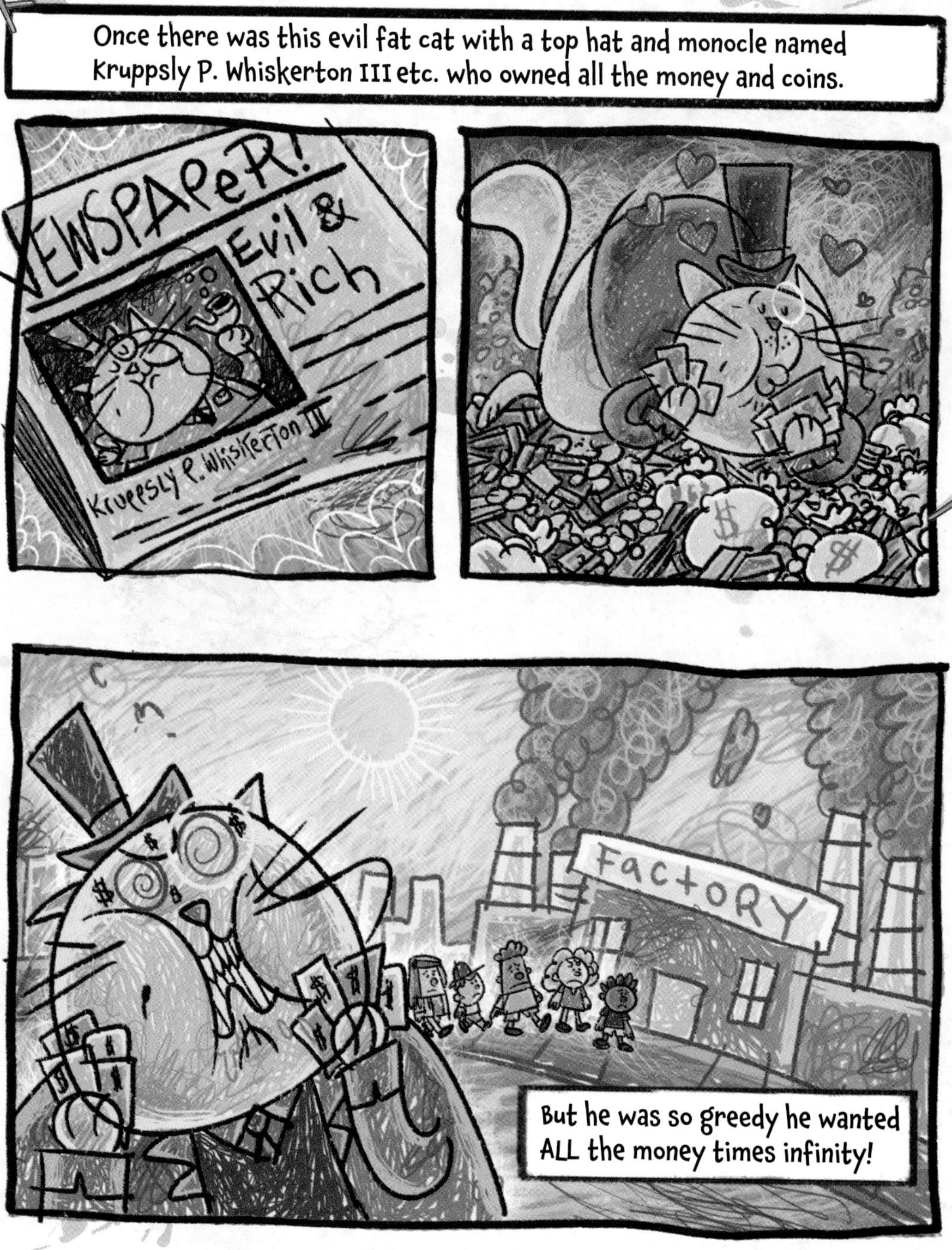
Once there was this evil fat cat with a top hat and monocle named Kruppsly P. Whiskerton III etc. who owned all the money and coins.
NEWSPAPER!
Evil & Rich
Kruppsly P. Whiskerton III
FACTORY
But he was so greedy he wanted ALL the money times infinity!

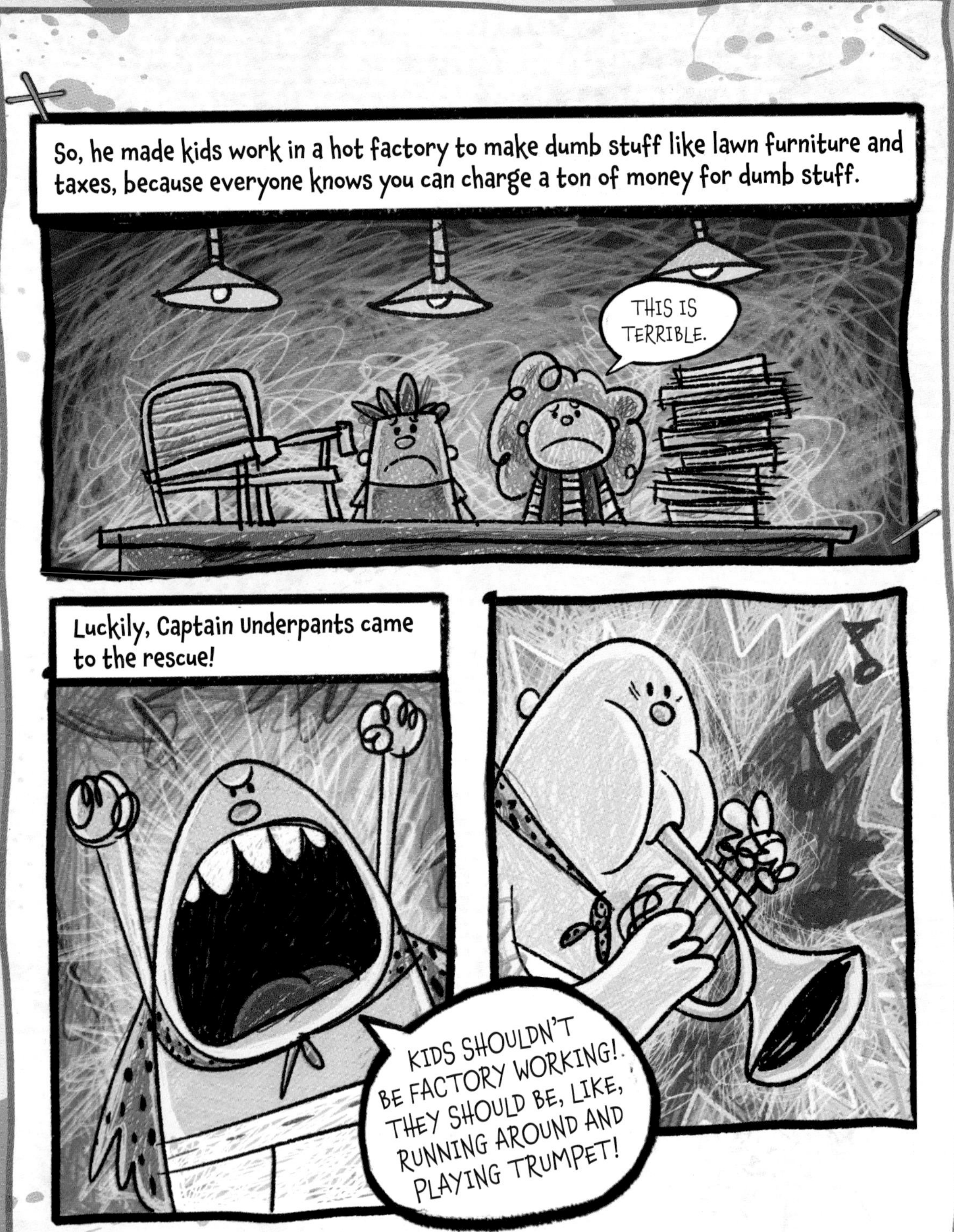

So, he made kids work in a hot factory to make dumb stuff like lawn furniture and taxes, because everyone knows you can charge a ton of money for dumb stuff.
THIS IS TERRIBLE.
Luckily, Captain Underpants came to the rescue!
KIDS SHOULDN'T BE FACTORY WORKING! THEY SHOULD BE, LIKE, RUNNING AROUND AND PLAYING TRUMPET!

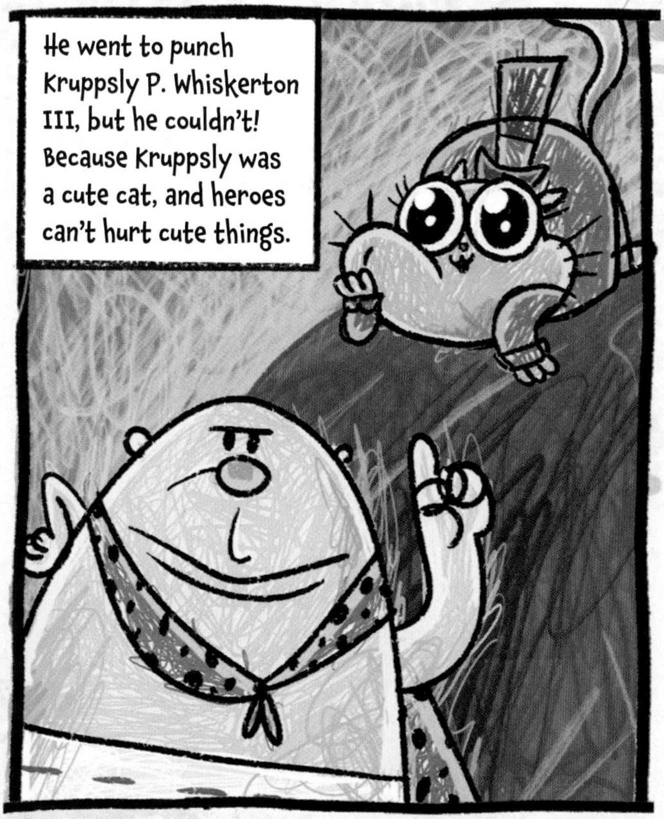
He went to punch Kruppsly P. Whiskerton III, but he couldn't! Because Kruppsly was a cute cat, and heroes can't hurt cute things.

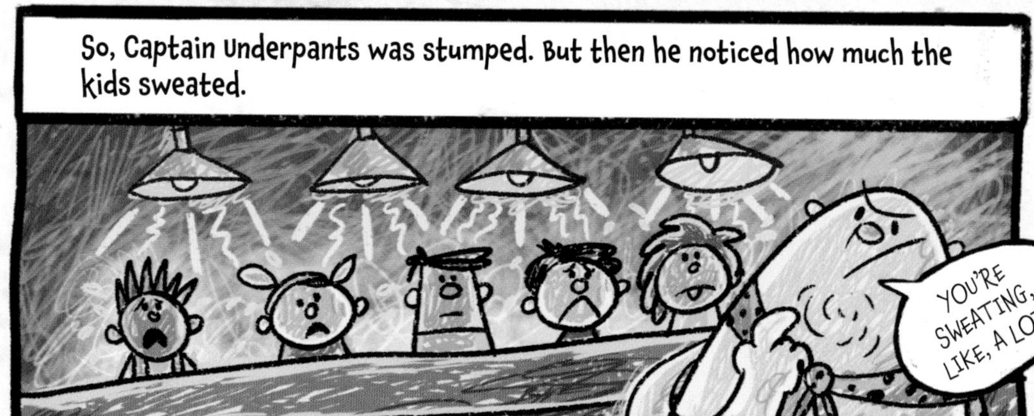
So, Captain Underpants was stumped. But then he noticed how much the kids sweated.
YOU'RE SWEATING, LIKE, A LOT.

So, he used his super-flying speed to fly in circles so fast it turned their sweat into a SWEATNAMI!

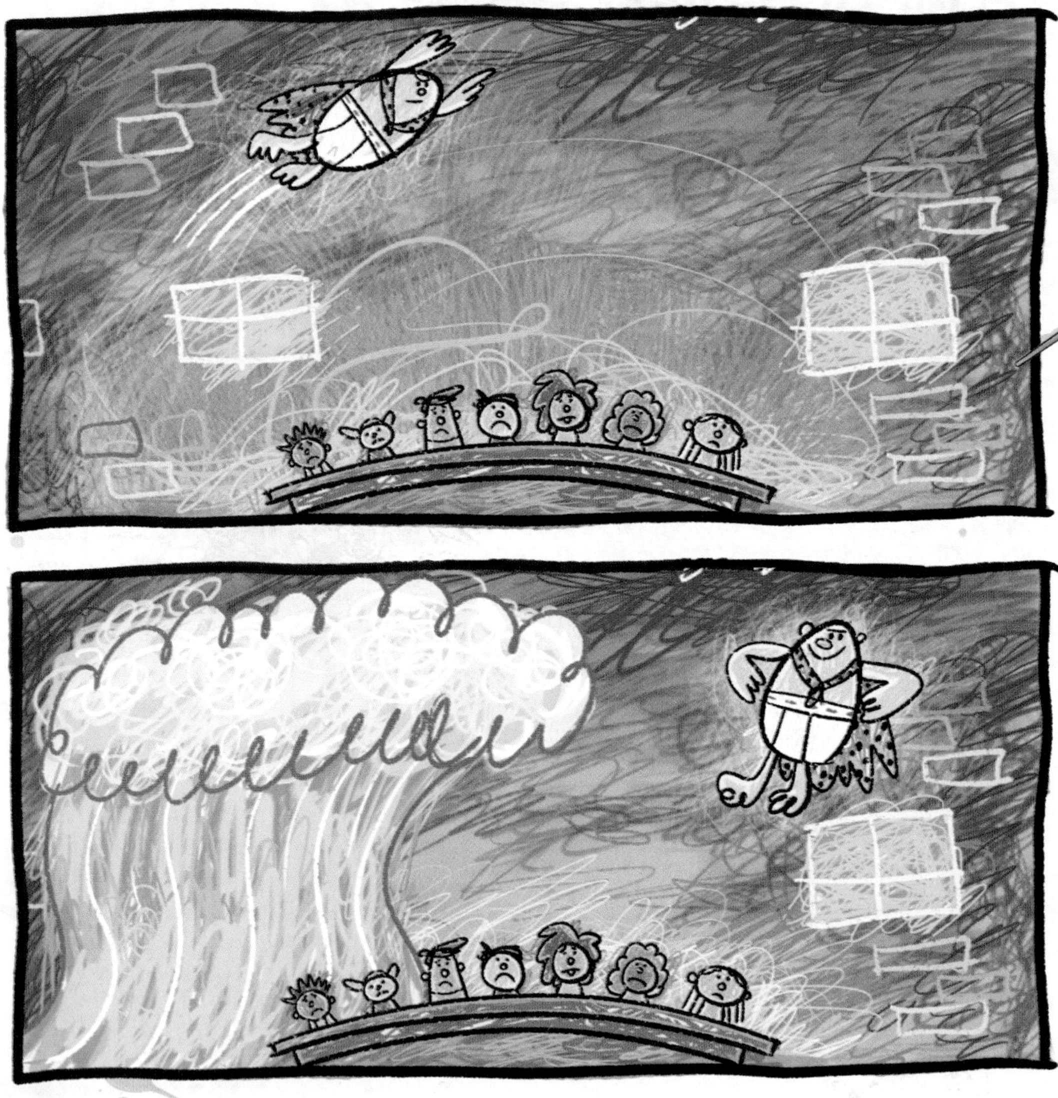

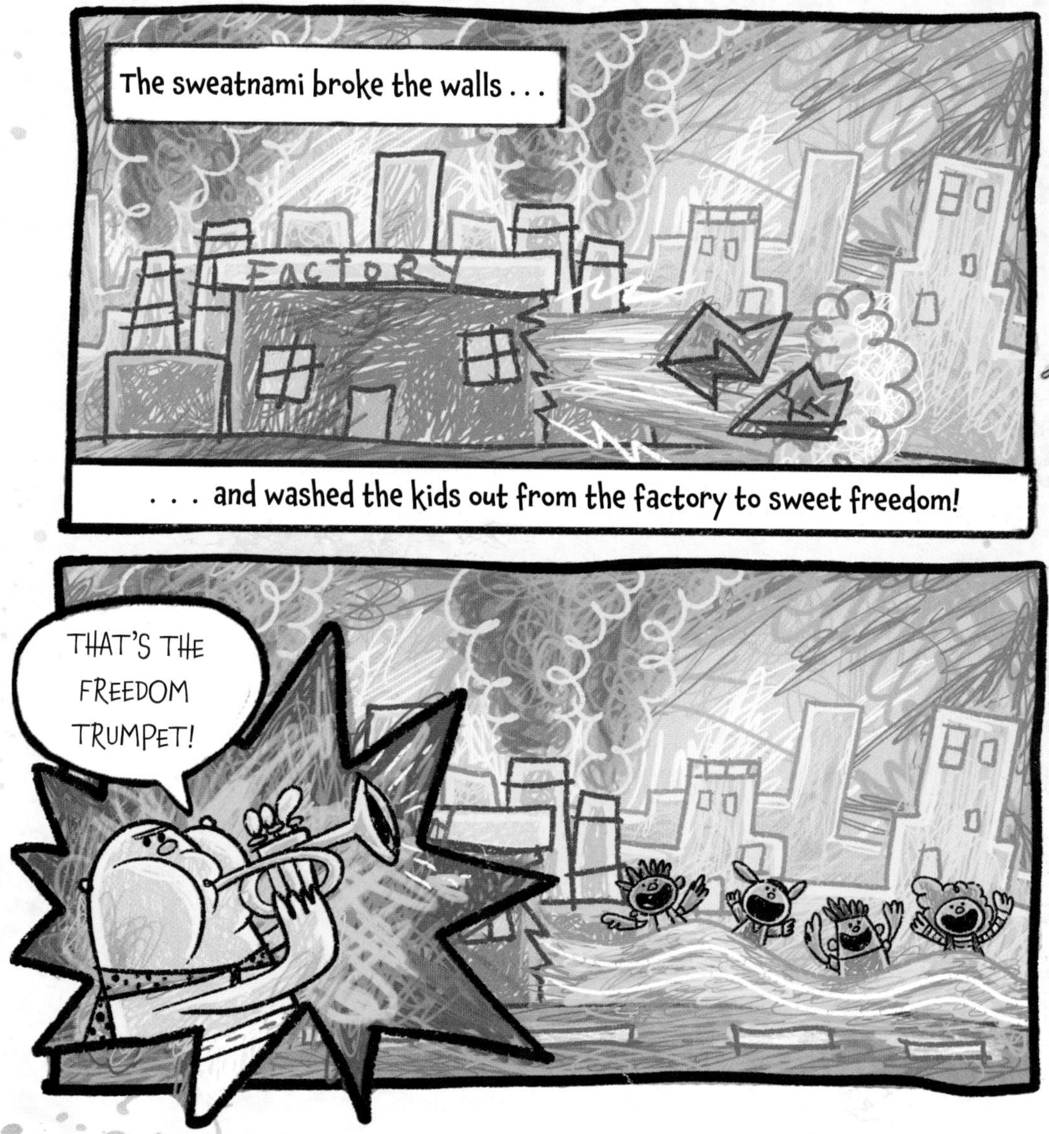
The sweatnami broke the walls . . .
FACTORY
. . . and washed the kids out from the factory to sweet freedom!
THAT'S THE FREEDOM TRUMPET!

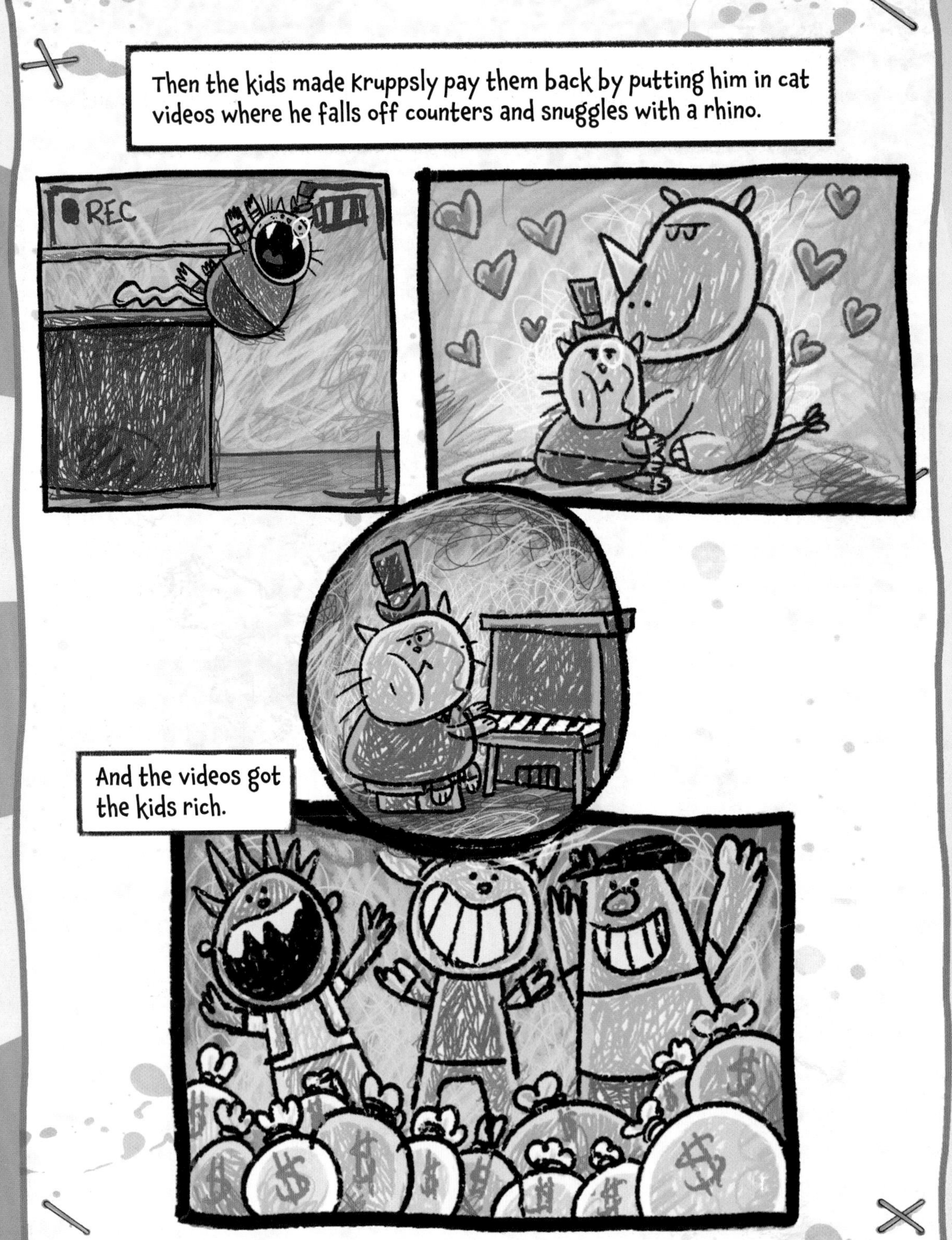
Then the kids made Kruppsly pay them back by putting him in cat videos where he falls off counters and snuggles with a rhino.
REC
And the videos got the kids rich.

And they used the money for good things, like building roads and bridges and hospitals and playgrounds and roller coasters and trumpet-practice rooms and ice cream–combat arenas.

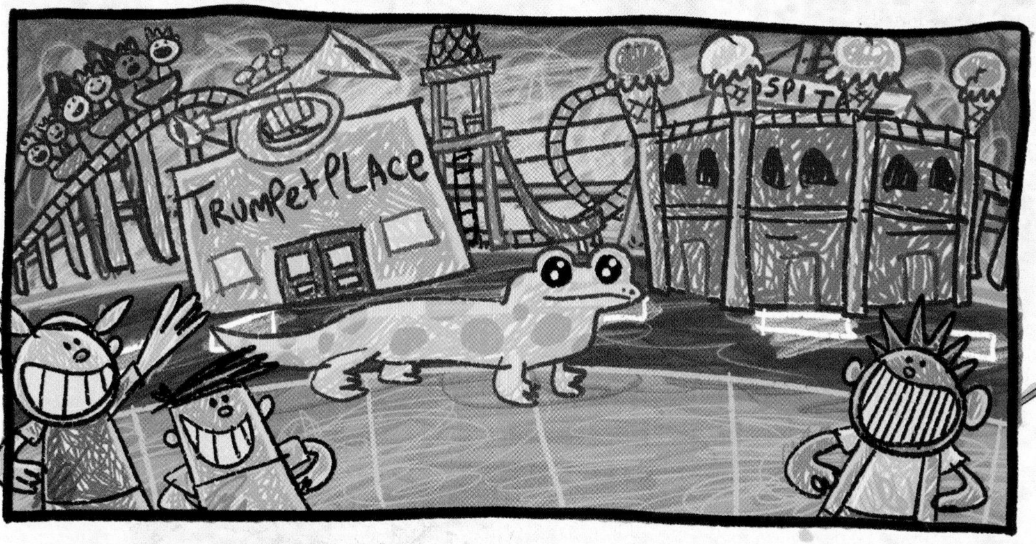
TRUMPet PLACE
SPIT

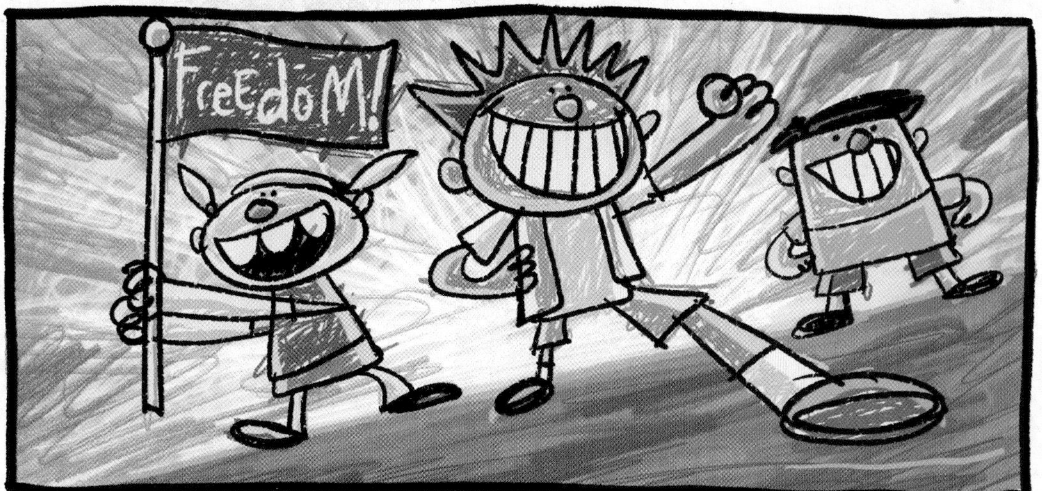
FreedoM!

The End!

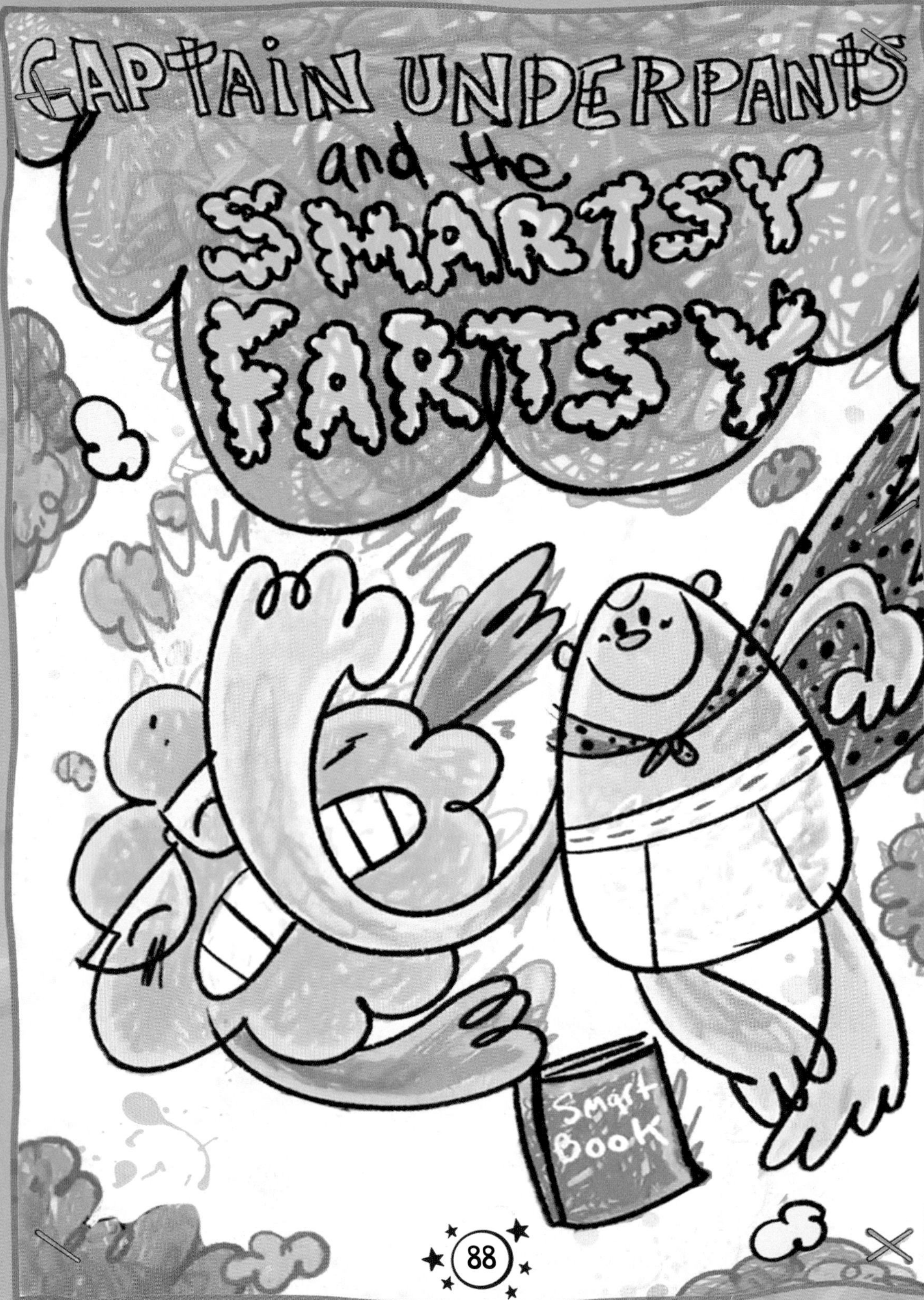
CAPTAIN UNDERPANTS
and the
SMARTSY FARTSY
Smart Book

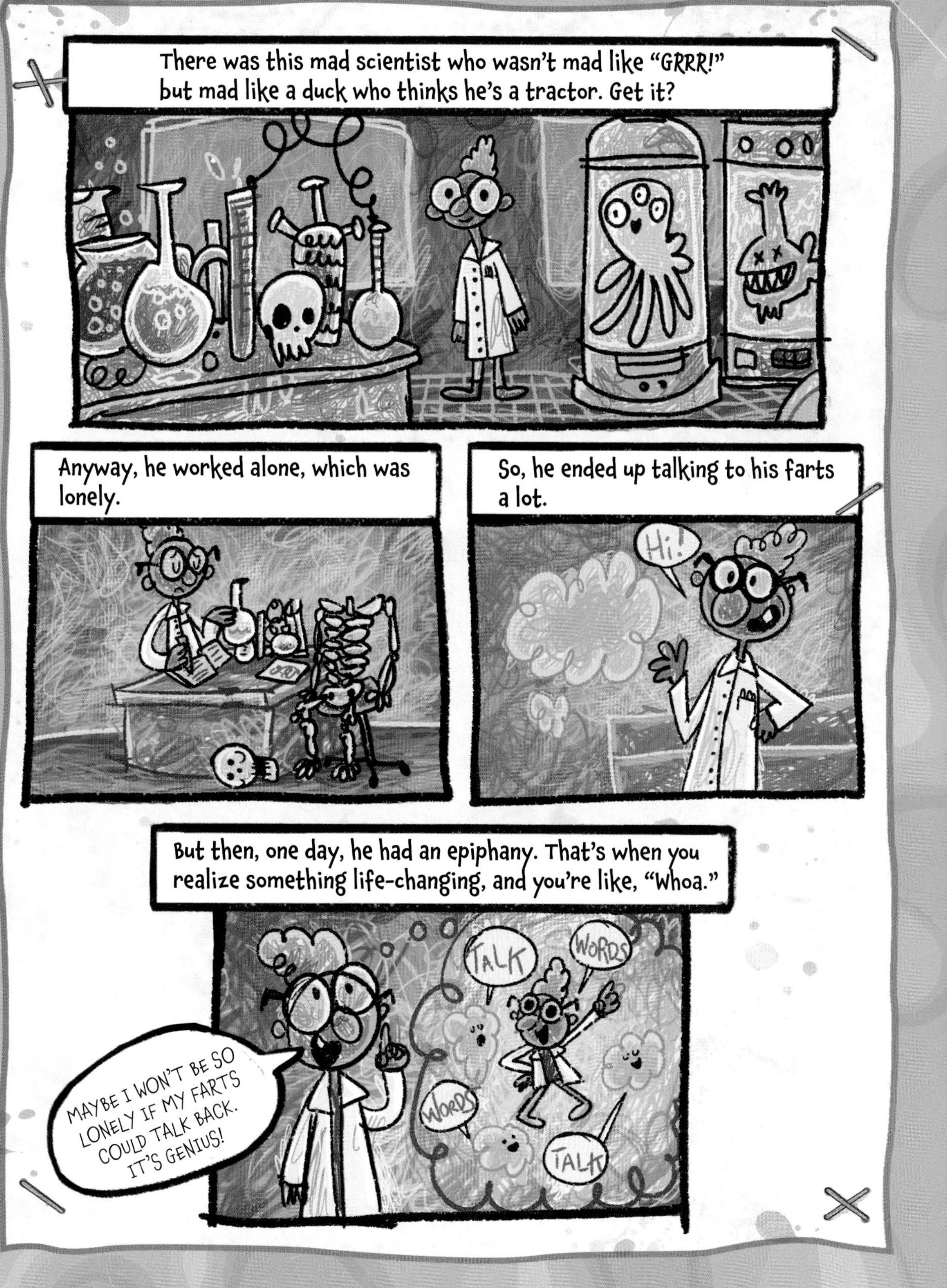

There was this mad scientist who wasn't mad like "GRRR!" but mad like a duck who thinks he's a tractor. Get it?
Anyway, he worked alone, which was lonely.
So, he ended up talking to his farts a lot.
Hi!
But then, one day, he had an epiphany. That's when you realize something life-changing, and you're like, "Whoa."
TALK
WORDS
MAYBE I WON'T BE SO LONELY IF MY FARTS COULD TALK BACK. IT'S GENIUS!
WORDS
TALK

So, he turned one of his farts from a stinker into a thinker. And he named it Smartsy Fartsy.

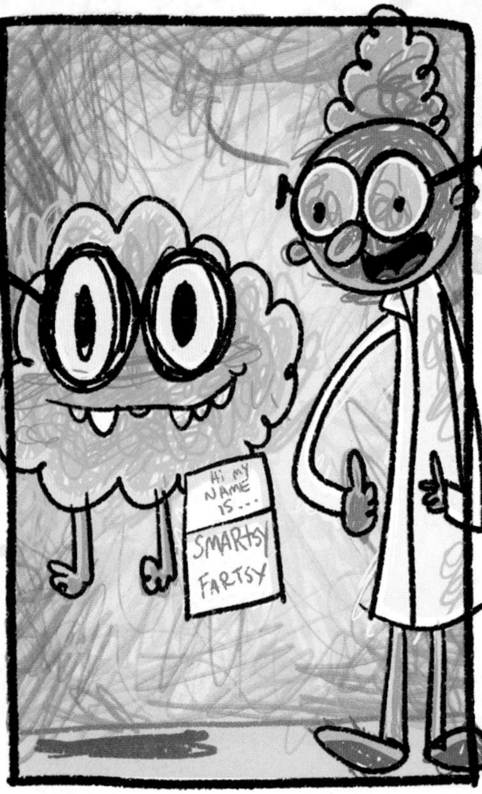
Hi MY NAME IS...
SMARTSY FARTSY

The scientist talked to Smartsy Fartsy about smart stuff like atomic molecule junk and Voltaire and his disappointing childhood.

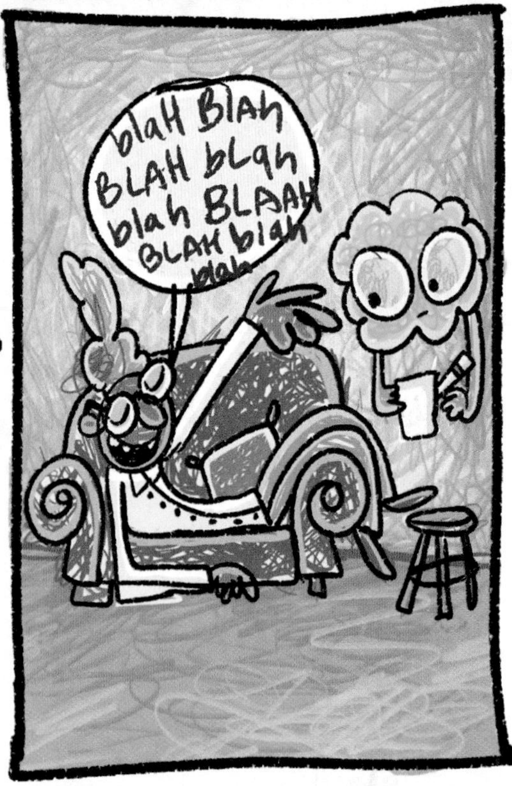
blaH Blah BLAH bLah blah BLAAH BLAH blah blah

But the mad scientist was in for a way crazy surprise . . .

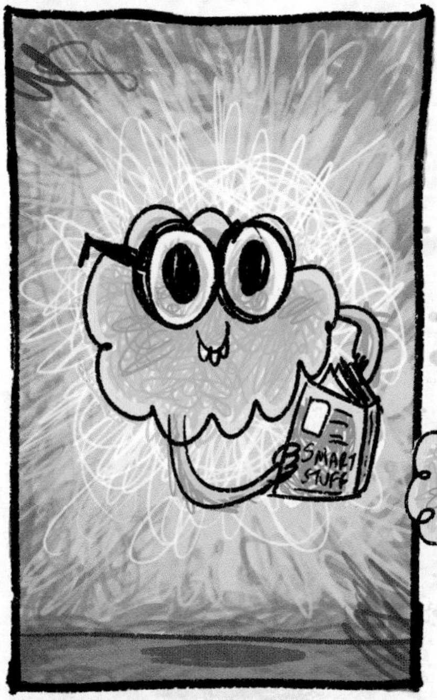
SMART STUFF

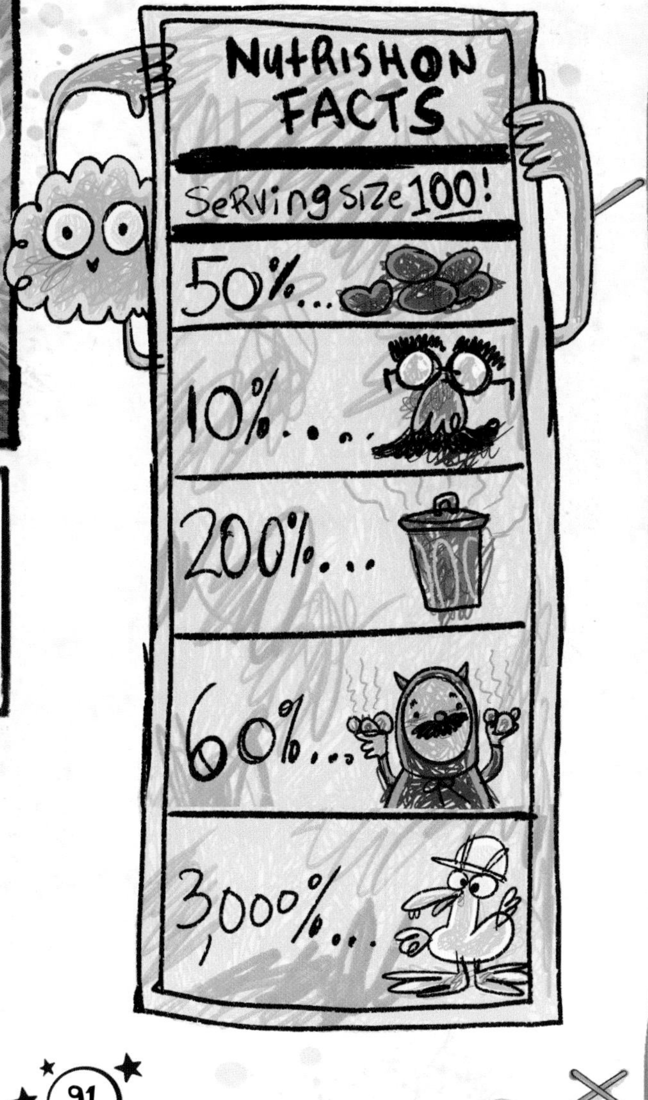
NutRISHON FACTS
SeRVing SIZe 100!
50%...
10%....
200%...
60%...
3,000%...

Smartsy Fartsy wasn't all that smart! Because farts are made of beans and stink and brimstone and egg and not smart stuff.

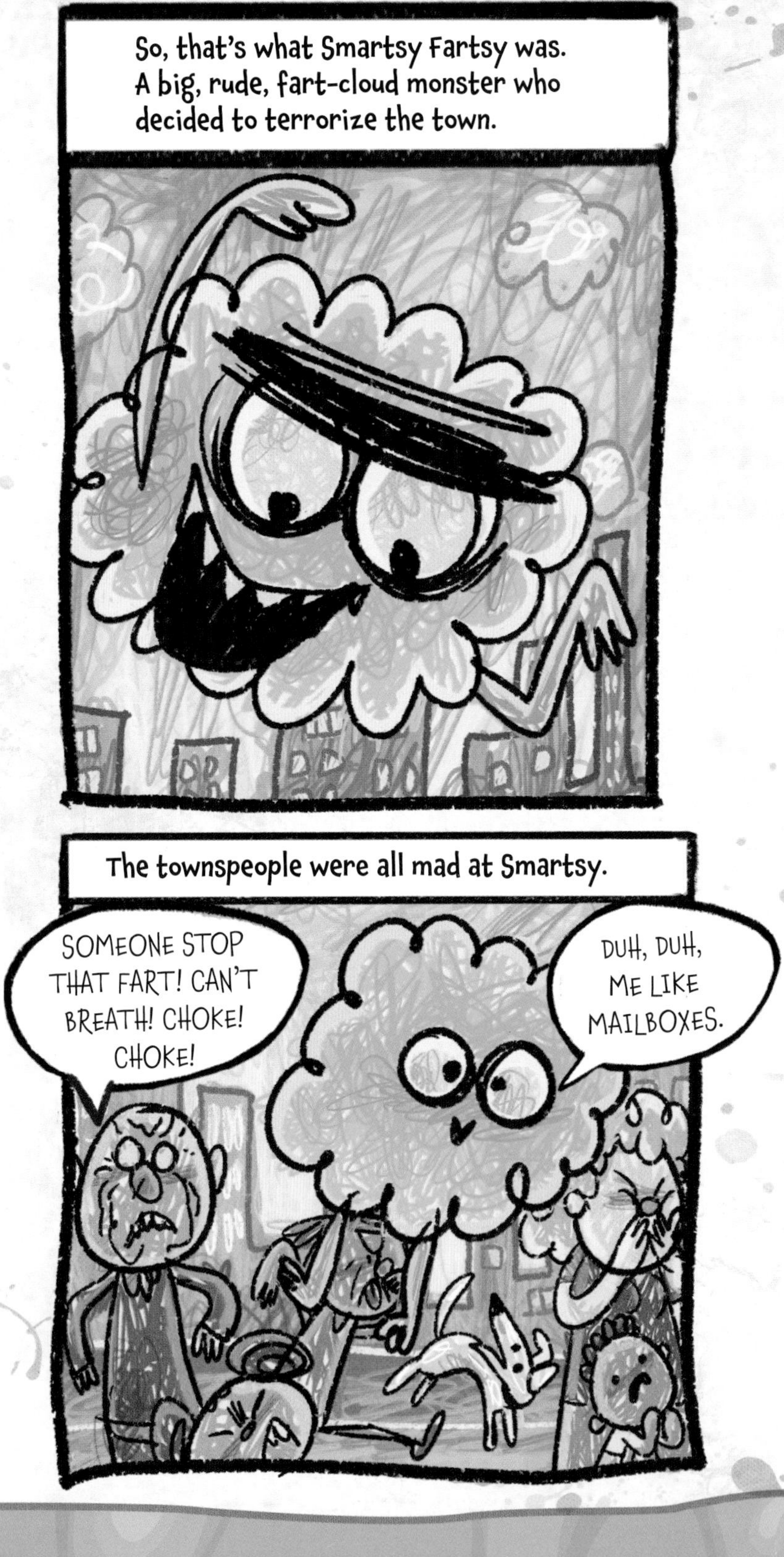
So, that's what Smartsy Fartsy was. A big, rude, fart-cloud monster who decided to terrorize the town.
The townspeople were all mad at Smartsy.
SOMEONE STOP THAT FART! CAN'T BREATH! CHOKE! CHOKE!
DUH, DUH, ME LIKE MAILBOXES.

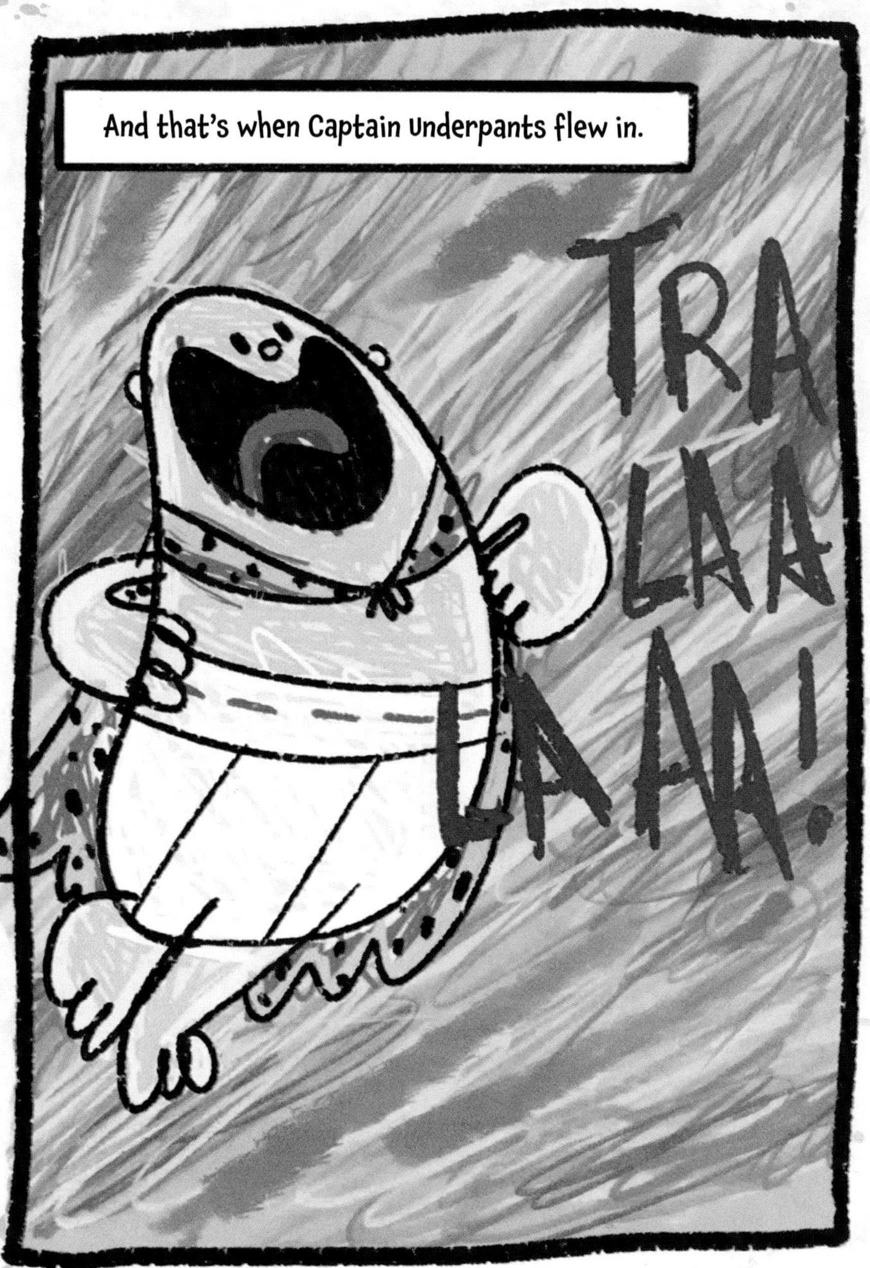
And that's when Captain Underpants flew in.
TRA LAA LAAA!

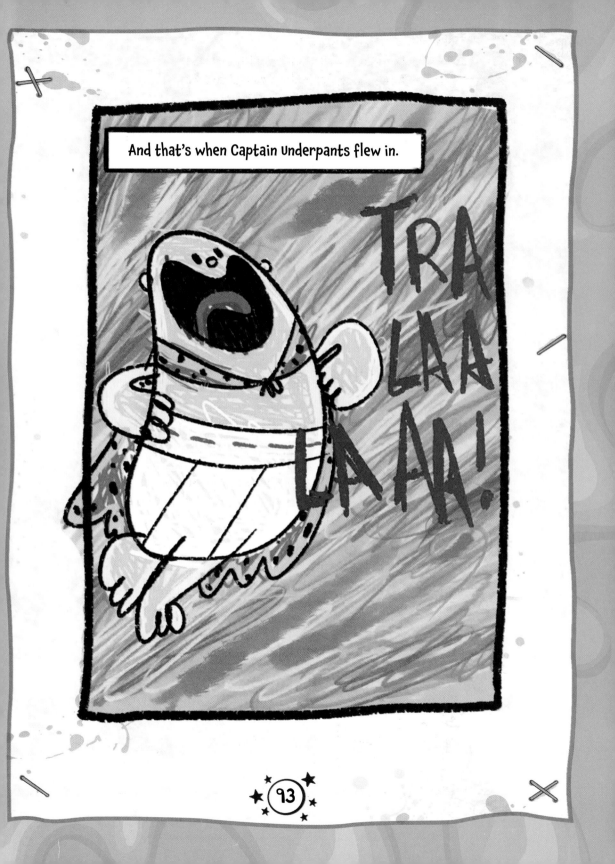

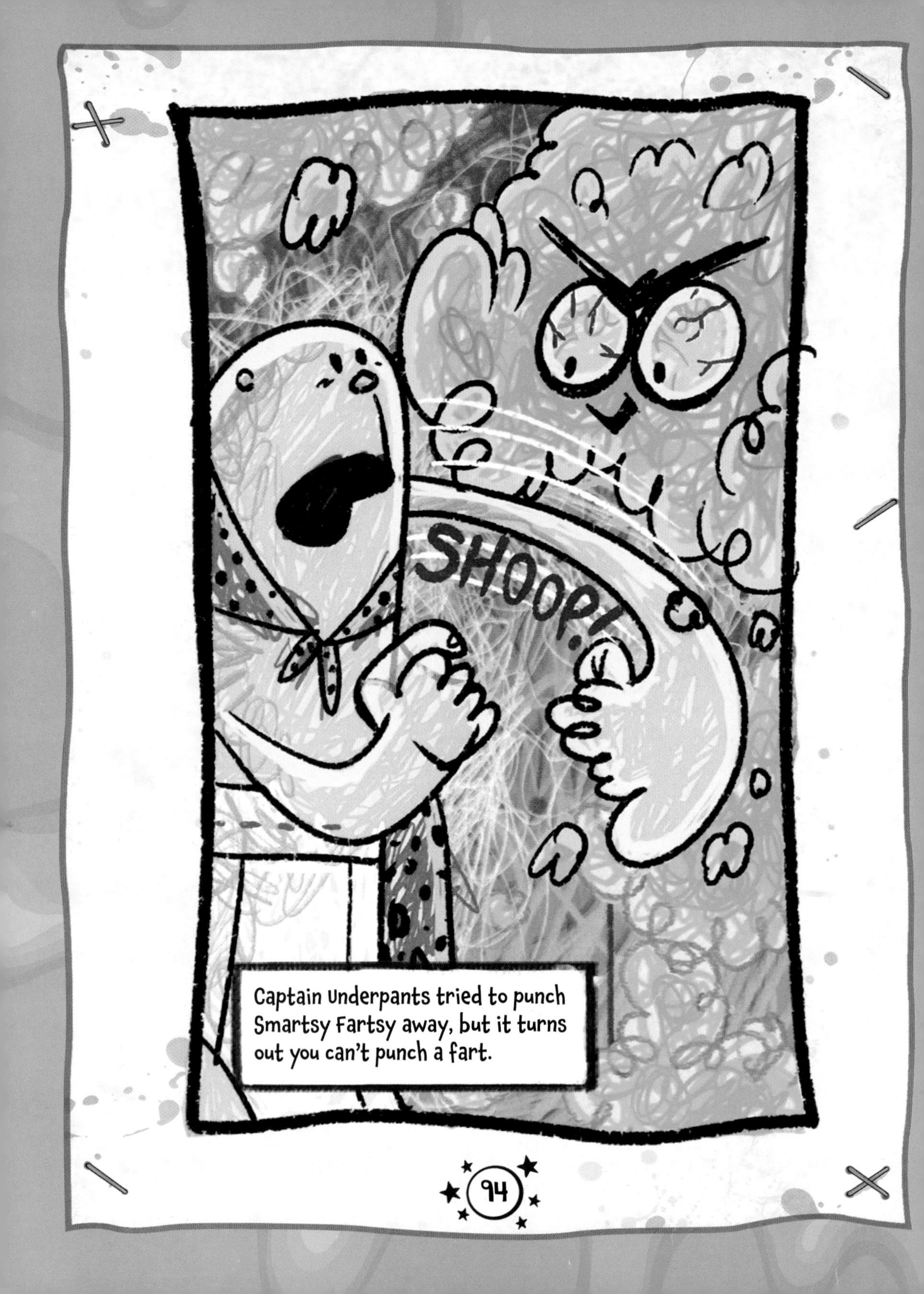
SHOOP!
Captain Underpants tried to punch Smartsy Fartsy away, but it turns out you can't punch a fart.

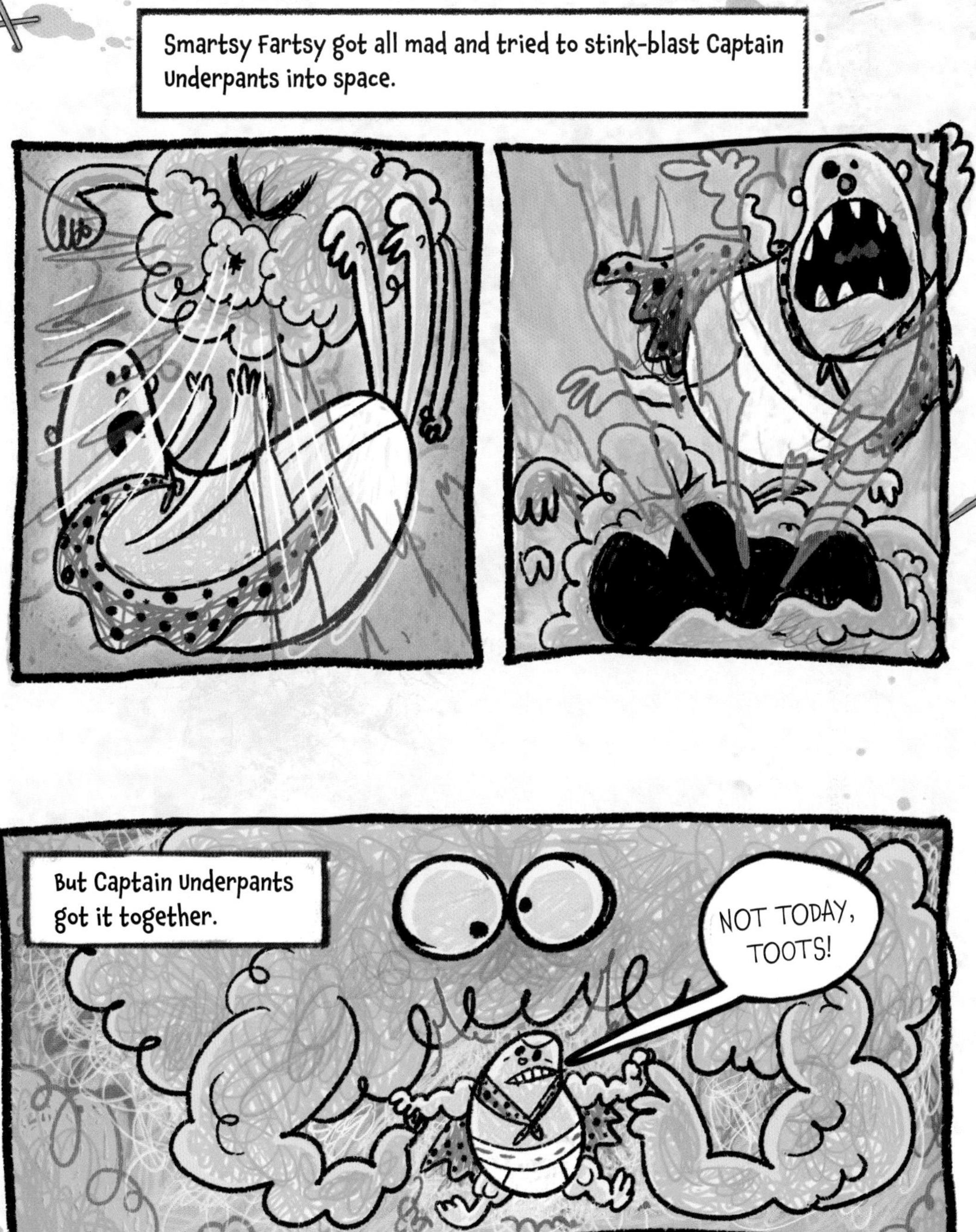
Smartsy Fartsy got all mad and tried to stink-blast Captain Underpants into space.
But Captain Underpants got it together.
NOT TODAY, TOOTS!

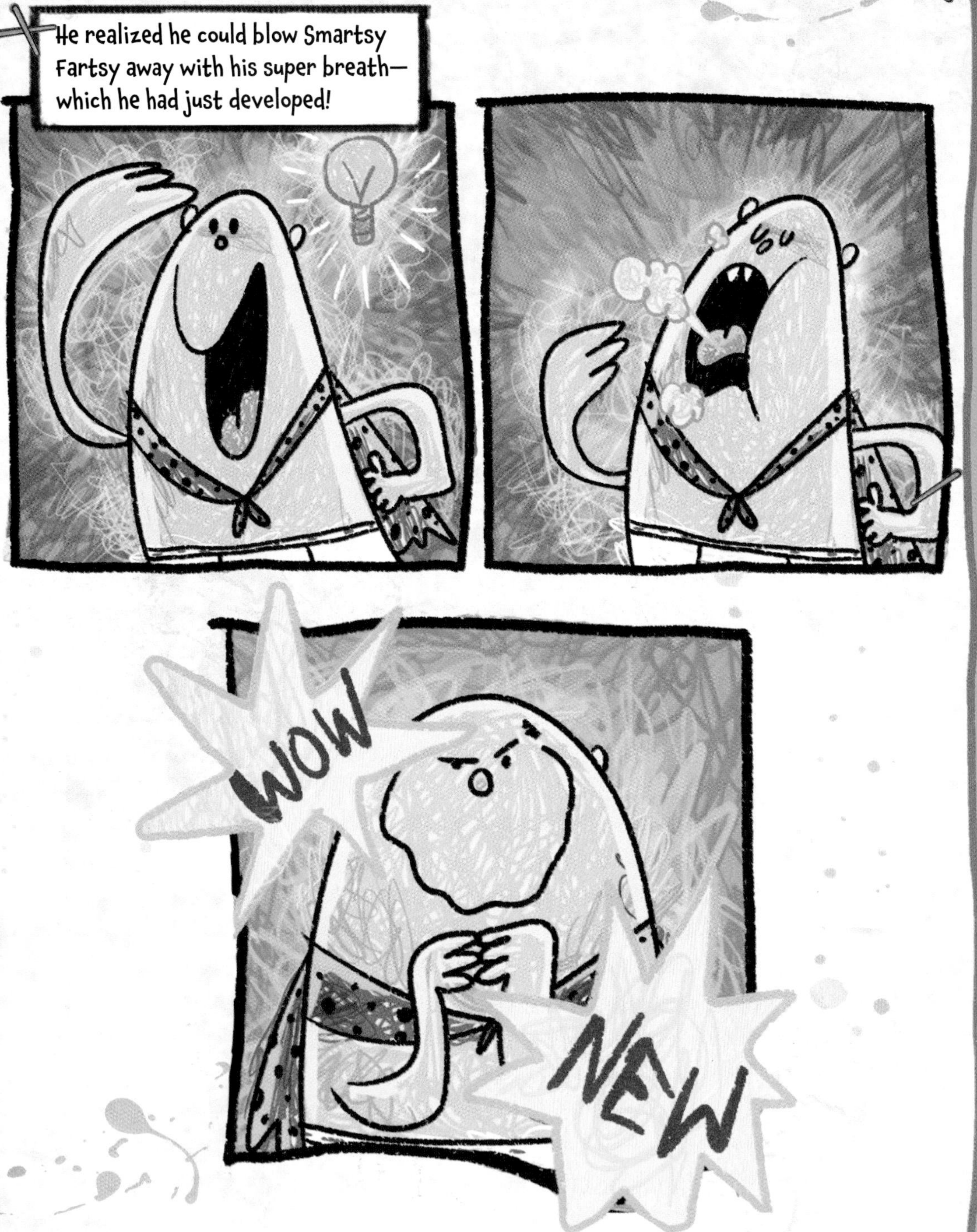
He realized he could blow Smartsy Fartsy away with his super breath—which he had just developed!
WOW
NEW

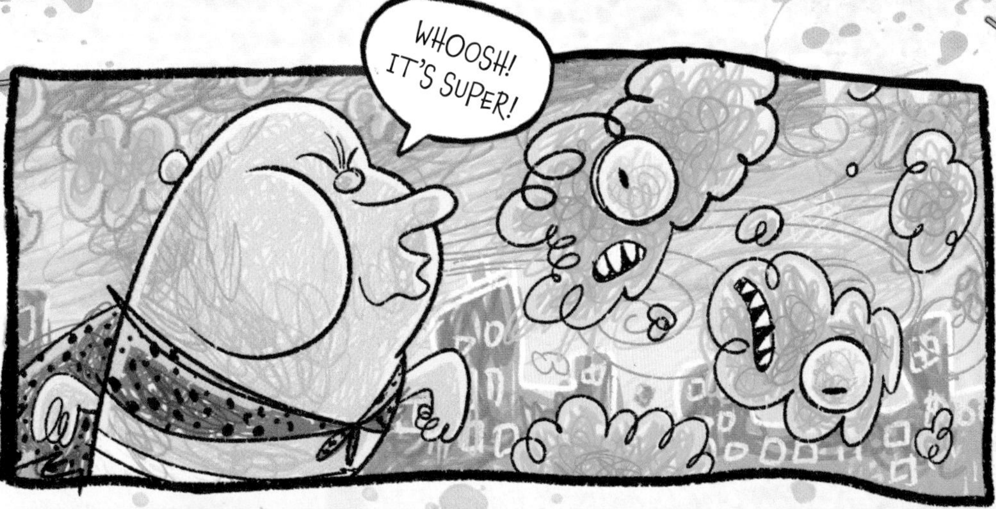
WHOOSH! IT'S SUPER!

And it worked! Everyone could breathe again, and they were all happy! Except for the mad scientist who was still lonely. So, Captain Underpants promised they could hang out every other Tuesday and maybe go bowling if there's not too much traffic.

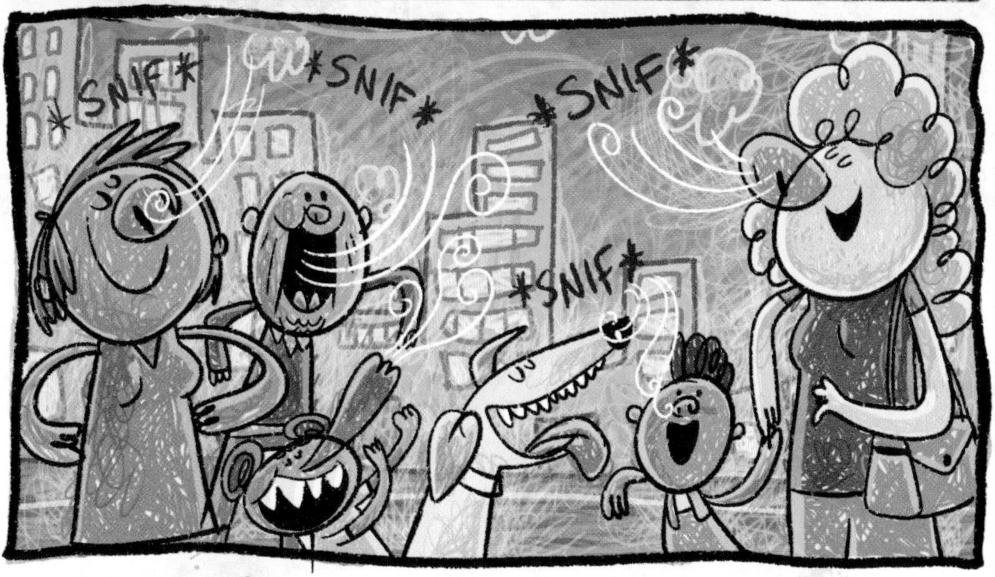
SNIF
SNIF
SNIF
SNIF

The End!

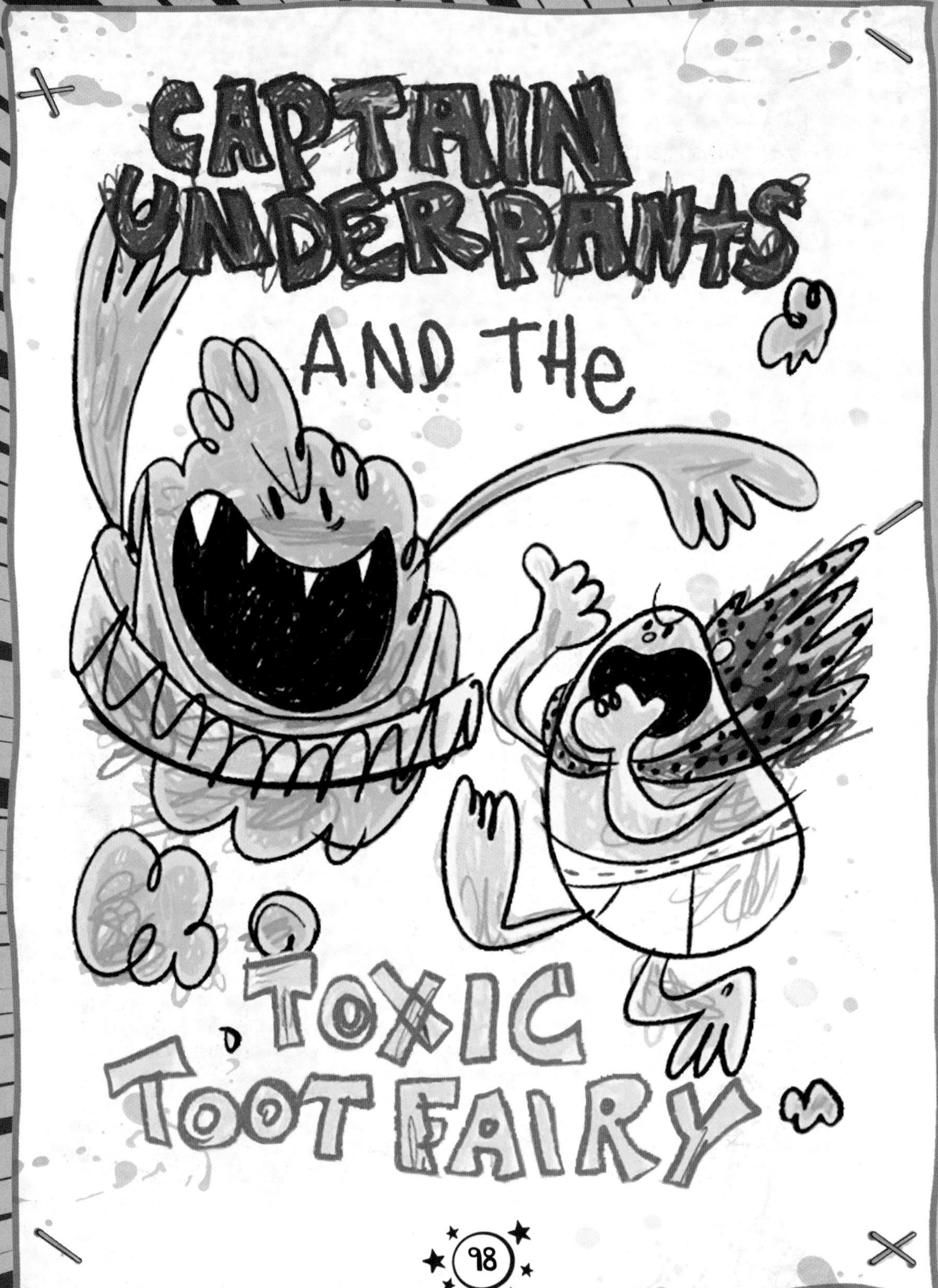
CAPTAIN UNDERPANTS
AND THE
TOXIC TOOT FAIRY

Everybody knows the Tooth Fairy, who flies around at night and trades teeth for money, which is weird, but okay. But the Tooth Fairy had a little brother named the Toot Fairy. And he was mean and instead of collecting teeth, he flew around at night swiping people's farts to build a SUPER FART BOMB.

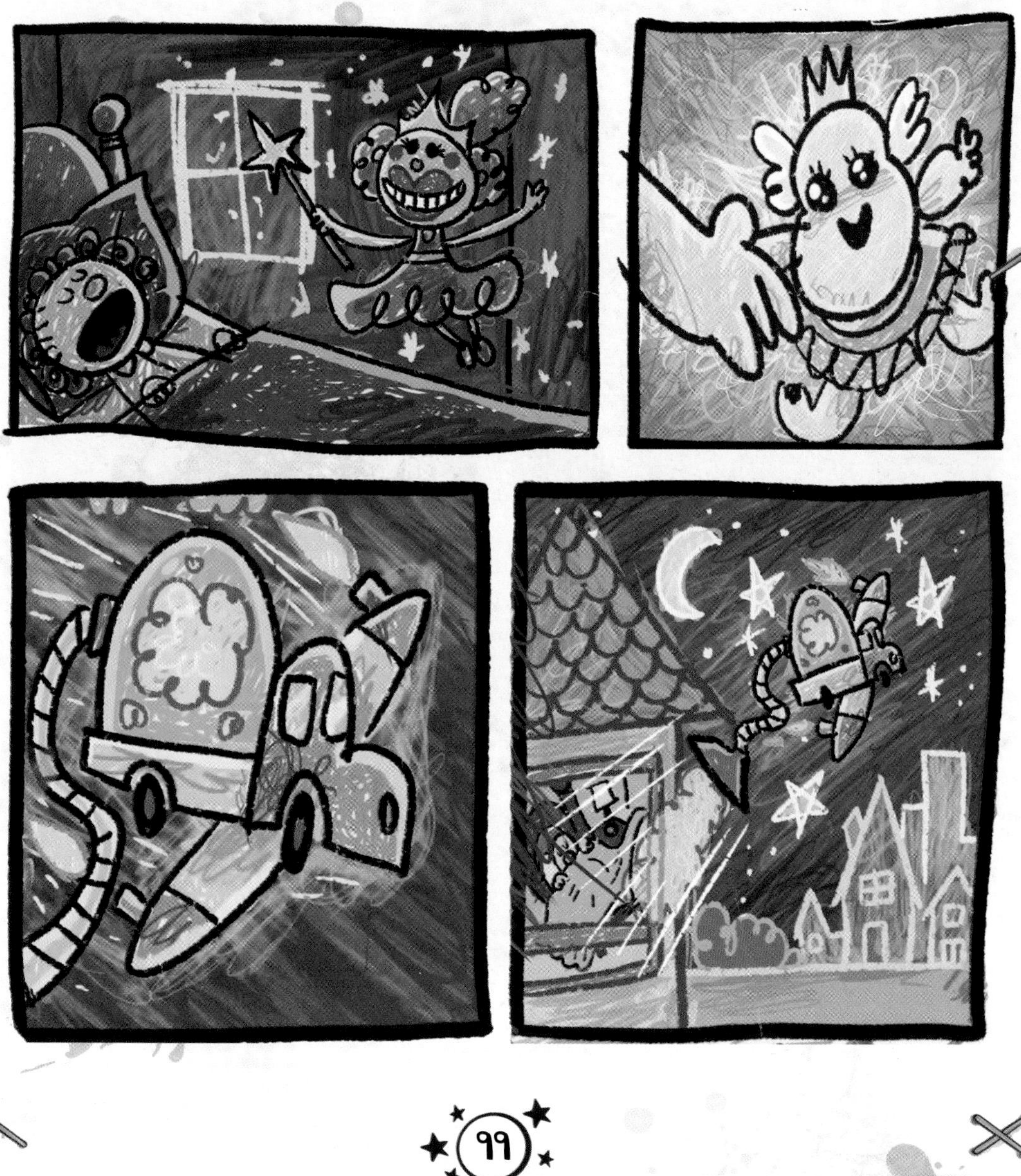

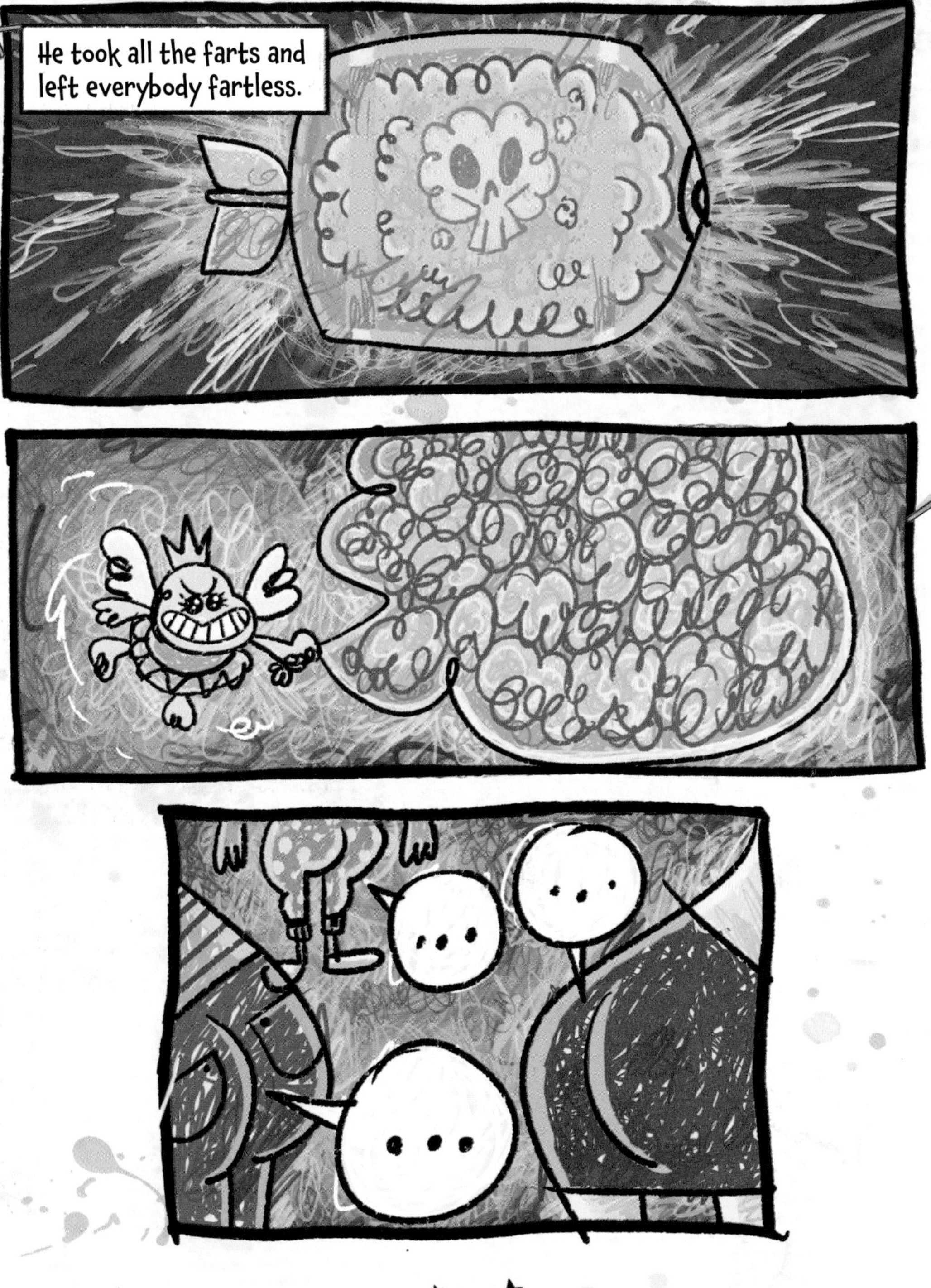
He took all the farts and left everybody fartless.
...
...
...

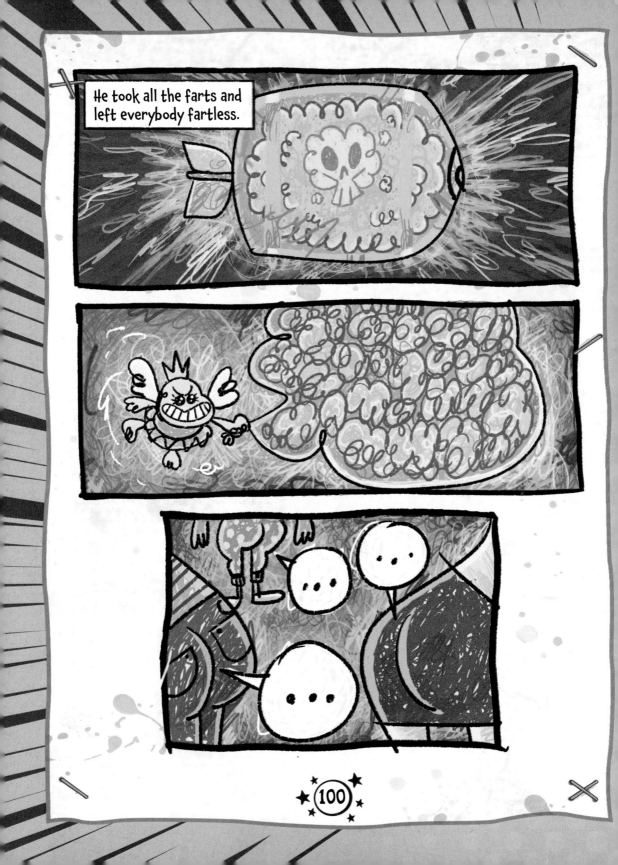

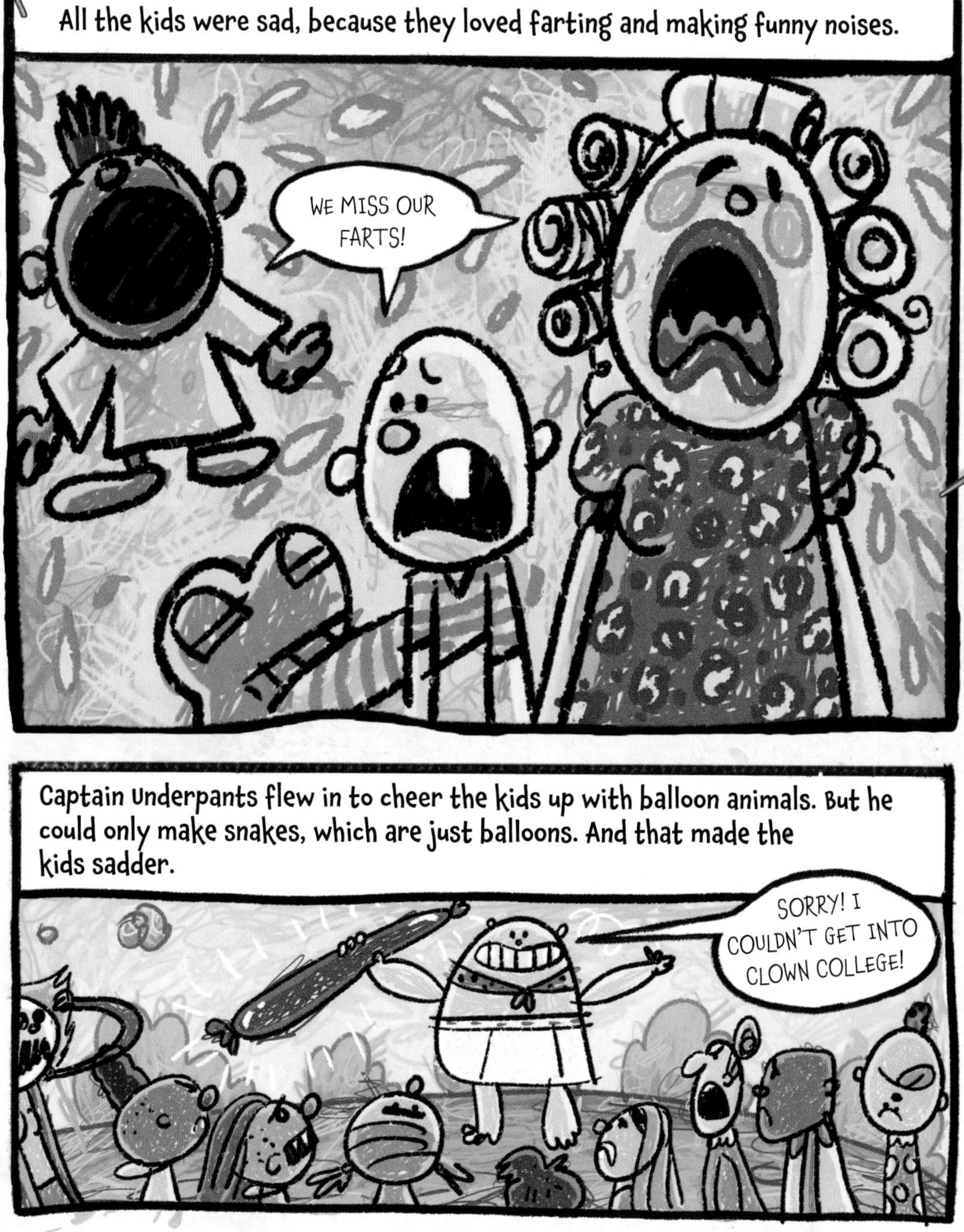
All the kids were sad, because they loved farting and making funny noises.
WE MISS OUR FARTS!
Captain Underpants flew in to cheer the kids up with balloon animals. But he could only make snakes, which are just balloons. And that made the kids sadder.
SORRY! I COULDN'T GET INTO CLOWN COLLEGE!

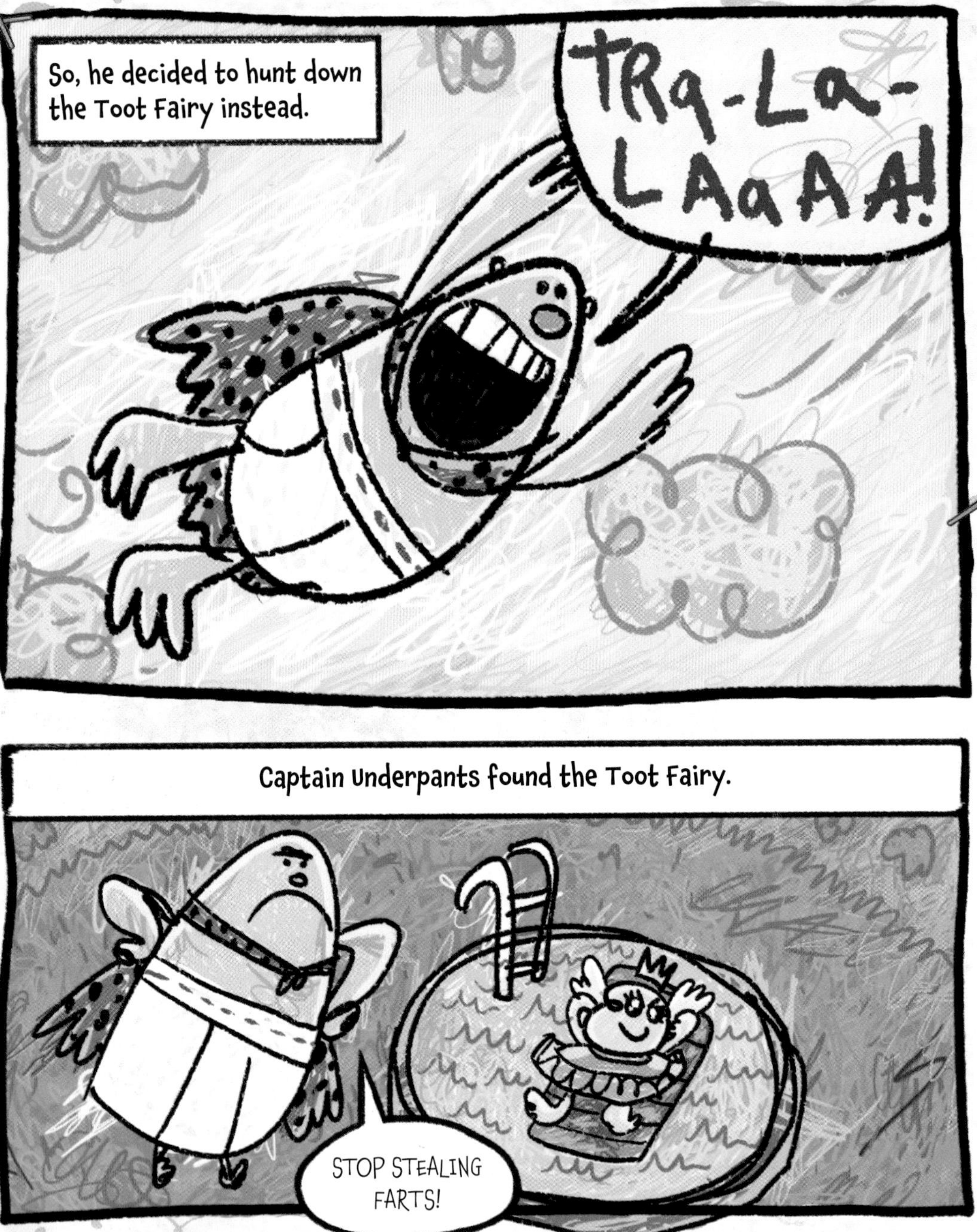
So, he decided to hunt down the Toot Fairy instead.
TRA-LA-LAAAA!
Captain Underpants found the Toot Fairy.
STOP STEALING FARTS!

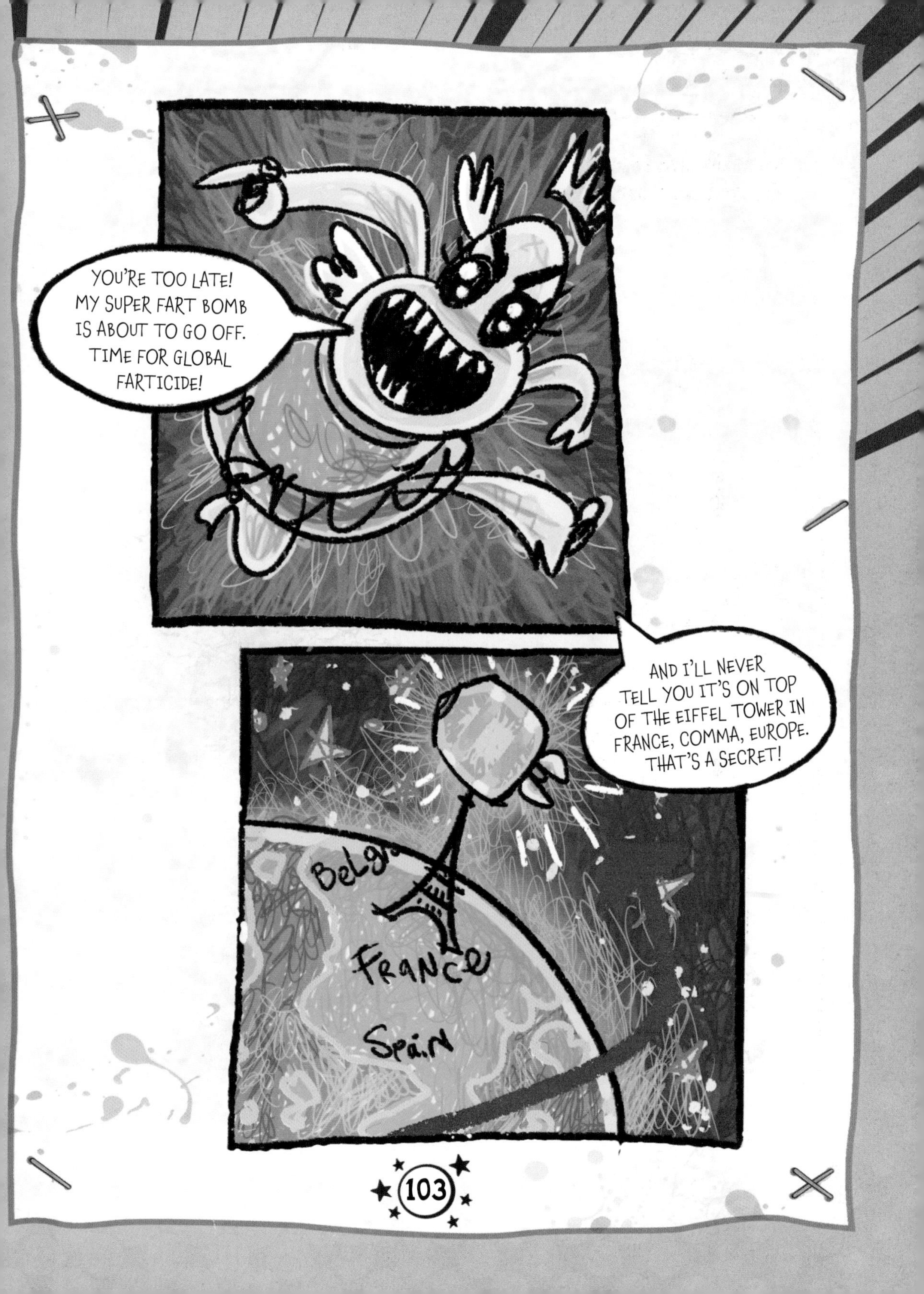
YOU'RE TOO LATE! MY SUPER FART BOMB IS ABOUT TO GO OFF. TIME FOR GLOBAL FARTICIDE!
AND I'LL NEVER TELL YOU IT'S ON TOP OF THE EIFFEL TOWER IN FRANCE, COMMA, EUROPE. THAT'S A SECRET!
FRANCE
Spain

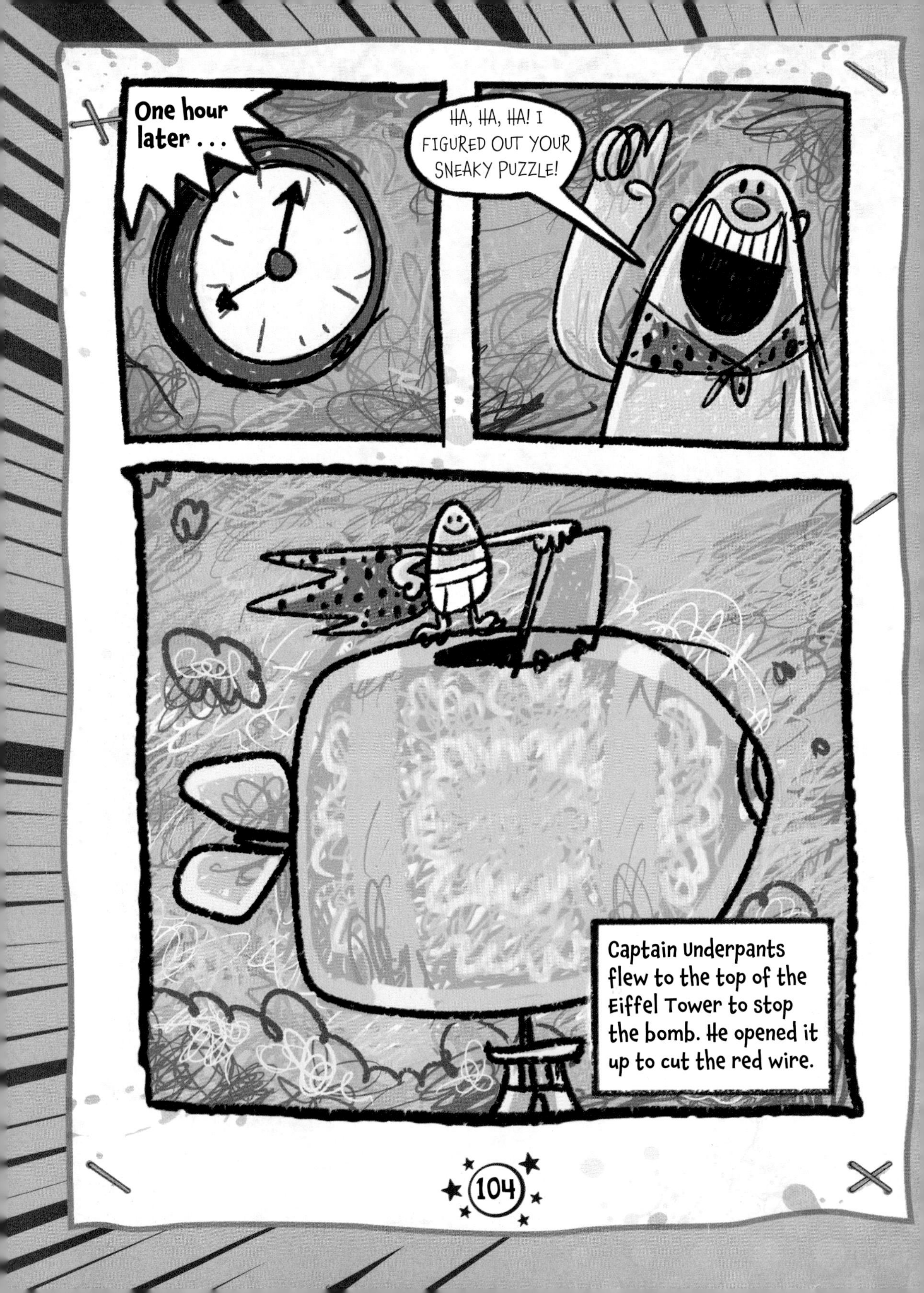
One hour later . . .
HA, HA, HA! I FIGURED OUT YOUR SNEAKY PUZZLE!
Captain Underpants flew to the top of the Eiffel Tower to stop the bomb. He opened it up to cut the red wire.

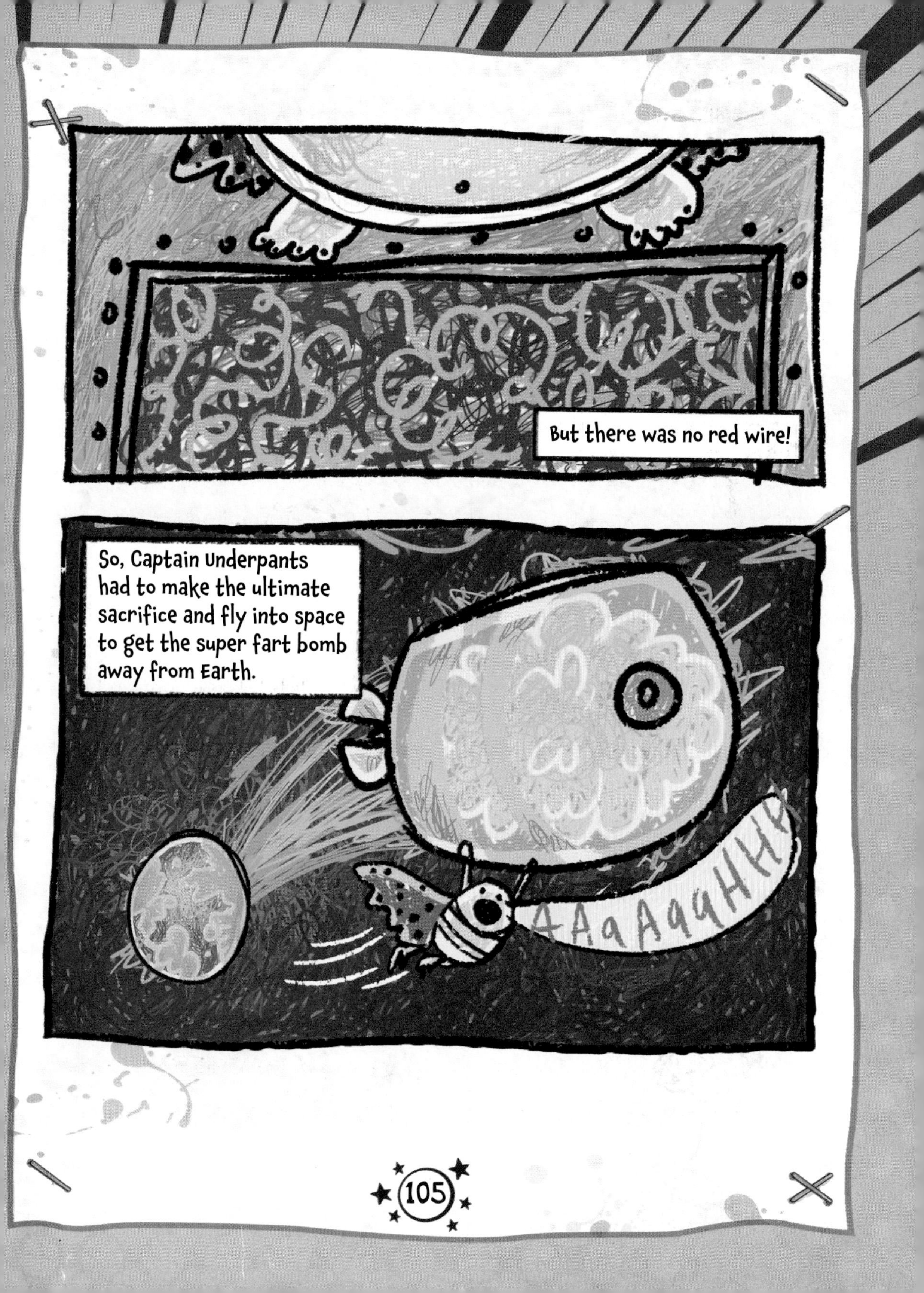
But there was no red wire!
So, Captain Underpants had to make the ultimate sacrifice and fly into space to get the super fart bomb away from Earth.
AAaAaaHHH

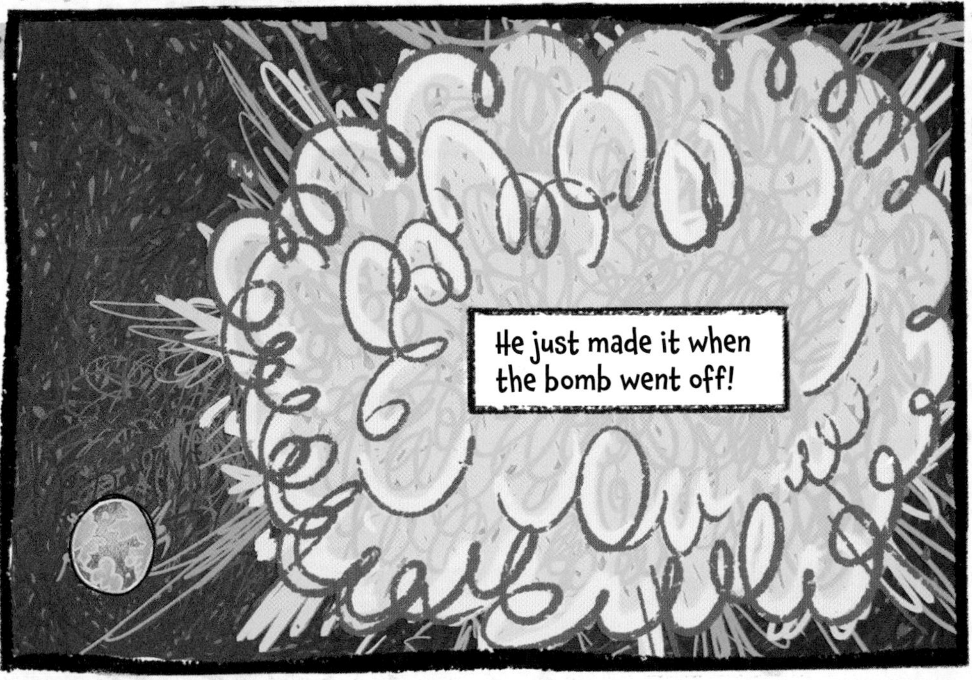
He just made it when the bomb went off!

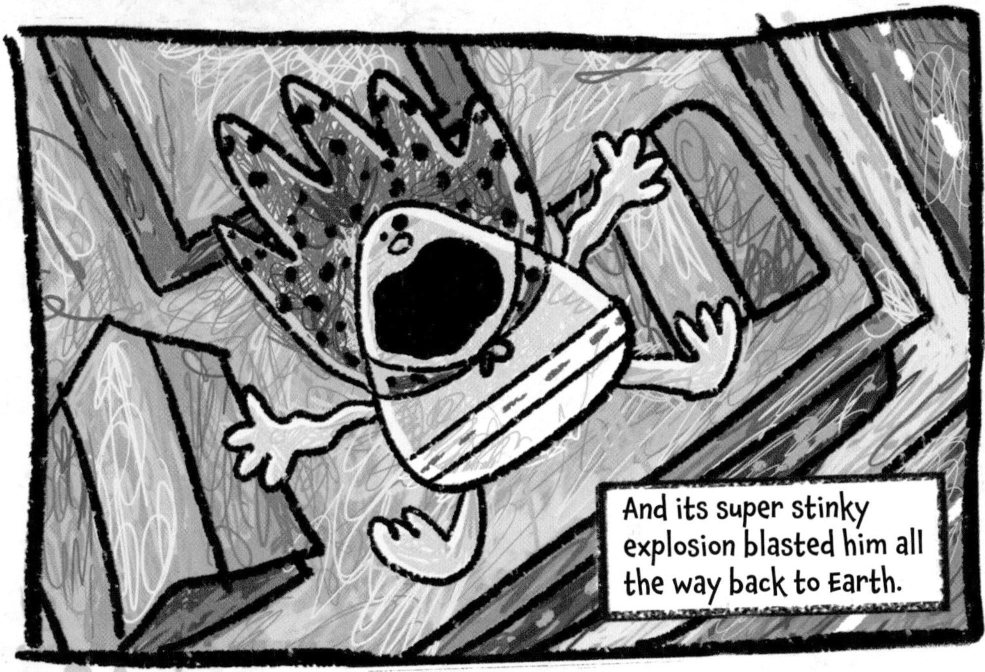
And its super stinky explosion blasted him all the way back to Earth.

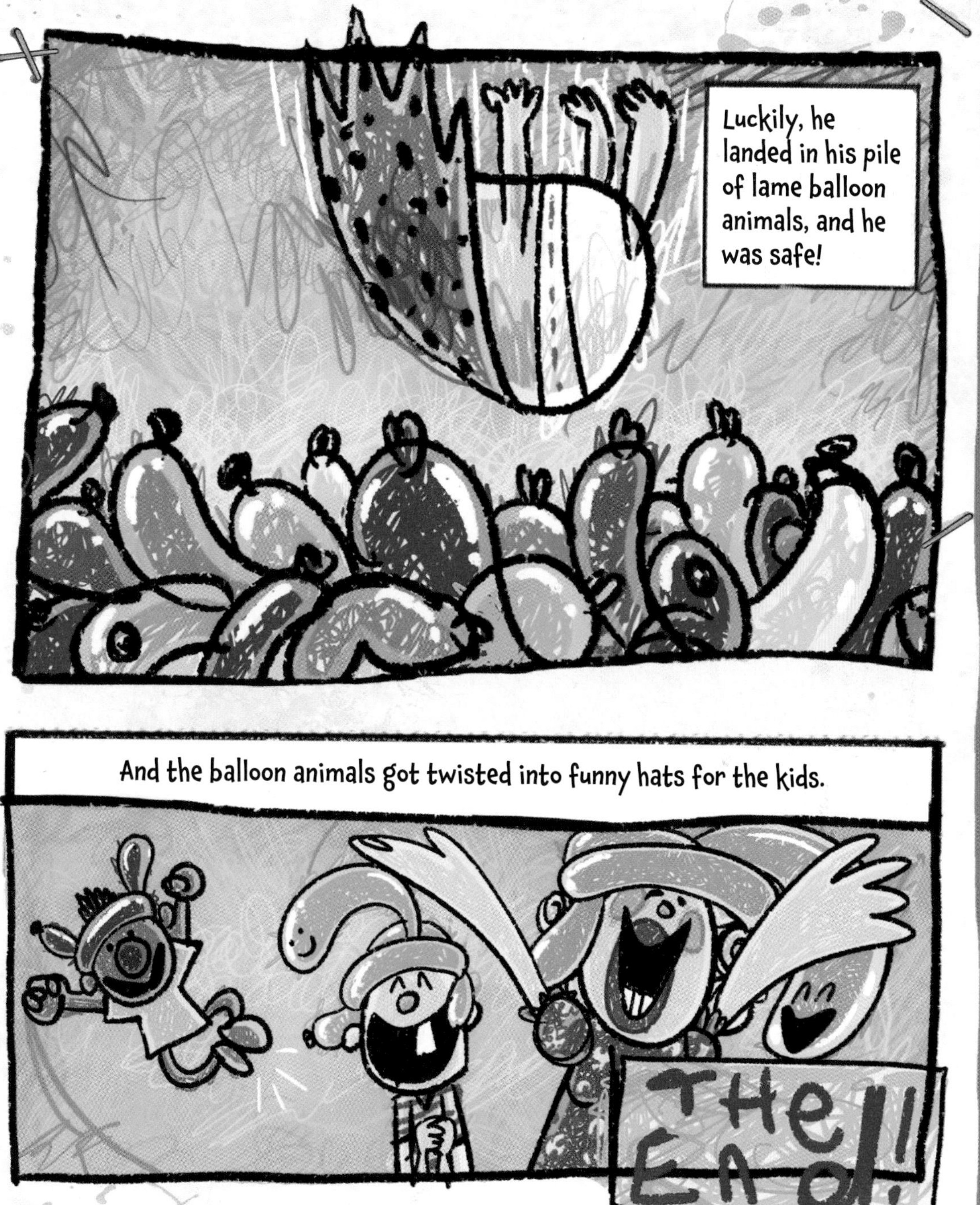
Luckily, he landed in his pile of lame balloon animals, and he was safe!
And the balloon animals got twisted into funny hats for the kids.
THE End!

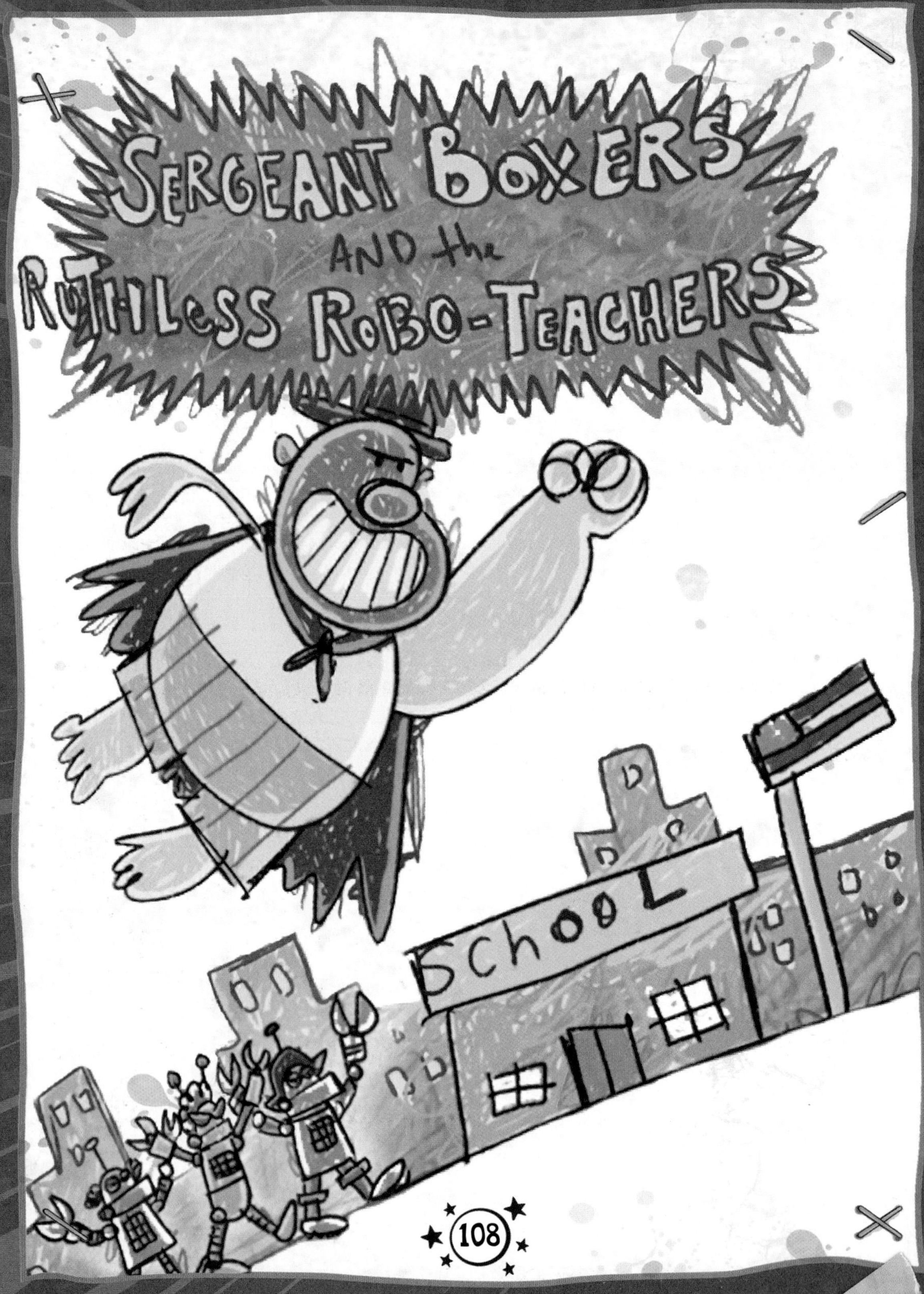
SERGEANT BOXERS
AND the
RUTHLESS ROBO-TEACHERS
SCHOOL

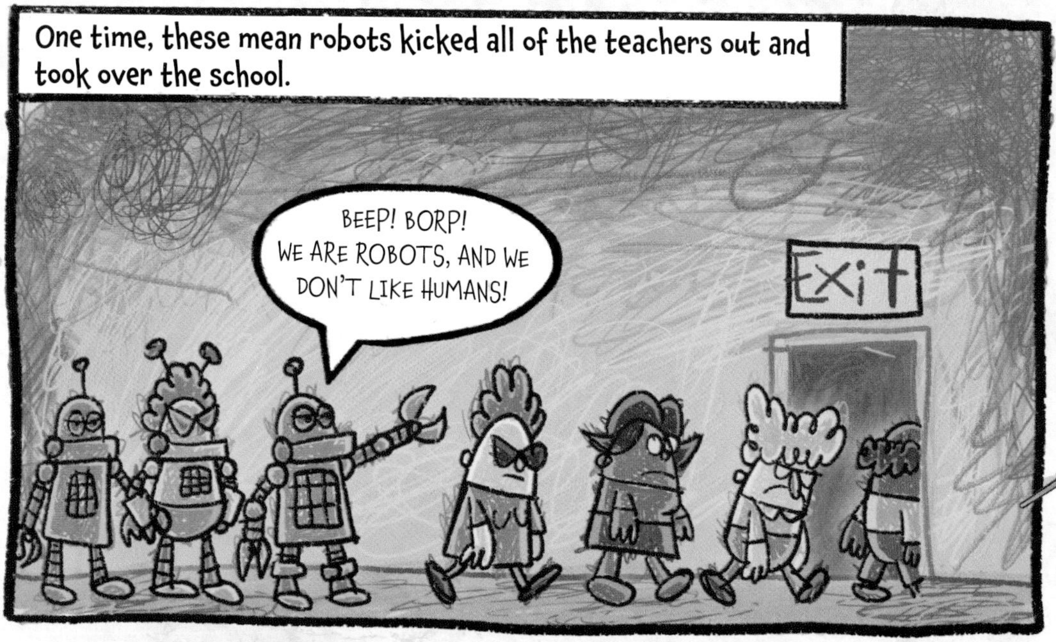
One time, these mean robots kicked all of the teachers out and took over the school.
BEEP! BORP! WE ARE ROBOTS, AND WE DON'T LIKE HUMANS!
Exit

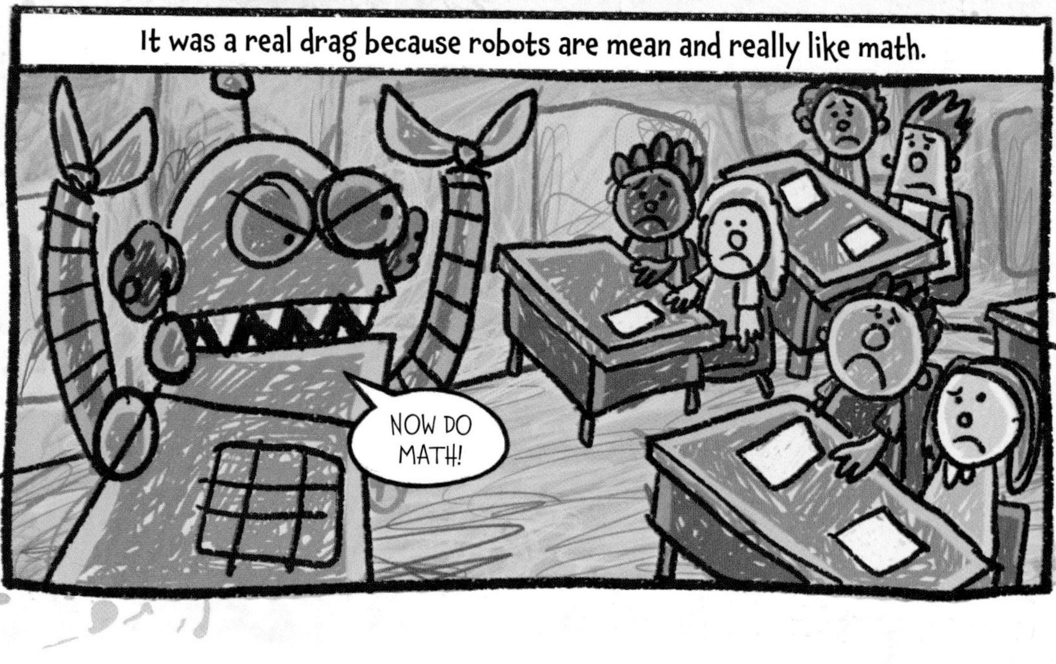
It was a real drag because robots are mean and really like math.
NOW DO MATH!

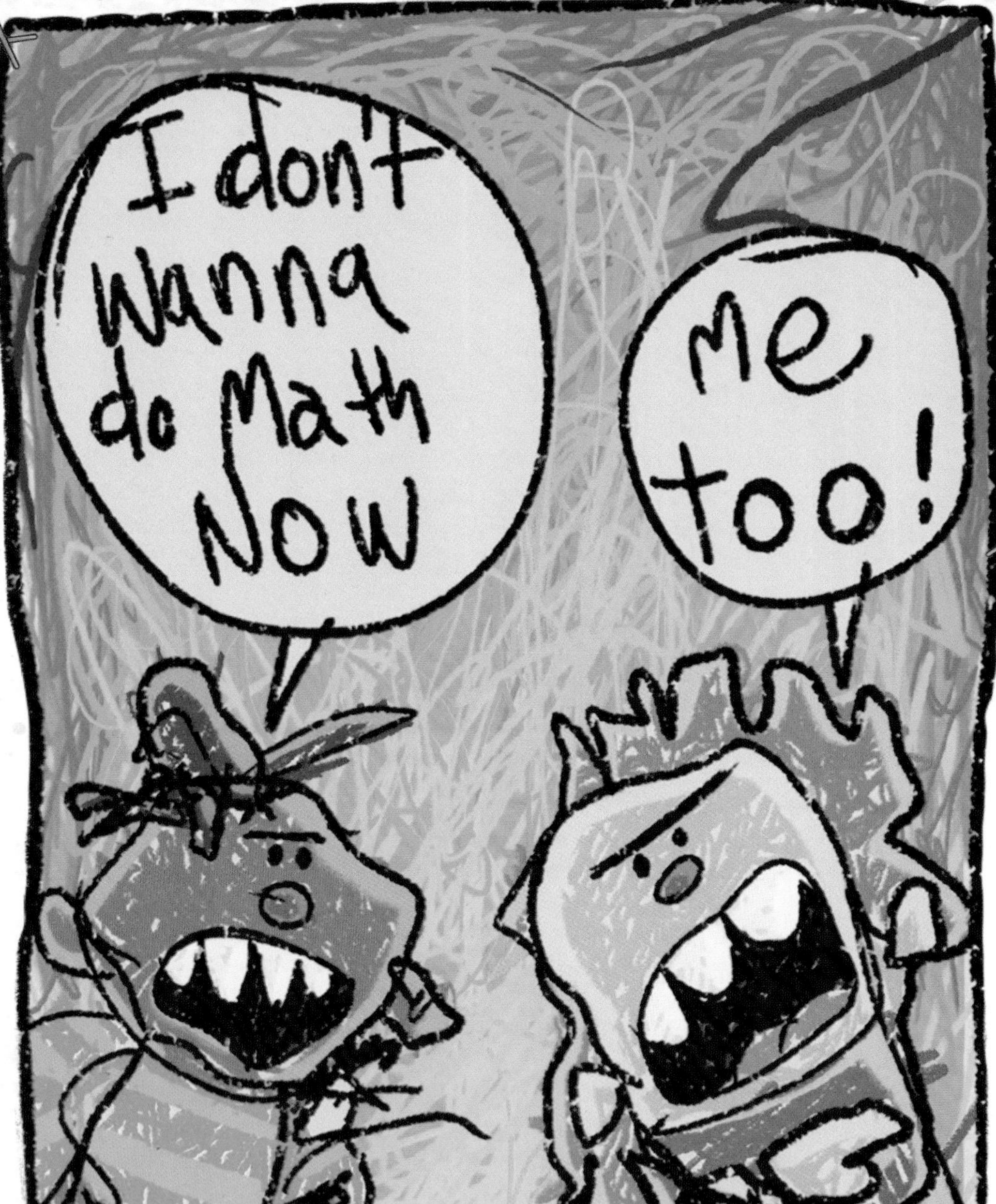
I don't wanna do Math NOW
Me too!

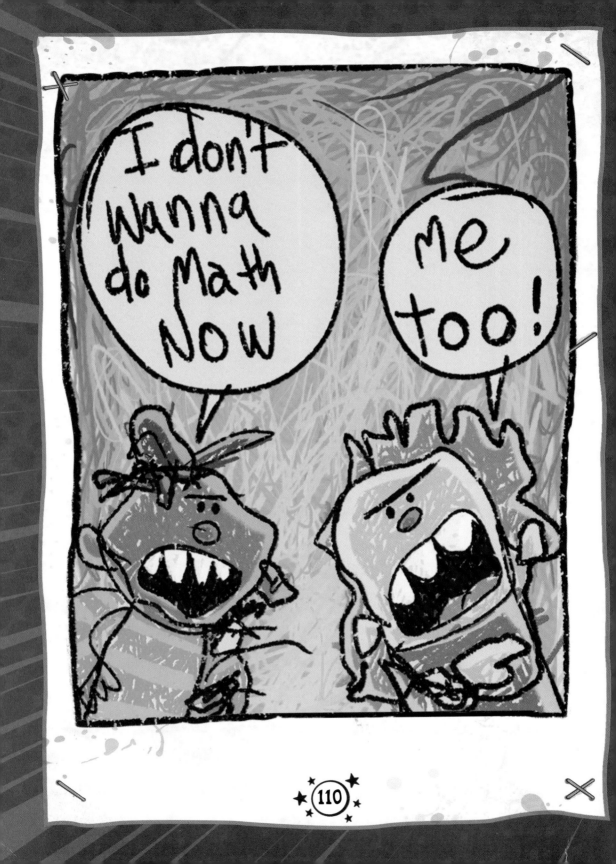

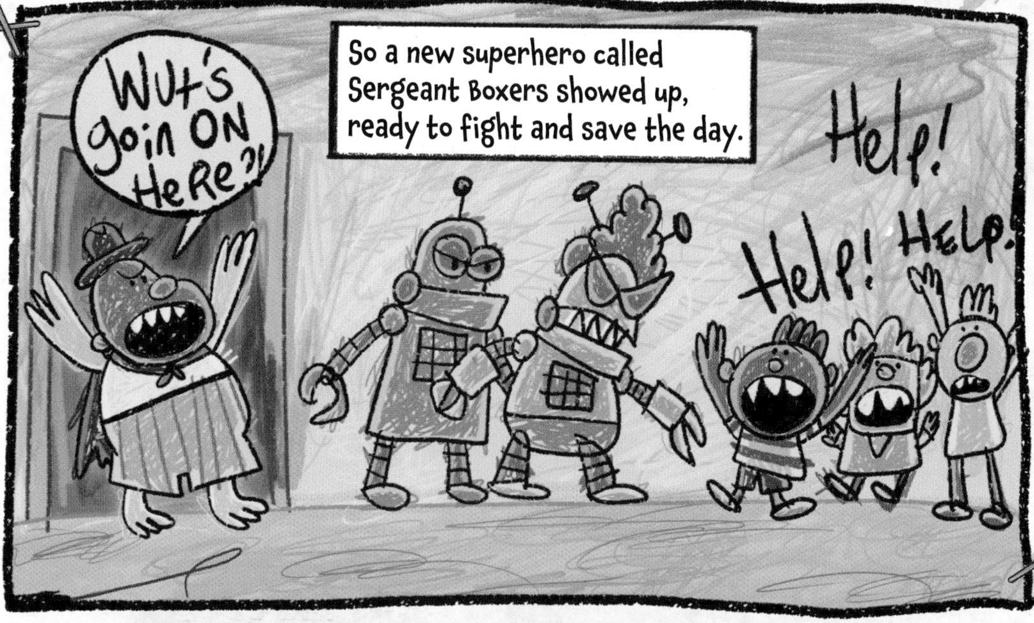
So a new superhero called Sergeant Boxers showed up, ready to fight and save the day.
Wut's goin ON HeRe?!
Help!
Help!
HELP!

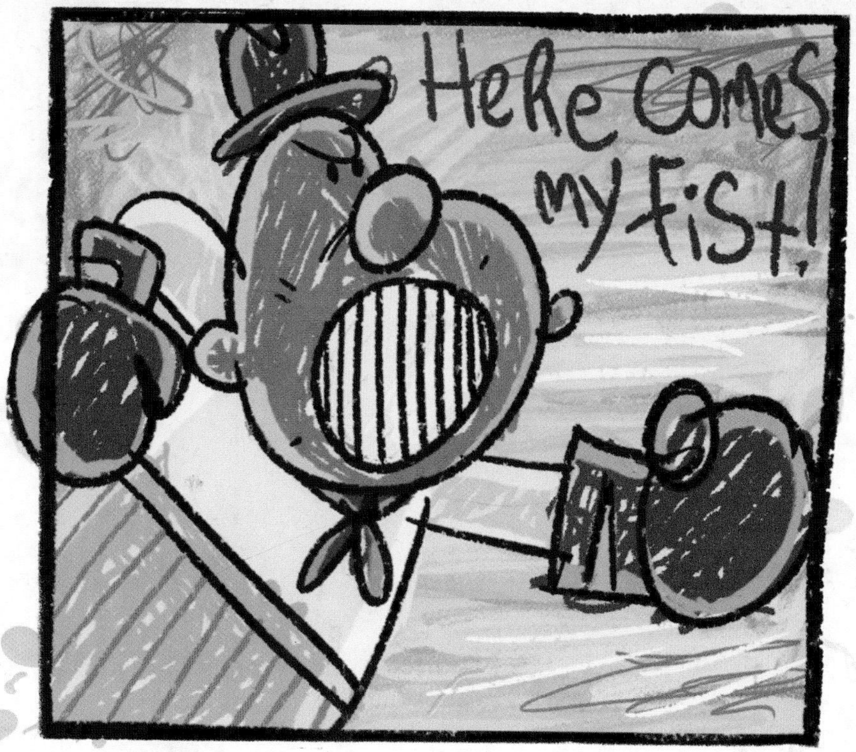
HeRe comes my fist!

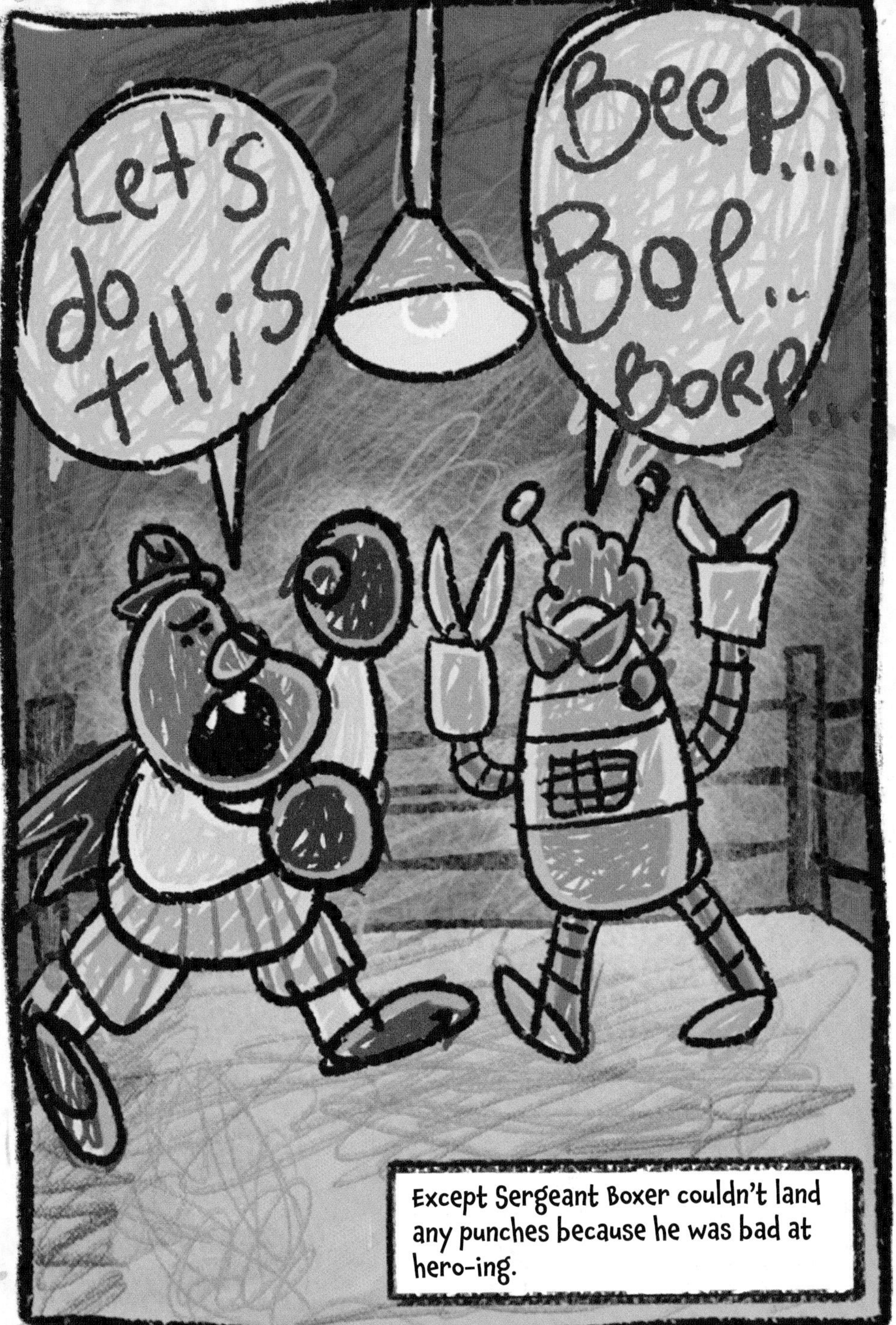
Let's do tHis
Beep... Bop... Borp...
Except Sergeant Boxer couldn't land any punches because he was bad at hero-ing.

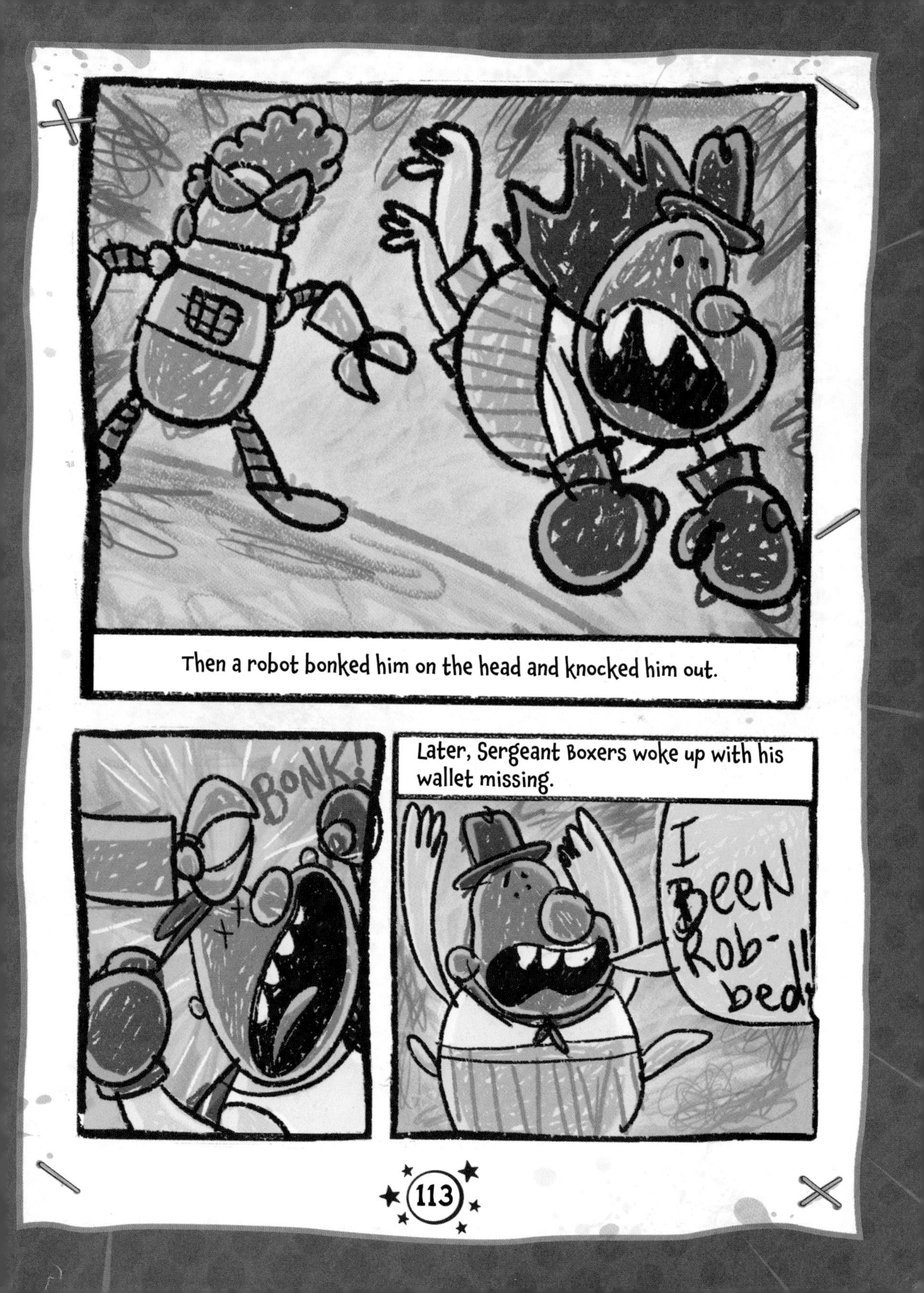
Then a robot bonked him on the head and knocked him out.
BONK!
Later, Sergeant Boxers woke up with his wallet missing.
I BEEN ROB-BED!!

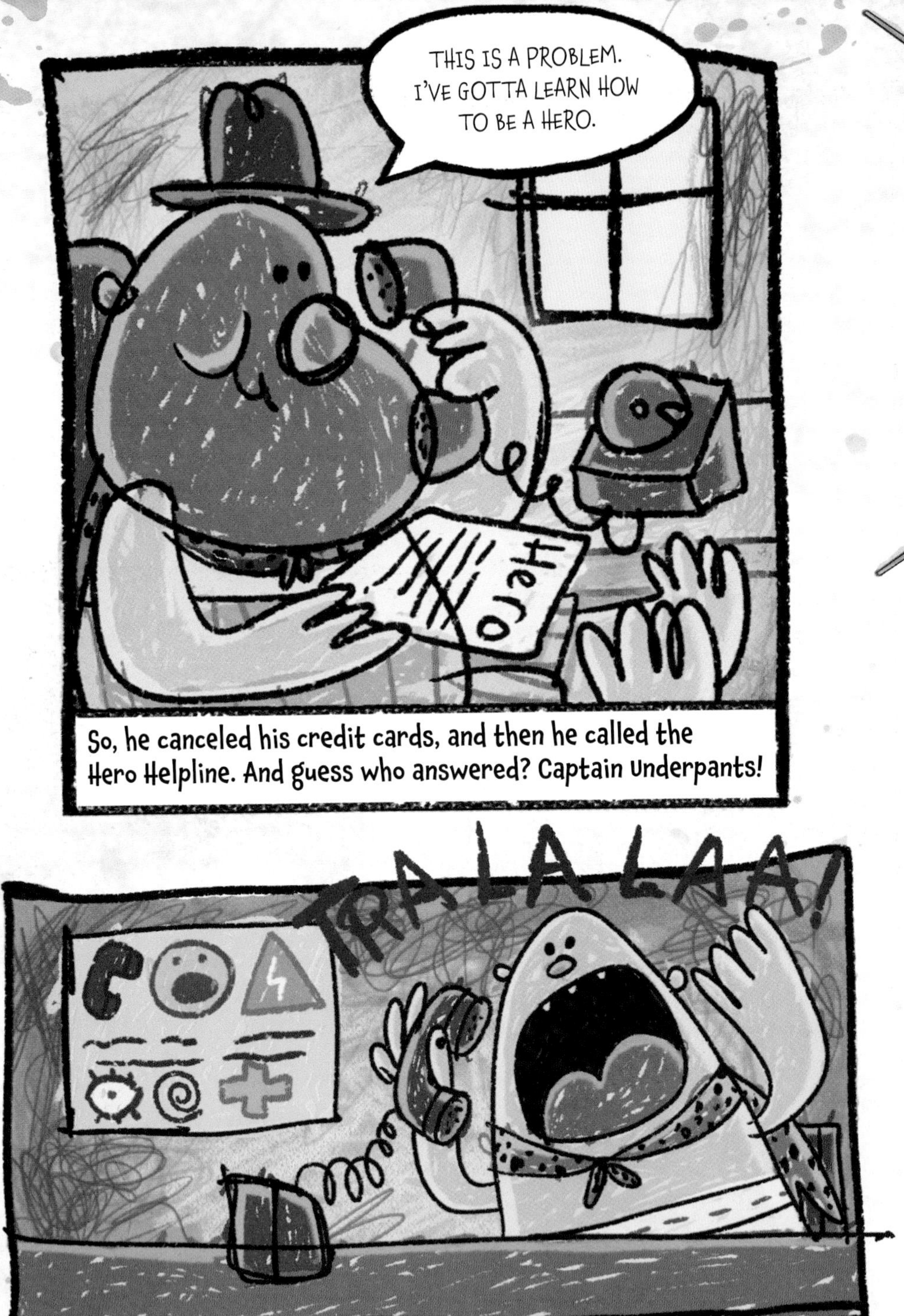
THIS IS A PROBLEM. I'VE GOTTA LEARN HOW TO BE A HERO.
Hero
So, he canceled his credit cards, and then he called the Hero Helpline. And guess who answered? Captain Underpants!
TRA LA LAA!

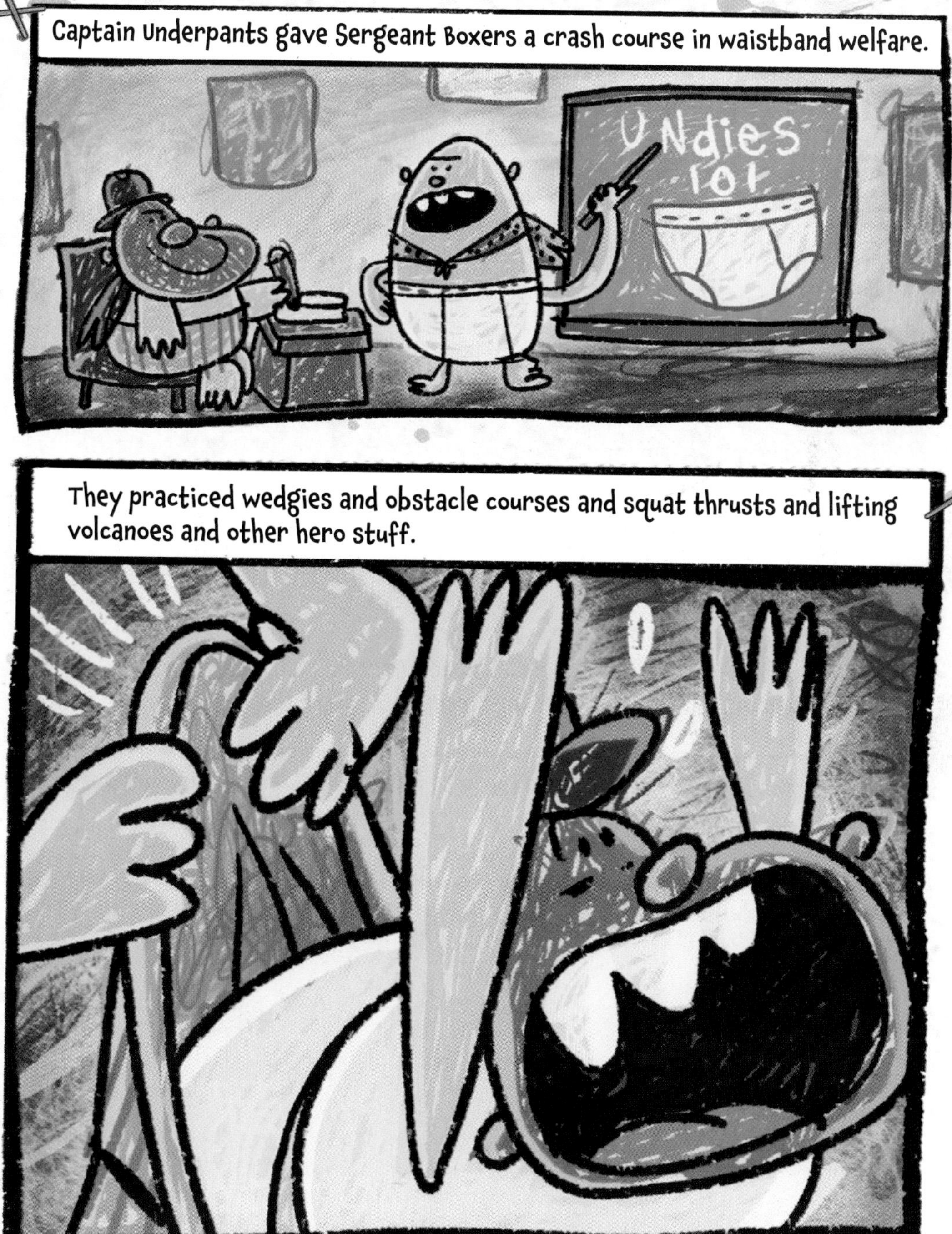
Captain Underpants gave Sergeant Boxers a crash course in waistband welfare.
Undies 101
They practiced wedgies and obstacle courses and squat thrusts and lifting volcanoes and other hero stuff.

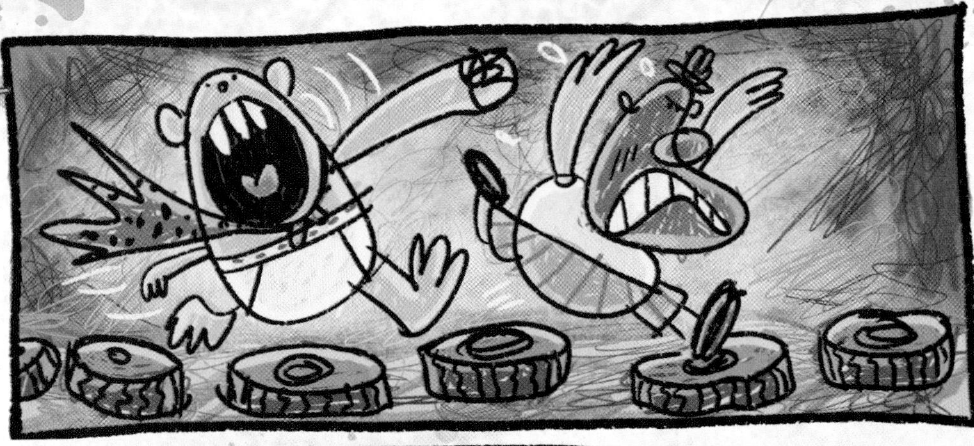

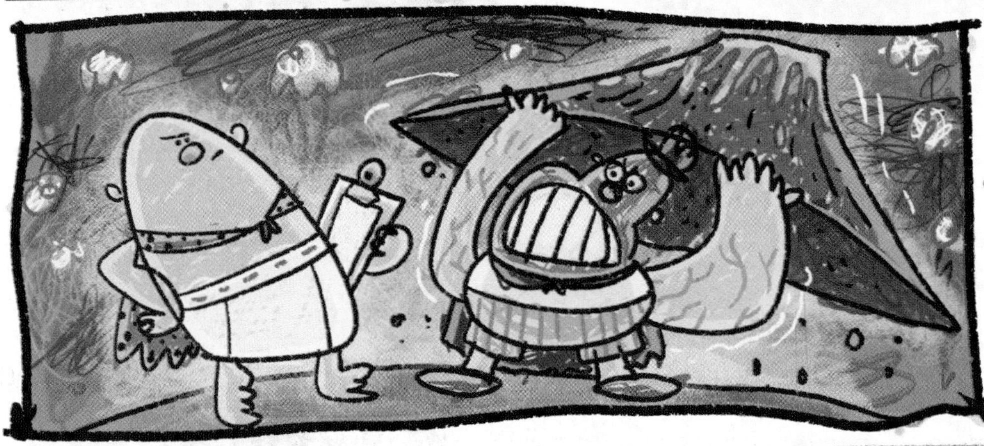

But Sergeant Boxers still didn't get how to be a hero. So, they did wind sprints and worked the heavy bag and peeled potatoes and cleaned toilets with a toothbrush and did shark sparring until, finally, Sergeant Boxers got it!

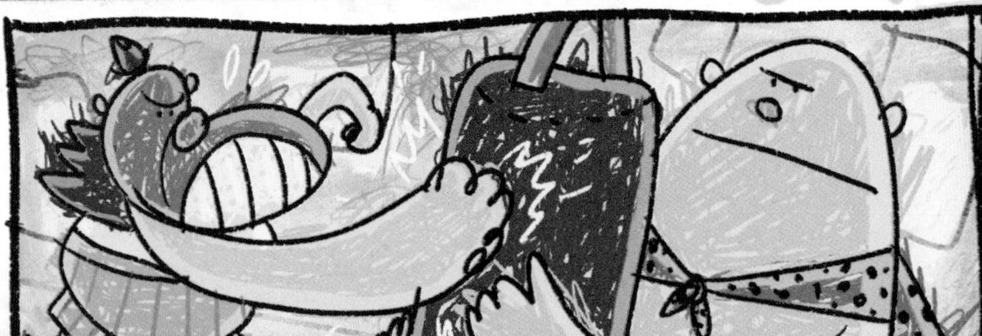

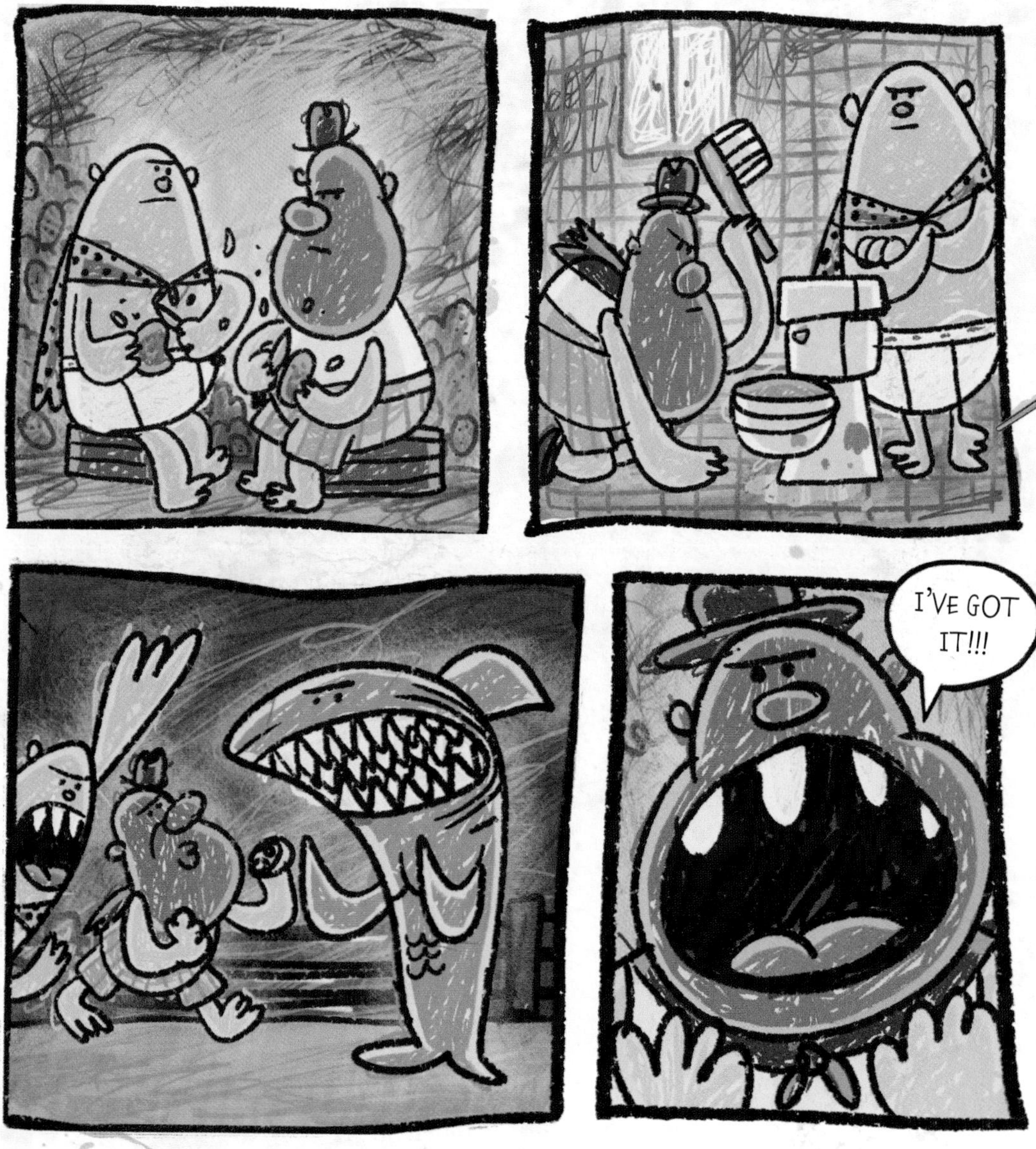
I'VE GOT IT!!!

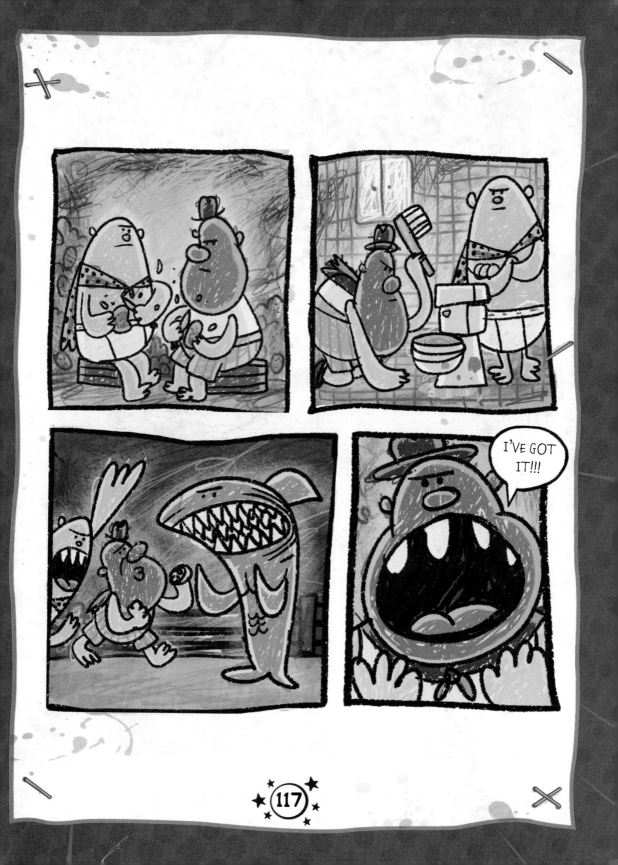

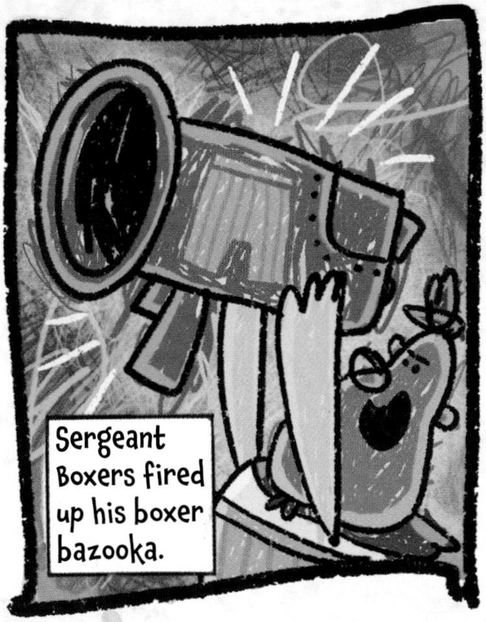
Sergeant Boxers fired up his boxer bazooka.

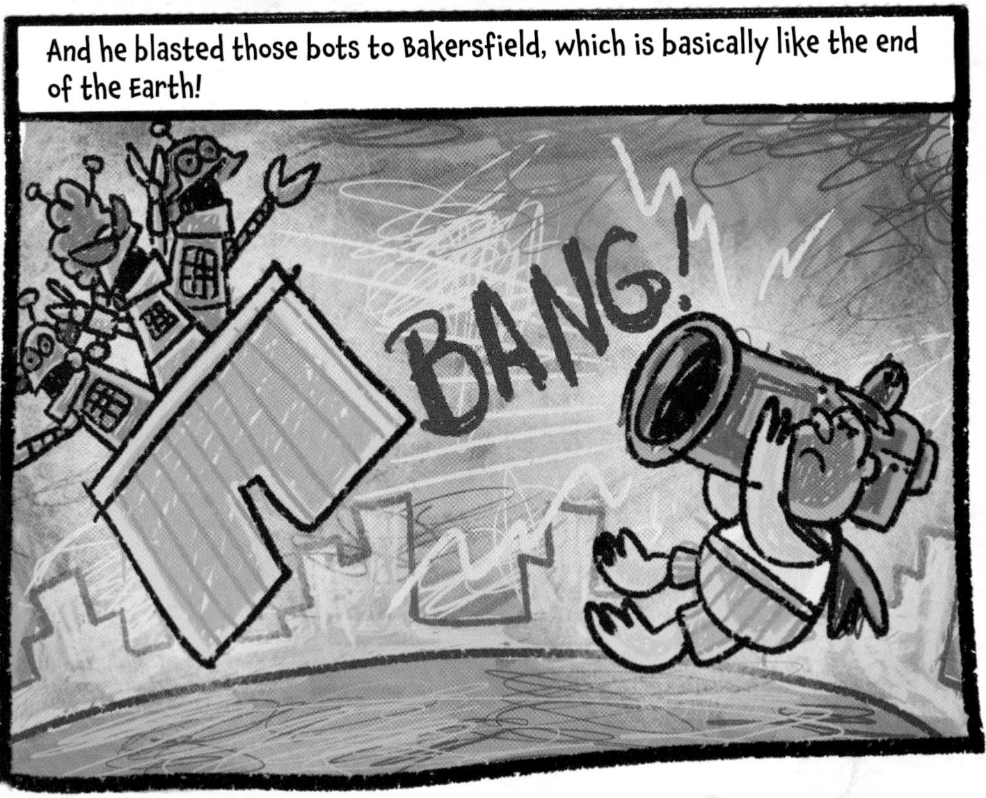
And he blasted those bots to Bakersfield, which is basically like the end of the Earth!
BANG!

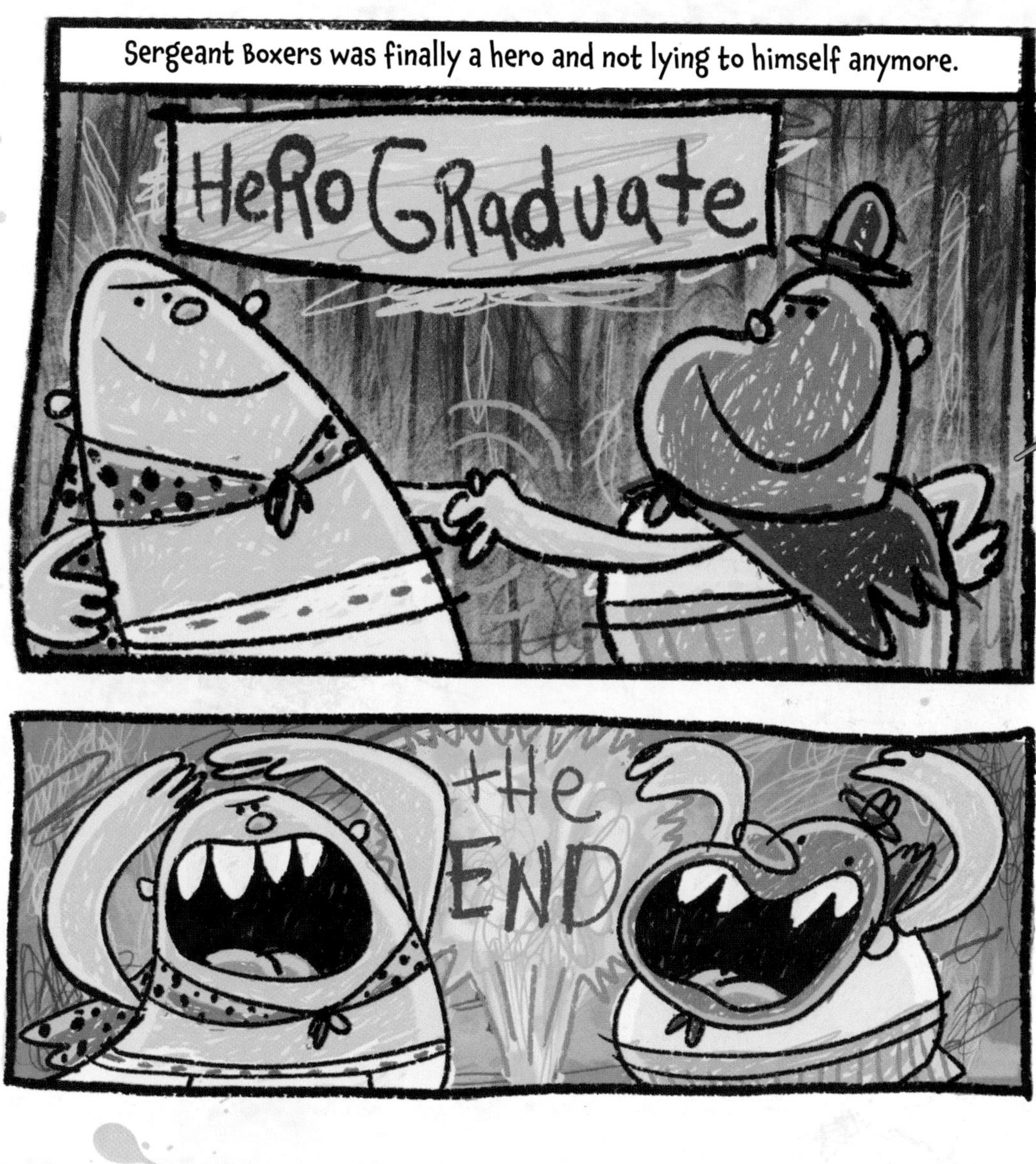

Sergeant Boxers was finally a hero and not lying to himself anymore.
HeRo GRaduate
tHe END

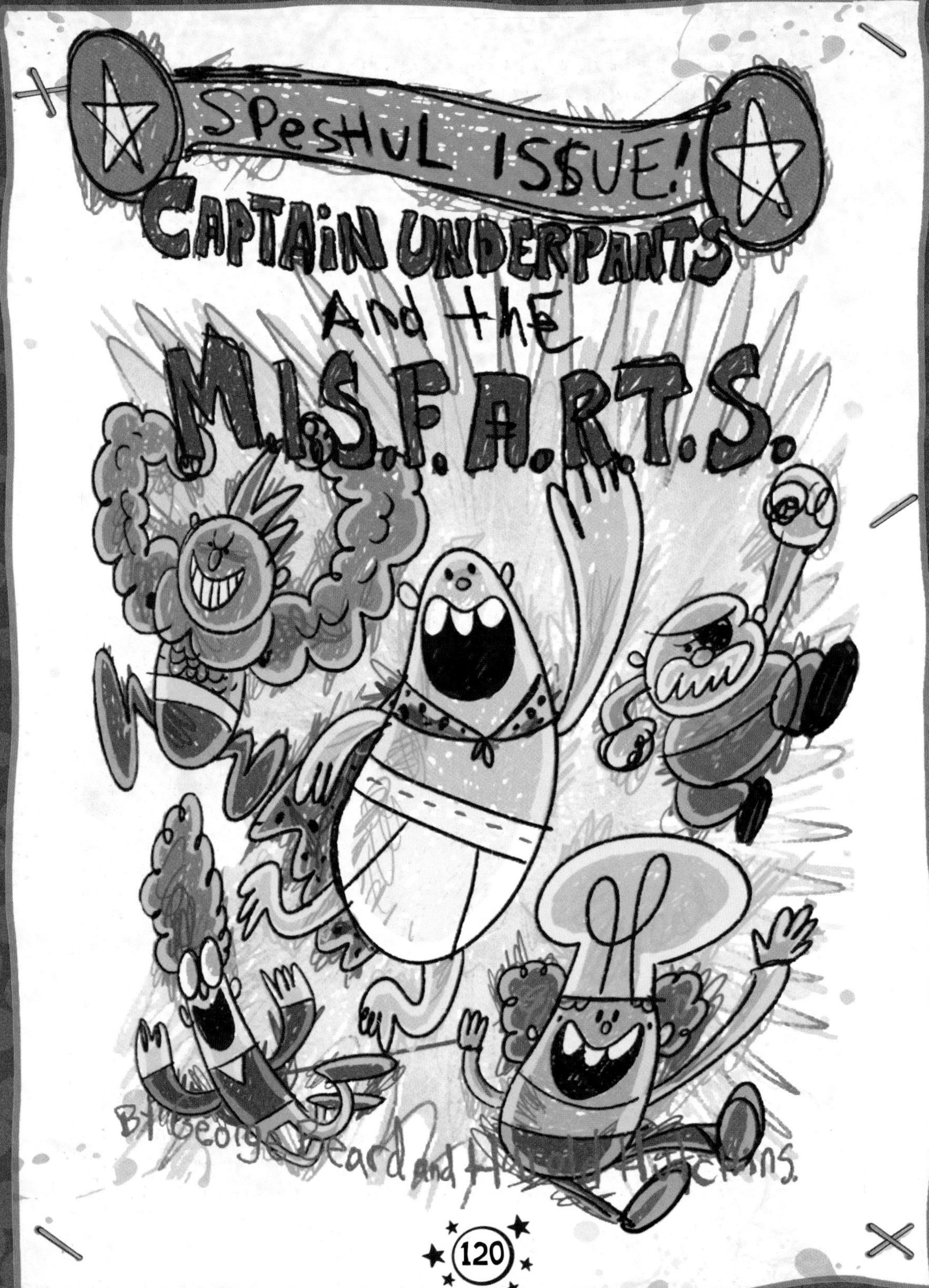
SPESHUL ISSUE!
CAPTAIN UNDERPANTS
and the
M.I.S.F.A.R.T.S.
By George Beard and Hutchins.

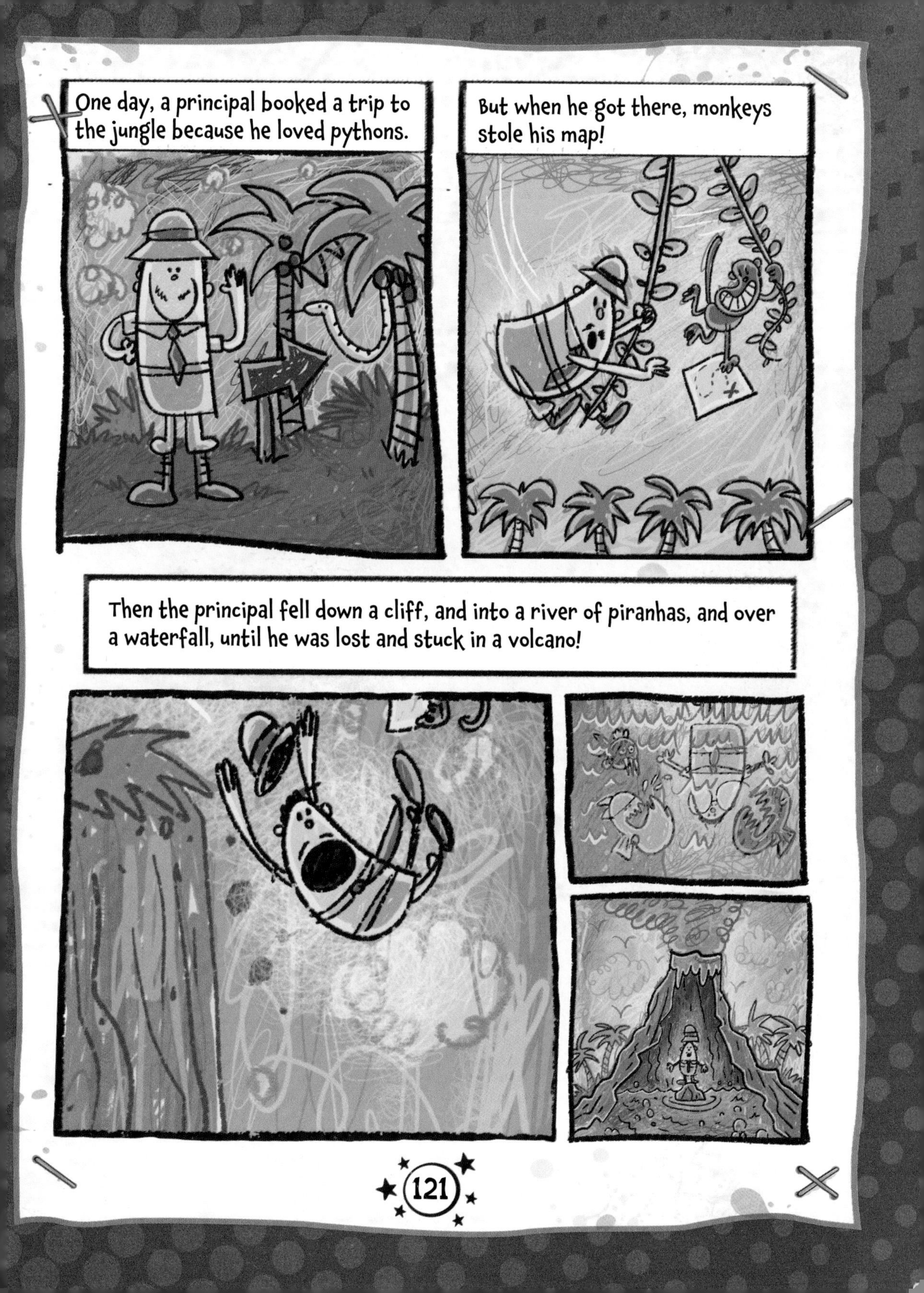
One day, a principal booked a trip to the jungle because he loved pythons.
But when he got there, monkeys stole his map!
Then the principal fell down a cliff, and into a river of piranhas, and over a waterfall, until he was lost and stuck in a volcano!

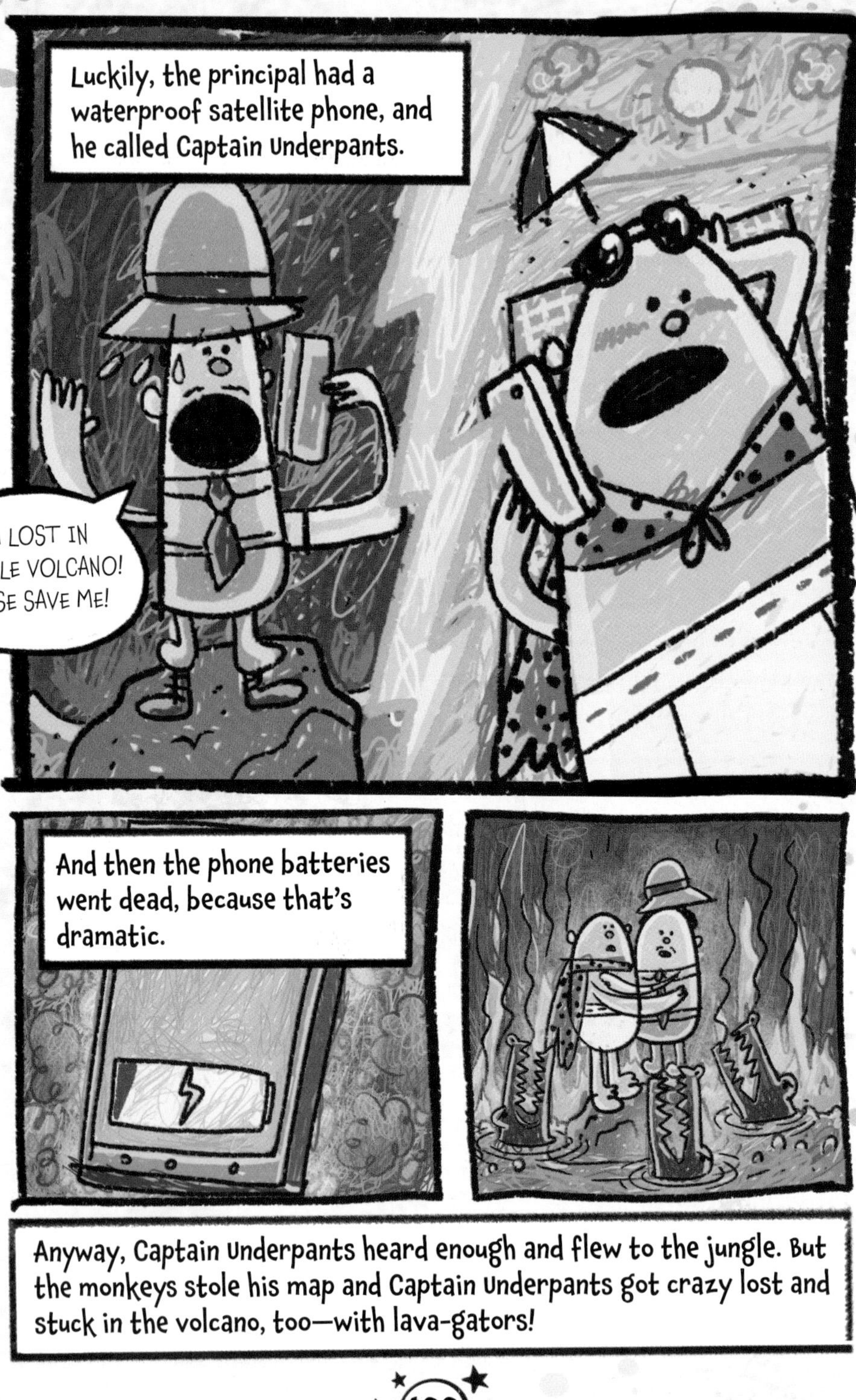
Luckily, the principal had a waterproof satellite phone, and he called Captain Underpants.
I'M LOST IN A JUNGLE VOLCANO! PLEASE SAVE ME!
And then the phone batteries went dead, because that's dramatic.
Anyway, Captain Underpants heard enough and flew to the jungle. But the monkeys stole his map and Captain Underpants got crazy lost and stuck in the volcano, too—with lava-gators!

Captain Underpants activated his emergency beacon, and the signal reached the M.I.S.F.A.R.T.S., a.k.a. the Mega! Incredible! Search! Force! Action! Rescue! Team! Squad!

M.I.S.F.A.R.T.S.

There was Thinks, the smart one. And Thumps, the strong one. And Winks, the grizzled vet. And Codes, the gizmo one. And there were some other ones, too, but they were in the bathroom.

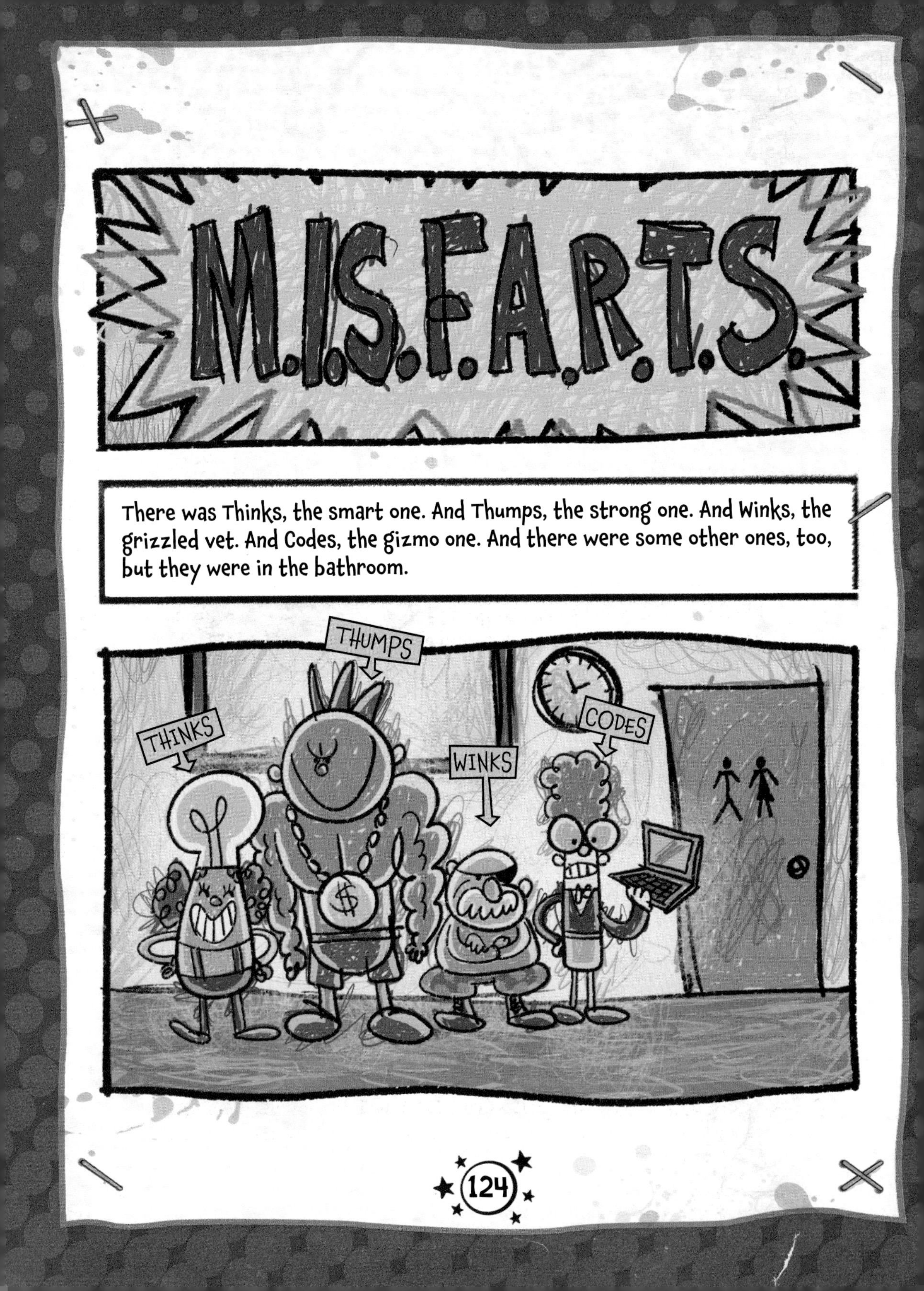
THUMPS
THINKS
WINKS
CODES

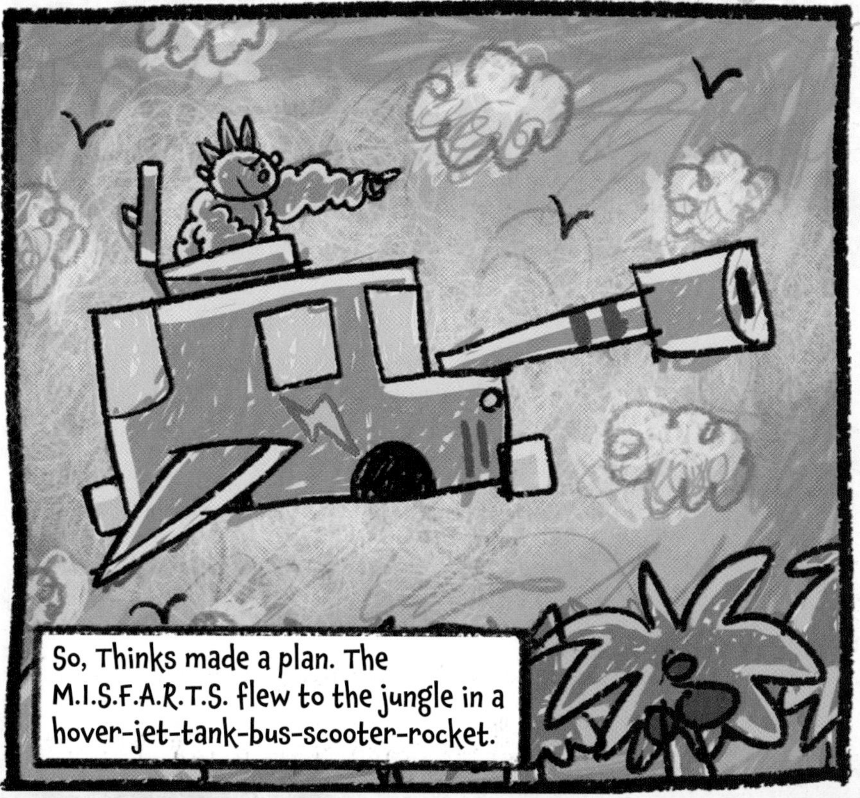
So, Thinks made a plan. The M.I.S.F.A.R.T.S. flew to the jungle in a hover-jet-tank-bus-scooter-rocket.

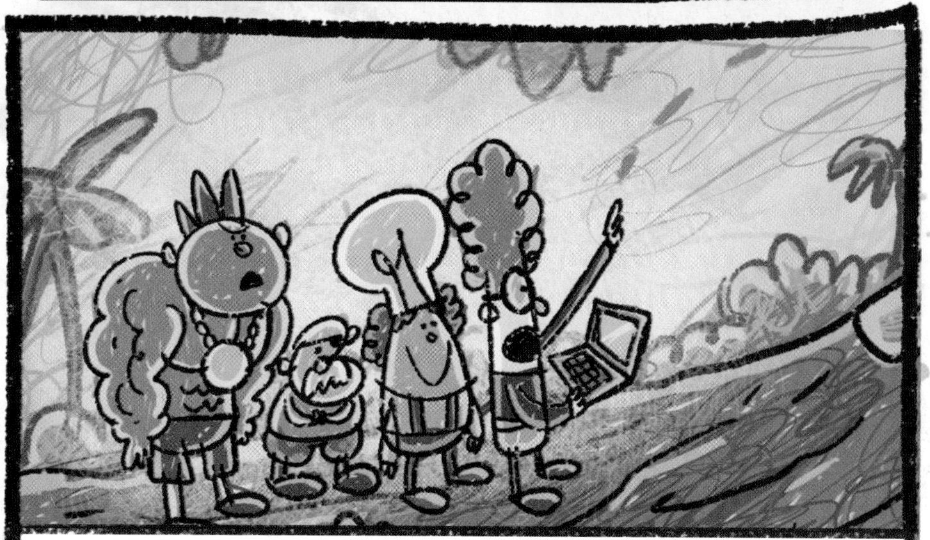
And Codes located the lost guys with a laser lost-guy-finder he built.

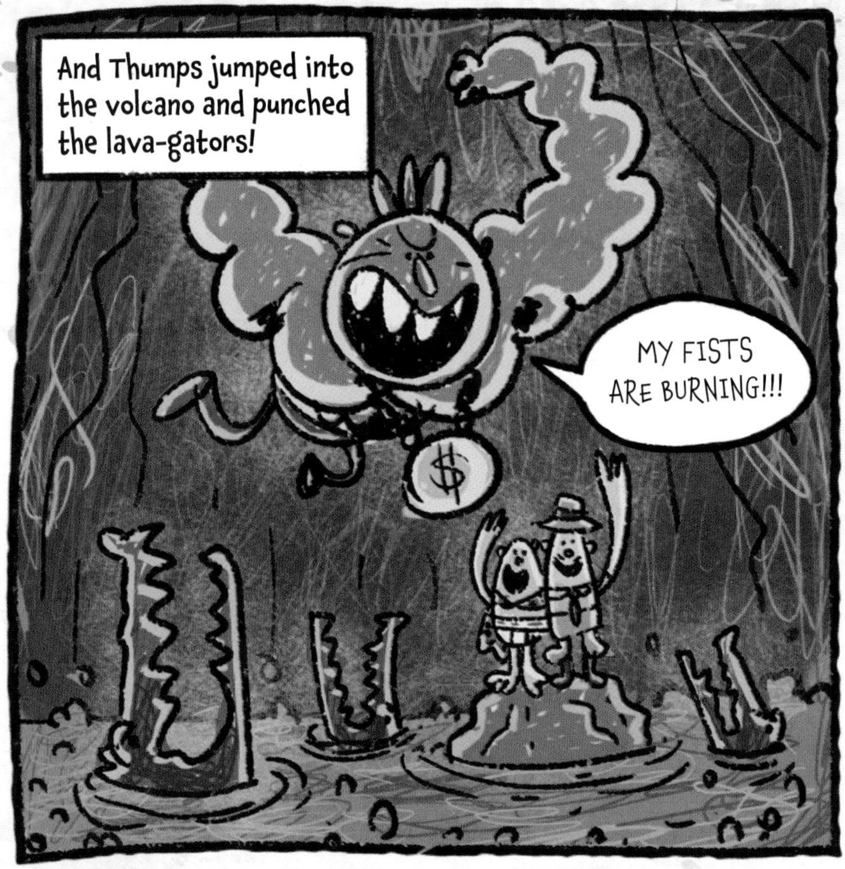
And Thumps jumped into the volcano and punched the lava-gators!
MY FISTS ARE BURNING!!!

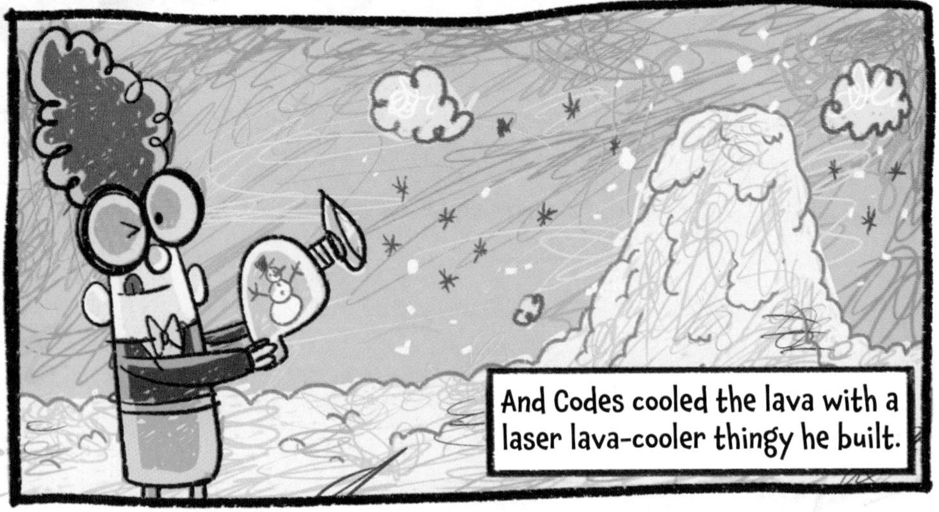
And Codes cooled the lava with a laser lava-cooler thingy he built.

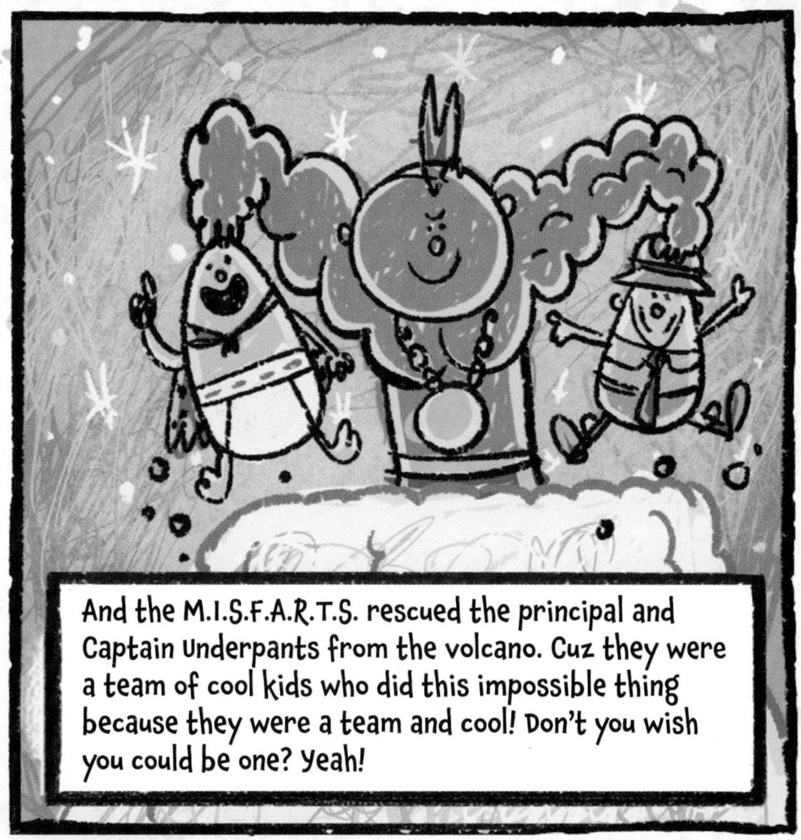
And the M.I.S.F.A.R.T.S. rescued the principal and Captain Underpants from the volcano. Cuz they were a team of cool kids who did this impossible thing because they were a team and cool! Don't you wish you could be one? Yeah!

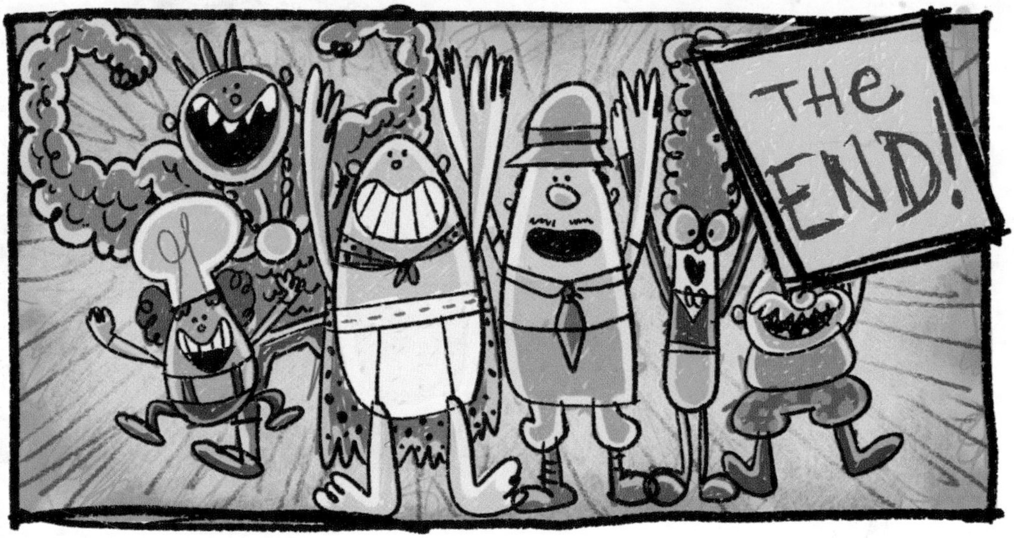
THE END!

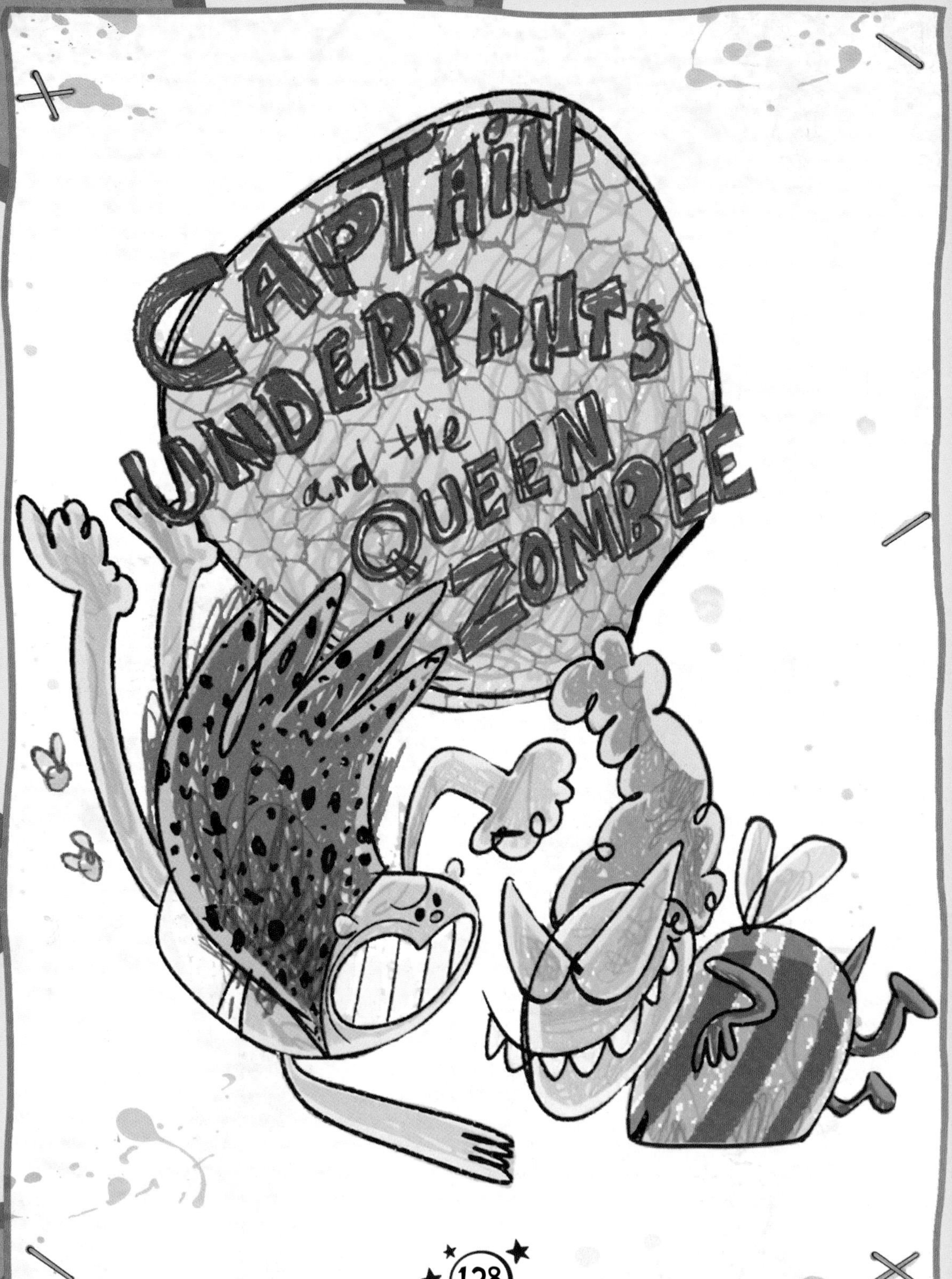
CAPTAIN UNDERPANTS and the QUEEN ZOMBEE

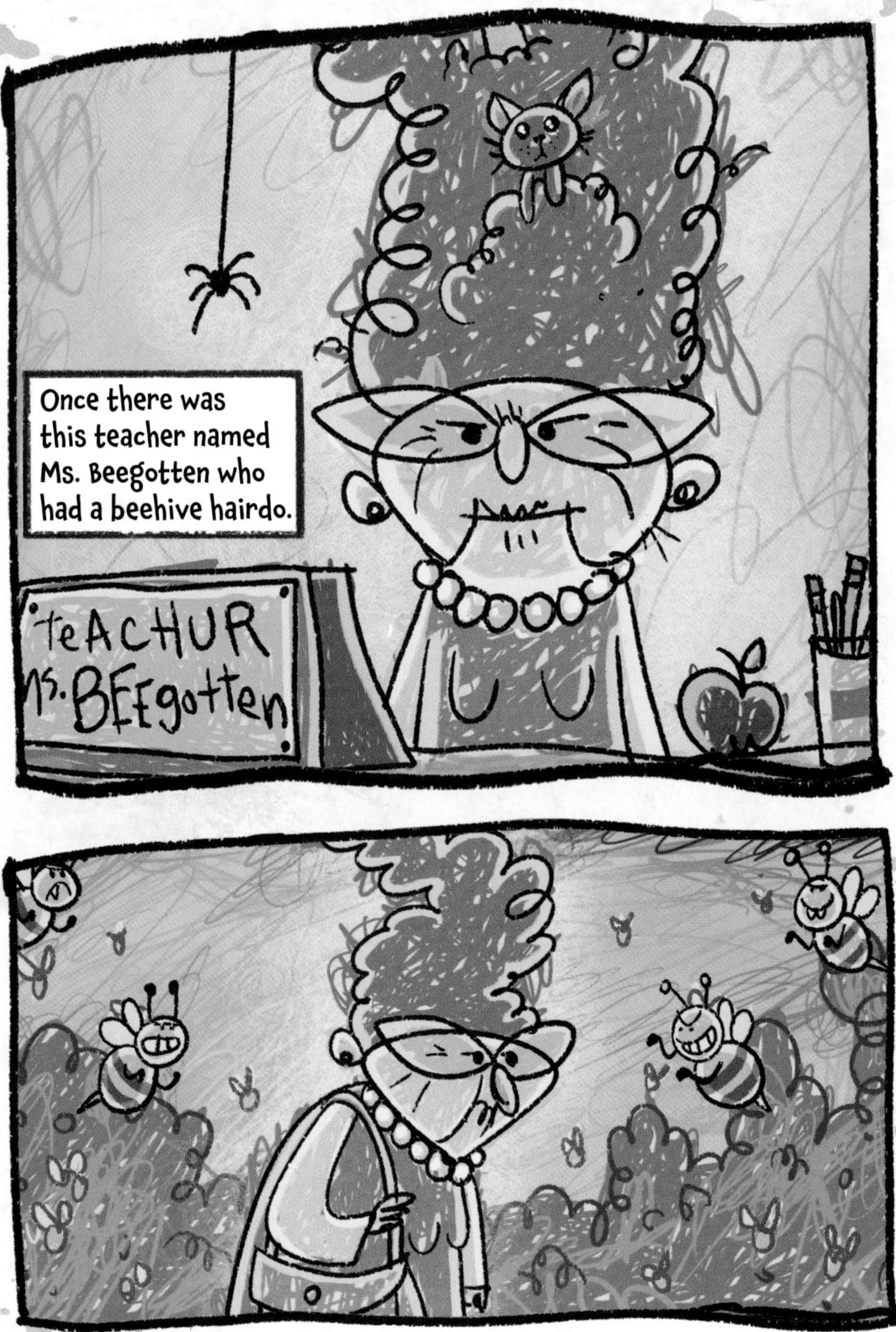
Once there was this teacher named Ms. Beegotten who had a beehive hairdo.
TeACHUR Ms. BEEgotten

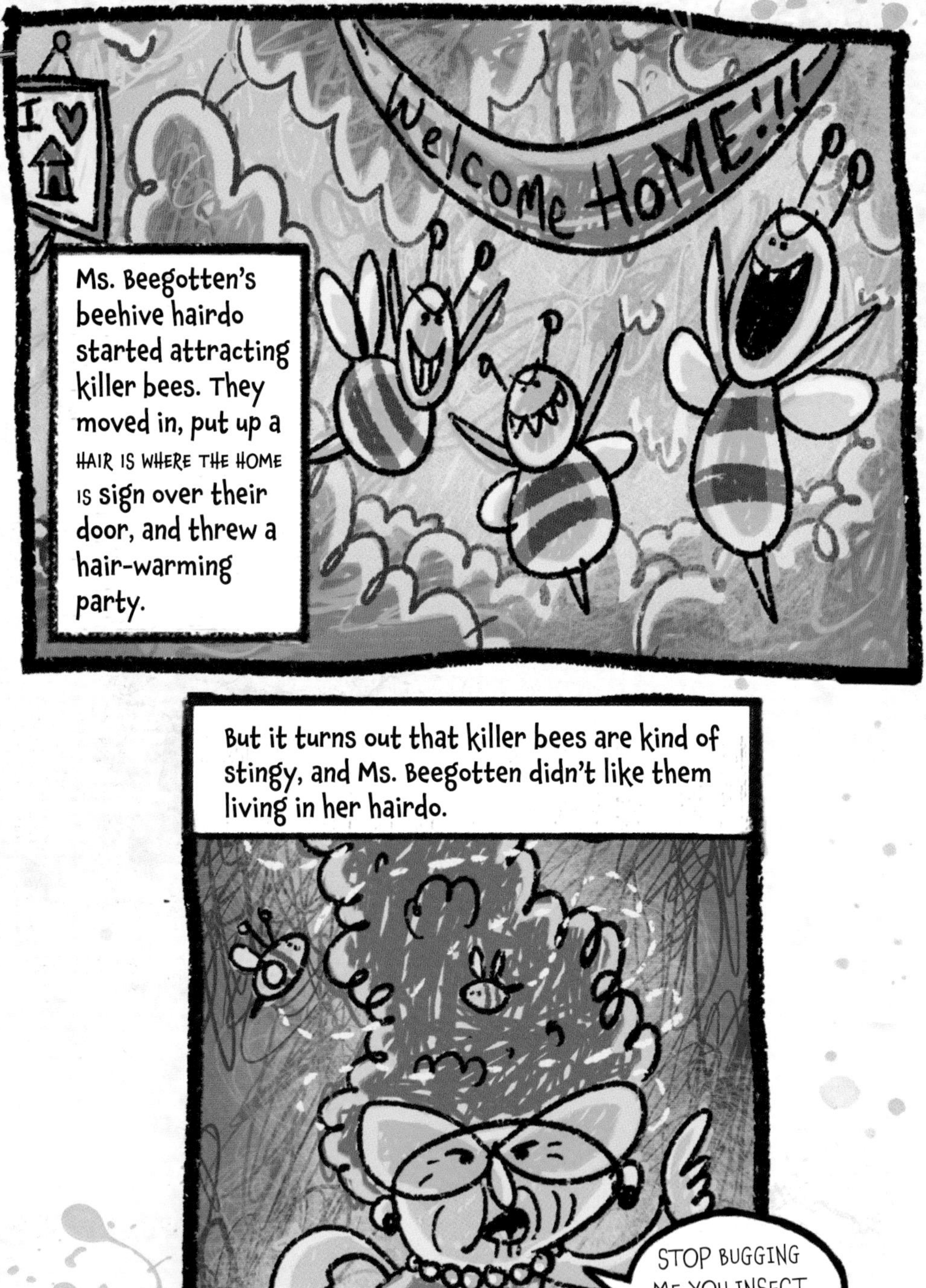
Welcome HOME!!!
Ms. Beegotten's beehive hairdo started attracting killer bees. They moved in, put up a HAIR IS WHERE THE HOME IS sign over their door, and threw a hair-warming party.
But it turns out that killer bees are kind of stingy, and Ms. Beegotten didn't like them living in her hairdo.
STOP BUGGING ME YOU INSECT BUZZKILLS!

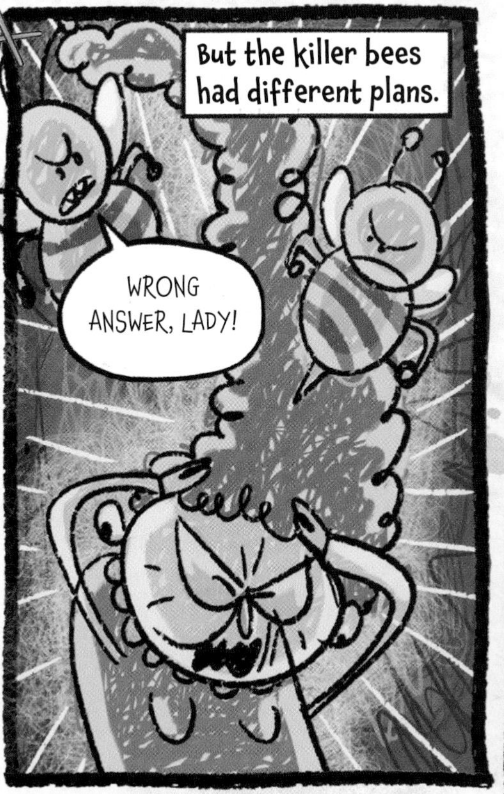
But the killer bees had different plans.
WRONG ANSWER, LADY!

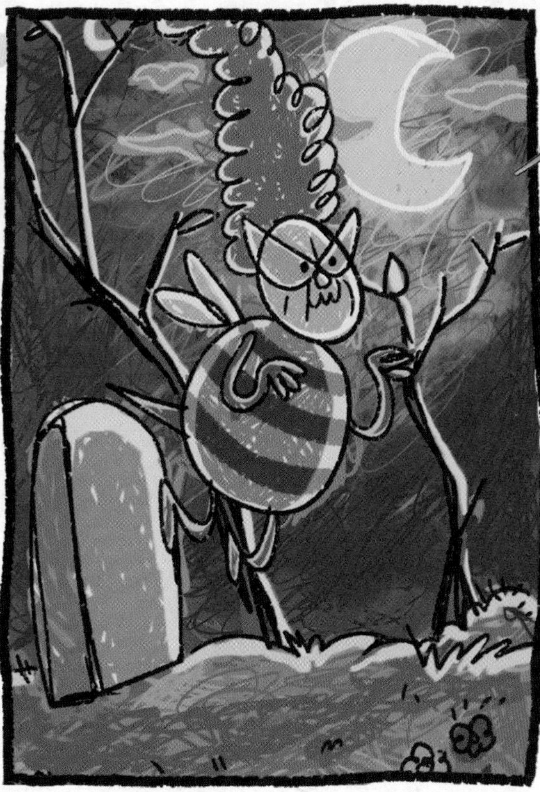

And they stung her like crazy to send her a message. Ms. Beegotten got stung so much she turned into the Queen Zombee!

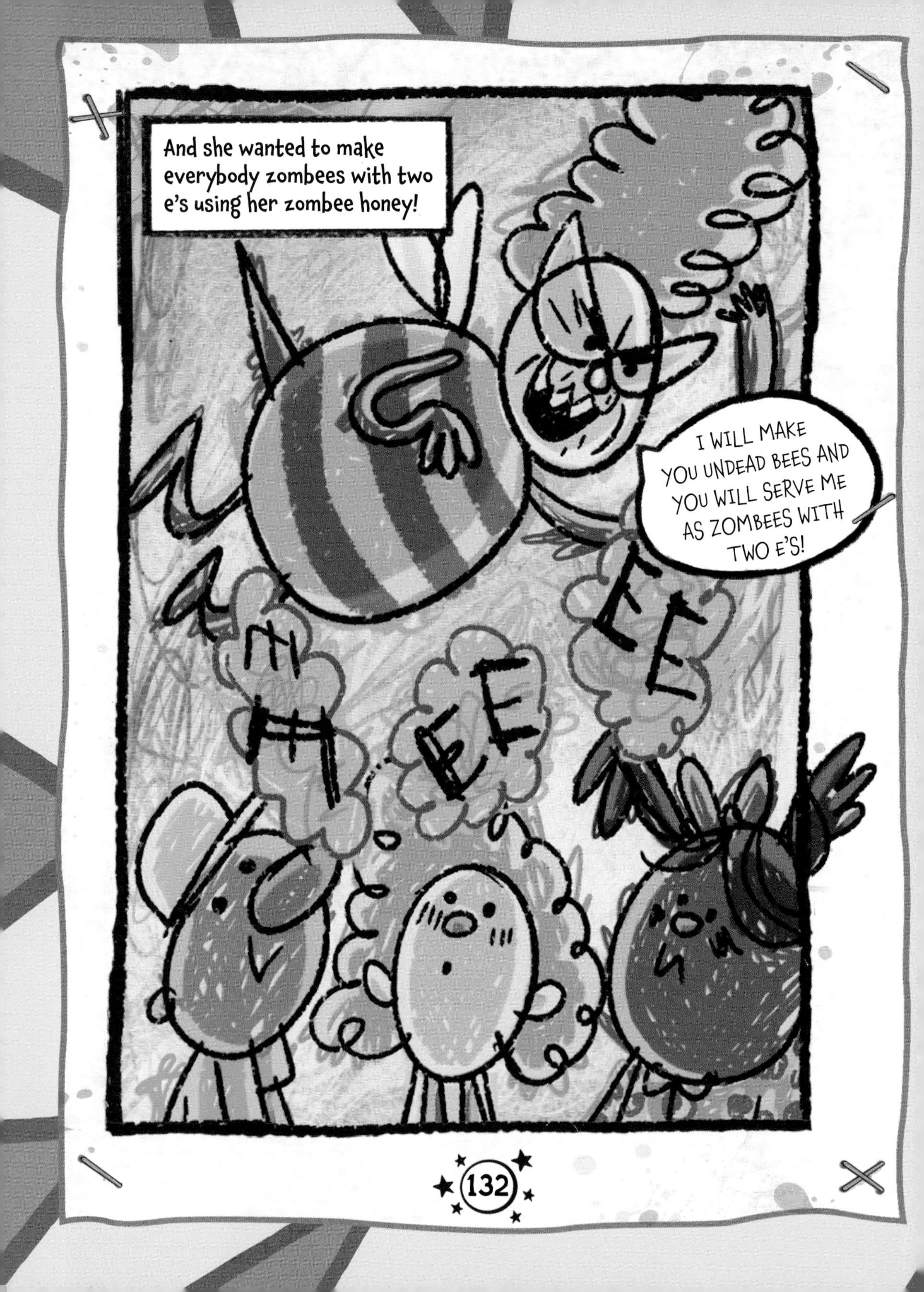
And she wanted to make everybody zombees with two e's using her zombee honey!
I WILL MAKE YOU UNDEAD BEES AND YOU WILL SERVE ME AS ZOMBEES WITH TWO E'S!
EEE
EE
EE

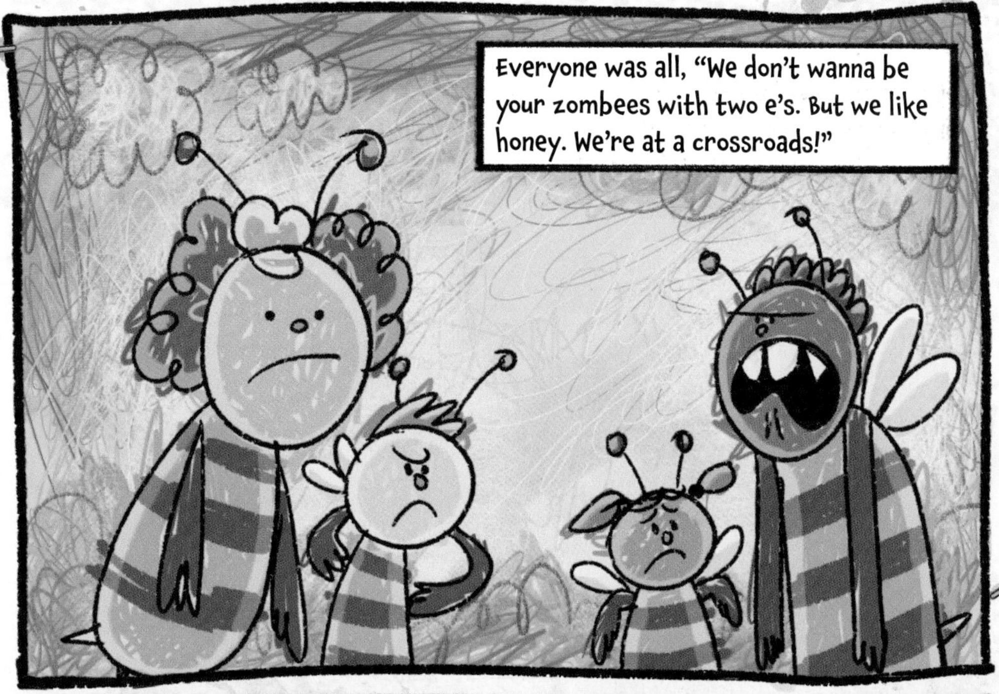
Everyone was all, "We don't wanna be your zombees with two e's. But we like honey. We're at a crossroads!"

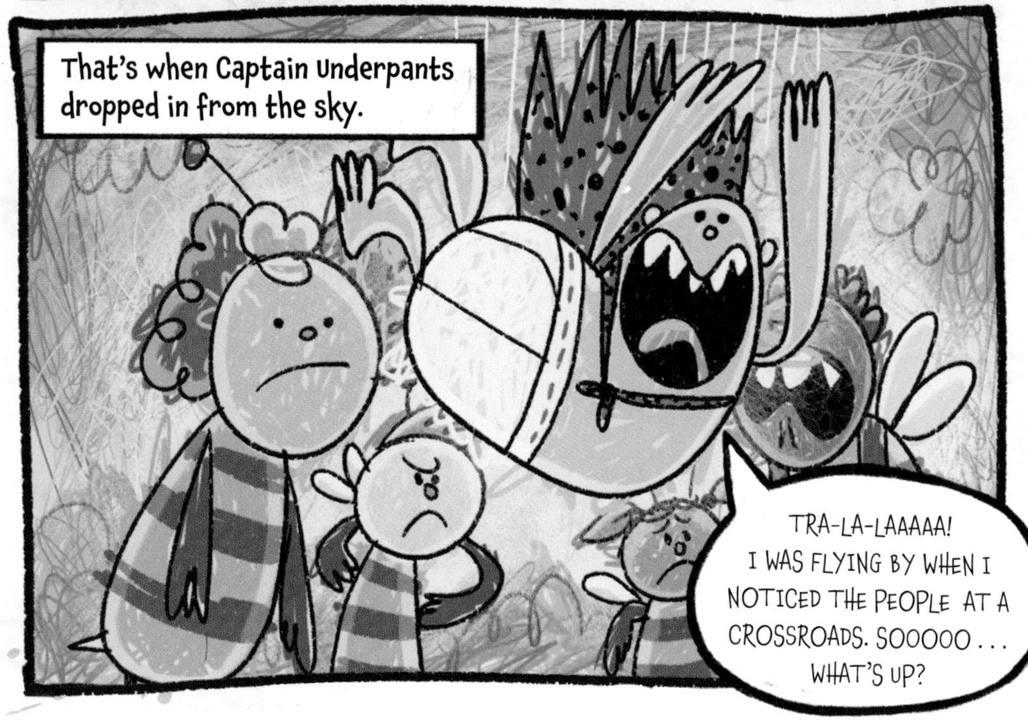
That's when Captain Underpants dropped in from the sky.
TRA-LA-LAAAAA! I WAS FLYING BY WHEN I NOTICED THE PEOPLE AT A CROSSROADS. SOOOOO . . . WHAT'S UP?

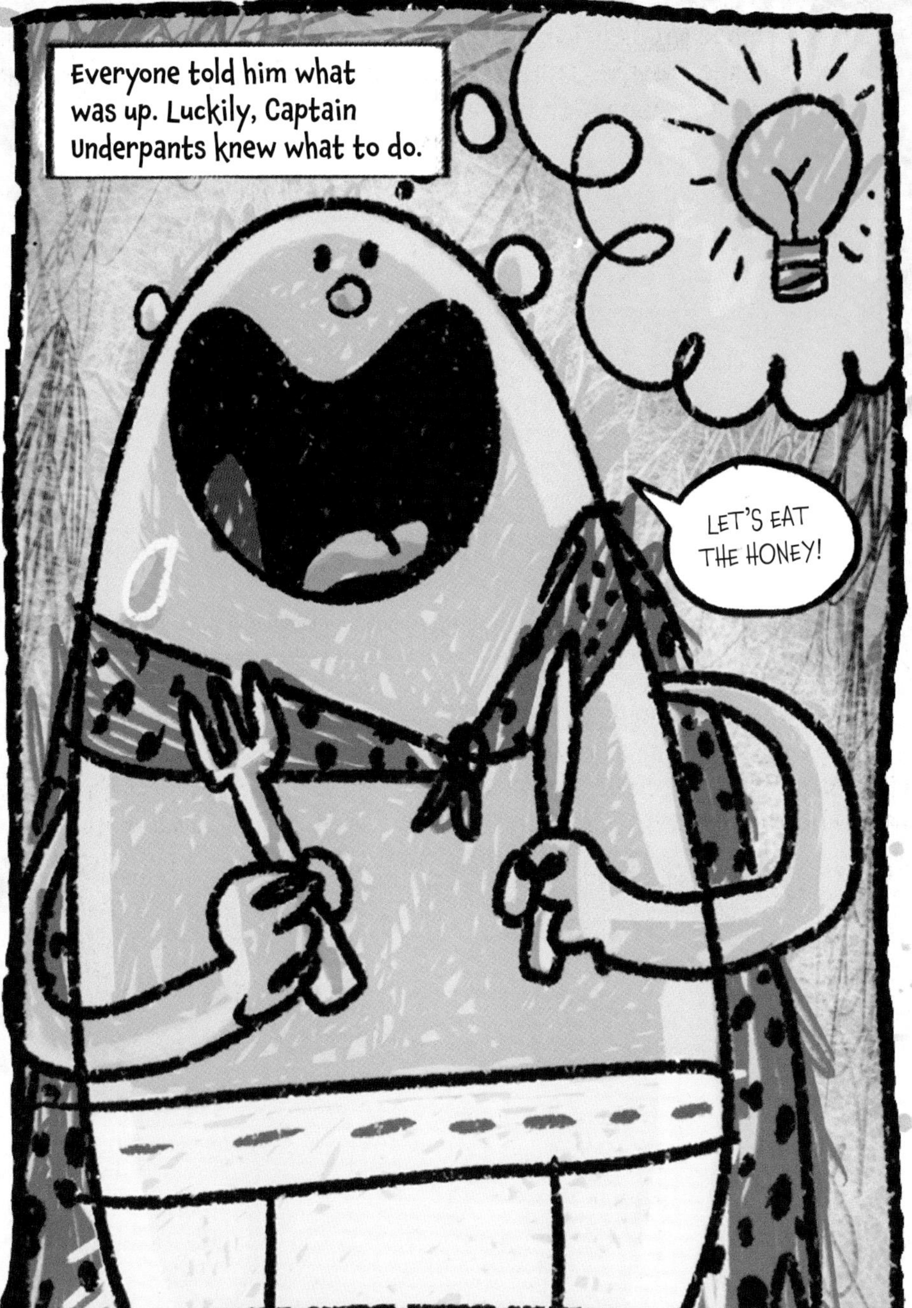
Everyone told him what was up. Luckily, Captain Underpants knew what to do.
LET'S EAT THE HONEY!

And Queen Zombee laughed. But more like "Bzzbzzz!" because she only spoke in bee talk and she thought Captain Underpants was falling into her bee trap and turning into a zombee with two e's.

But Captain Underpants super-loved honey, so he ate it all and got crazy-fat dinosaur big. And he didn't become a zombee with two e's because he has a super stomach.

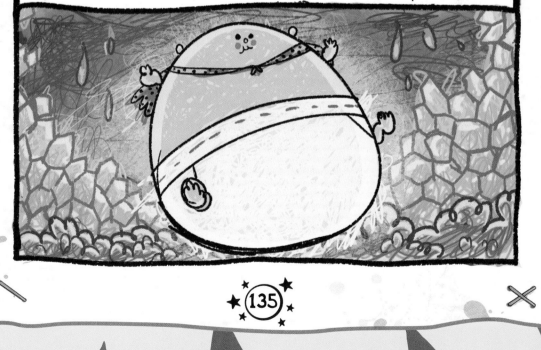

Captain Underpants tried to fly away. But he was over his maximum launch weight.

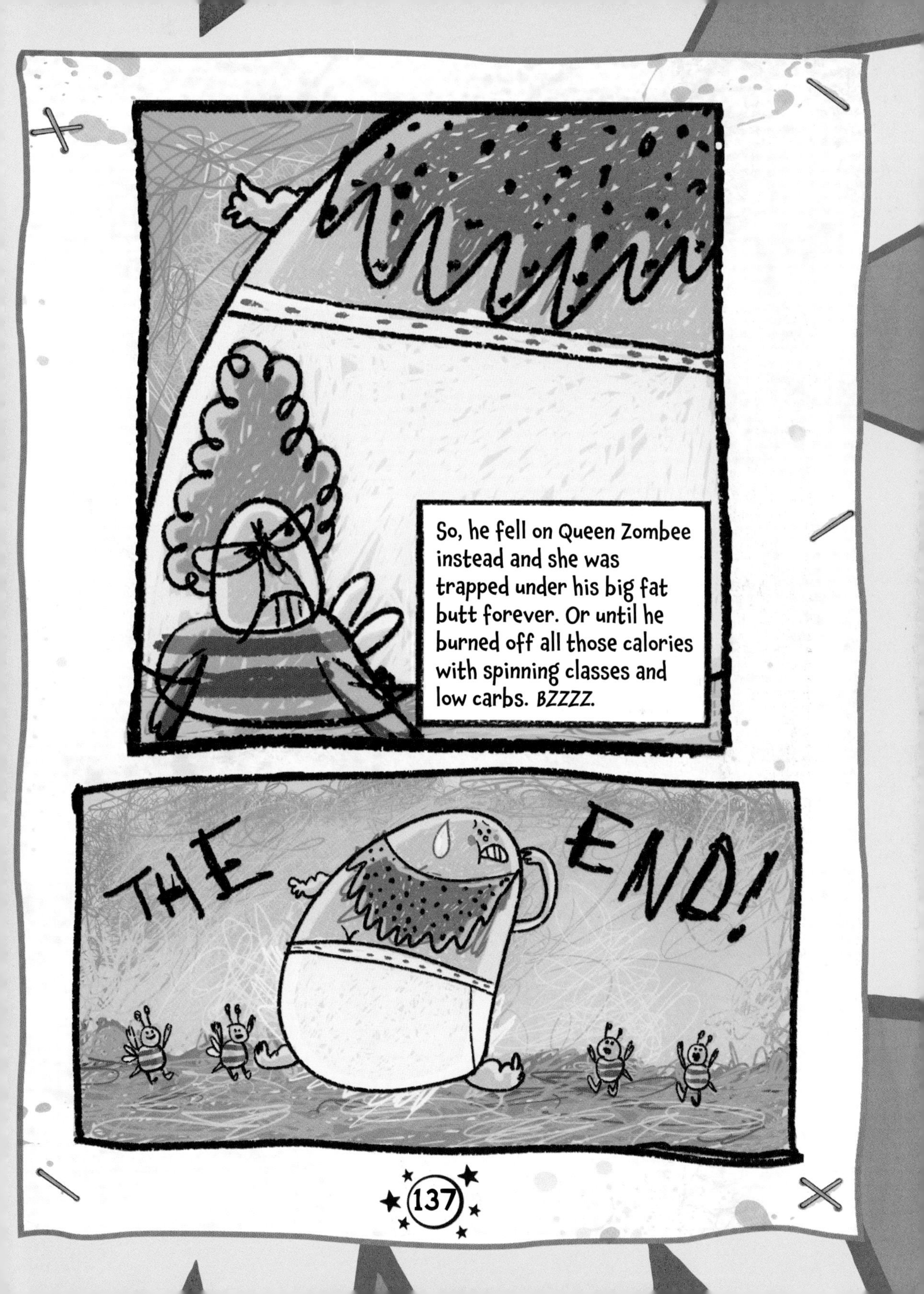
So, he fell on Queen Zombee instead and she was trapped under his big fat butt forever. Or until he burned off all those calories with spinning classes and low carbs. BZZZZ.
THE END!

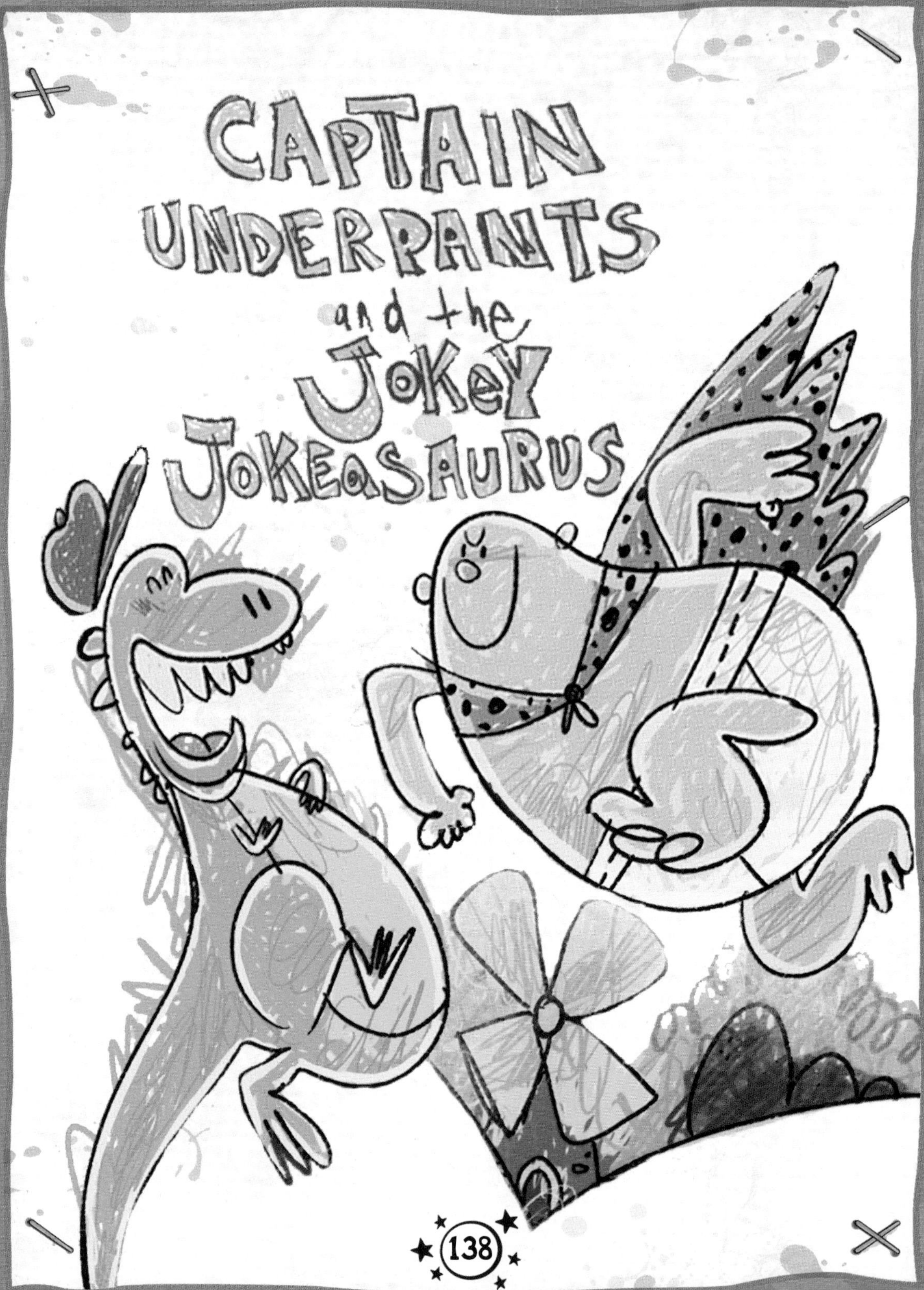
CAPTAIN
UNDERPANTS
and the
JOKEY
JOKEASAURUS

This scientist guy wanted to write a dinosaur book. So, he went to the time-machine store, rented a time machine, and zapped back to dinosaur times!

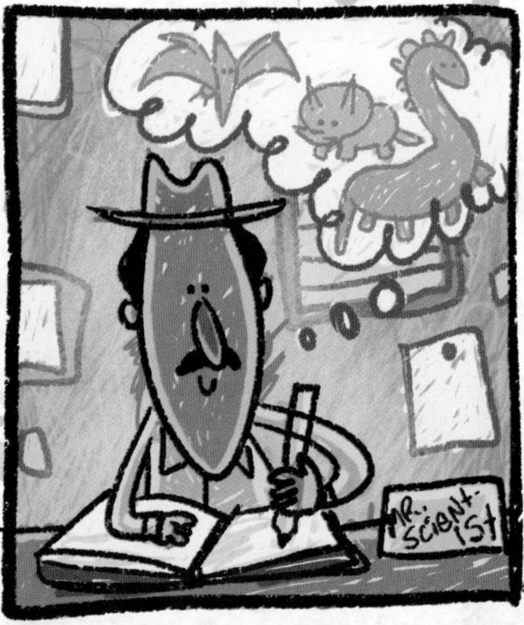
MR. SCIENT-IST

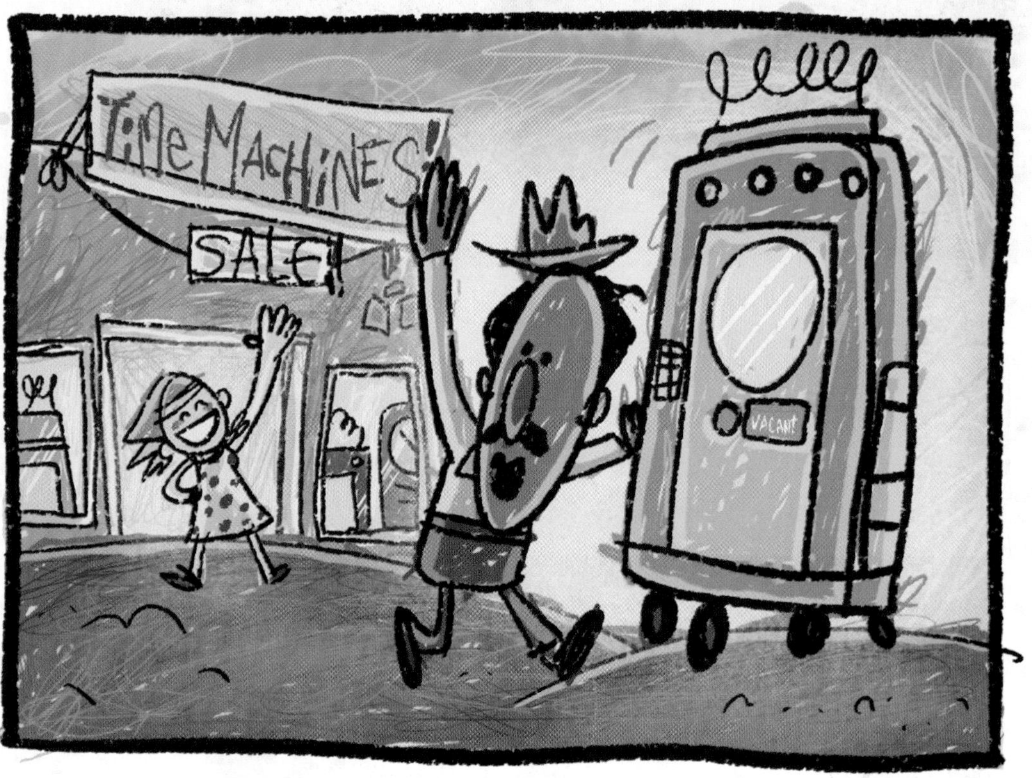
TIME MACHINES!
SALE!
VACANT

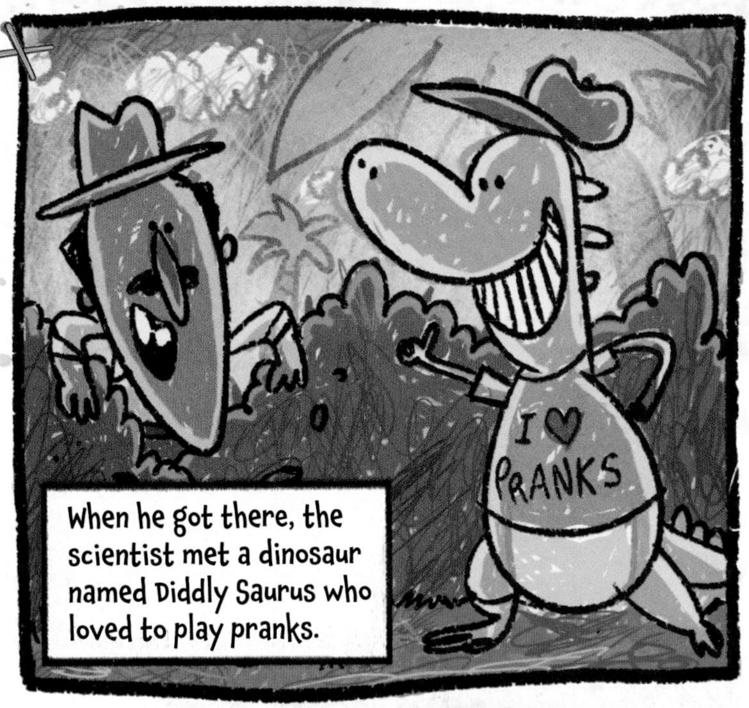
I ♥ PRANKS
When he got there, the scientist met a dinosaur named Diddly Saurus who loved to play pranks.

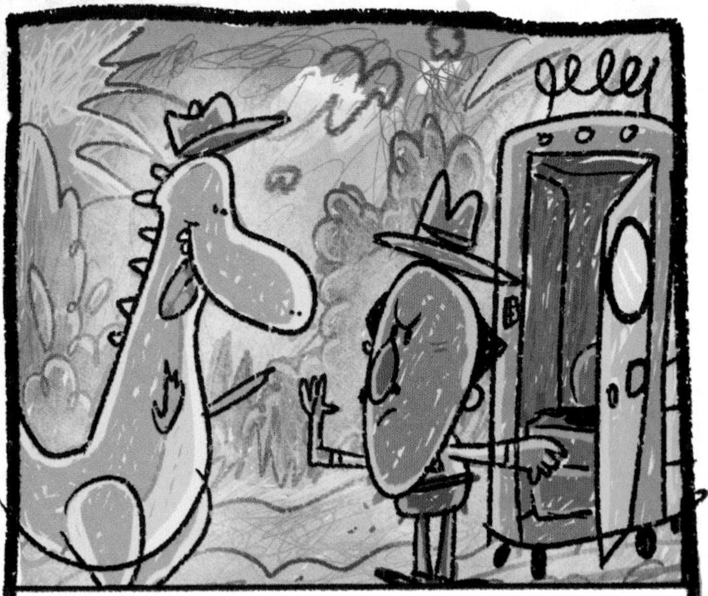
Diddly Saurus wanted to borrow the time machine. But the scientist wouldn't let him.

So, Diddly pulled the old, “Oh hey, look! What’s that over there and stuff?” prank and stole the time machine, anyway!

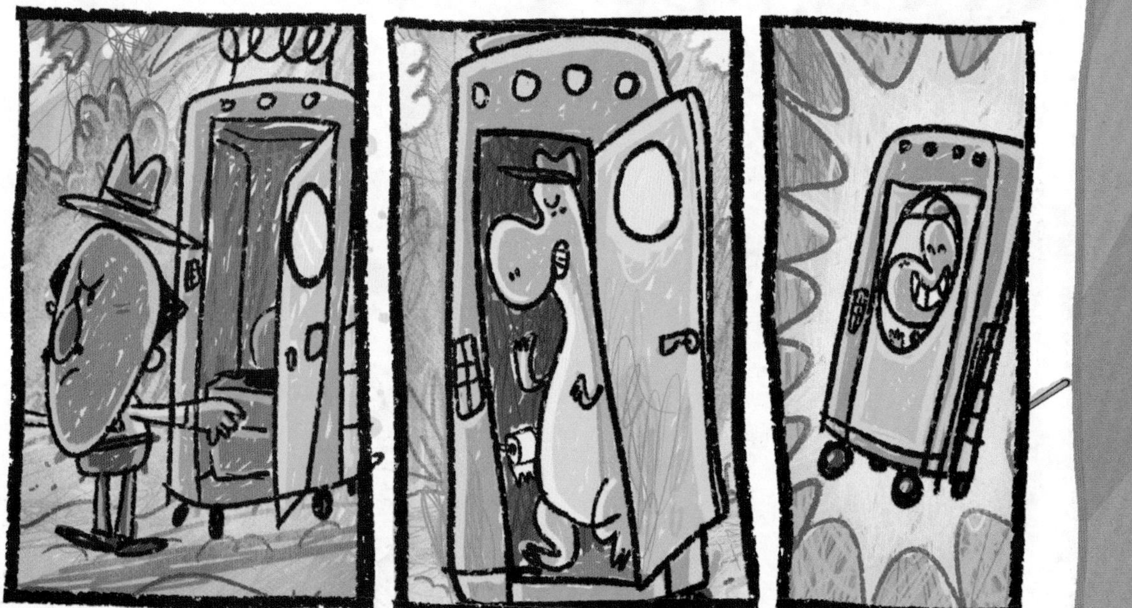

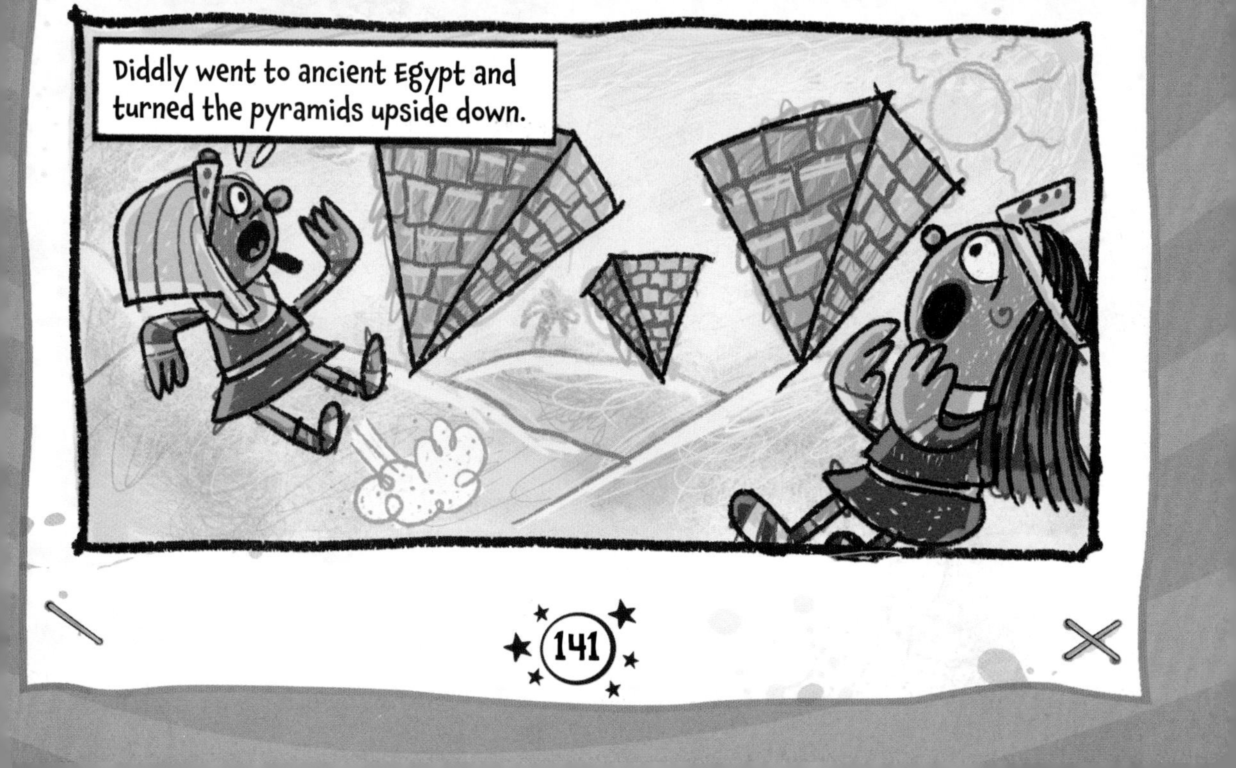
Diddly went to ancient Egypt and turned the pyramids upside down.

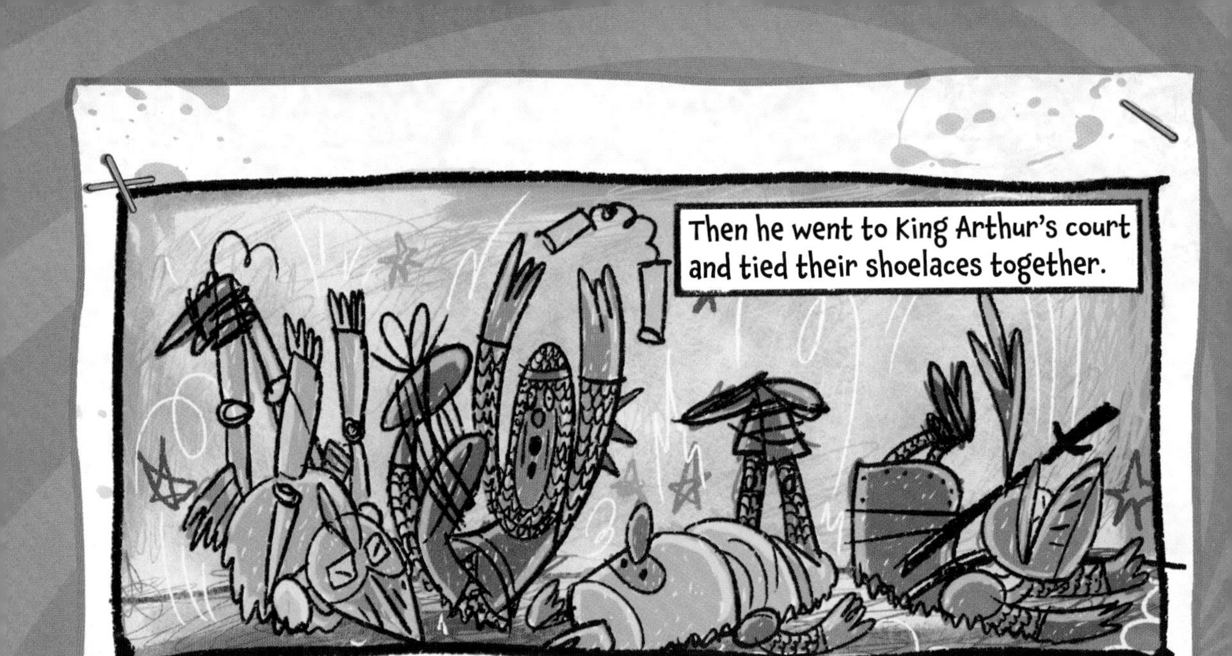
Then he went to King Arthur's court and tied their shoelaces together.

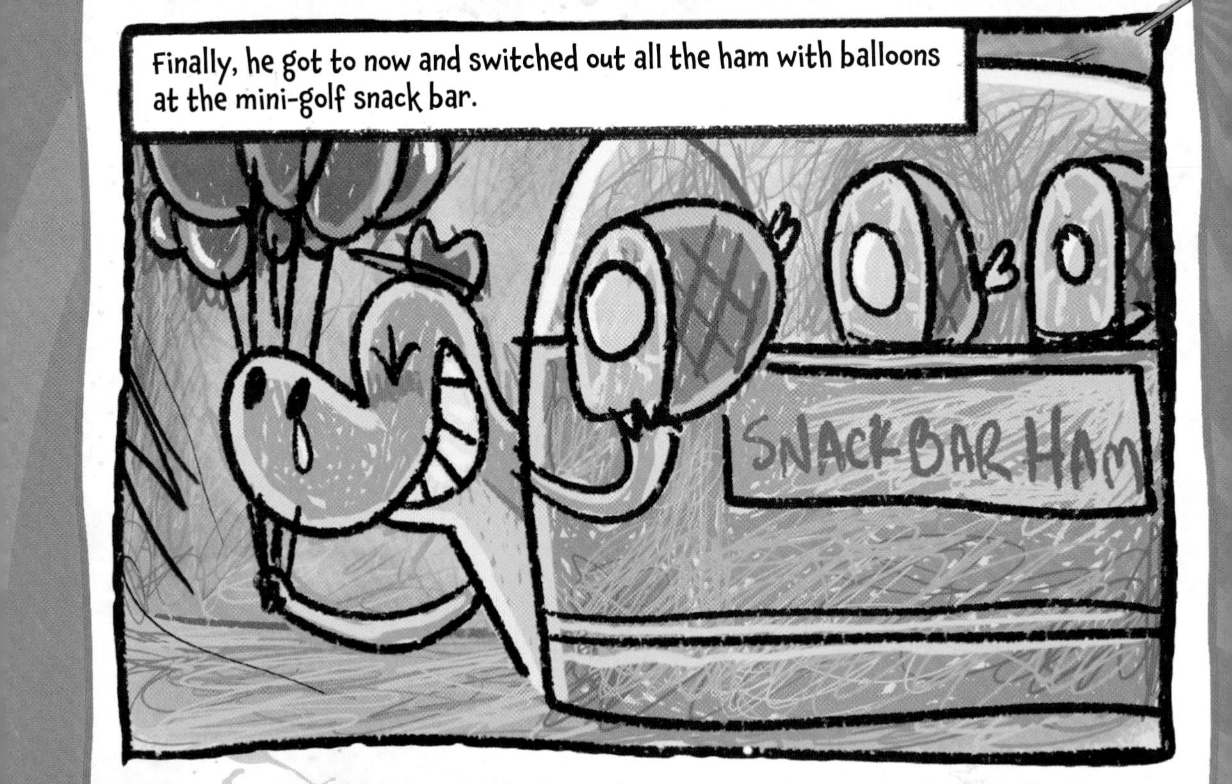
Finally, he got to now and switched out all the ham with balloons at the mini-golf snack bar.
SNACK BAR HAM

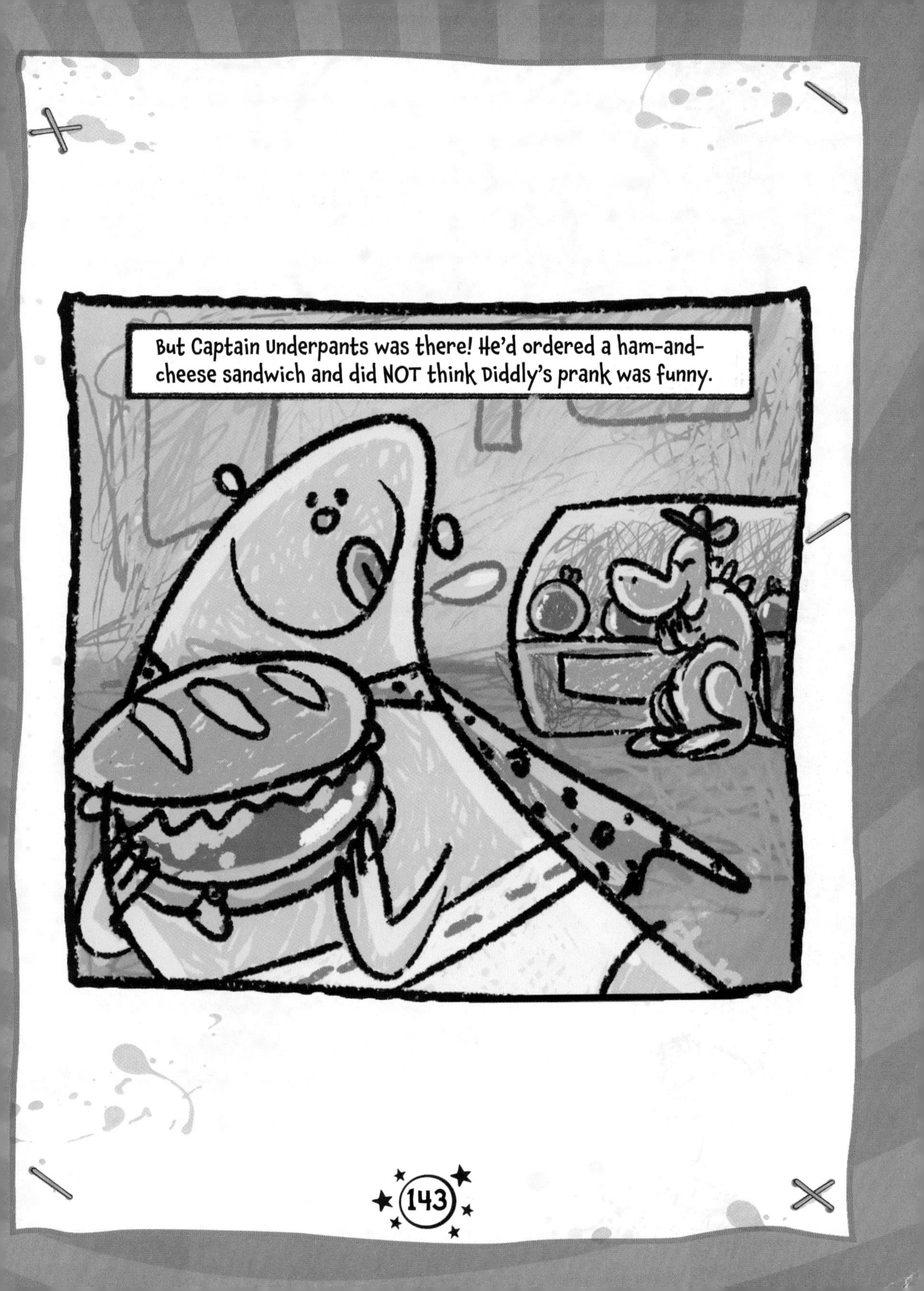
But Captain Underpants was there! He'd ordered a ham-and-cheese sandwich and did NOT think Diddly's prank was funny.

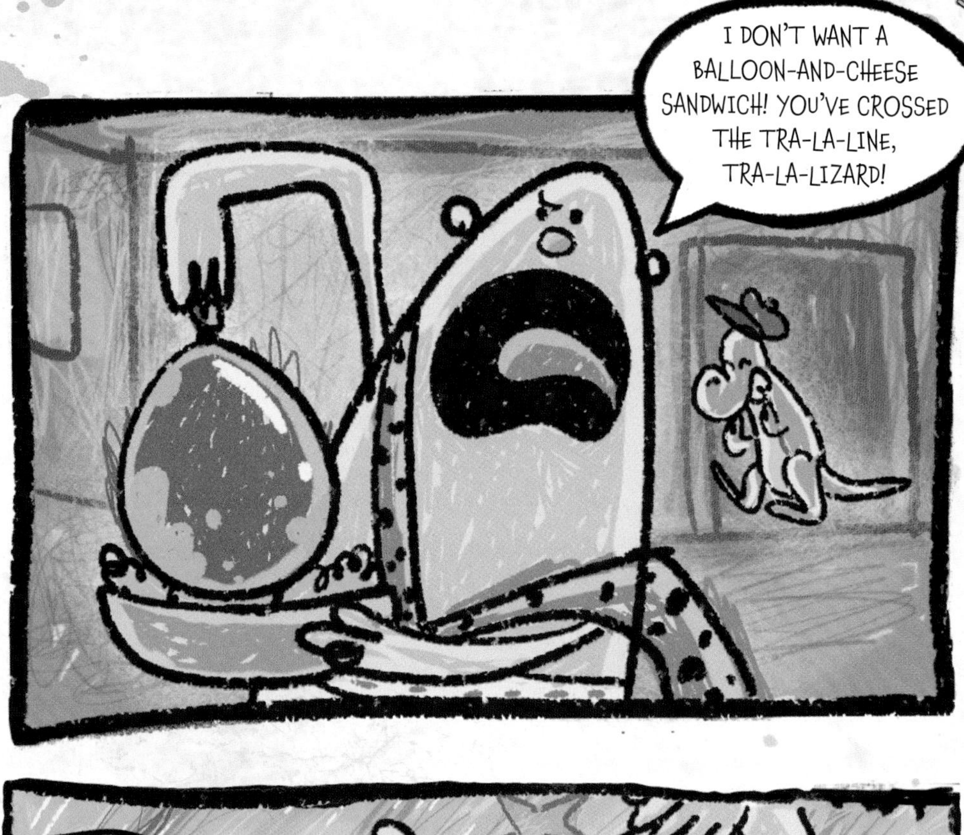
I DON'T WANT A BALLOON-AND-CHEESE SANDWICH! YOU'VE CROSSED THE TRA-LA-LINE, TRA-LA-LIZARD!

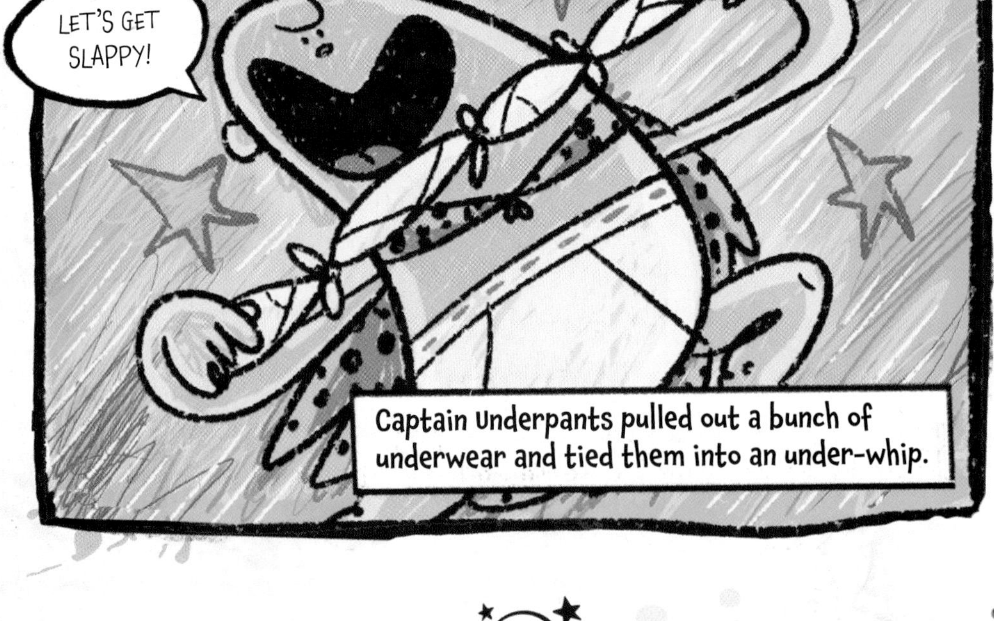
LET'S GET SLAPPY!
Captain Underpants pulled out a bunch of underwear and tied them into an under-whip.

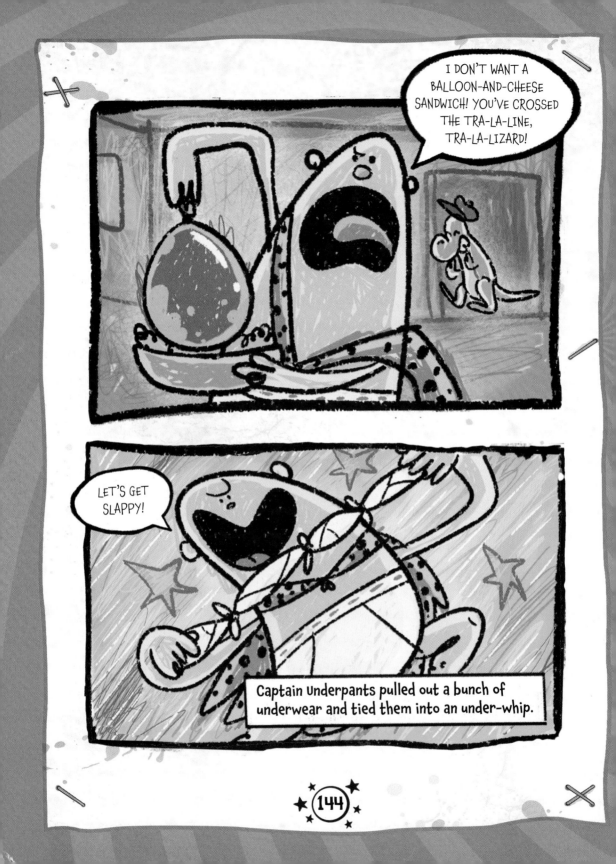

Then it was on like mastodon! Tighty-whitey versus taily-whaley!

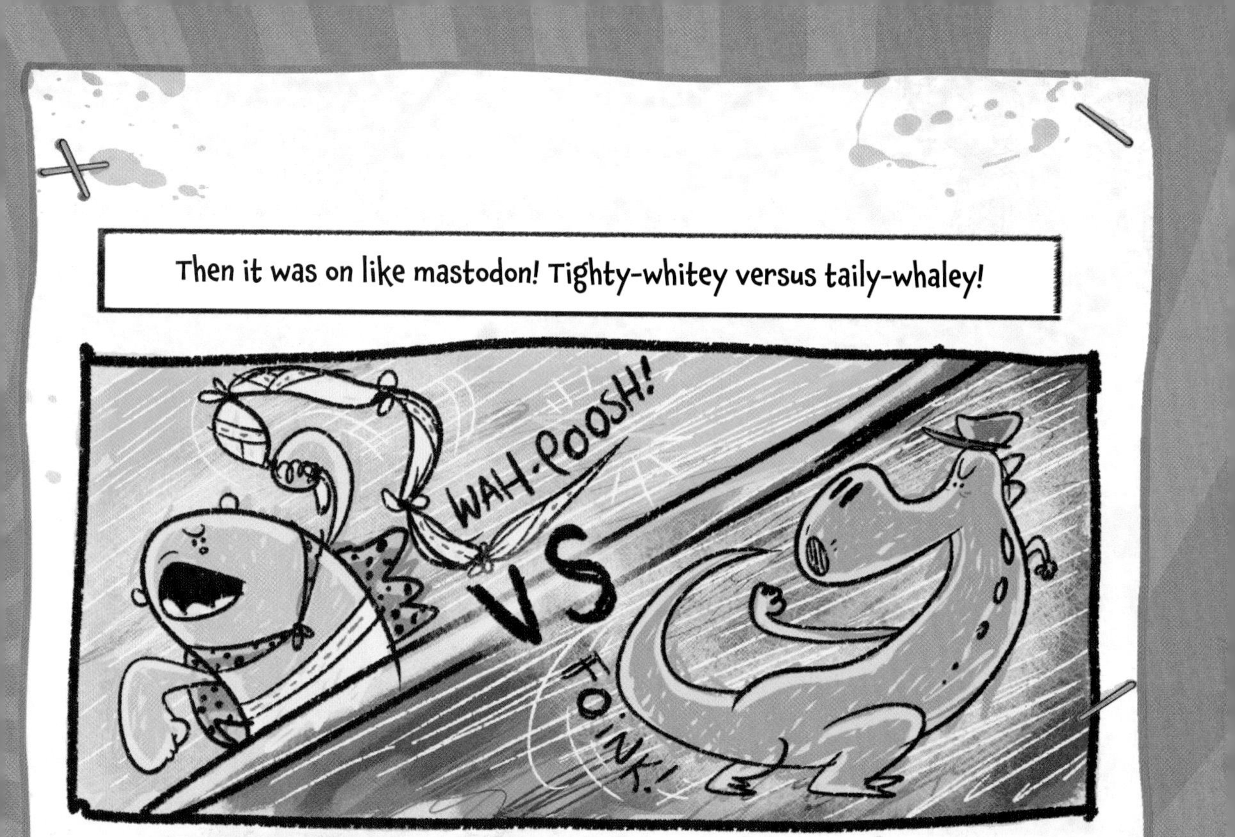
WAH-POOSH!
VS
FOINK!

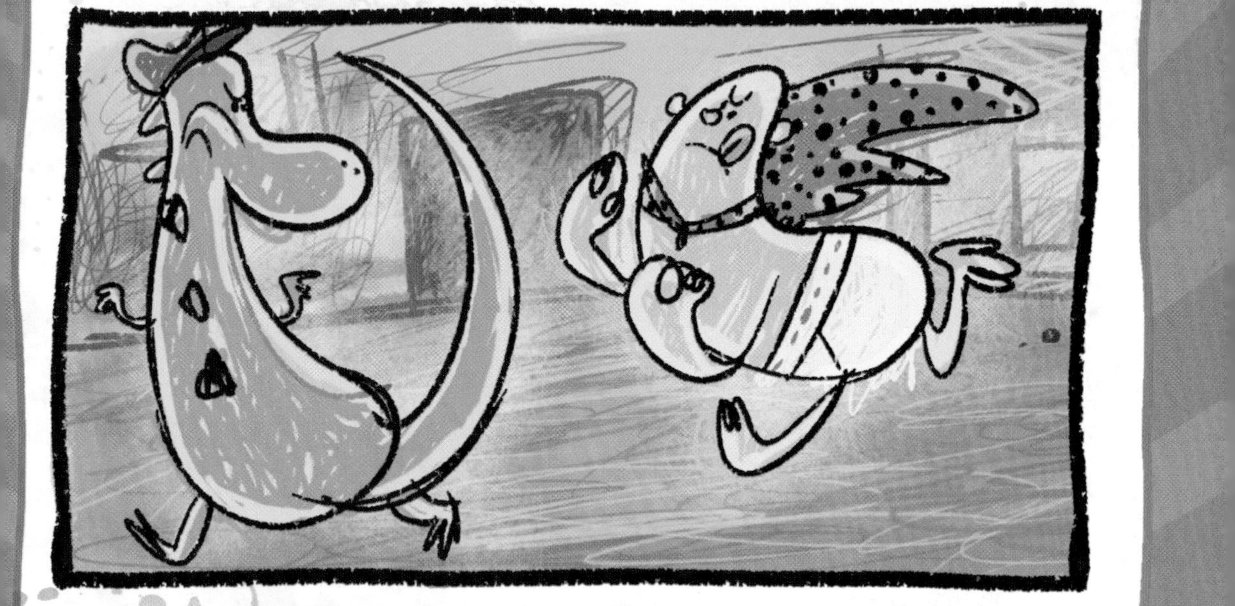

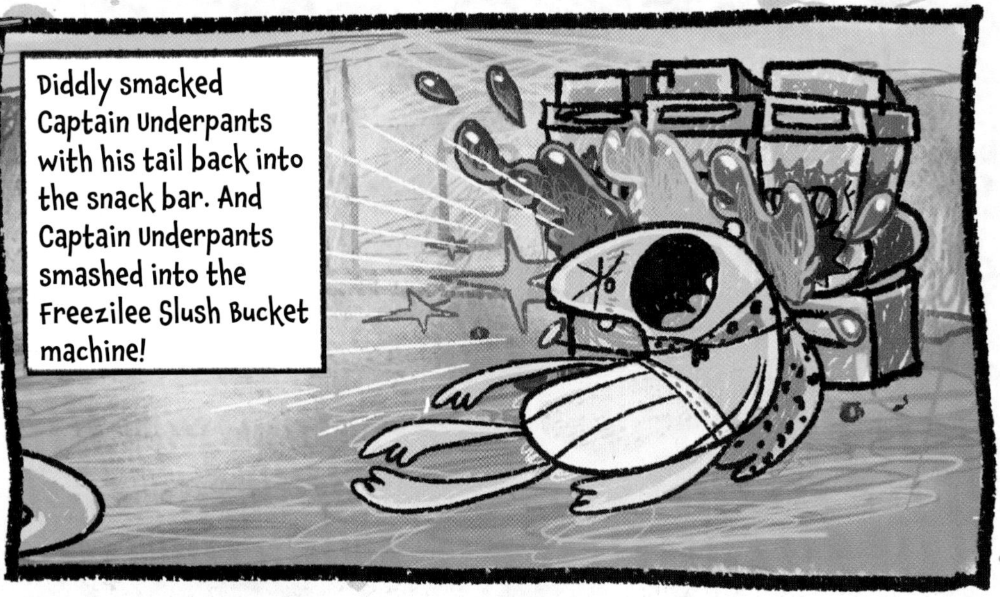
Diddly smacked Captain Underpants with his tail back into the snack bar. And Captain Underpants smashed into the Freezilee Slush Bucket machine!

But as Diddly got real close, Captain Underpants blasted him with the Freezilee Slush Bucket machine and stopped him cold!

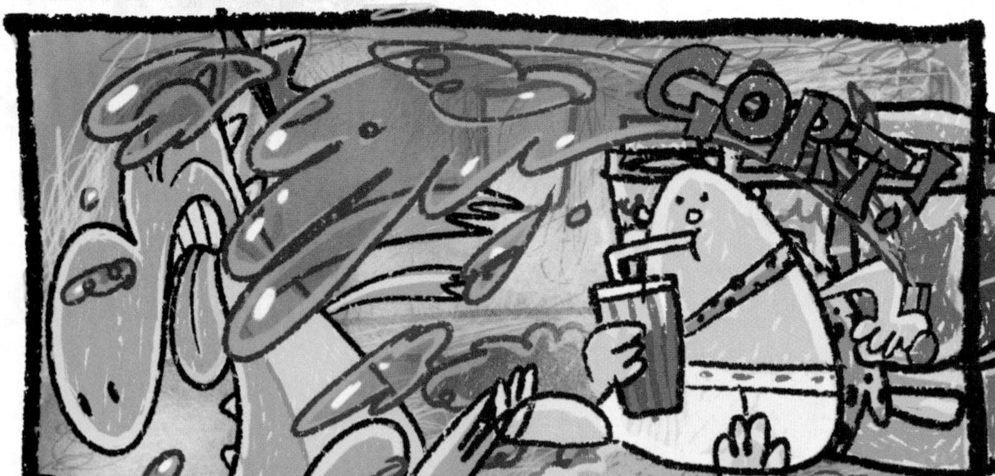

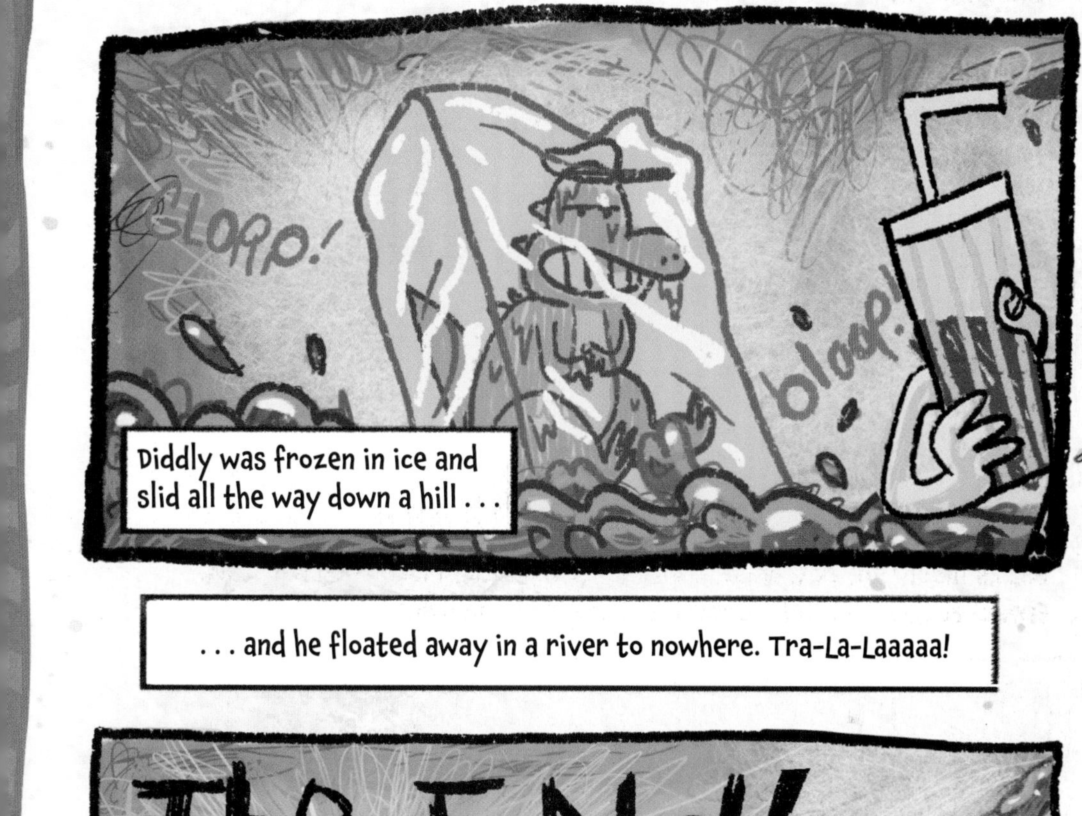
bloop!
Diddly was frozen in ice and slid all the way down a hill . . .

. . . and he floated away in a river to nowhere. Tra-La-Laaaaa!

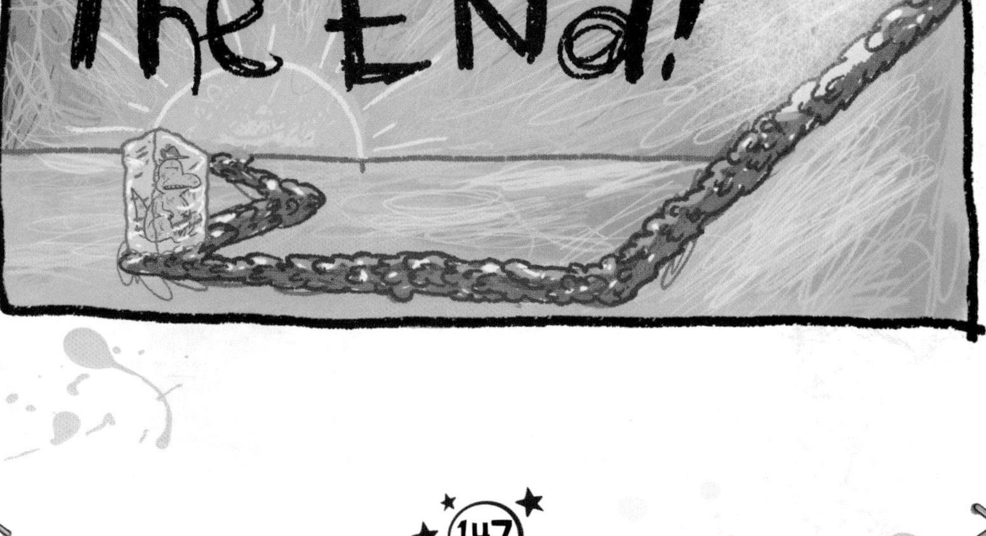
The End!

CAPTAIN UNDERPANTS & the CROC-O-BAT BUTT-ERFLY CONUNDRUM BLUNDER

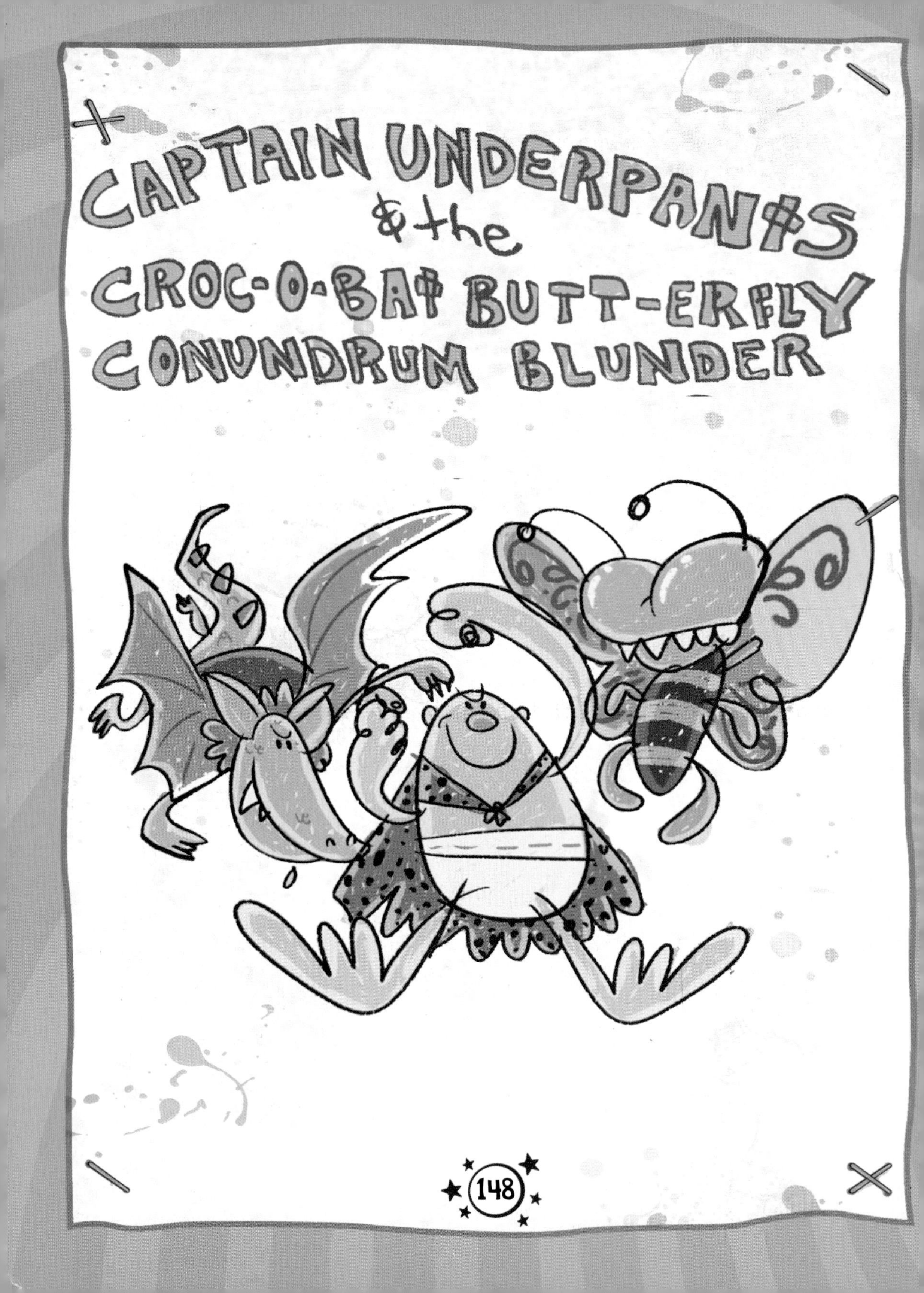

Recess is a time for fun with running and jumping, but also being careful so you don't skin your knee or bonk your head because that's definitely not fun.

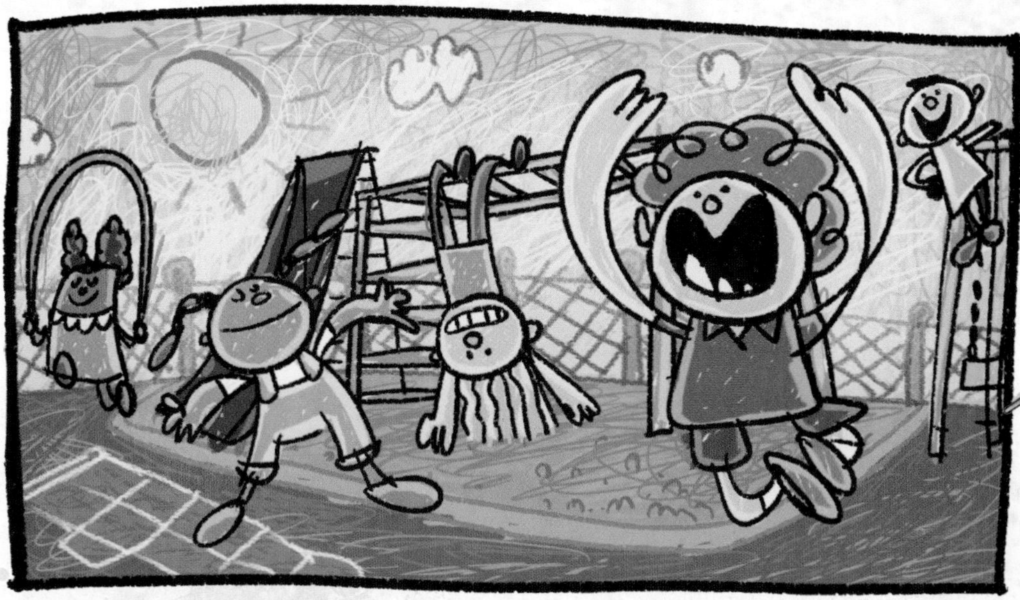

But one day there was a smart kid who loved science and hated fun. His name was Nelvin.

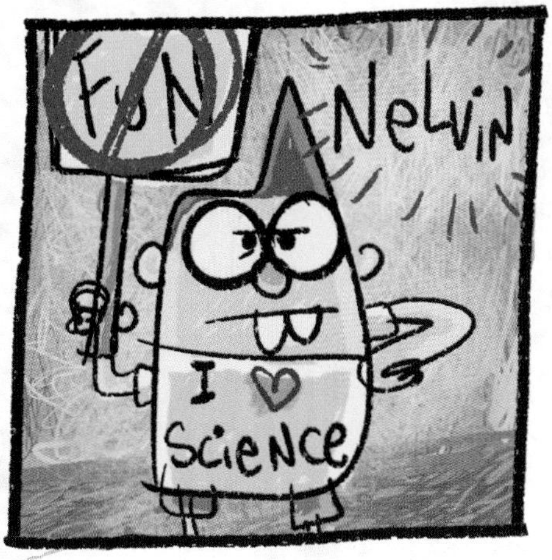
FUN
NELVIN
I ♥ SCIENCE

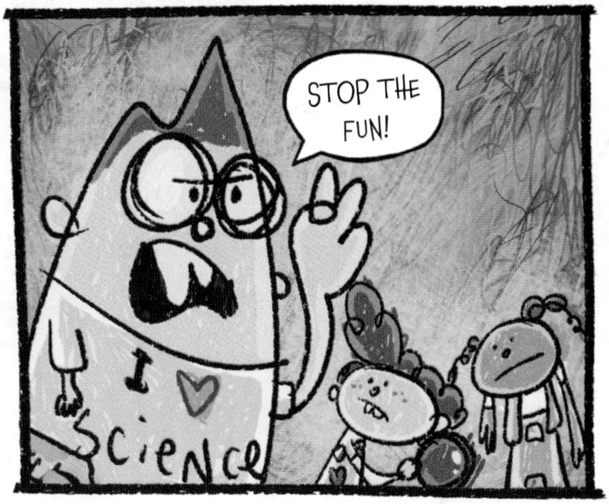
STOP THE FUN!
I ♥ SCIENCE

Then Nelvin built a machine that could combine two different things into one totally awesome new thing. He combined crocodiles and bats in order to make croc-o-bats!

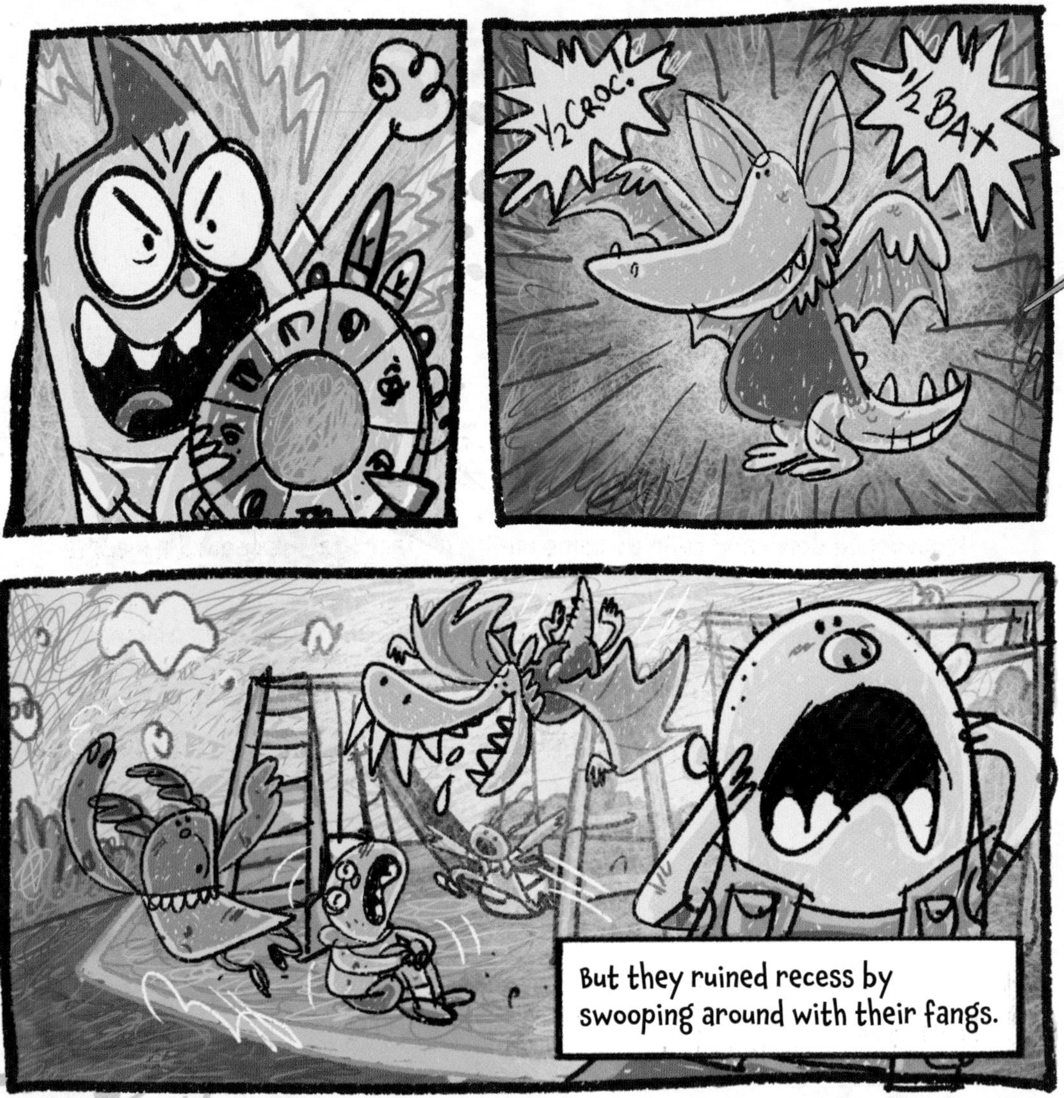
½ CROC!
½ BAT
But they ruined recess by swooping around with their fangs.

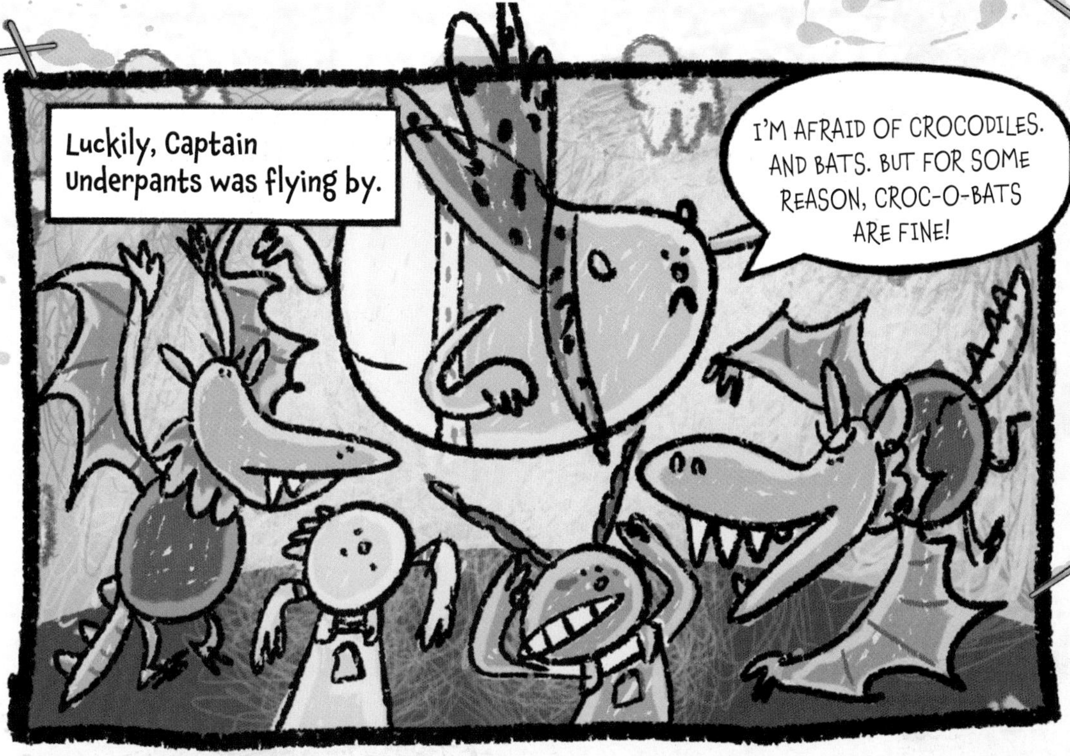
Luckily, Captain Underpants was flying by.
I'M AFRAID OF CROCODILES. AND BATS. BUT FOR SOME REASON, CROC-O-BATS ARE FINE!

He swooped down and twirled some undies so fast that he opened a wedgie wormhole!

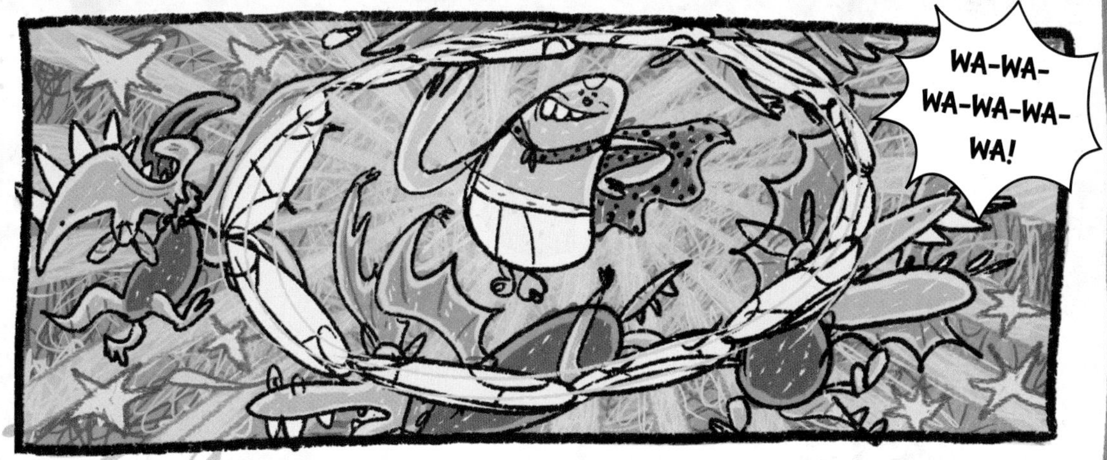
WA-WA-WA-WA-WA-WA!

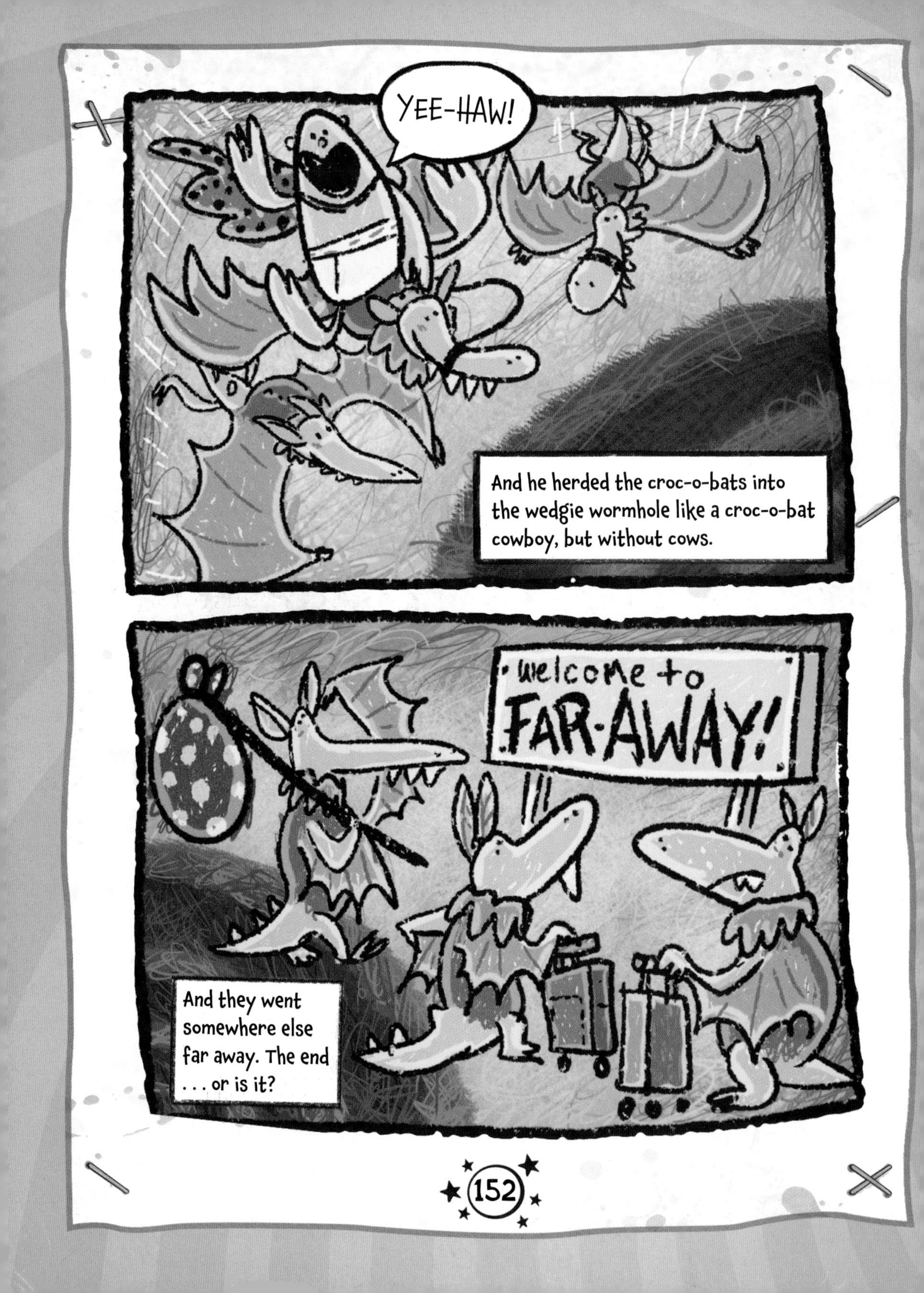
YEE-HAW!
And he herded the croc-o-bats into the wedgie wormhole like a croc-o-bat cowboy, but without cows.
welcome to FAR-AWAY!
And they went somewhere else far away. The end . . . or is it?

You see, the kids were so happy, they wanted to celebrate. Especially some kids named George and Harold, who may be inspired by actual persons and events.

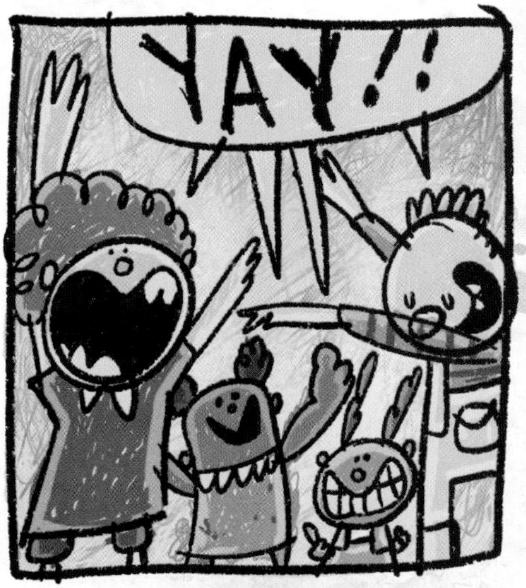
YAY!!

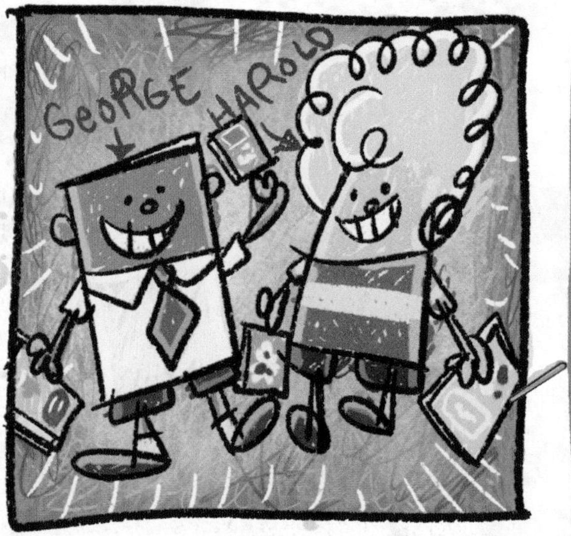
GEORGE
HAROLD

George and Harold borrowed—NOT stole—Nelvin's machine in order to celebrate.

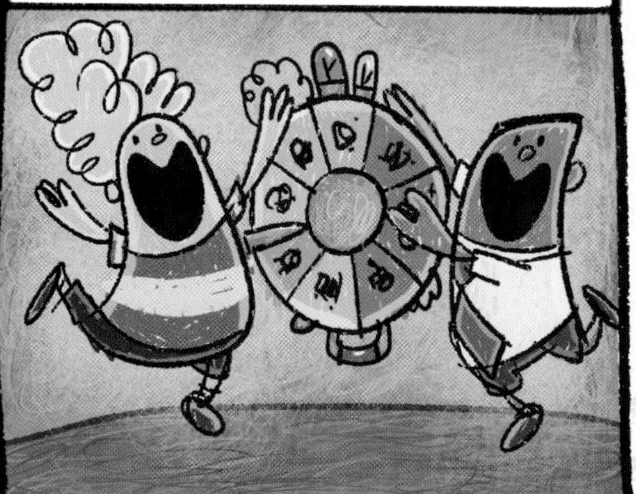

And they combined butts and flies to make butt-erflies, because that's quality comedy right there.

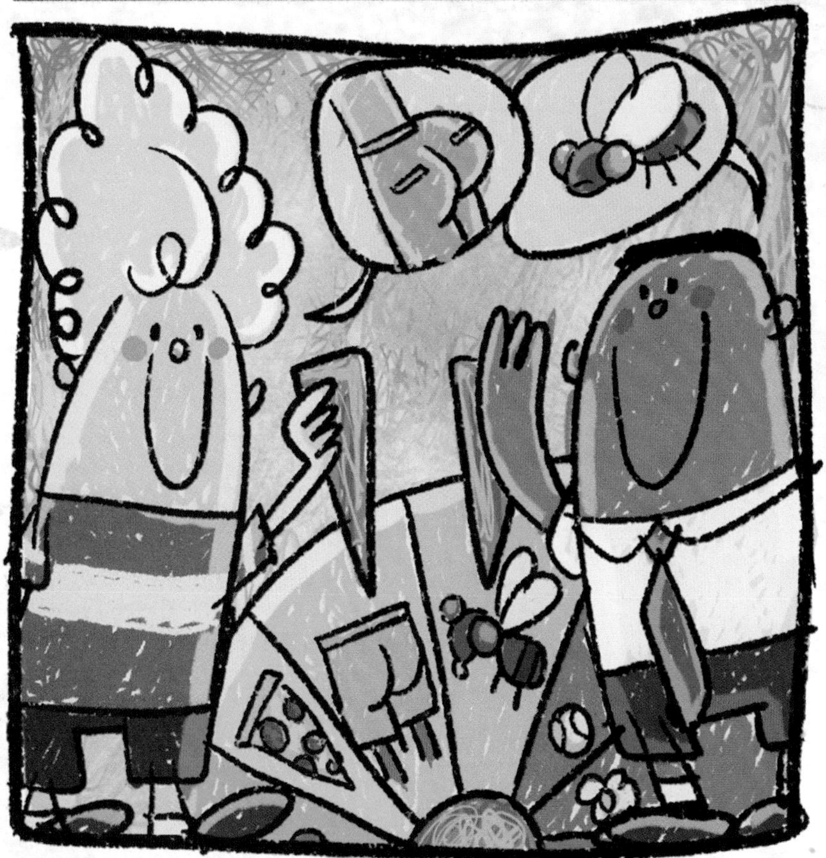

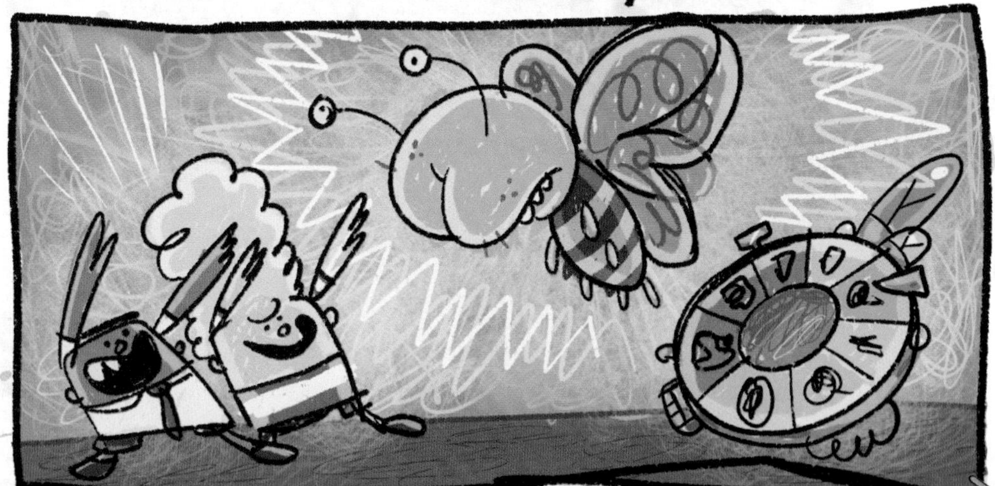

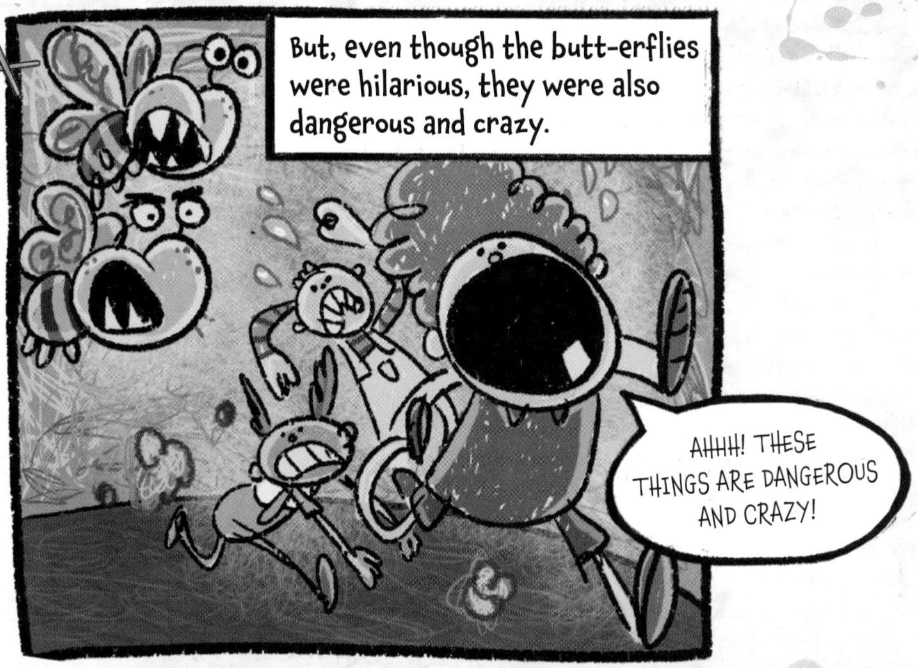
But, even though the butt-erflies were hilarious, they were also dangerous and crazy.
AHHH! THESE THINGS ARE DANGEROUS AND CRAZY!

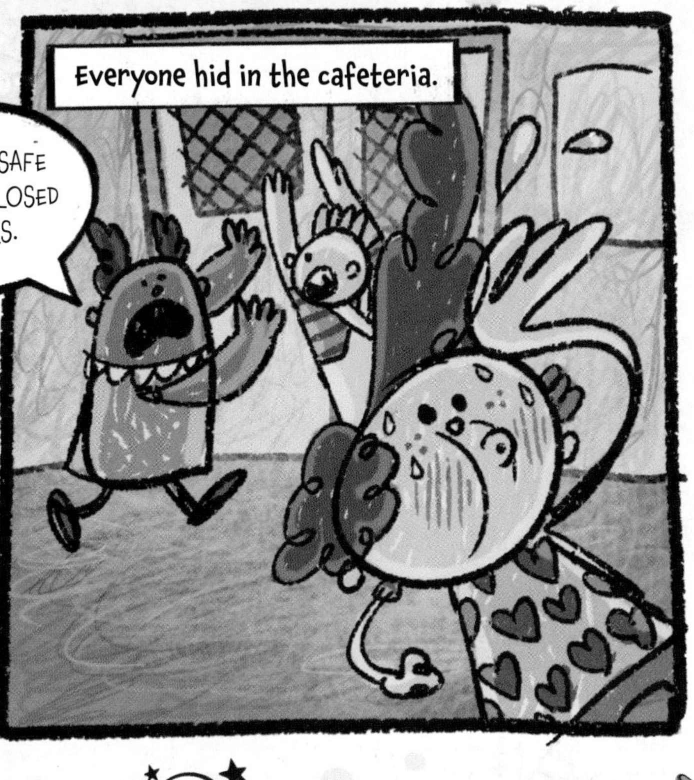
Everyone hid in the cafeteria.
WHEW, WE'RE SAFE BECAUSE WE CLOSED THE DOORS.

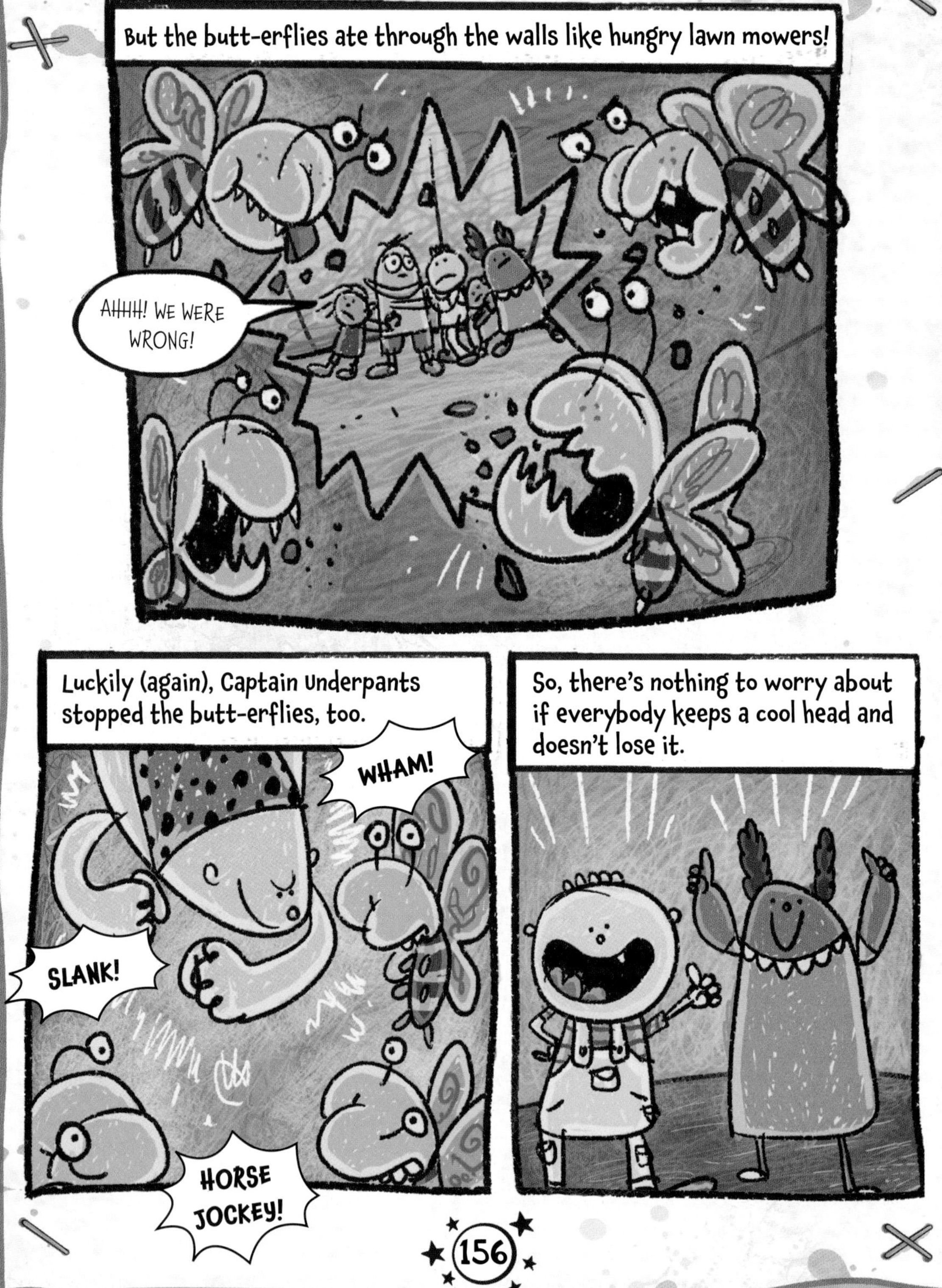

But the butt-erflies ate through the walls like hungry lawn mowers!
AHHH! WE WERE WRONG!
Luckily (again), Captain Underpants stopped the butt-erflies, too.
WHAM!
SLANK!
HORSE JOCKEY!
So, there's nothing to worry about if everybody keeps a cool head and doesn't lose it.

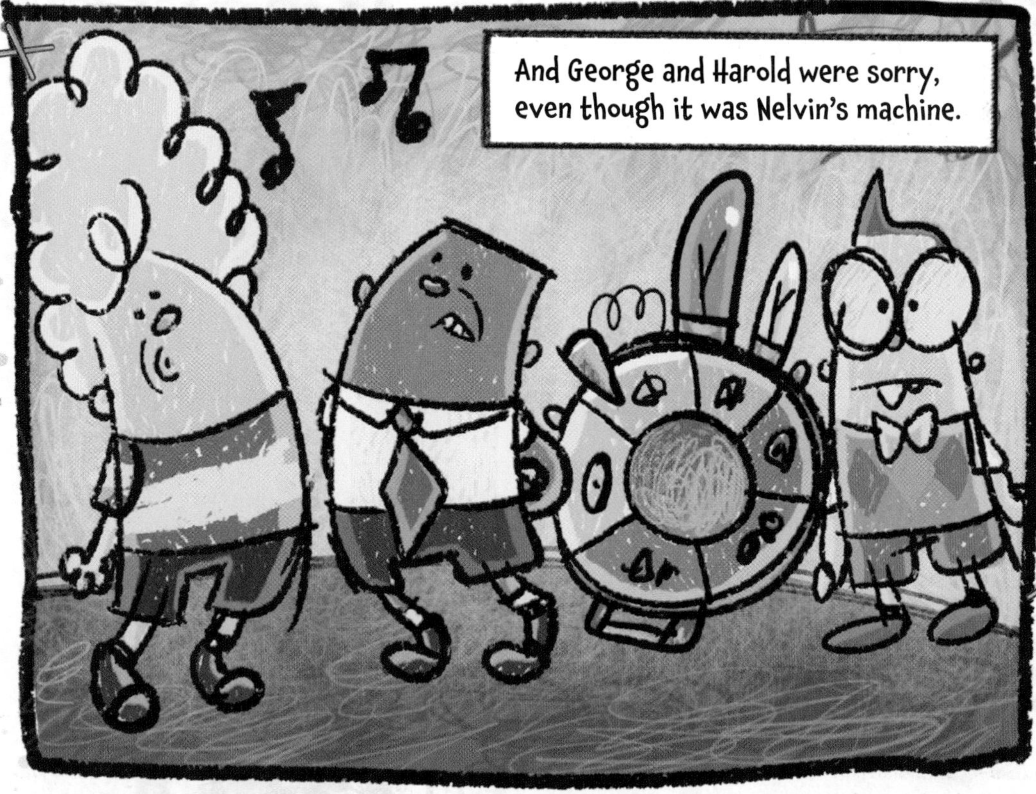
And George and Harold were sorry, even though it was Nelvin's machine.

They felt so bad they got everyone ice cream. And everyone forgave them and didn't hand them over to the butt monsters. The end. For real this time.

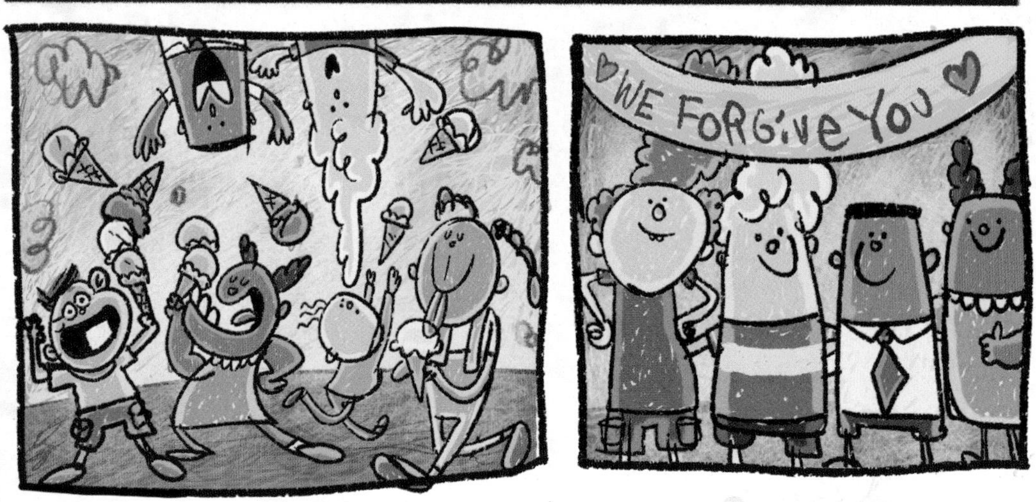
WE FORGIVE YOU

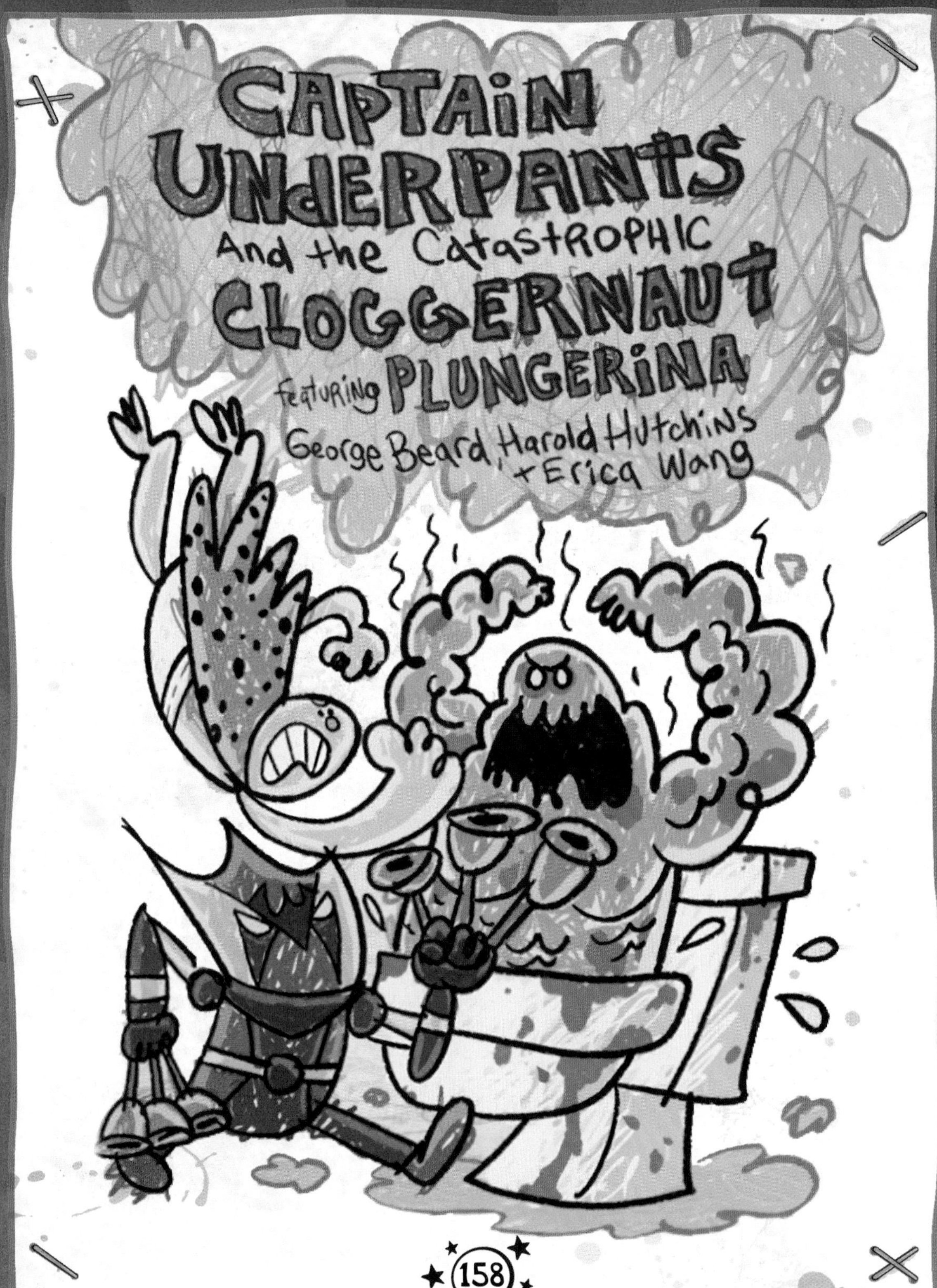
CAPTAIN UNDERPANTS
And the Catastrophic
CLOGGERNAUT
featuring PLUNGERINA
George Beard, Harold Hutchins + Erica Wang

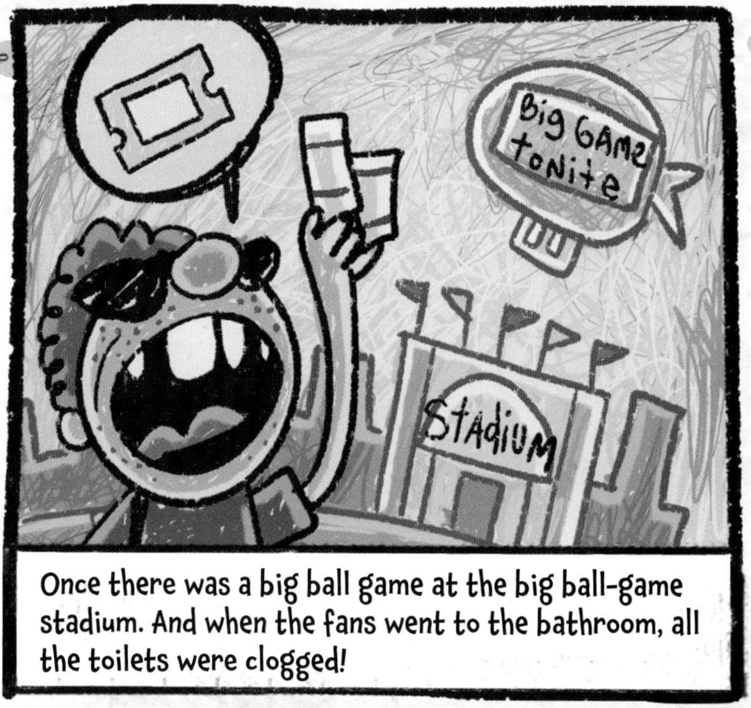
Big GAMe toNite
STADIUM
Once there was a big ball game at the big ball-game stadium. And when the fans went to the bathroom, all the toilets were clogged!

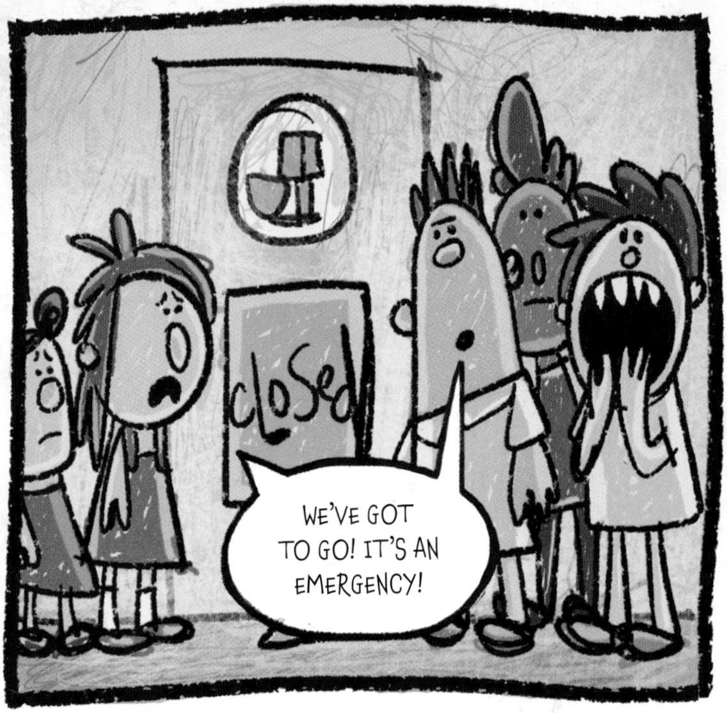
CLOSED
WE'VE GOT TO GO! IT'S AN EMERGENCY!

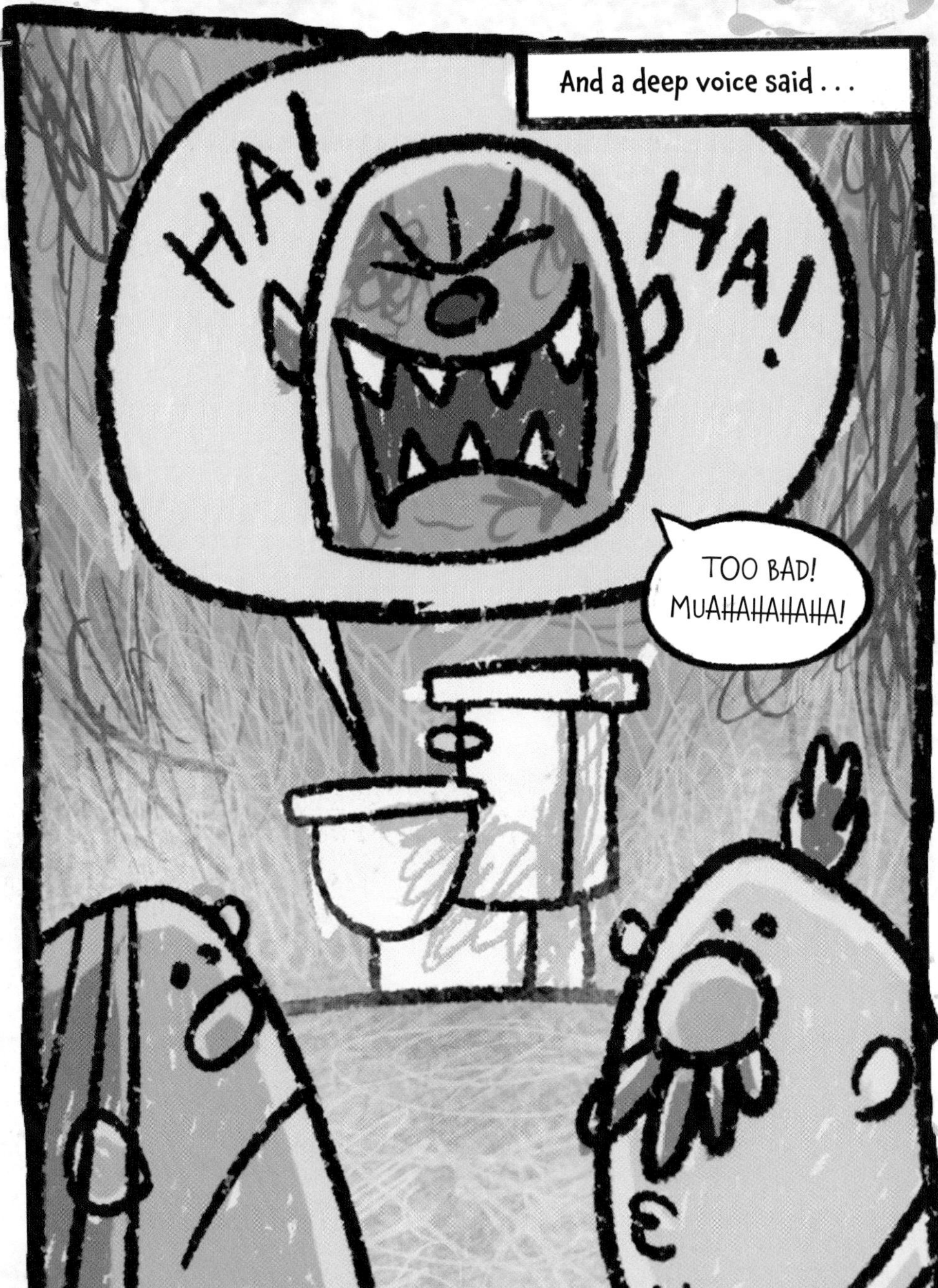
And a deep voice said . . .
HA! HA!
TOO BAD! MUAHAHAHAHA!

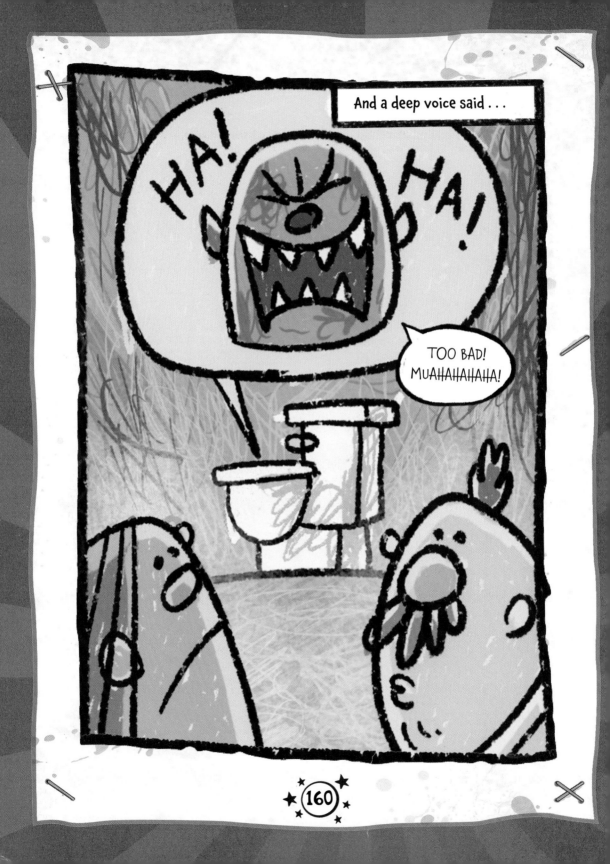

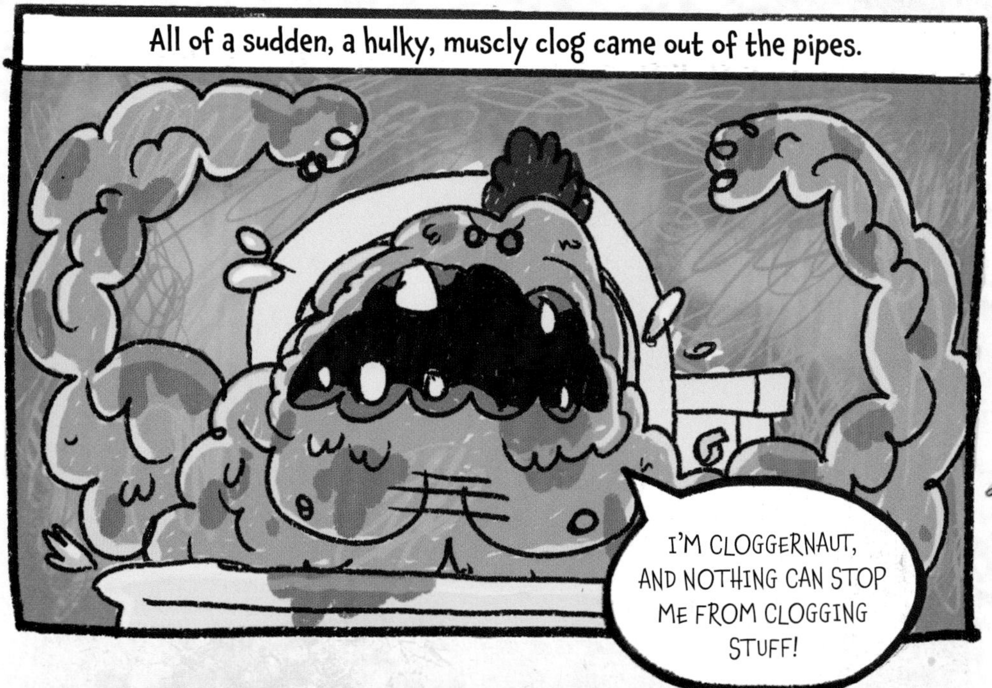
All of a sudden, a hulky, muscly clog came out of the pipes.
I'M CLOGGERNAUT, AND NOTHING CAN STOP ME FROM CLOGGING STUFF!

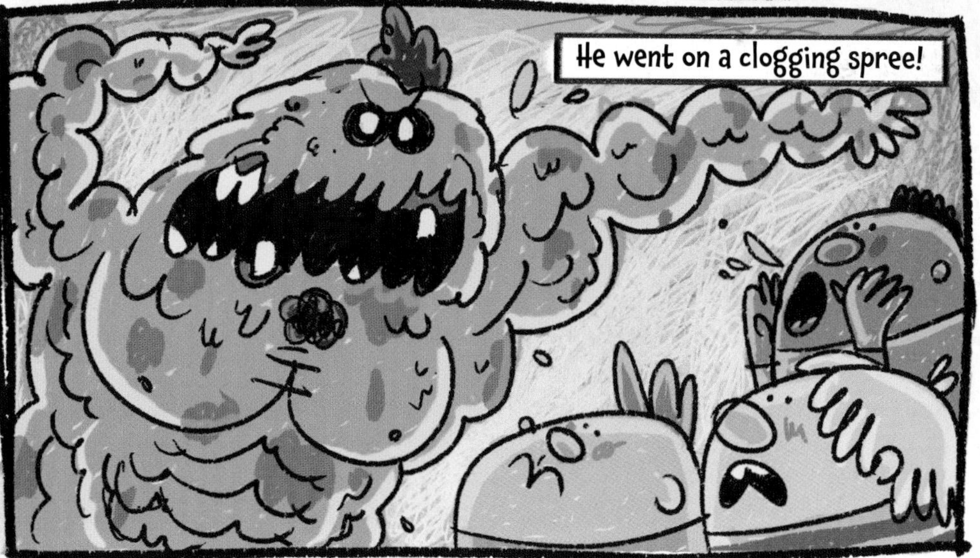
He went on a clogging spree!

He clogged the field, the peanut guy, and the overpriced souvenir stand where they sell those expensive foam fingers.

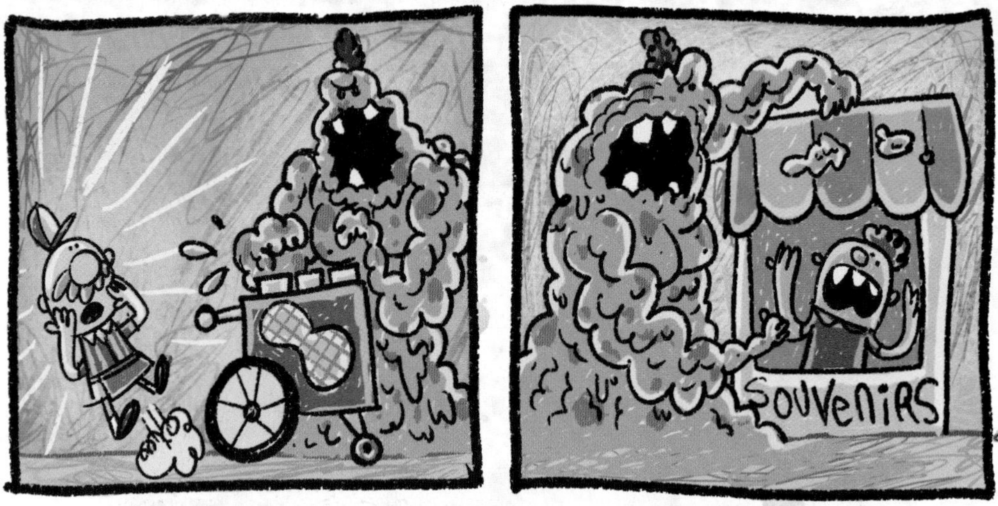
SOUVENIRS

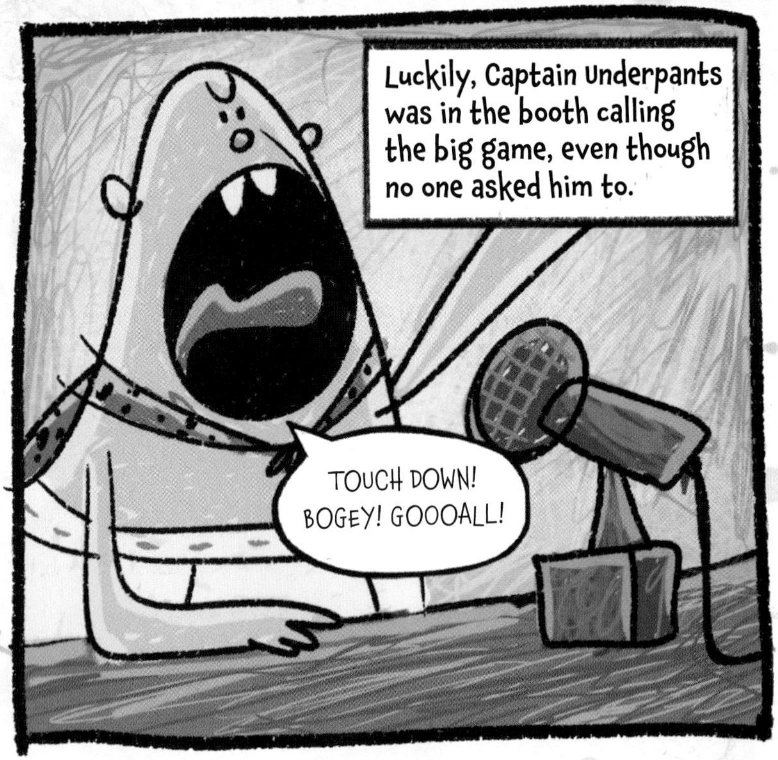
Luckily, Captain Underpants was in the booth calling the big game, even though no one asked him to.
TOUCH DOWN! BOGEY! GOOOALL!

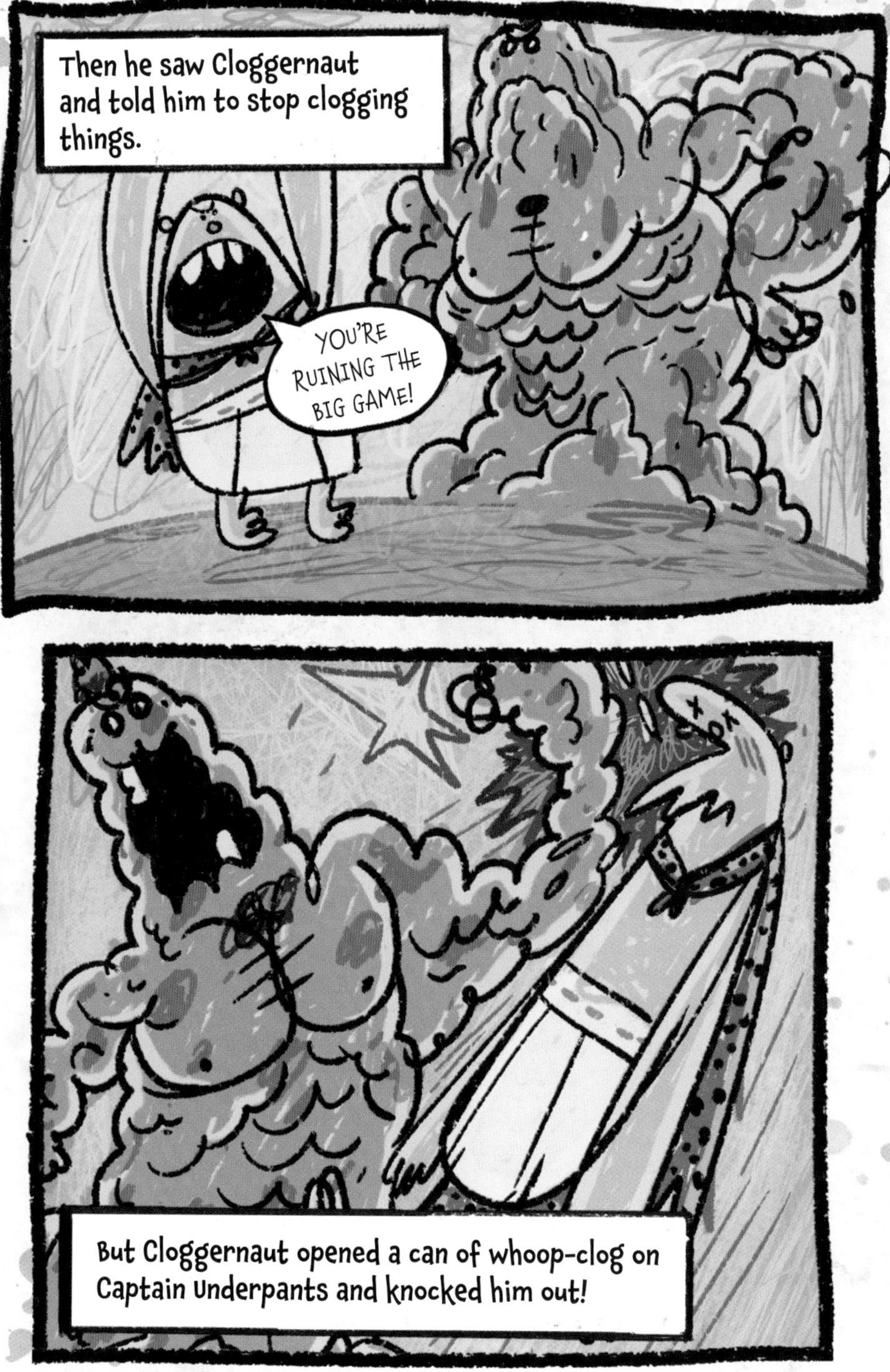
Then he saw Cloggernaut and told him to stop clogging things.
YOU'RE RUINING THE BIG GAME!
But Cloggernaut opened a can of whoop-clog on Captain Underpants and knocked him out!

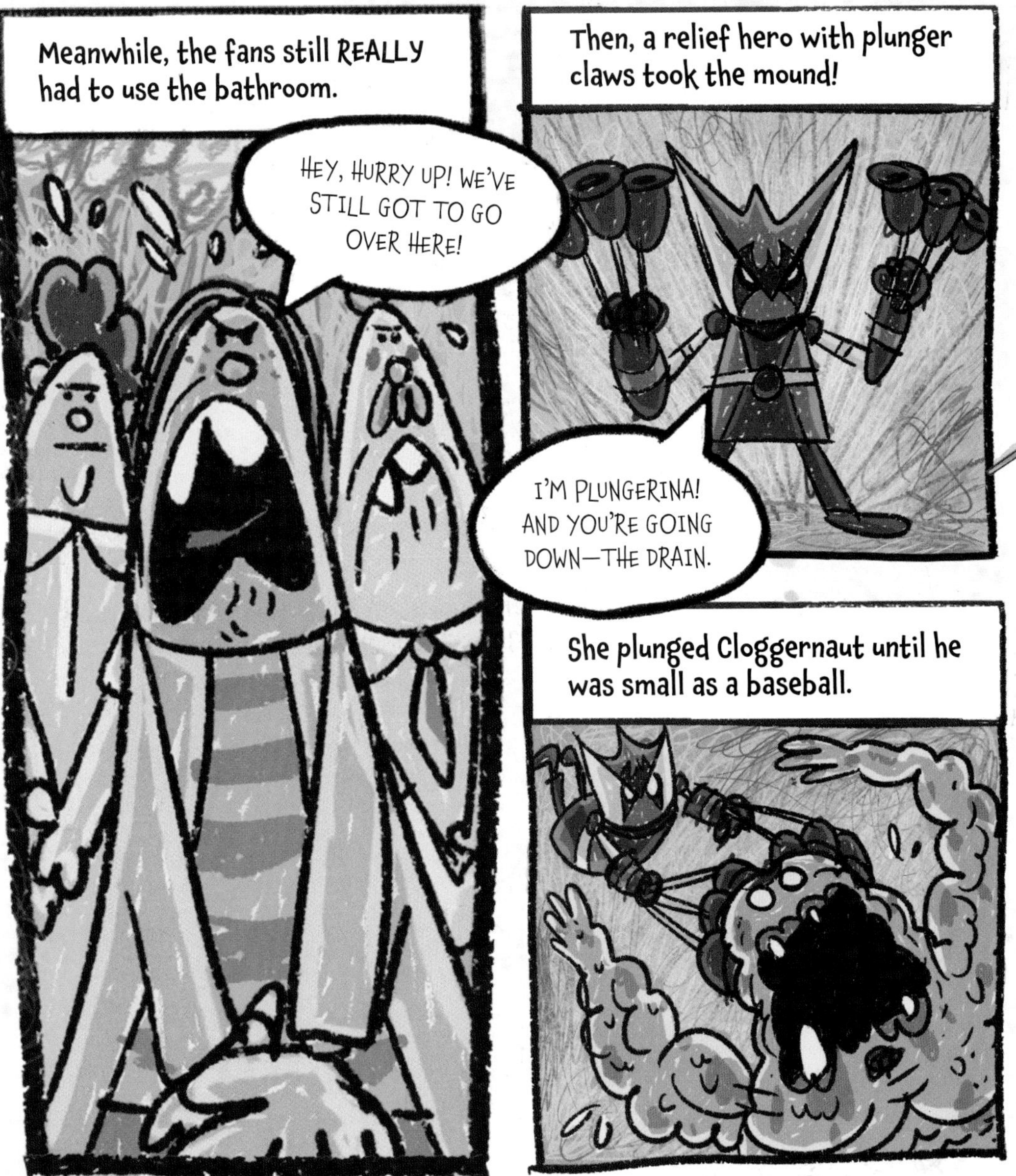
Meanwhile, the fans still REALLY had to use the bathroom.
HEY, HURRY UP! WE'VE STILL GOT TO GO OVER HERE!
Then, a relief hero with plunger claws took the mound!
I'M PLUNGERINA! AND YOU'RE GOING DOWN—THE DRAIN.
She plunged Cloggernaut until he was small as a baseball.

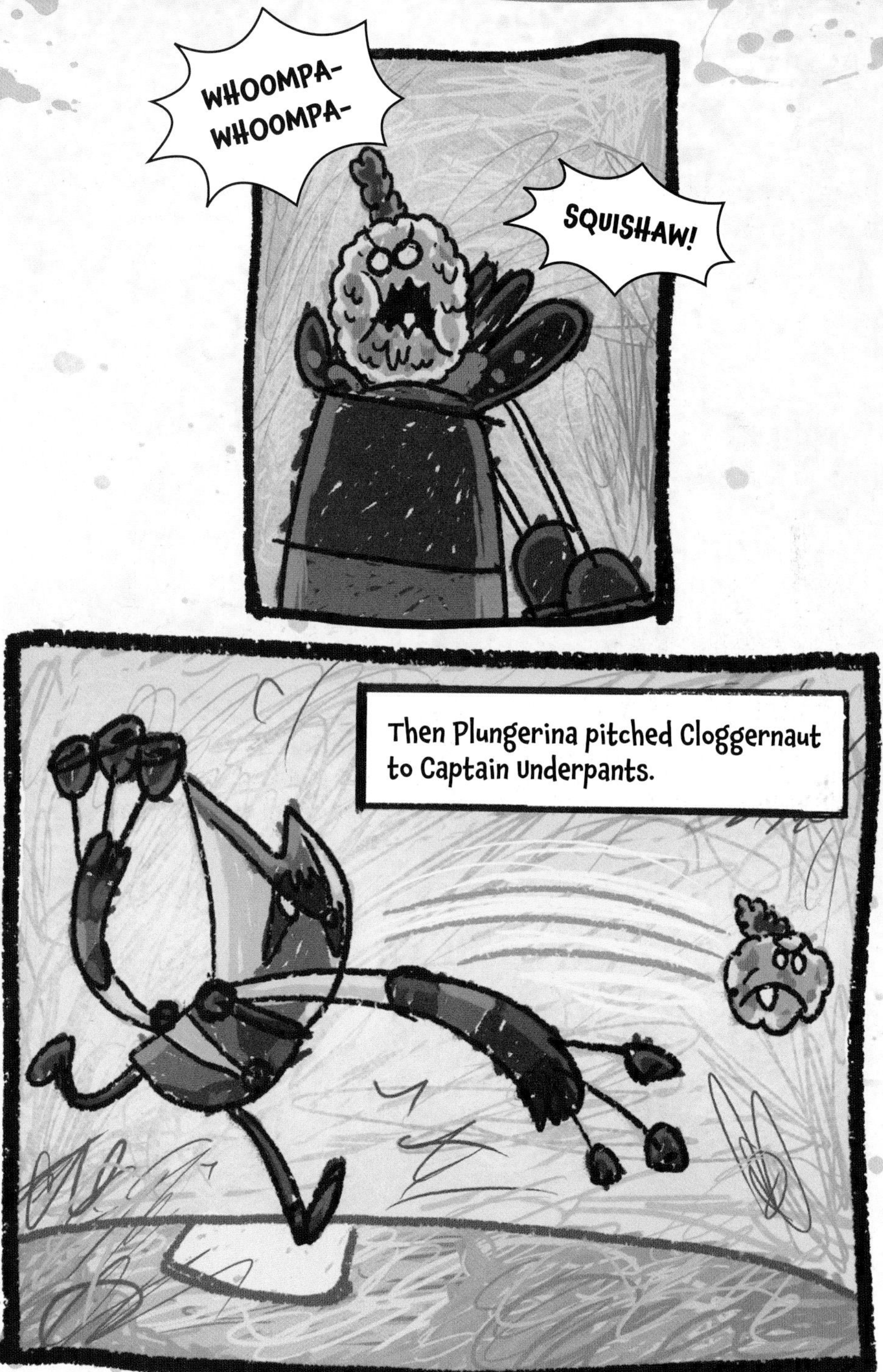
WHOOMPA-
WHOOMPA-
SQUISHAW!
Then Plungerina pitched Cloggernaut to Captain Underpants.

And Captain Underpants knocked Cloggernaut outta the park!

Captain Underpants rounded the bases and ran up to Plungerina.

HEY, PLUNGERINA, WANT TO BE ON MY UNDIE TEAM?

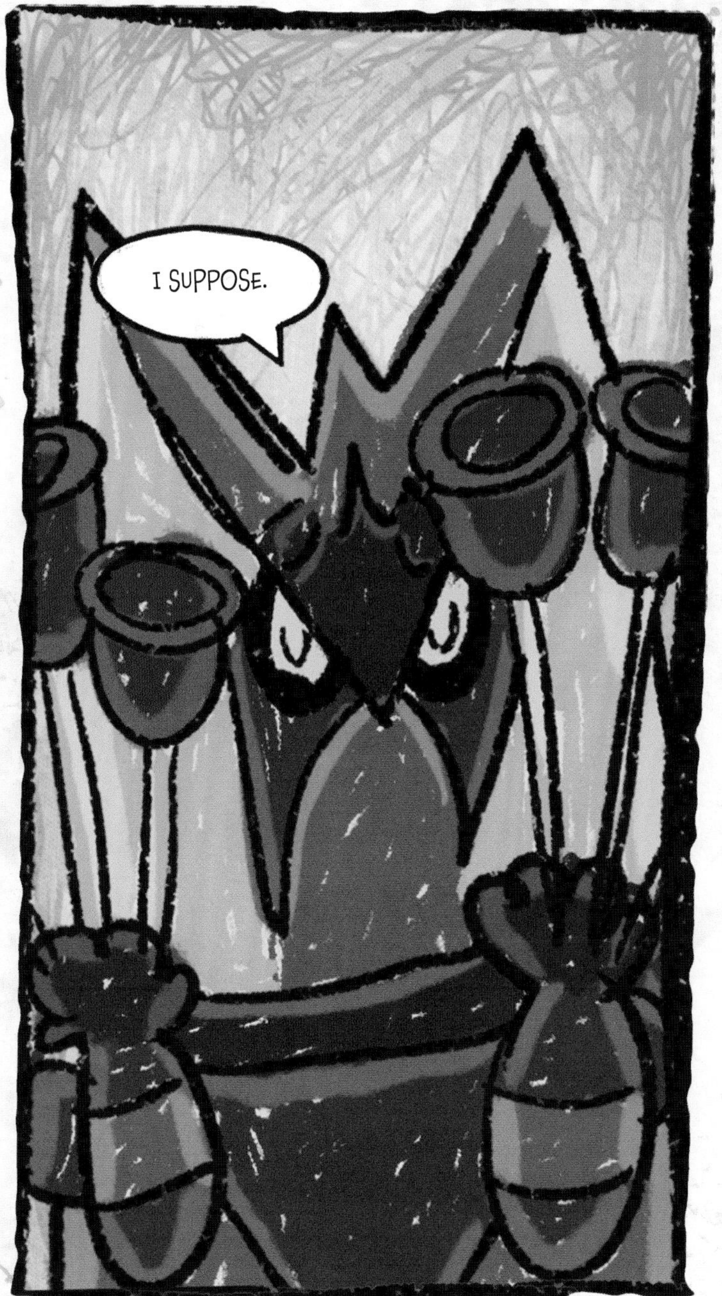
I SUPPOSE.

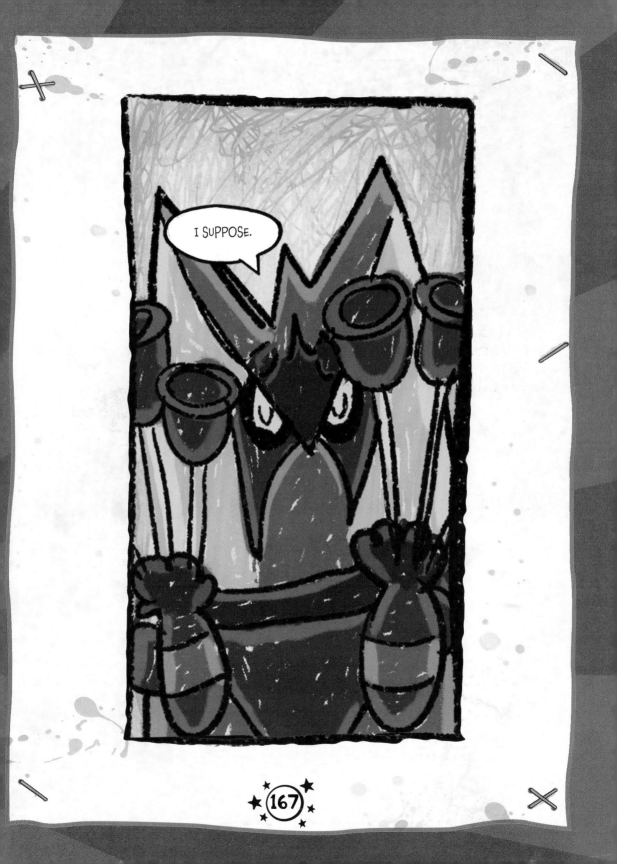

So, Captain Underpants poured a jug of sports drink on her to celebrate, even though no one likes that.

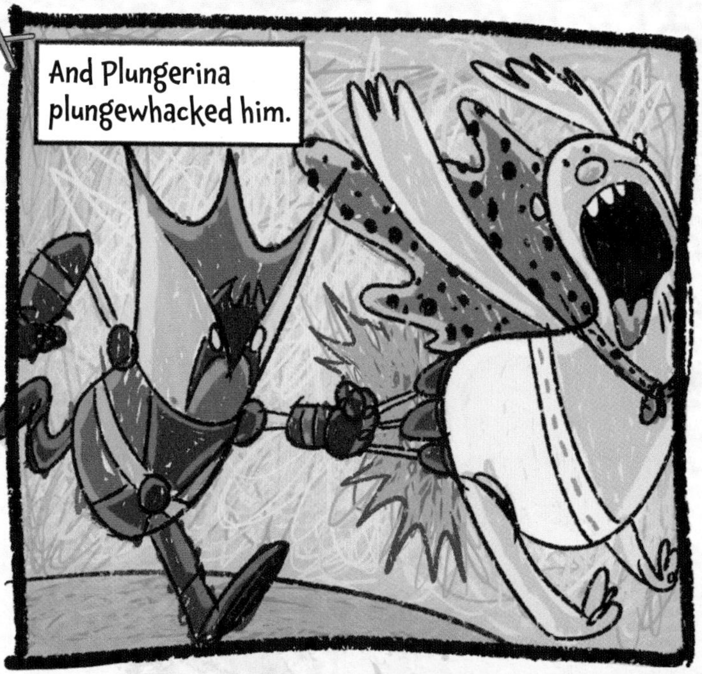
And Plungerina plungewhacked him.

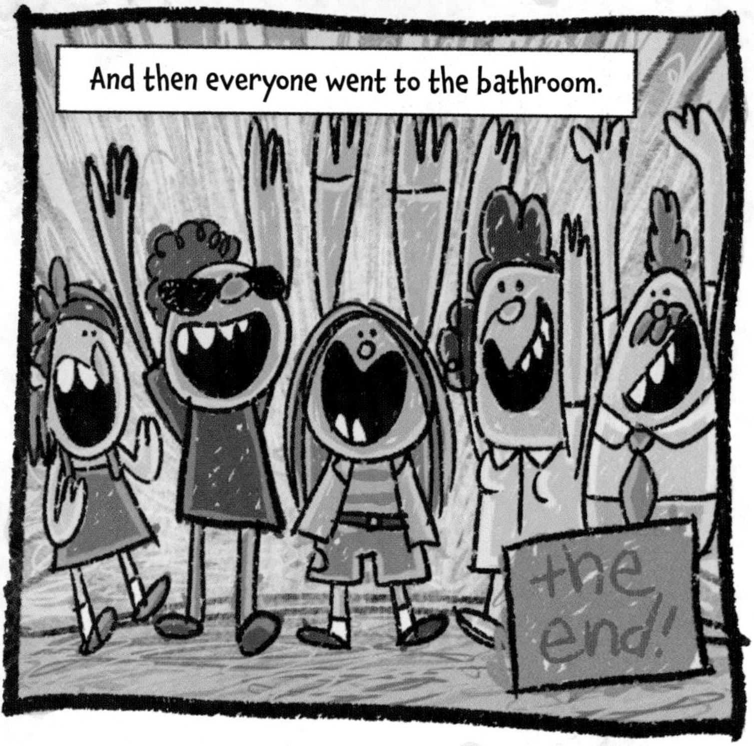
And then everyone went to the bathroom.
the end!

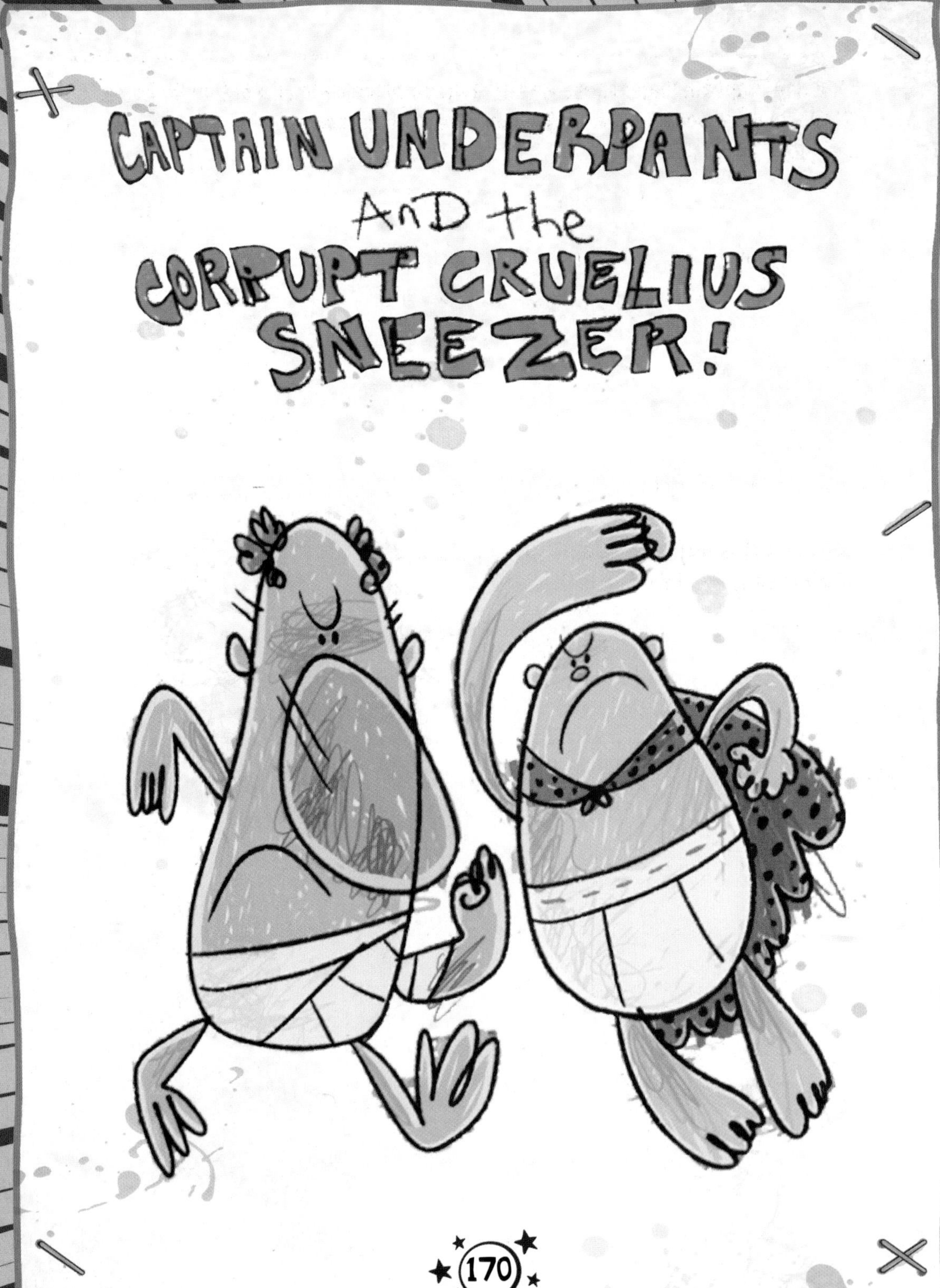
CAPTAIN UNDERPANTS
AnD the
CORRUPT CRUELIUS
SNEEZER!

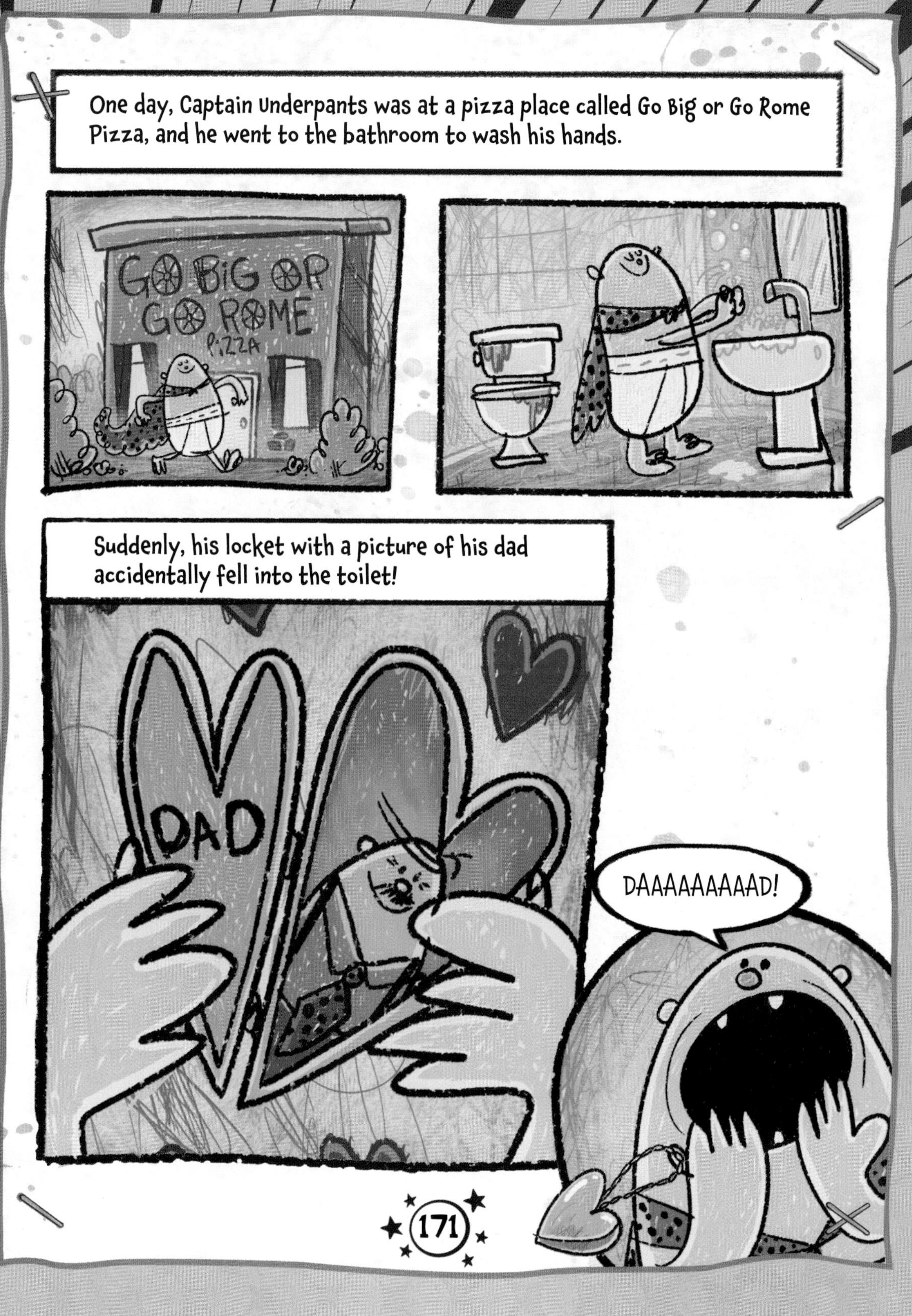
One day, Captain Underpants was at a pizza place called Go Big or Go Rome Pizza, and he went to the bathroom to wash his hands.
GO BIG OR GO ROME PIZZA
Suddenly, his locket with a picture of his dad accidentally fell into the toilet!
DAD
DAAAAAAAAAD!

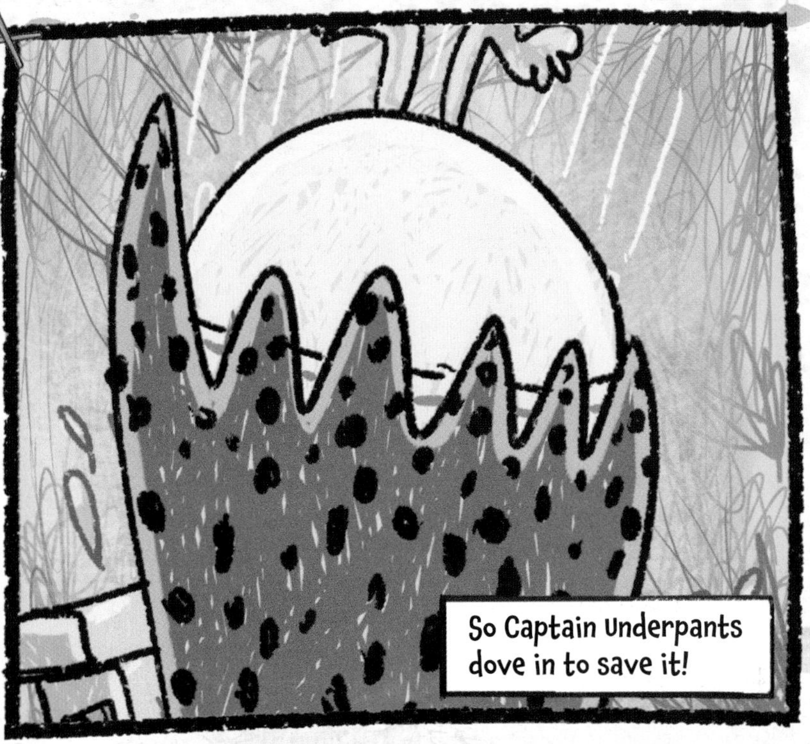
So Captain Underpants dove in to save it!

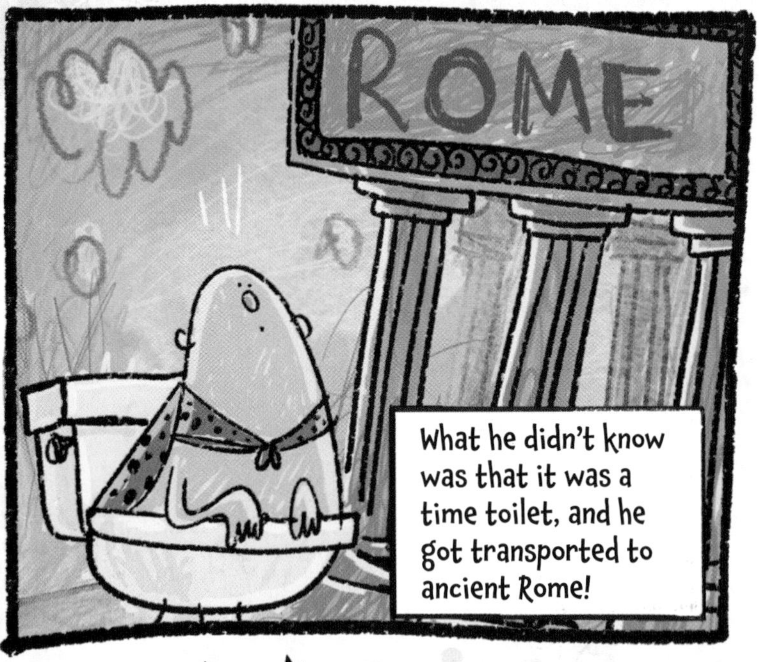
ROME
What he didn't know was that it was a time toilet, and he got transported to ancient Rome!

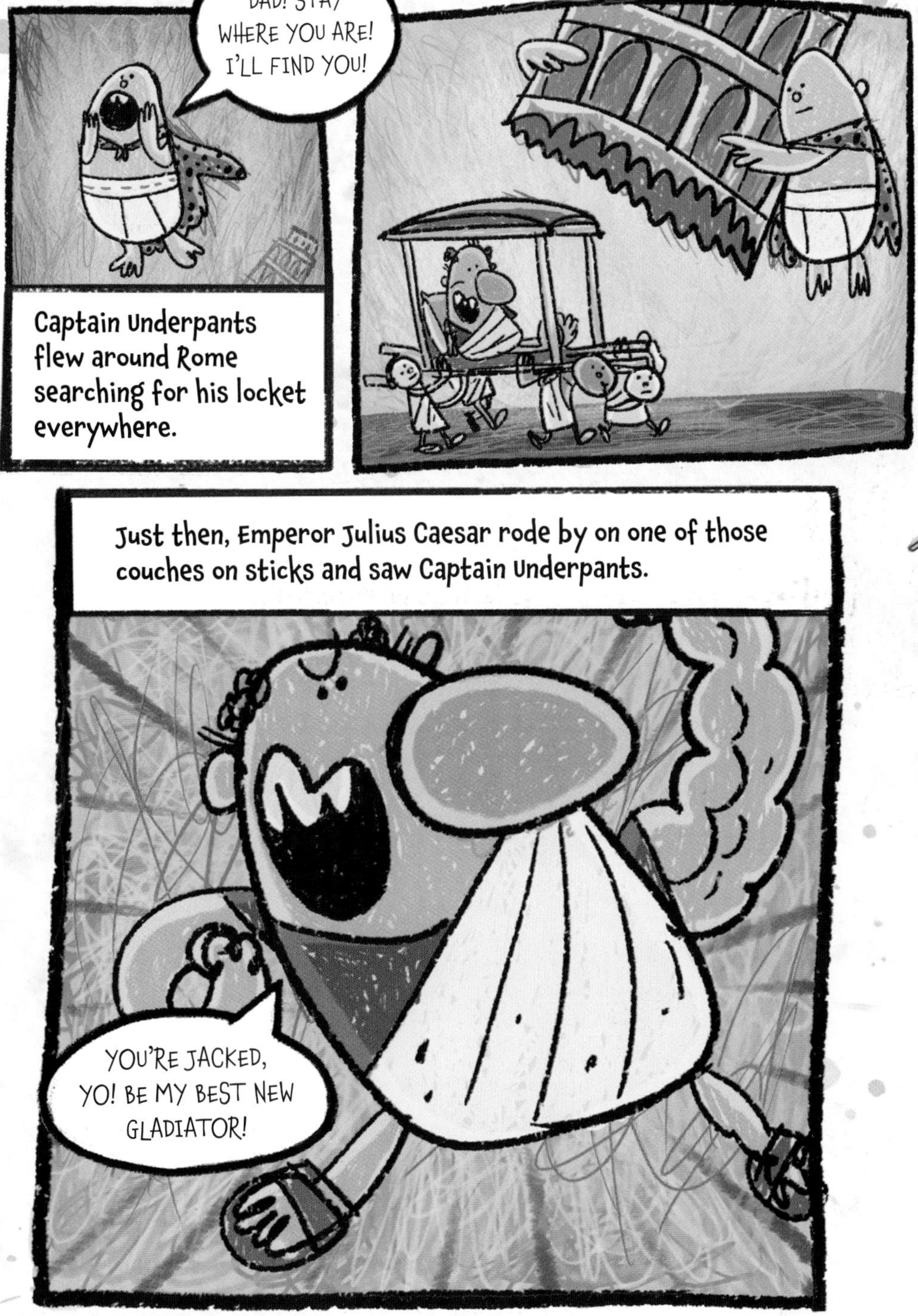
DAD! STAY WHERE YOU ARE! I'LL FIND YOU!
Captain Underpants flew around Rome searching for his locket everywhere.
Just then, Emperor Julius Caesar rode by on one of those couches on sticks and saw Captain Underpants.
YOU'RE JACKED, YO! BE MY BEST NEW GLADIATOR!

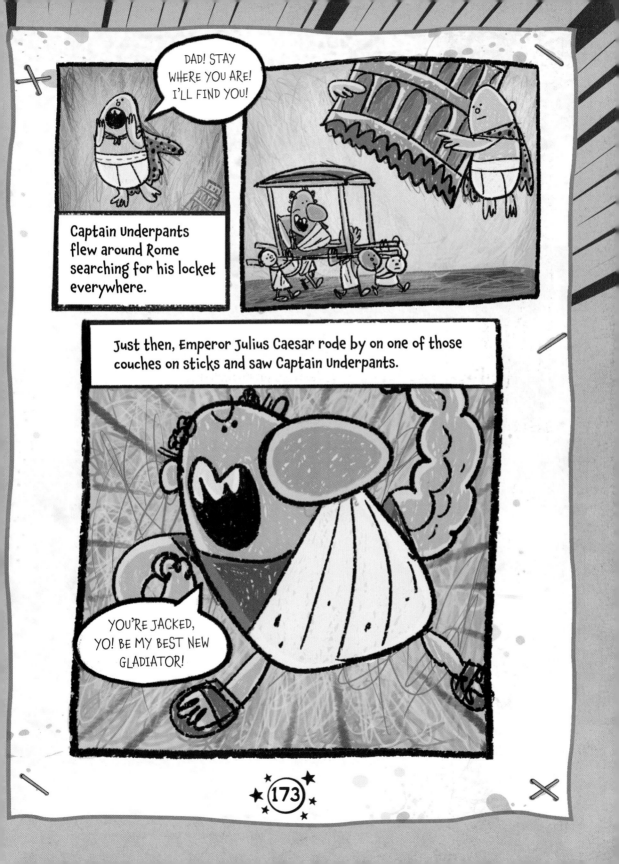

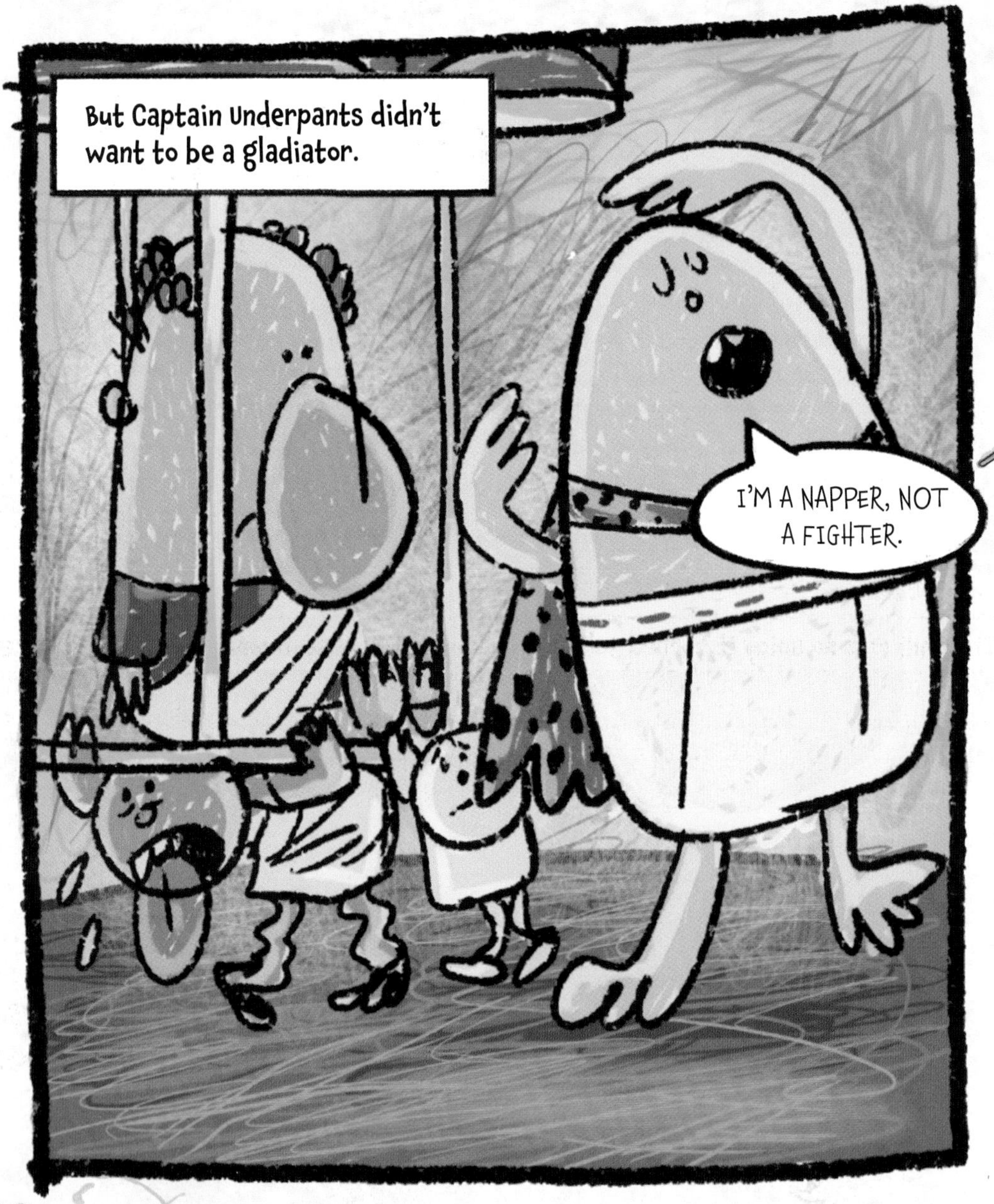
But Captain Underpants didn't want to be a gladiator.
I'M A NAPPER, NOT A FIGHTER.

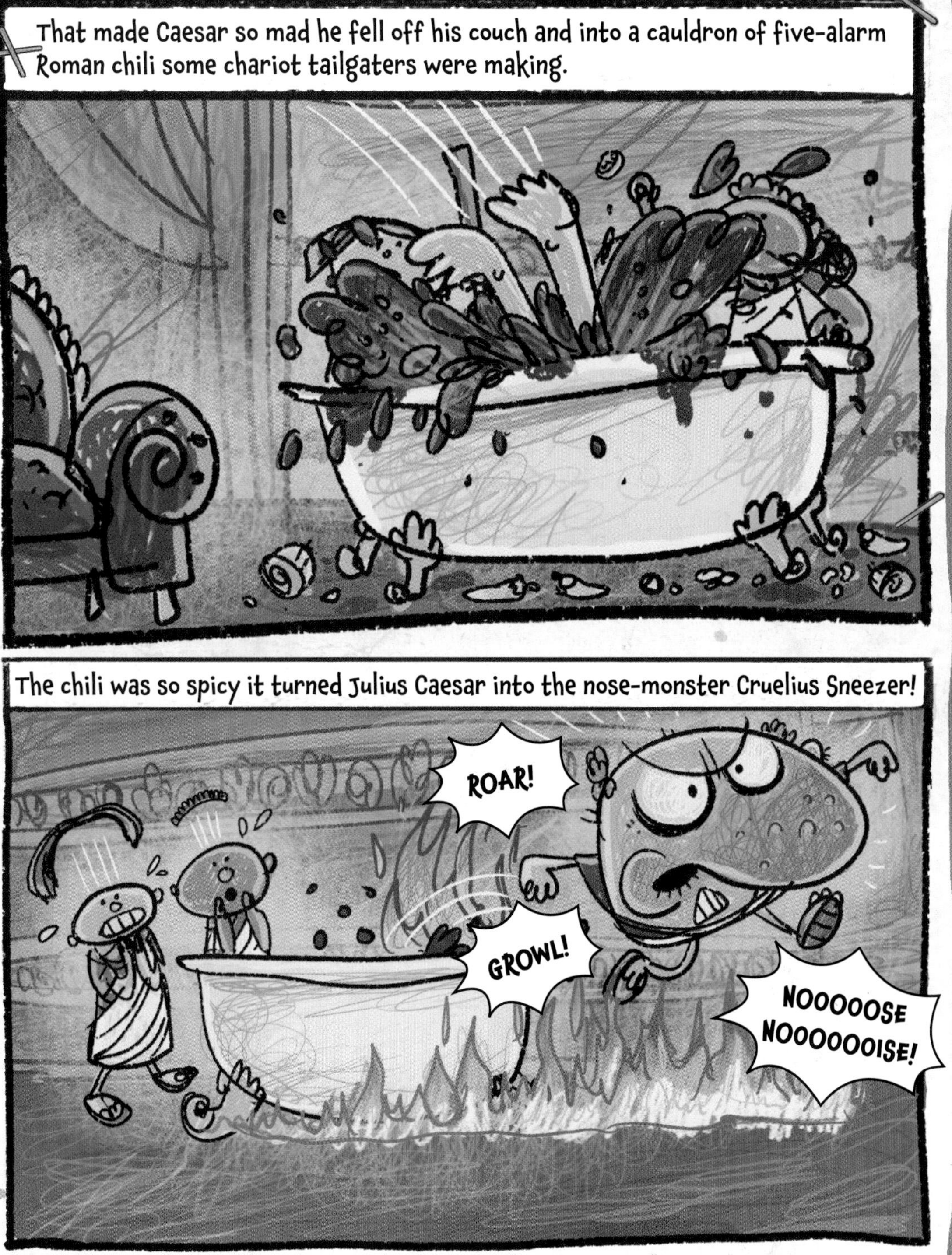
That made Caesar so mad he fell off his couch and into a cauldron of five-alarm Roman chili some chariot tailgaters were making.
The chili was so spicy it turned Julius Caesar into the nose-monster Cruelius Sneezer!
ROAR!
GROWL!
NOOOOOSE NOOOOOOISE!

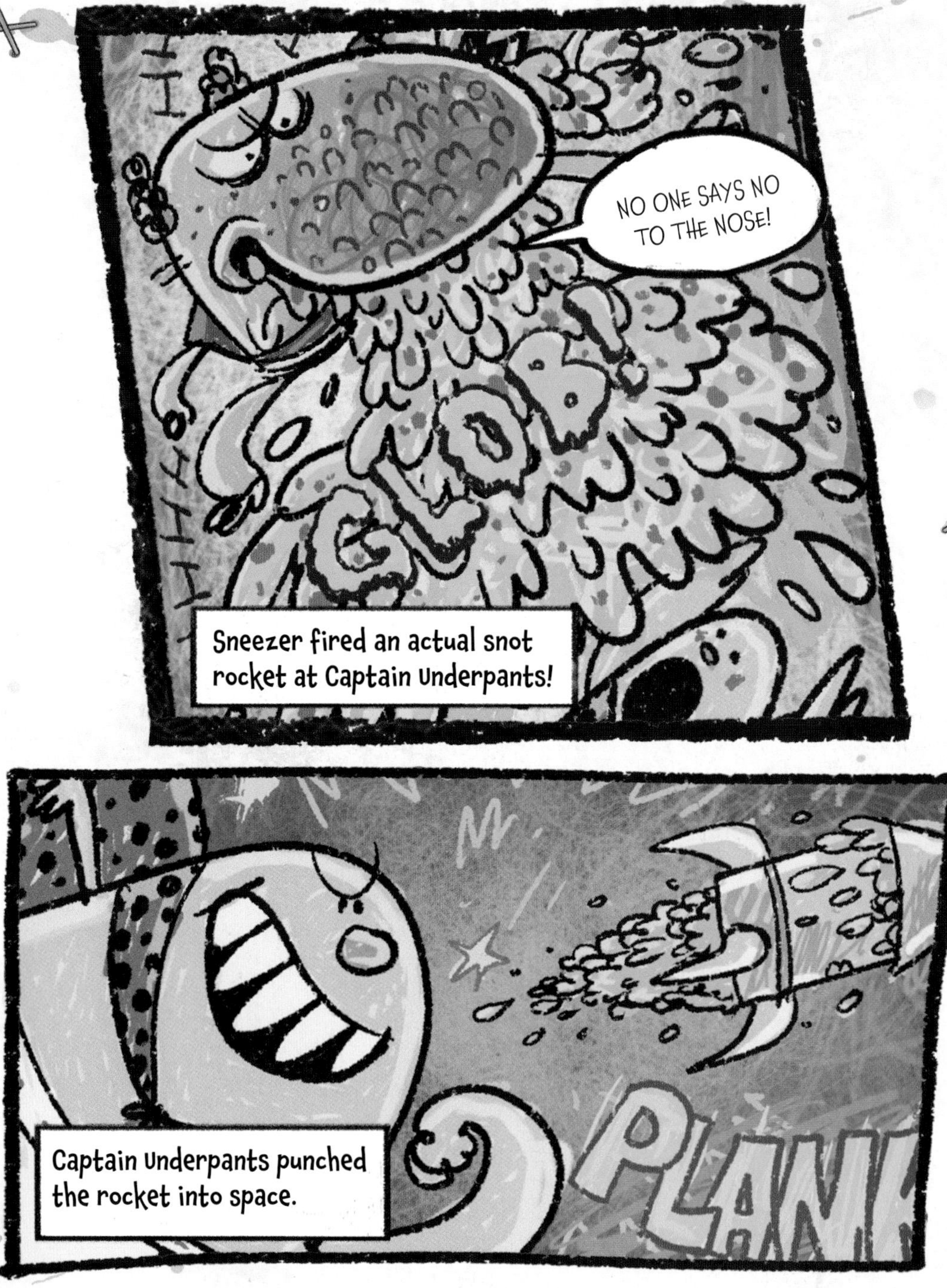
NO ONE SAYS NO TO THE NOSE!
Sneezer fired an actual snot rocket at Captain Underpants!
Captain Underpants punched the rocket into space.

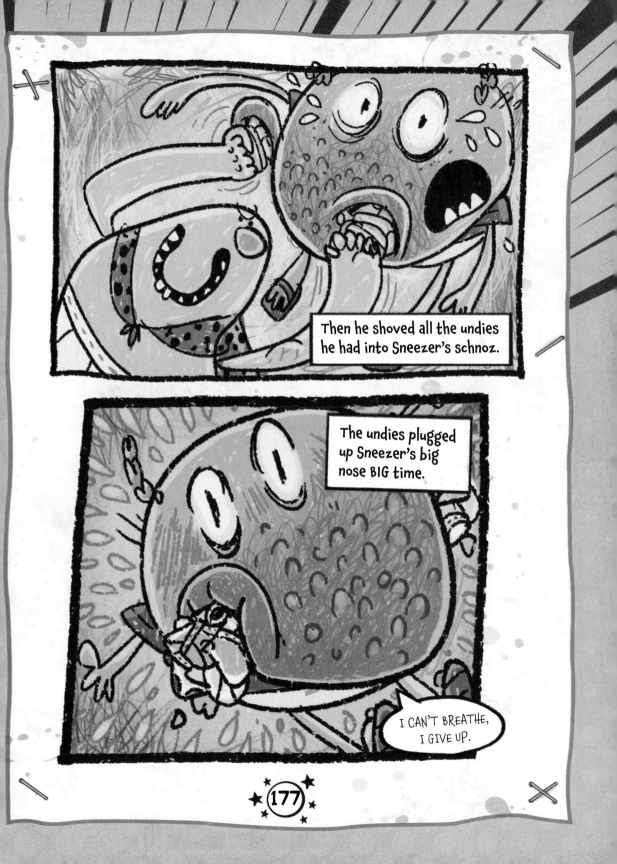

Then he shoved all the undies he had into Sneezer's schnoz.

The undies plugged up Sneezer's big nose BIG time.

I CAN'T BREATHE, I GIVE UP.

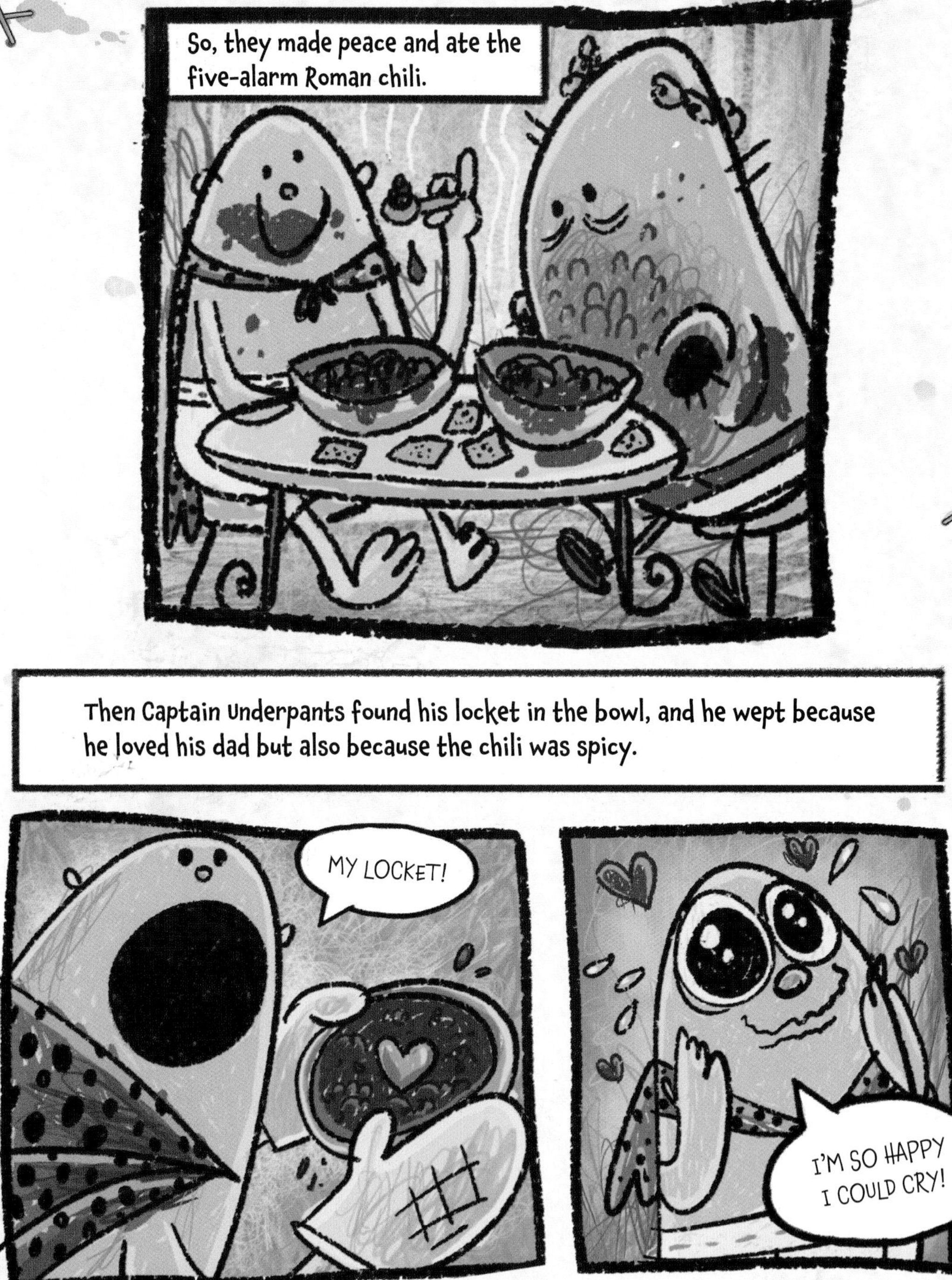
So, they made peace and ate the five-alarm Roman chili.
Then Captain Underpants found his locket in the bowl, and he wept because he loved his dad but also because the chili was spicy.
MY LOCKET!
I'M SO HAPPY I COULD CRY!

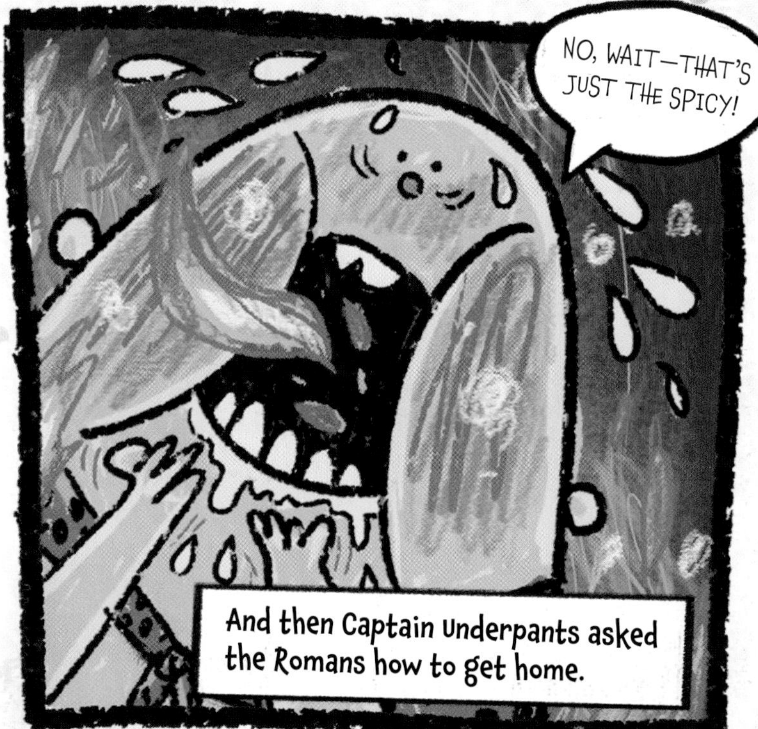

NO, WAIT—THAT'S JUST THE SPICY!
And then Captain Underpants asked the Romans how to get home.

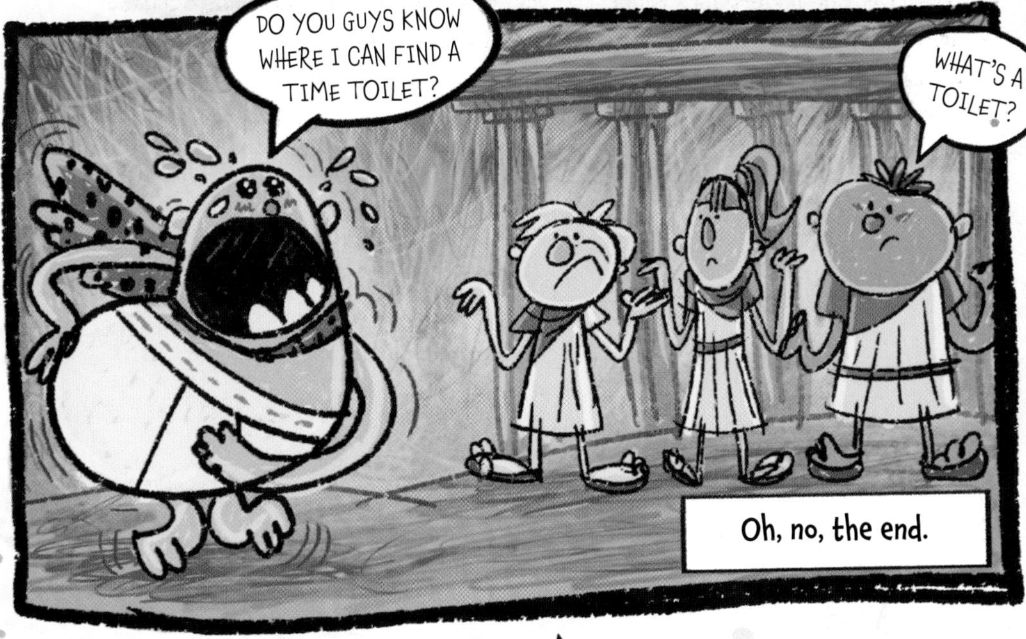

DO YOU GUYS KNOW WHERE I CAN FIND A TIME TOILET?
WHAT'S A TOILET?
Oh, no, the end.

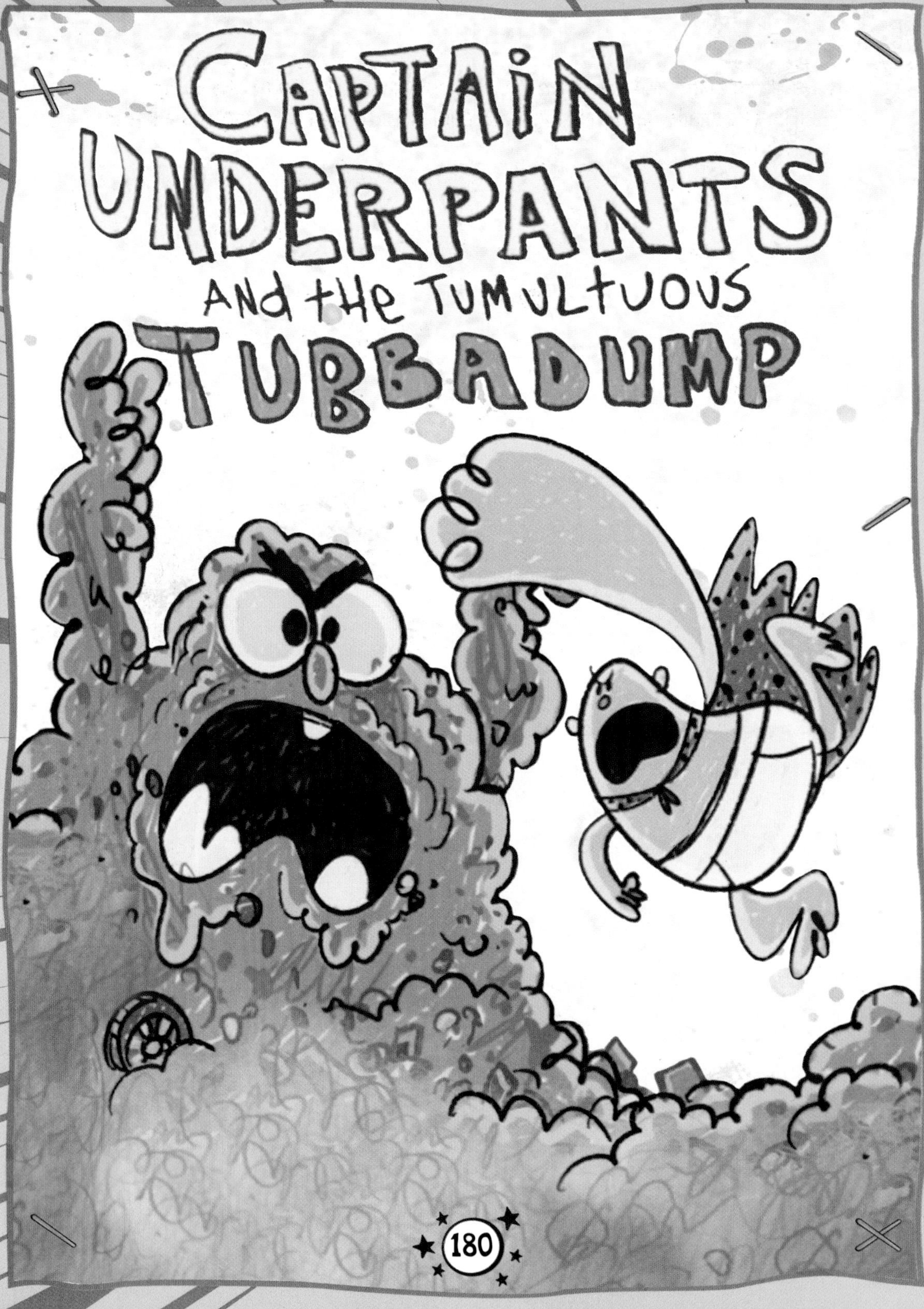
CAPTAIN UNDERPANTS
AND THE TUMULTUOUS
TUBBADUMP

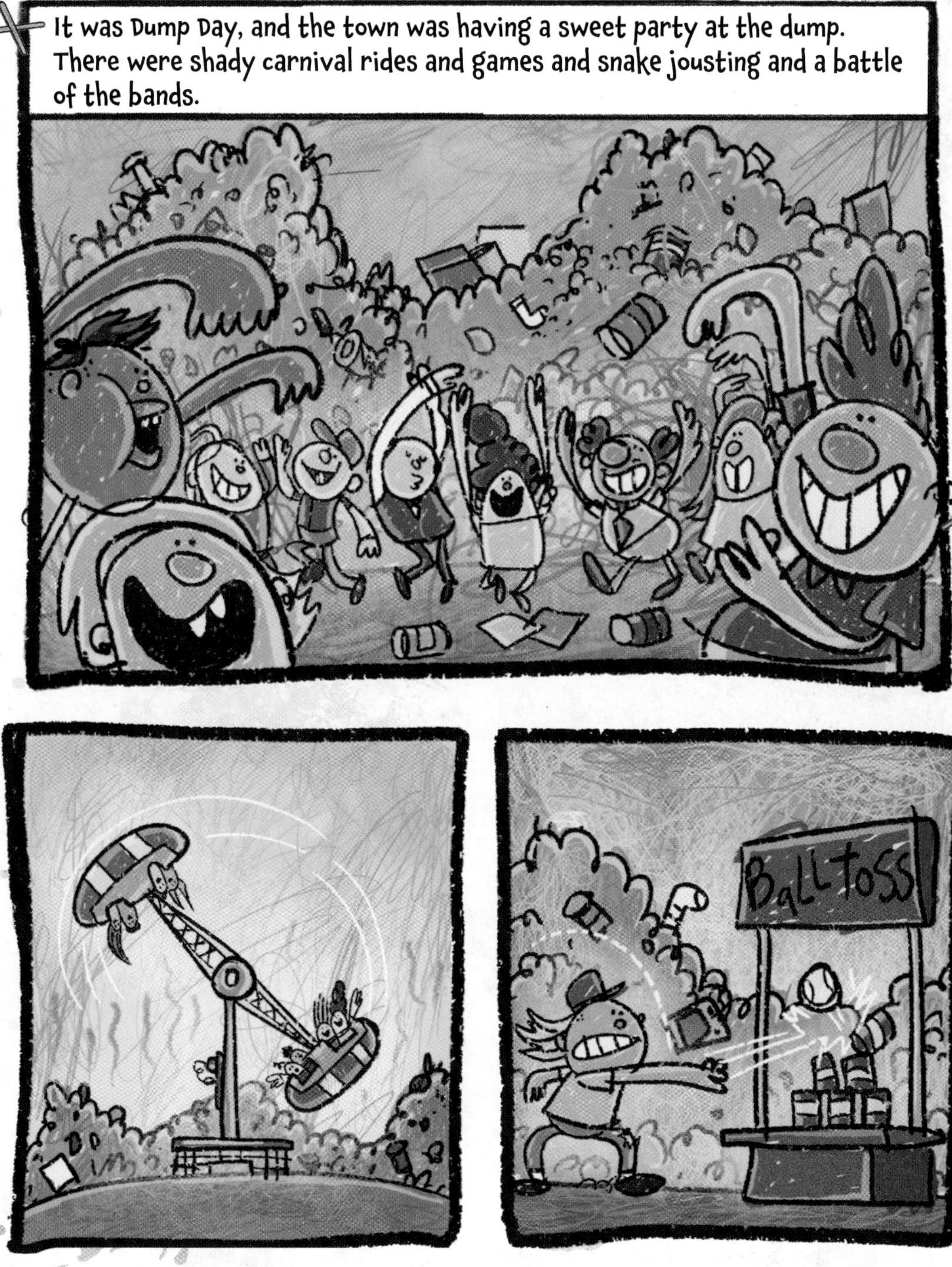
It was Dump Day, and the town was having a sweet party at the dump. There were shady carnival rides and games and snake jousting and a battle of the bands.
BaLL toss

It was a blast and loud enough to raise the dead, which it did, because Horatio Dump's final resting place was at the dump. And his ghost woke up!

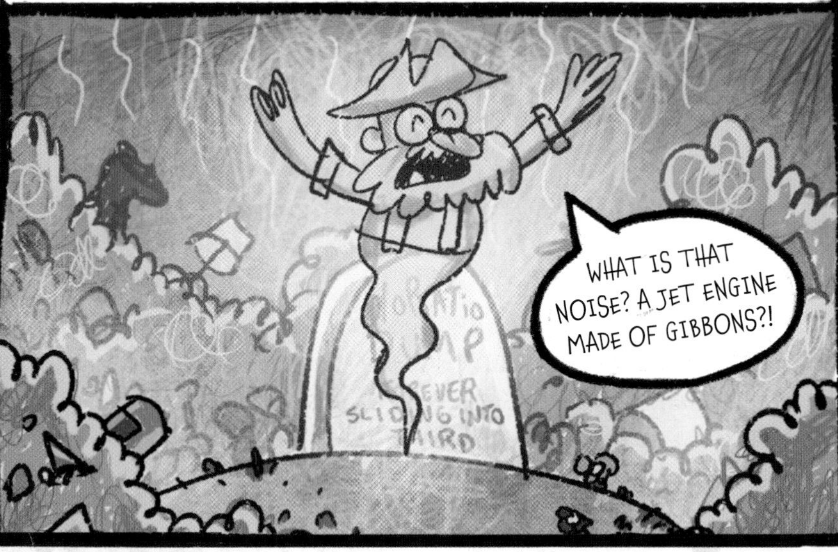
WHAT IS THAT NOISE? A JET ENGINE MADE OF GIBBONS?!

And he saw people eating caramel burgers and garbage skiing and arm-wrestling rats, and that made him angry.

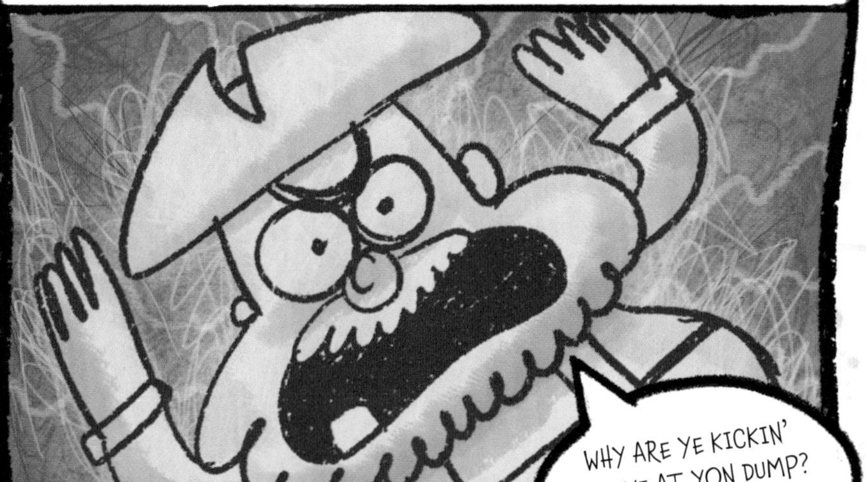
WHY ARE YE KICKIN' IT LIVE AT YON DUMP? TIS FOR TRASH, NOT PARTIES!

He asked the people to take the noise down a notch. And what did they say?

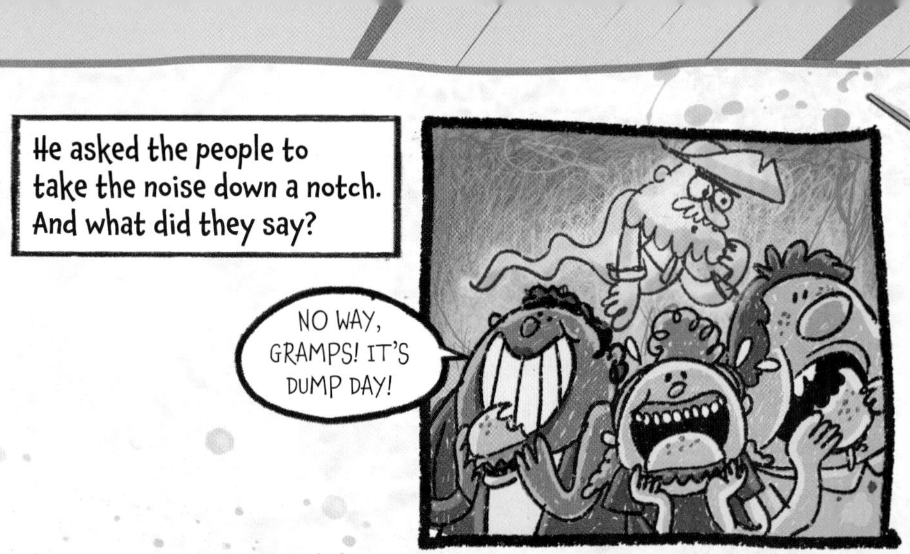
NO WAY, GRAMPS! IT'S DUMP DAY!

So Horatio raised his ghost arms and trash-piled onto him until he was a huge trash monster! And he started using his trash fists to throw trash everywhere!

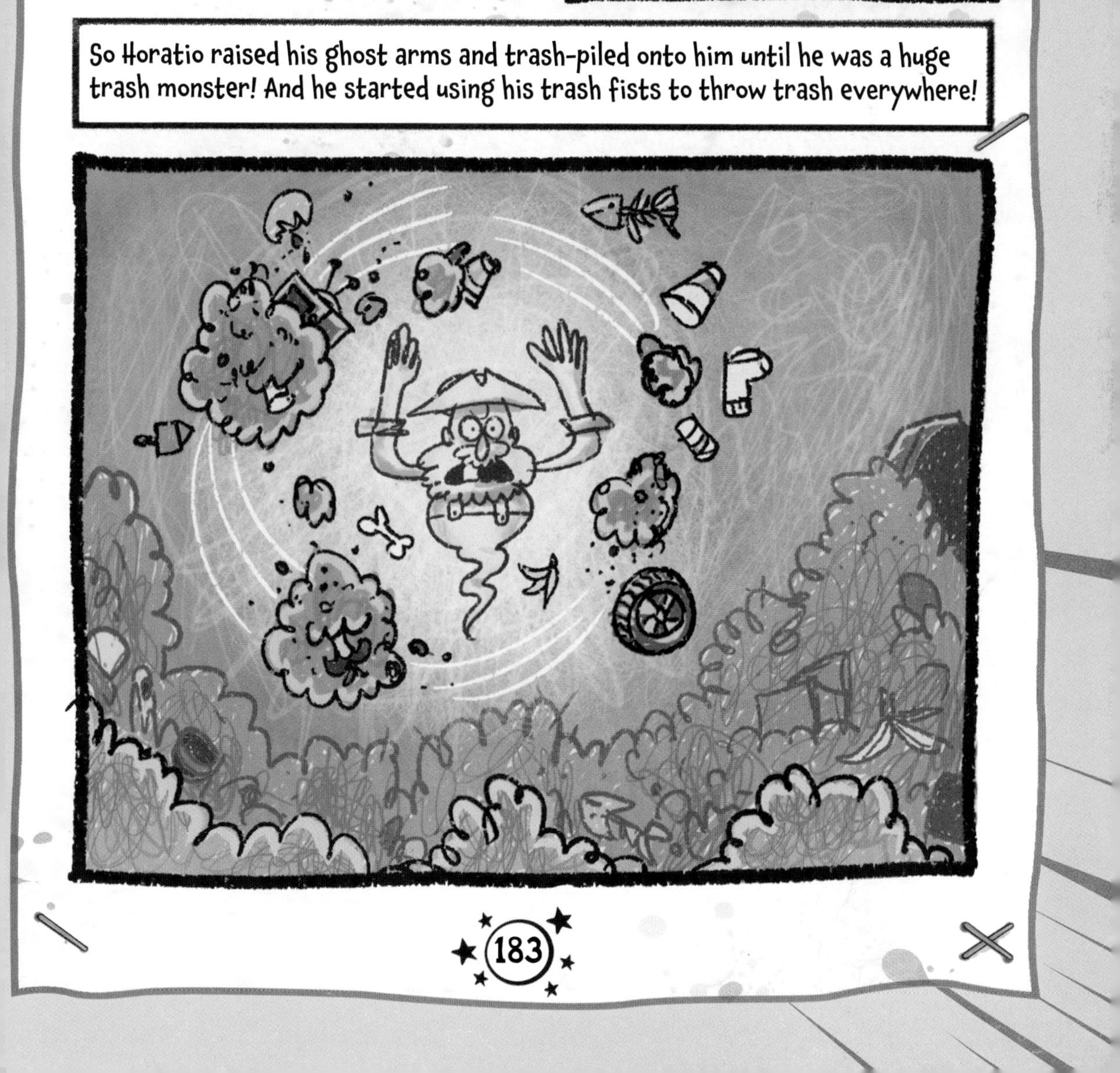

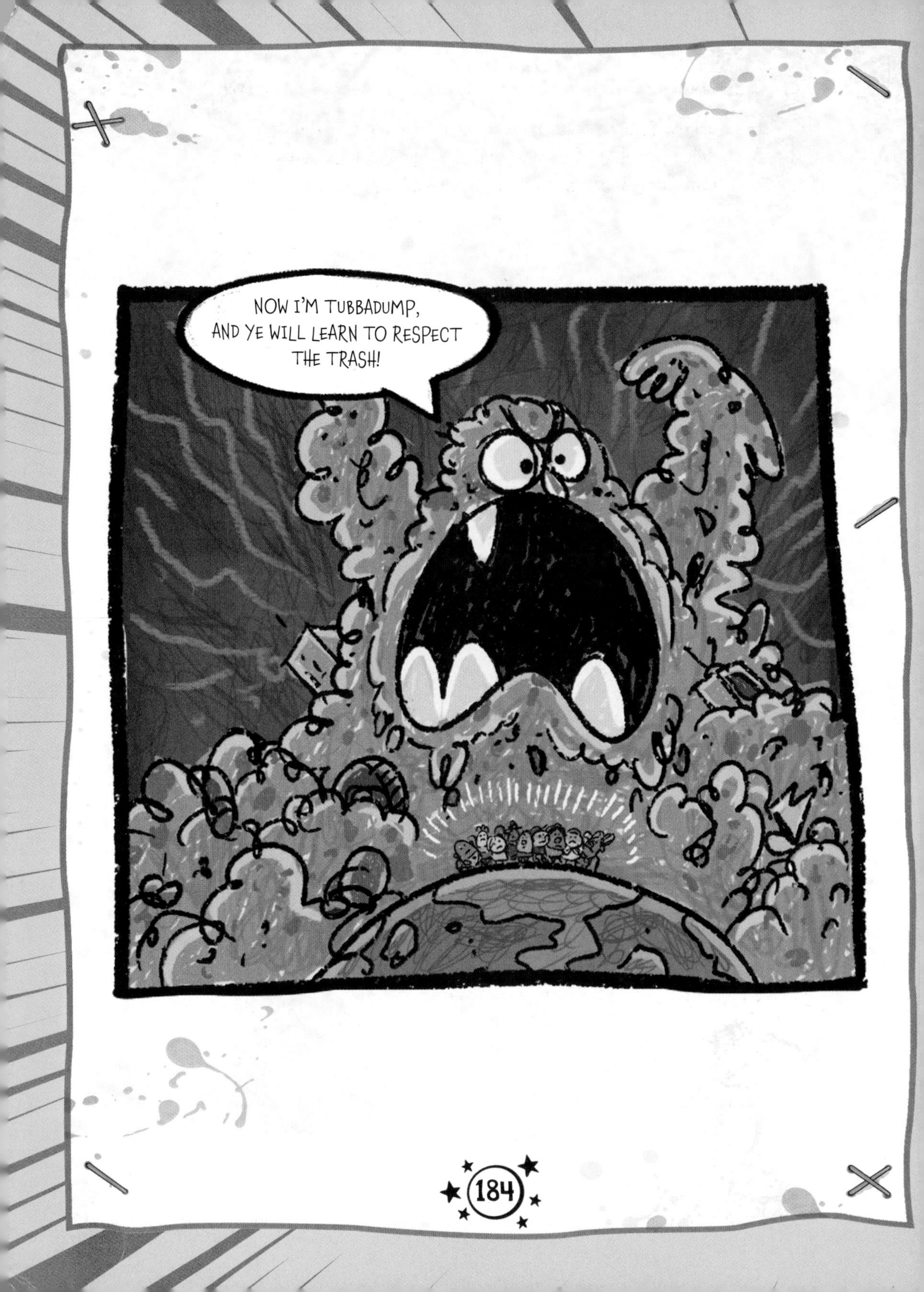
NOW I'M TUBBADUMP, AND YE WILL LEARN TO RESPECT THE TRASH!

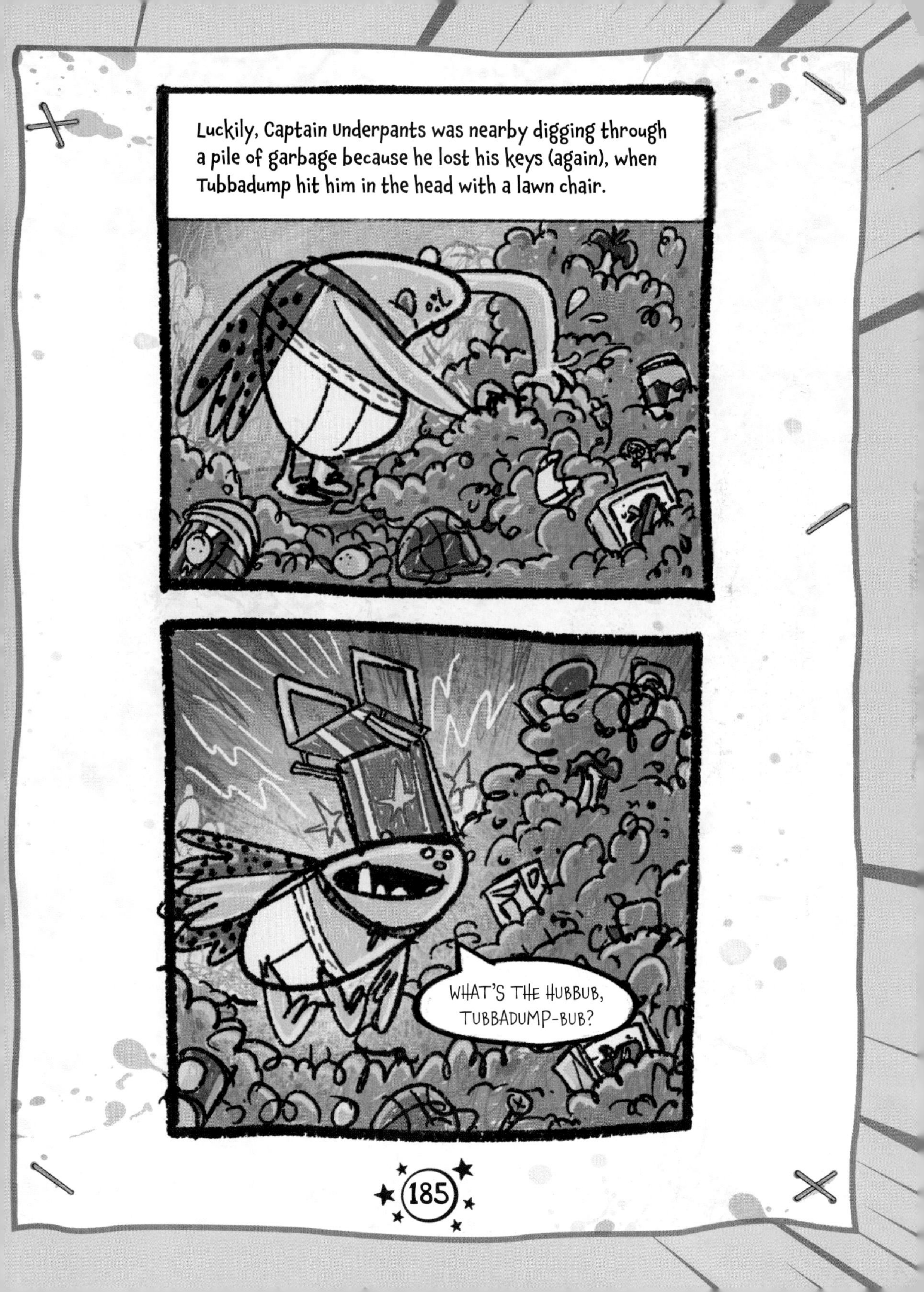
Luckily, Captain Underpants was nearby digging through a pile of garbage because he lost his keys (again), when Tubbadump hit him in the head with a lawn chair.
WHAT'S THE HUBBUB, TUBBADUMP-BUB?

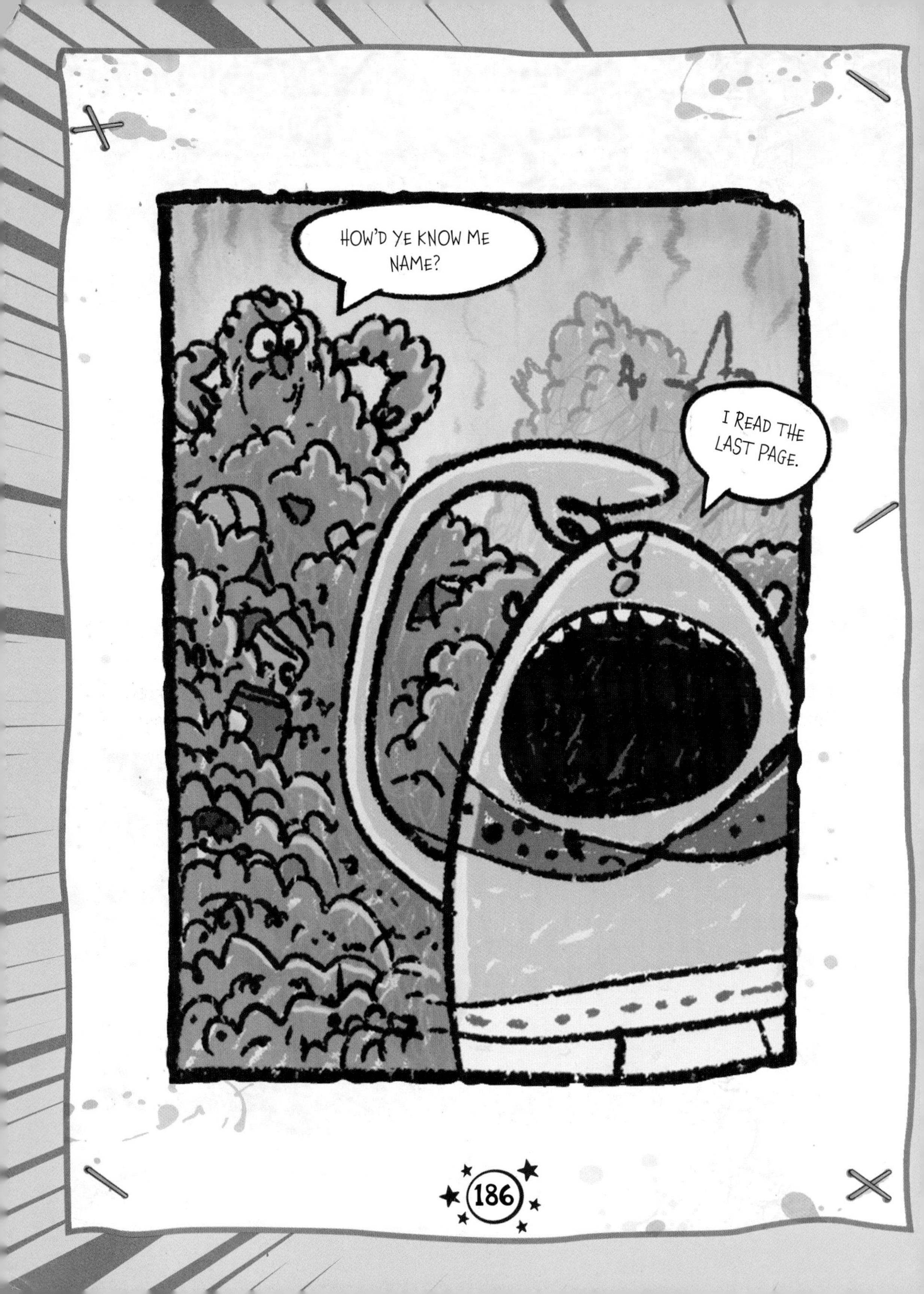
HOW'D YE KNOW ME NAME?
I READ THE LAST PAGE.

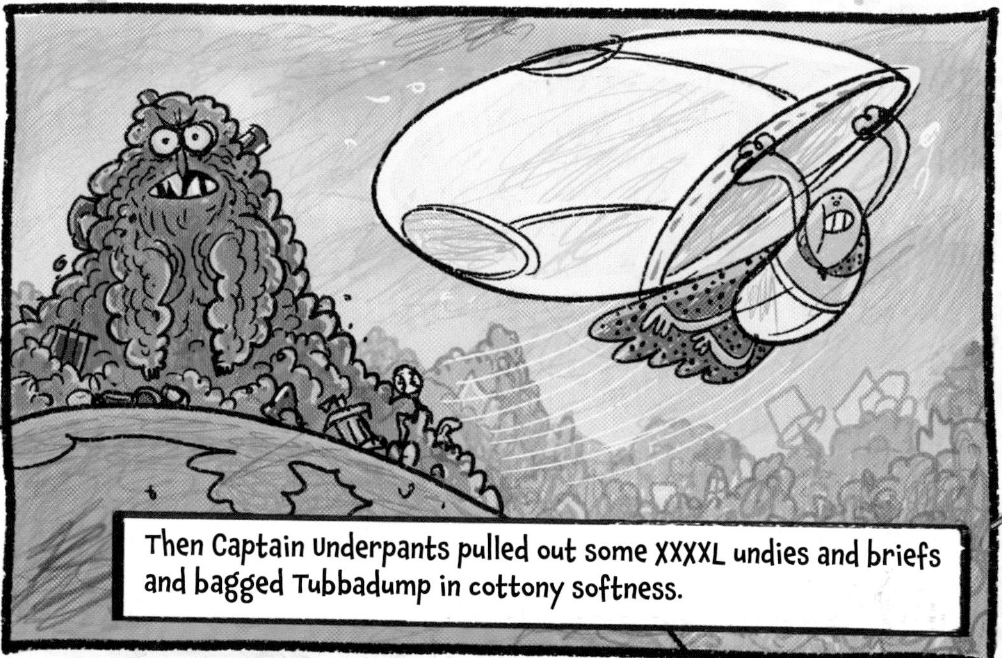
Then Captain Underpants pulled out some XXXXL undies and briefs and bagged Tubbadump in cottony softness.

But Tubbadump broke free because trash is sharp so you need to double brief. Then Captain Underpants saw a teetering trash mountain behind Tubbadump.

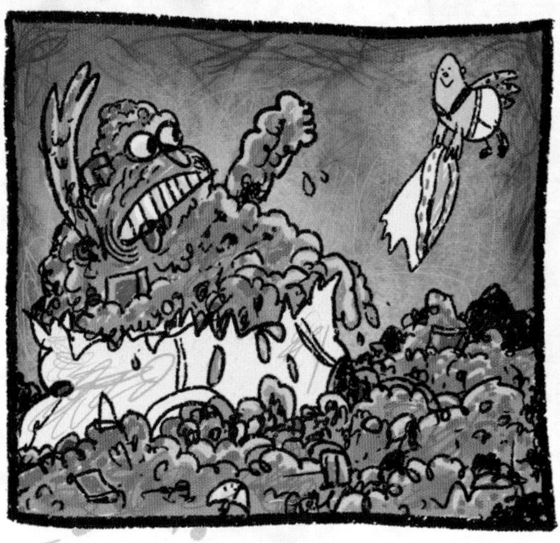

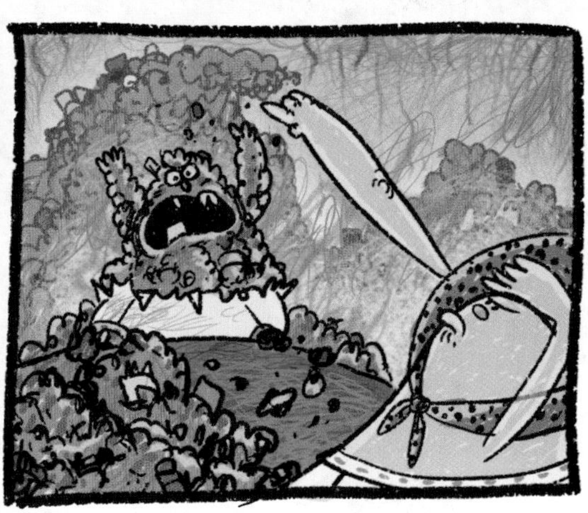

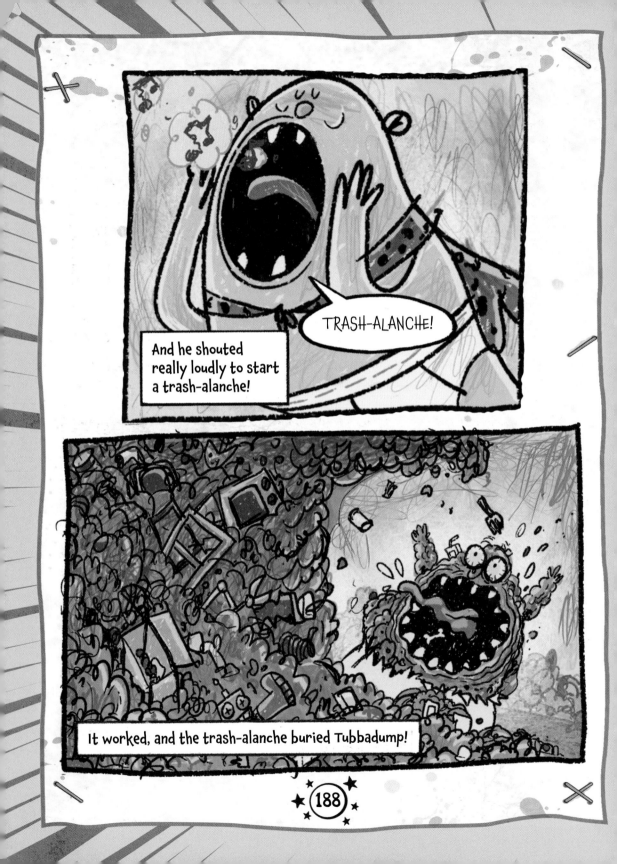

TRASH-ALANCHE!

And he shouted really loudly to start a trash-alanche!

It worked, and the trash-alanche buried Tubbadump!

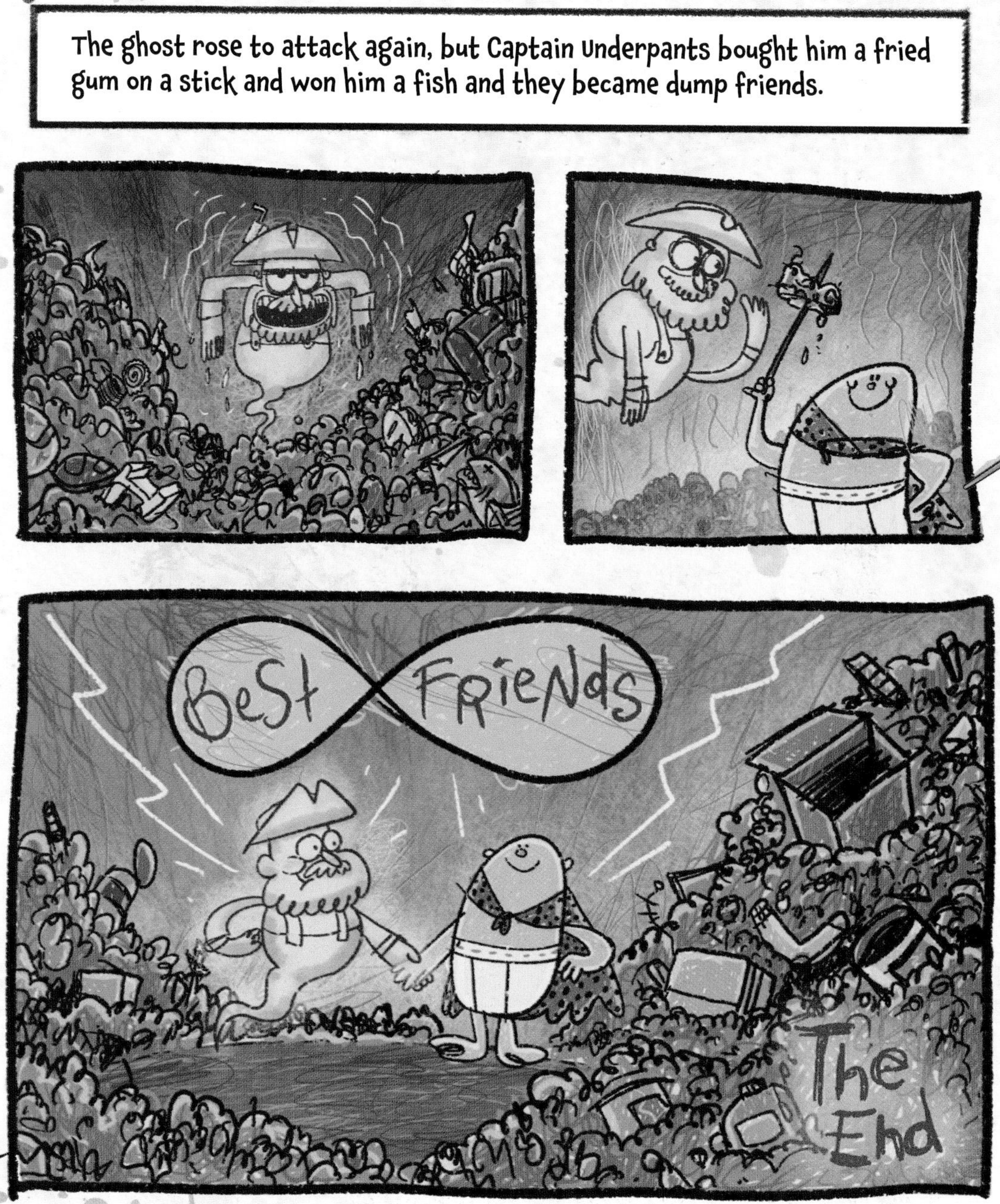
The ghost rose to attack again, but Captain Underpants bought him a fried gum on a stick and won him a fish and they became dump friends.
Best Friends
The End

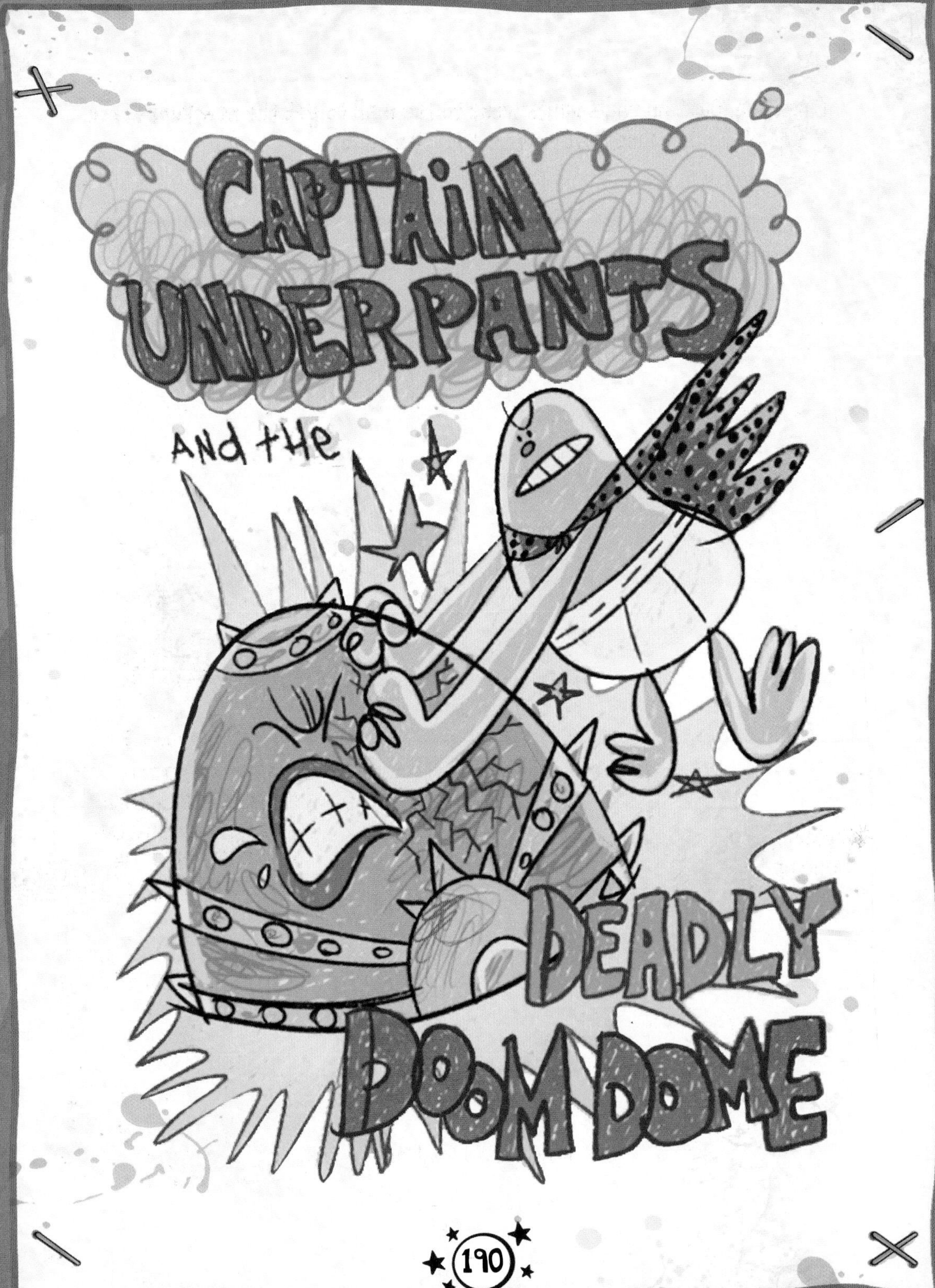
CAPTAIN UNDERPANTS
and the
DEADLY DOOM DOME

One time, Captain Underpants went to the mall to get the new Punt Force Mama album because that was his favorite band.

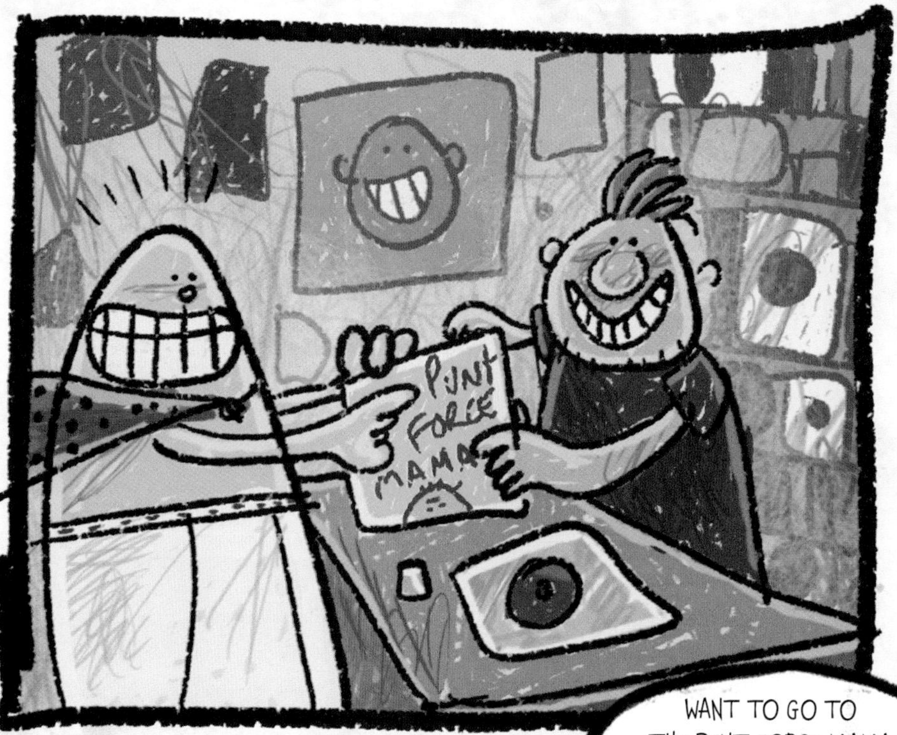
PUNT FORCE MAMA

Suddenly, this cool dude with a sweet mustache came up to him.

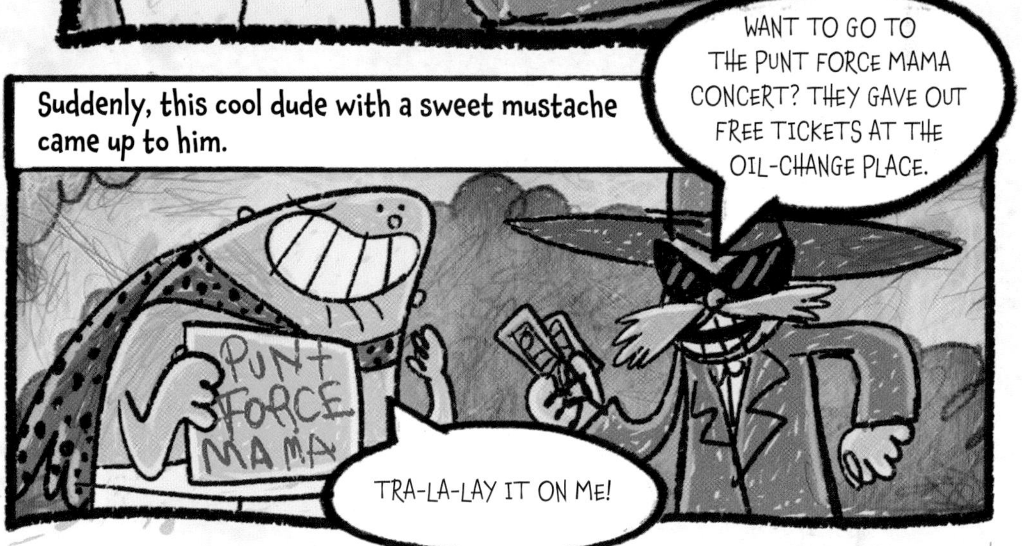
WANT TO GO TO THE PUNT FORCE MAMA CONCERT? THEY GAVE OUT FREE TICKETS AT THE OIL-CHANGE PLACE.
PUNT FORCE MAMA
TRA-LA-LAY IT ON ME!

So they went to the new ThisIsn'tATrap Dome, which sounds suspicious, but nobody noticed because they were so psyched for the sweet concert.

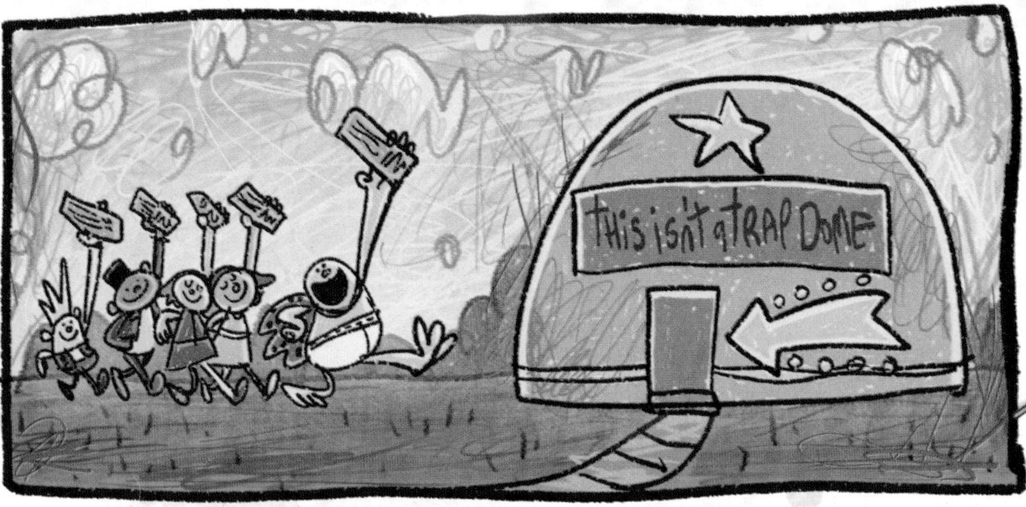
THIS isn't a TRAP DOME

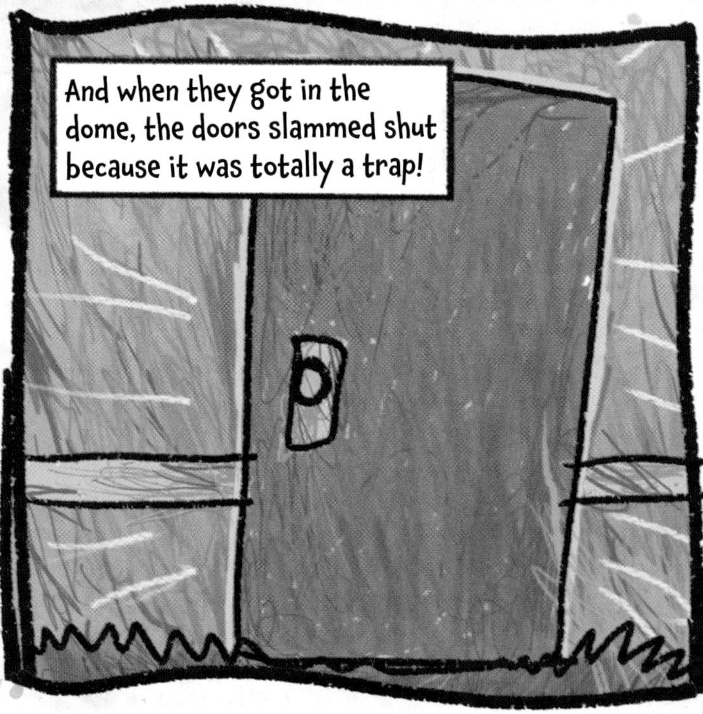
And when they got in the dome, the doors slammed shut because it was totally a trap!

And the cool dude turned into Dr. Disgruntled, a cranky villain who built a doom dome to be evil.

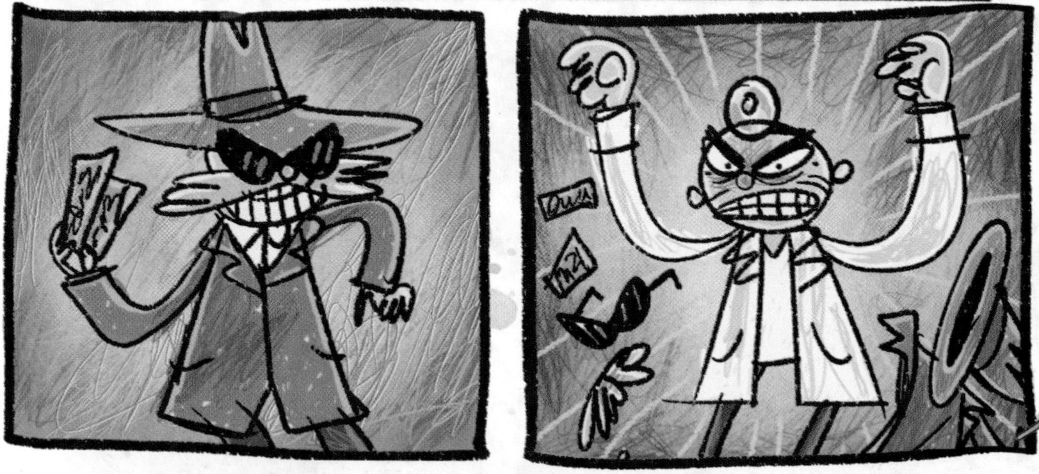

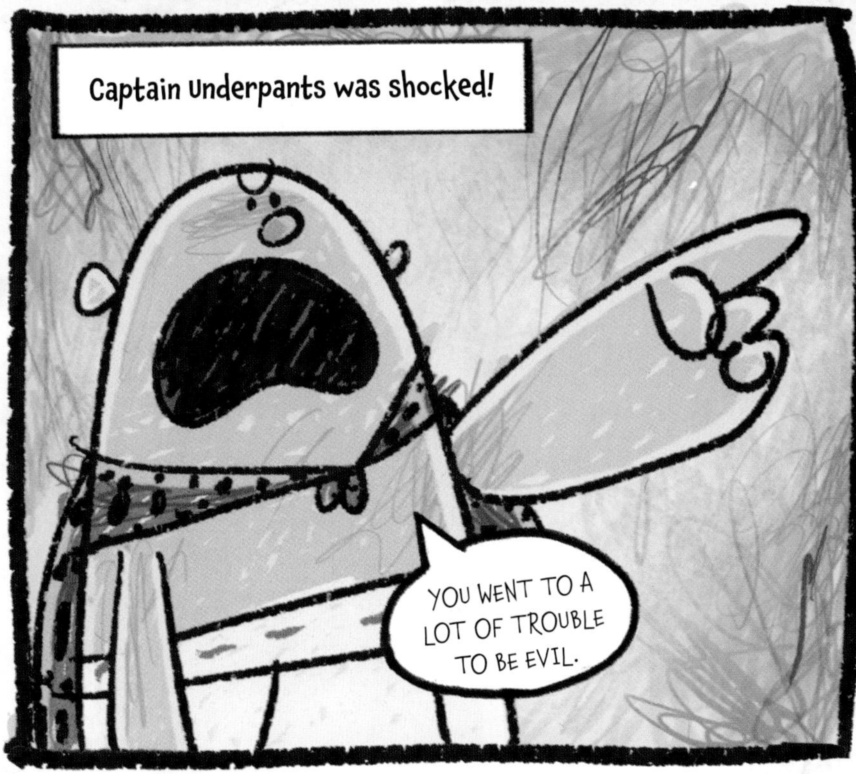
Captain Underpants was shocked!
YOU WENT TO A LOT OF TROUBLE TO BE EVIL.

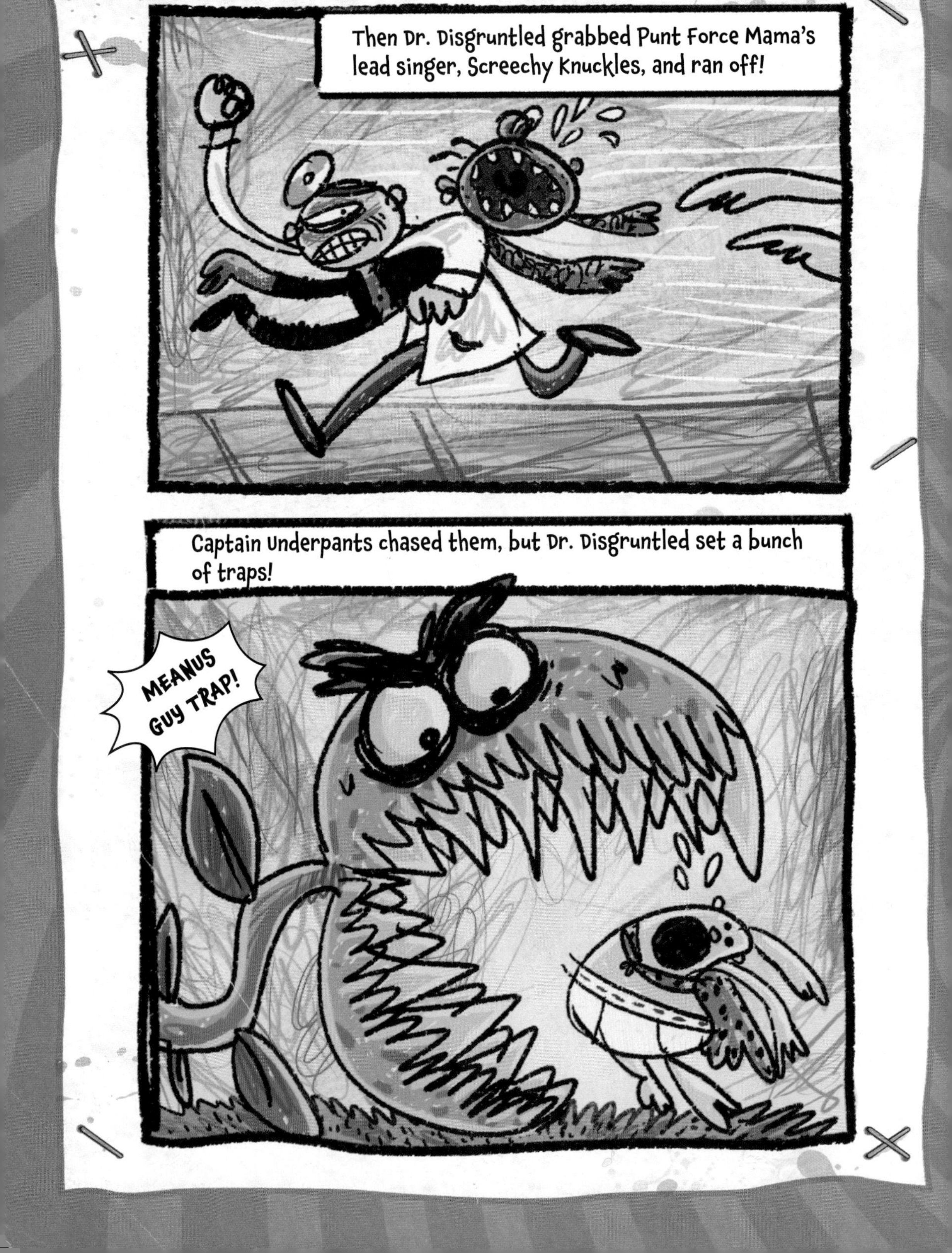
Then Dr. Disgruntled grabbed Punt Force Mama's lead singer, Screechy Knuckles, and ran off!
Captain Underpants chased them, but Dr. Disgruntled set a bunch of traps!
MEANUS GUY TRAP!

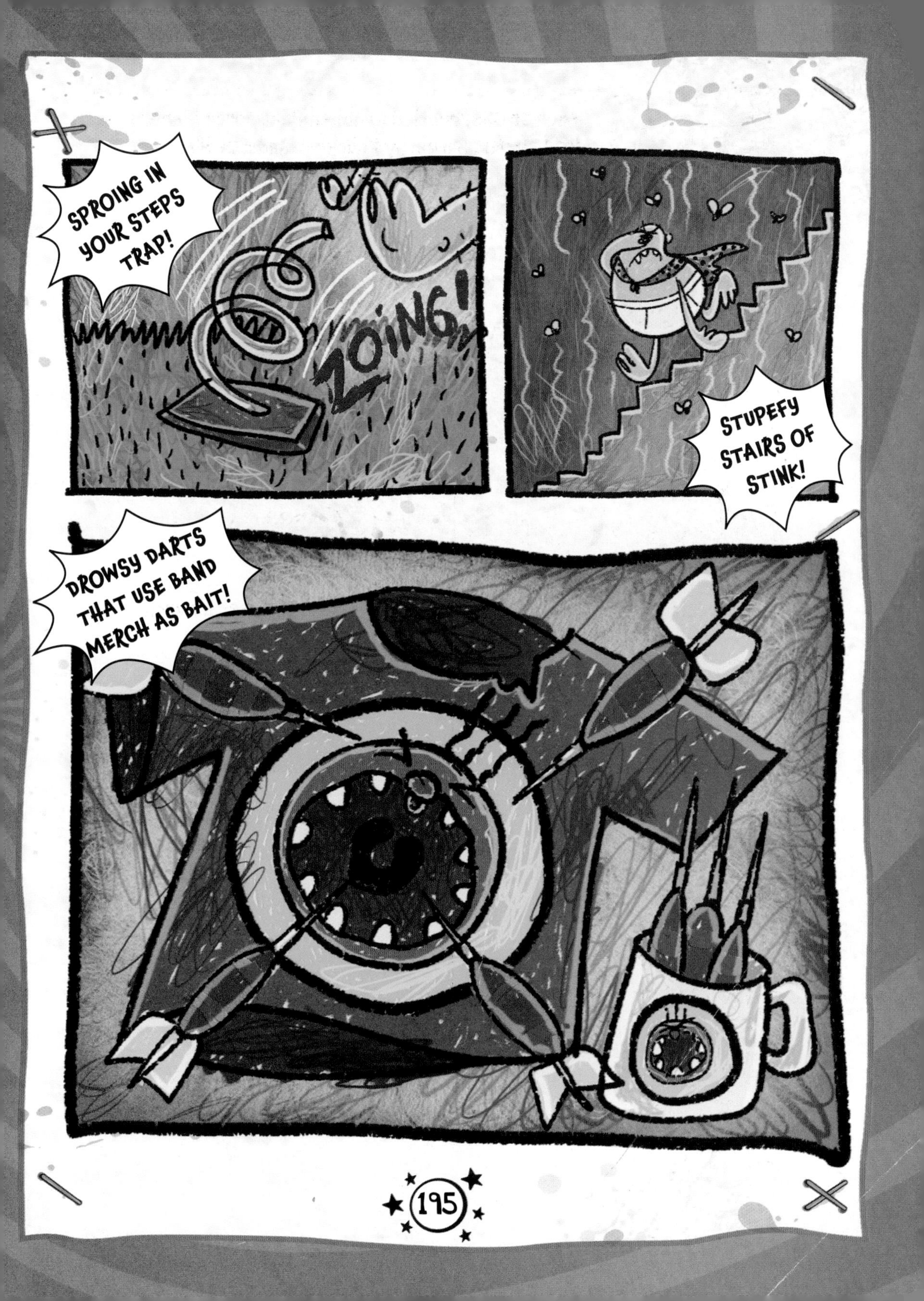
SPROING IN YOUR STEPS TRAP!
ZOING!
STUPEFY STAIRS OF STINK!
DROWSY DARTS THAT USE BAND MERCH AS BAIT!

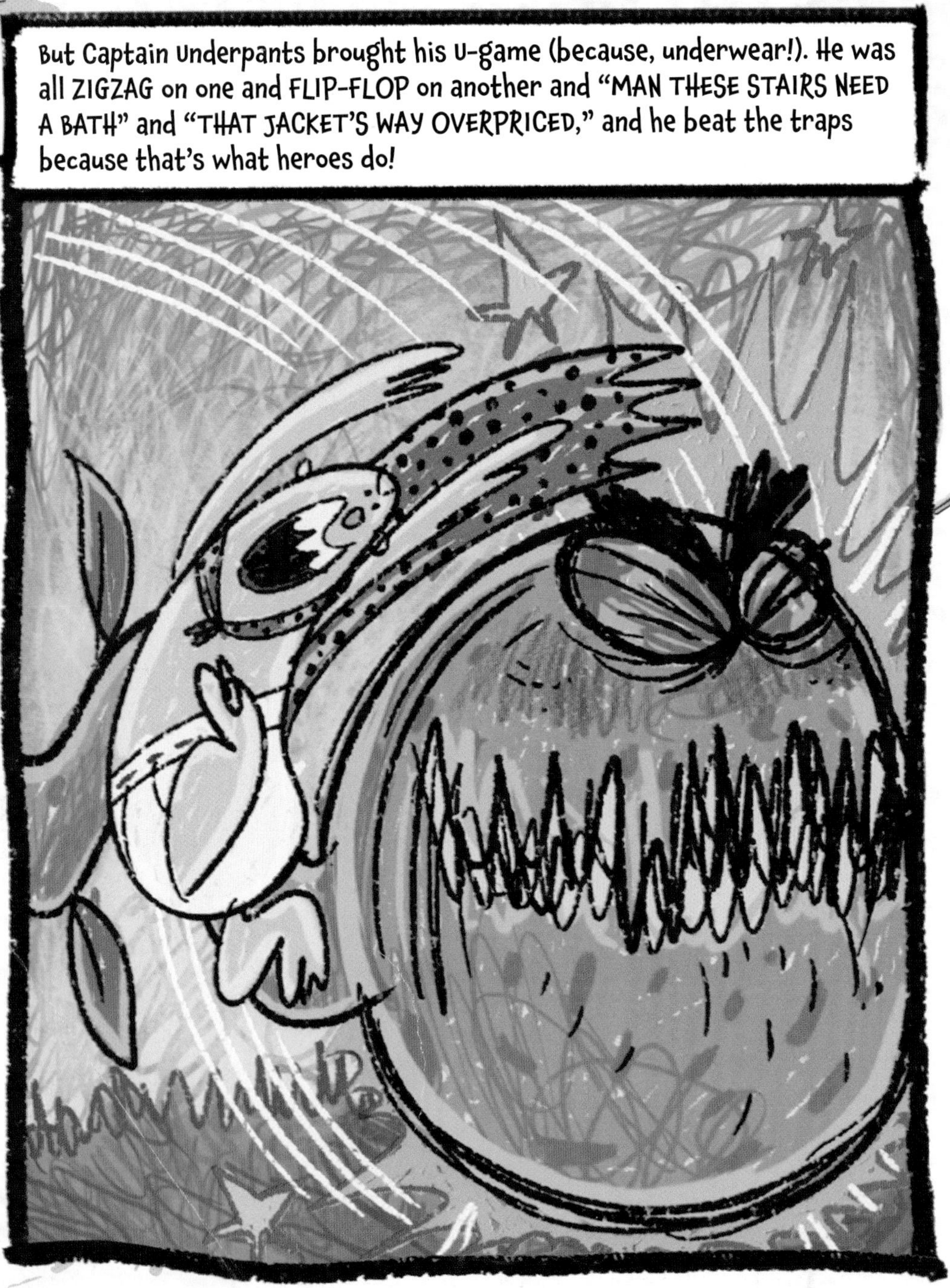
But Captain Underpants brought his U-game (because, underwear!). He was all ZIGZAG on one and FLIP-FLOP on another and "MAN THESE STAIRS NEED A BATH" and "THAT JACKET'S WAY OVERPRICED," and he beat the traps because that's what heroes do!

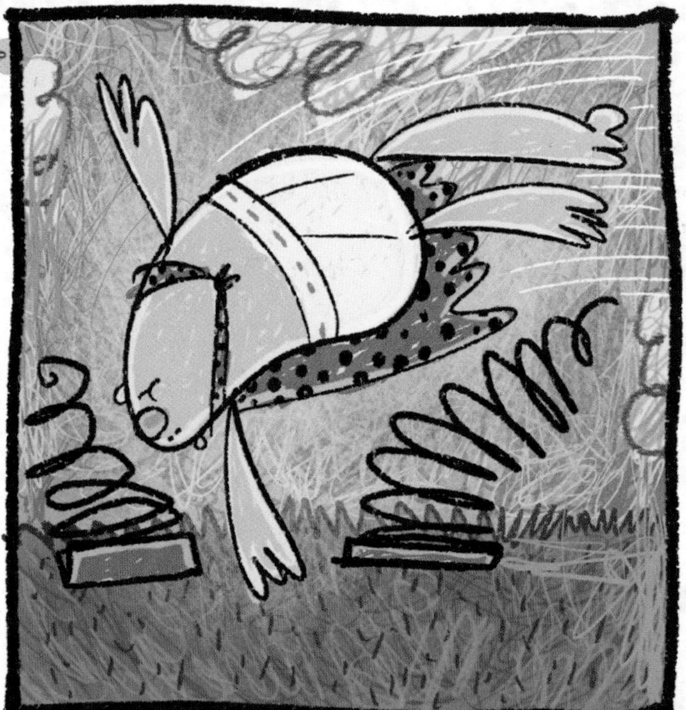

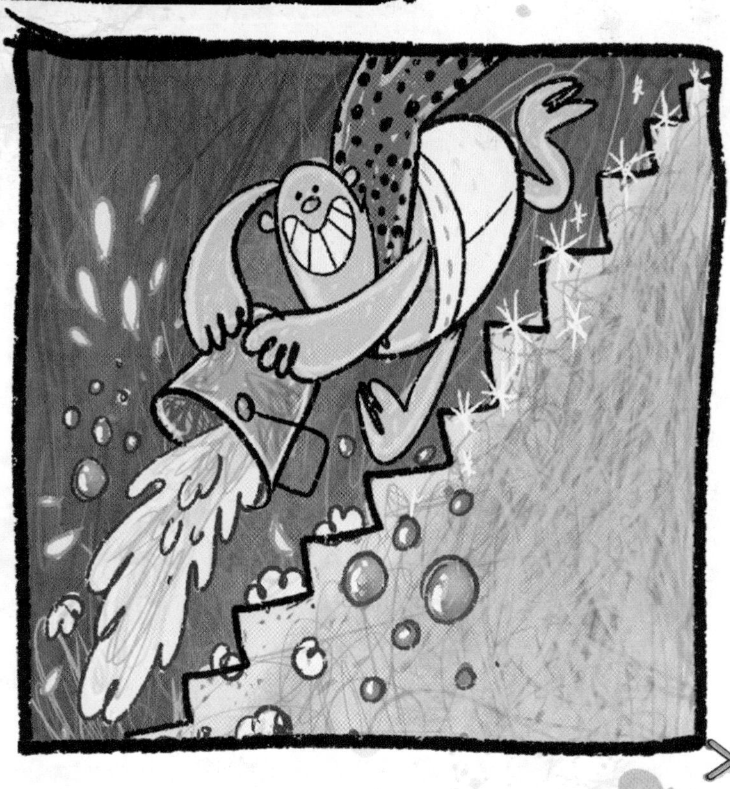

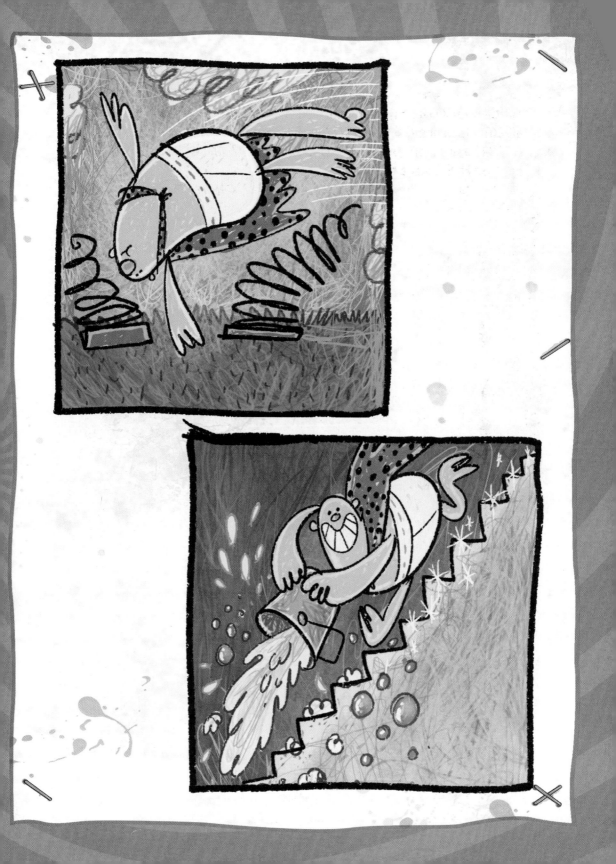

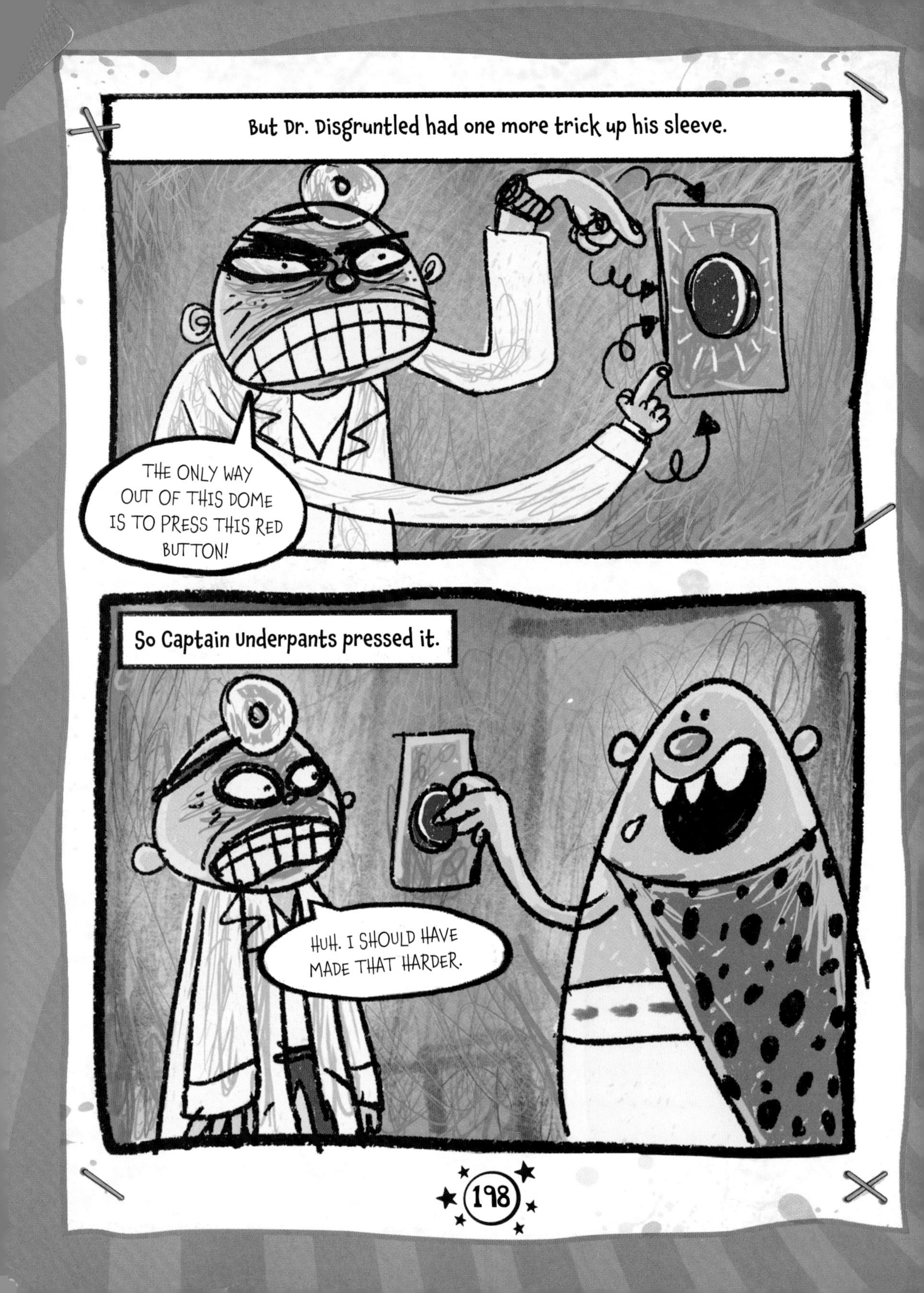

But Dr. Disgruntled had one more trick up his sleeve.
THE ONLY WAY OUT OF THIS DOME IS TO PRESS THIS RED BUTTON!
So Captain Underpants pressed it.
HUH. I SHOULD HAVE MADE THAT HARDER.

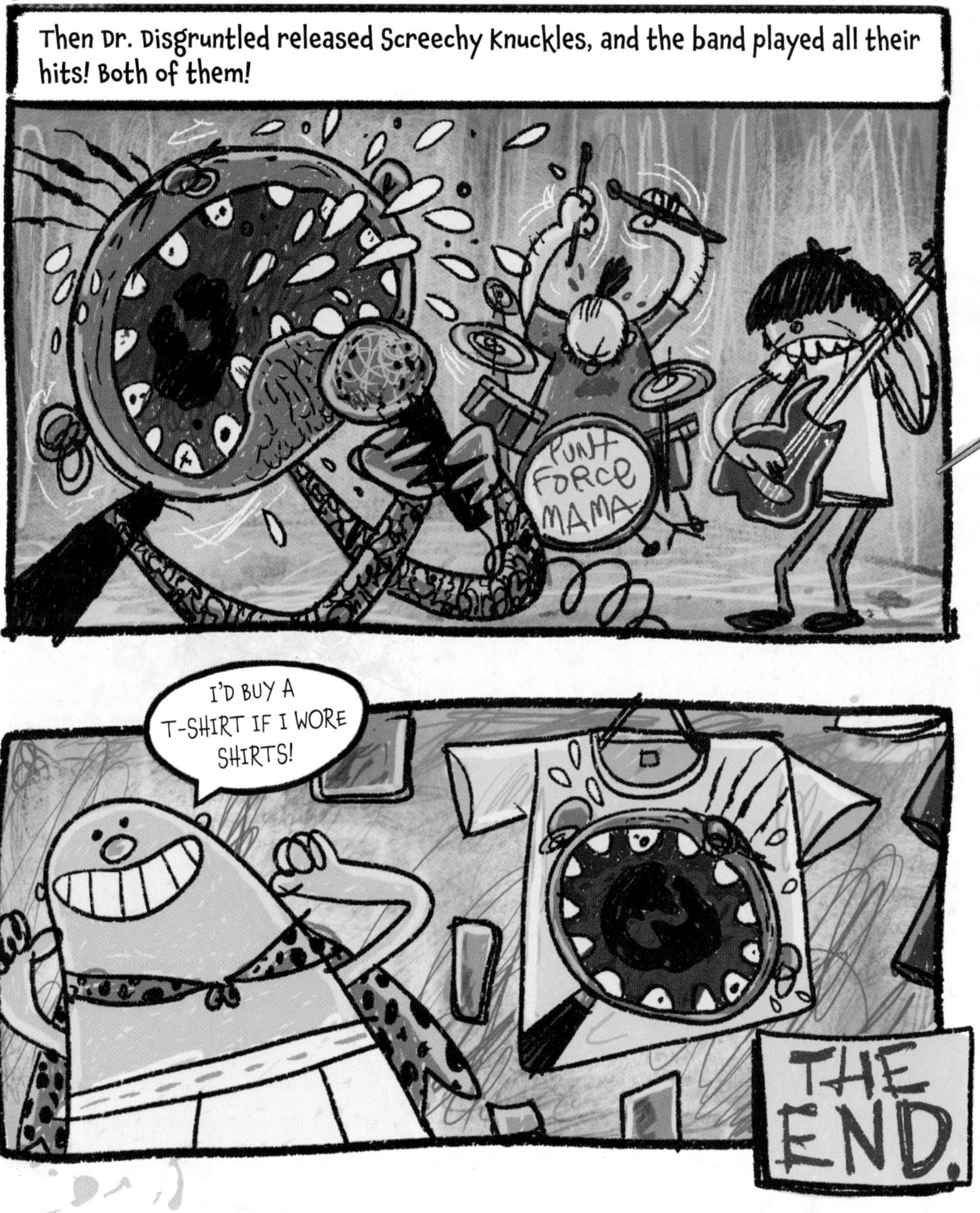
Then Dr. Disgruntled released Screechy Knuckles, and the band played all their hits! Both of them!
PUNK FORCE MAMA
I'D BUY A T-SHIRT IF I WORE SHIRTS!
THE END.

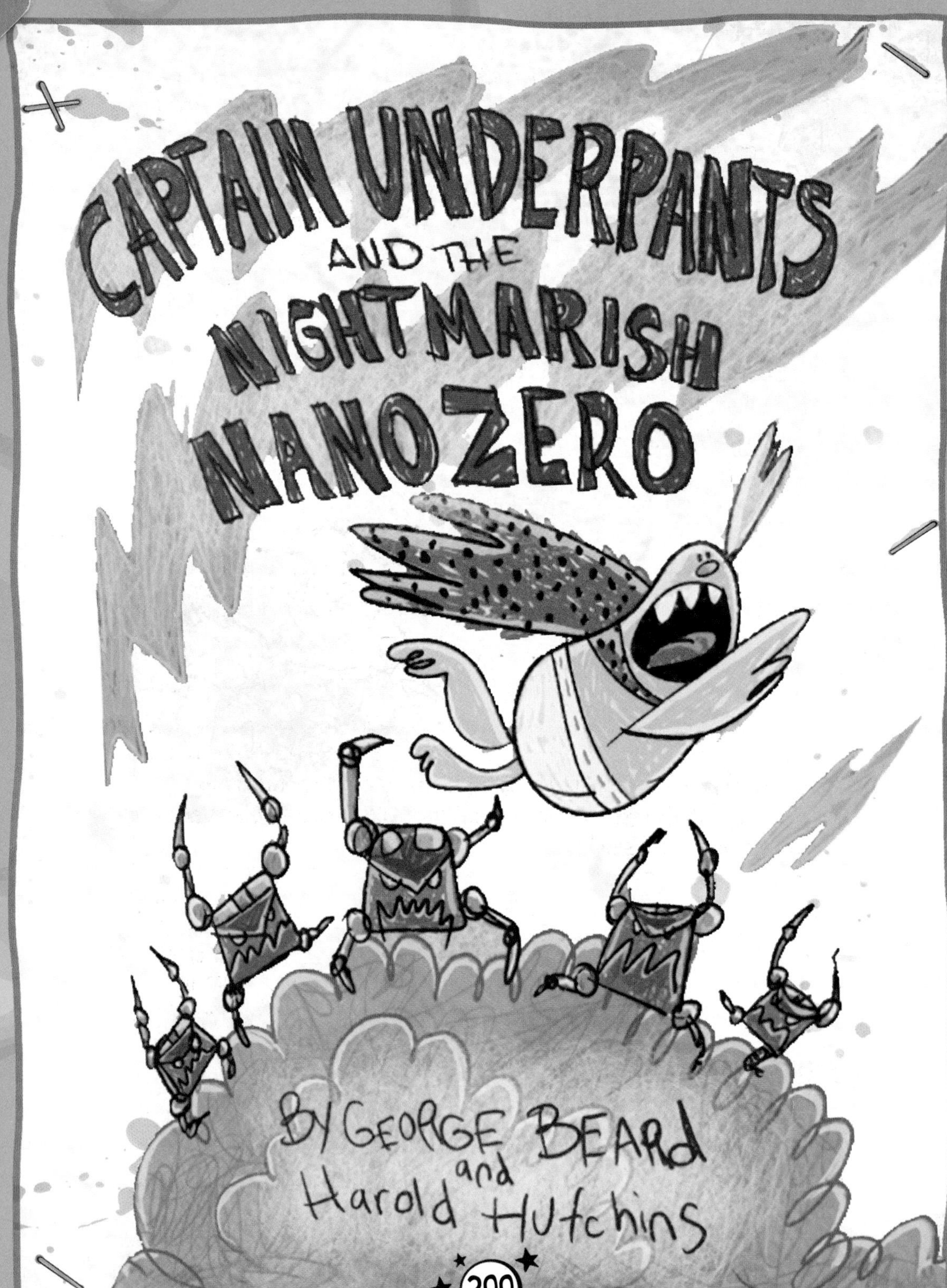
CAPTAIN UNDERPANTS
AND THE
NIGHTMARISH
NANO ZERO
By GEORGE BEARD
and
Harold Hutchins

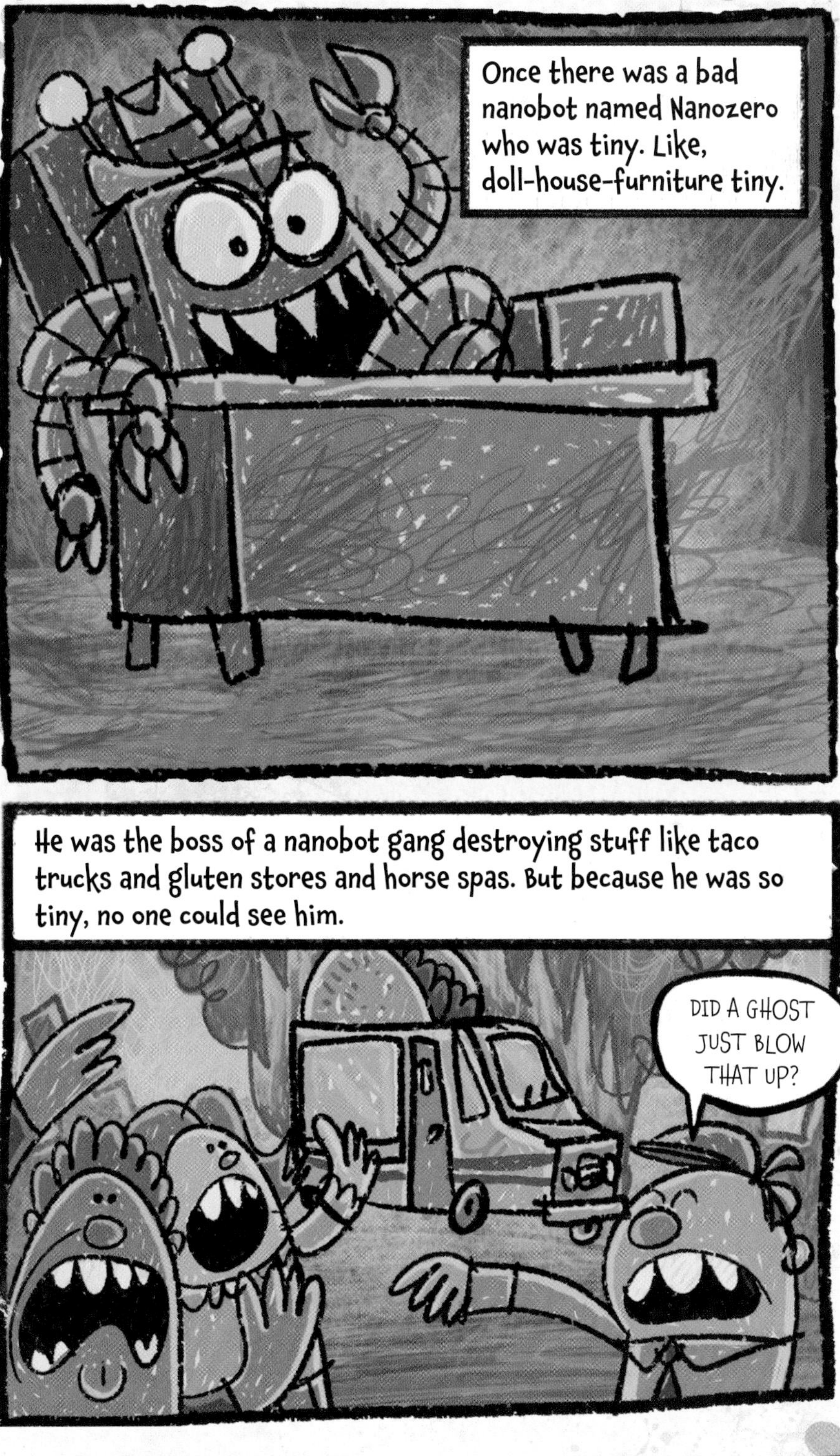
Once there was a bad nanobot named Nanozero who was tiny. Like, doll-house-furniture tiny.
He was the boss of a nanobot gang destroying stuff like taco trucks and gluten stores and horse spas. But because he was so tiny, no one could see him.
DID A GHOST JUST BLOW THAT UP?

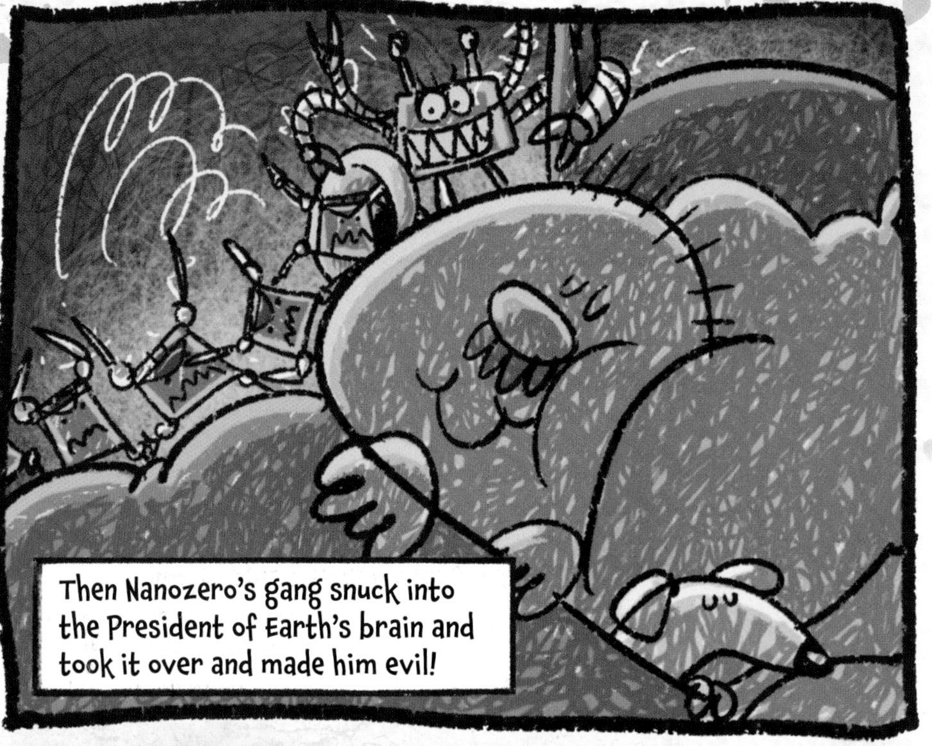
Then Nanozero's gang snuck into the President of Earth's brain and took it over and made him evil!

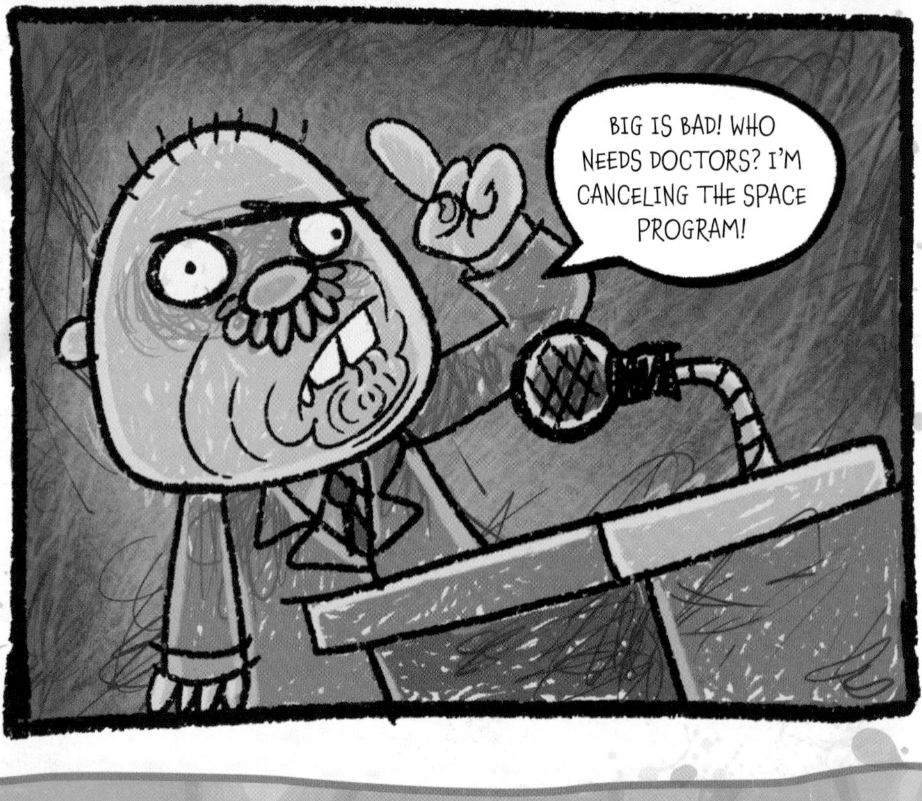
BIG IS BAD! WHO NEEDS DOCTORS? I'M CANCELING THE SPACE PROGRAM!

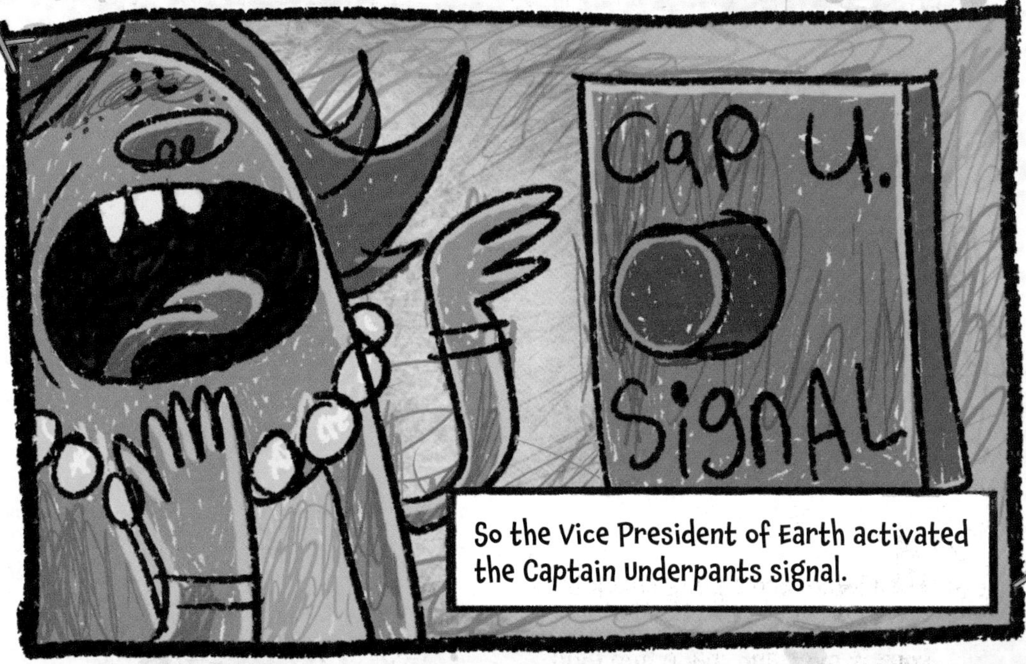
Cap U.
signAL
So the Vice President of Earth activated the Captain Underpants signal.

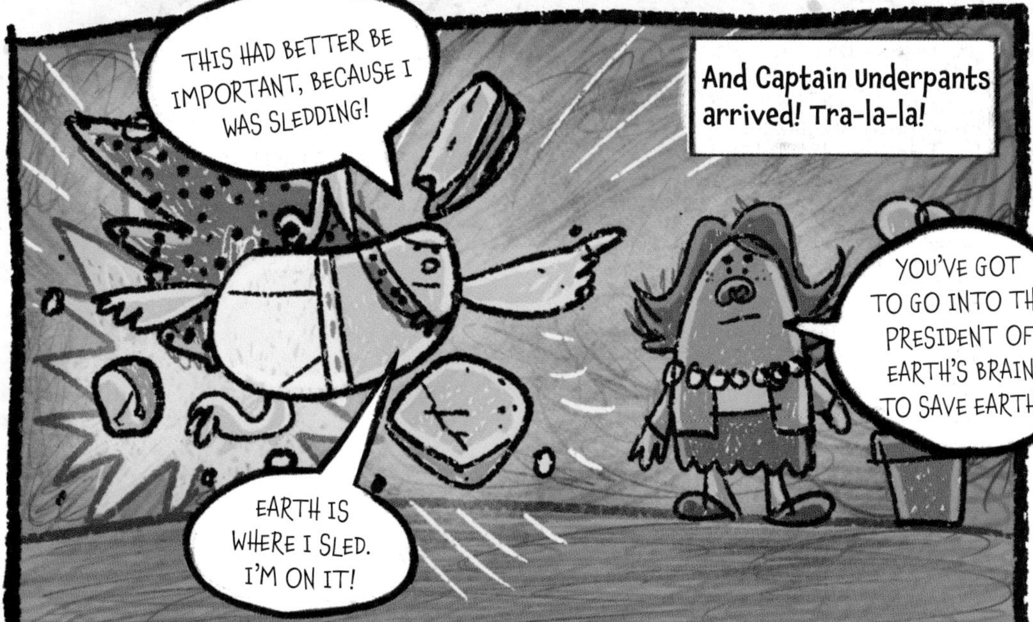
THIS HAD BETTER BE IMPORTANT, BECAUSE I WAS SLEDDING!
And Captain Underpants arrived! Tra-la-la!
YOU'VE GOT TO GO INTO THE PRESIDENT OF EARTH'S BRAIN TO SAVE EARTH!
EARTH IS WHERE I SLED. I'M ON IT!

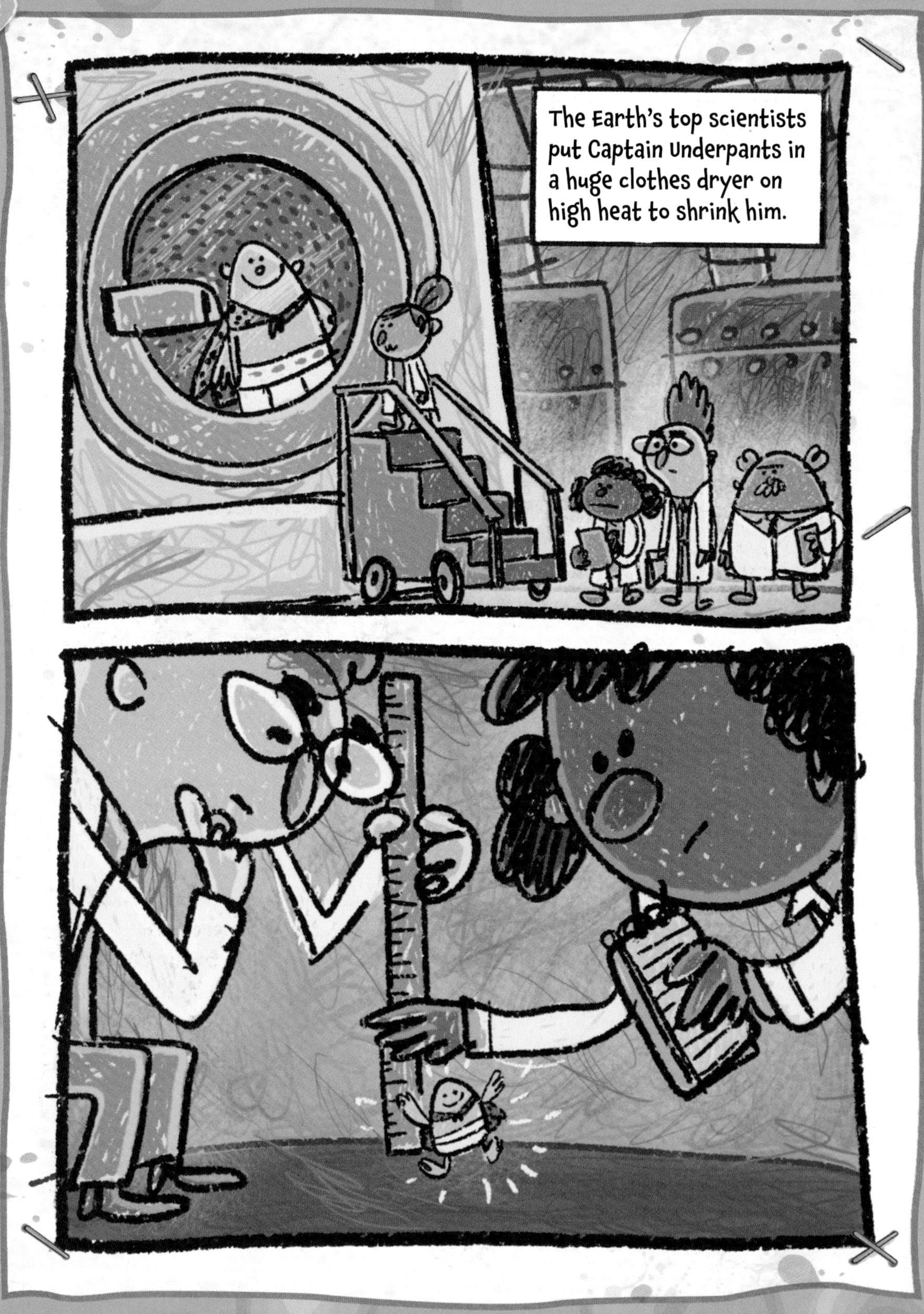
The Earth's top scientists put Captain Underpants in a huge clothes dryer on high heat to shrink him.

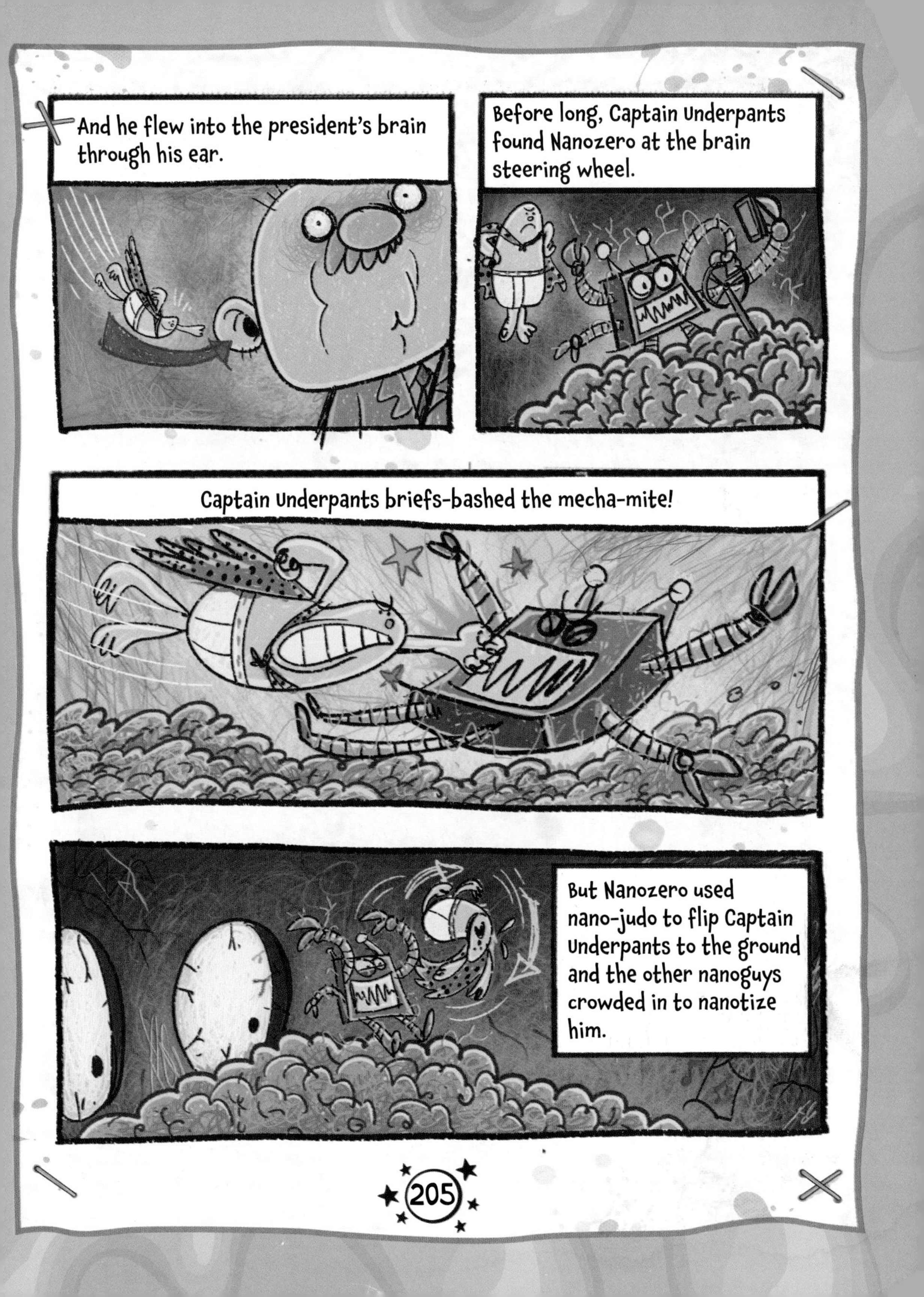
And he flew into the president's brain through his ear.
Before long, Captain Underpants found Nanozero at the brain steering wheel.
Captain Underpants briefs-bashed the mecha-mite!
But Nanozero used nano-judo to flip Captain Underpants to the ground and the other nanoguys crowded in to nanotize him.

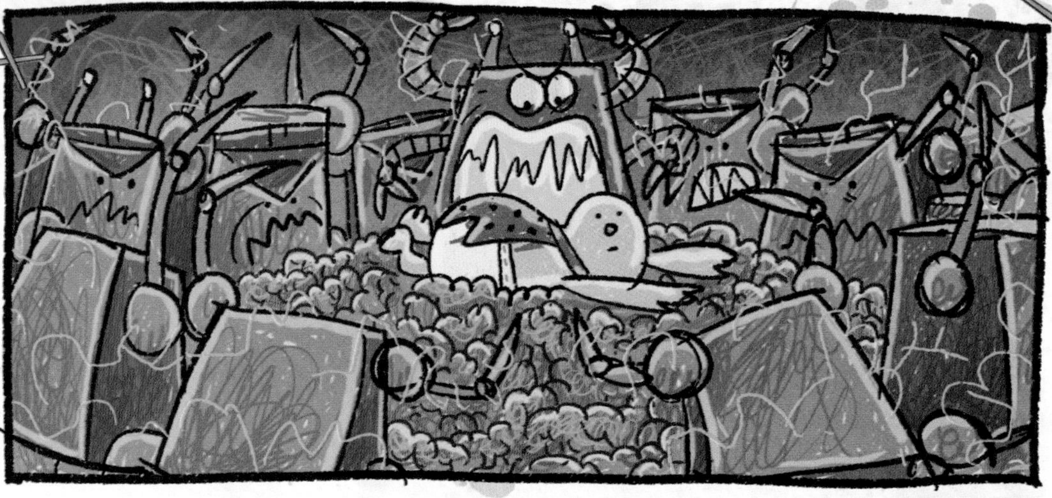

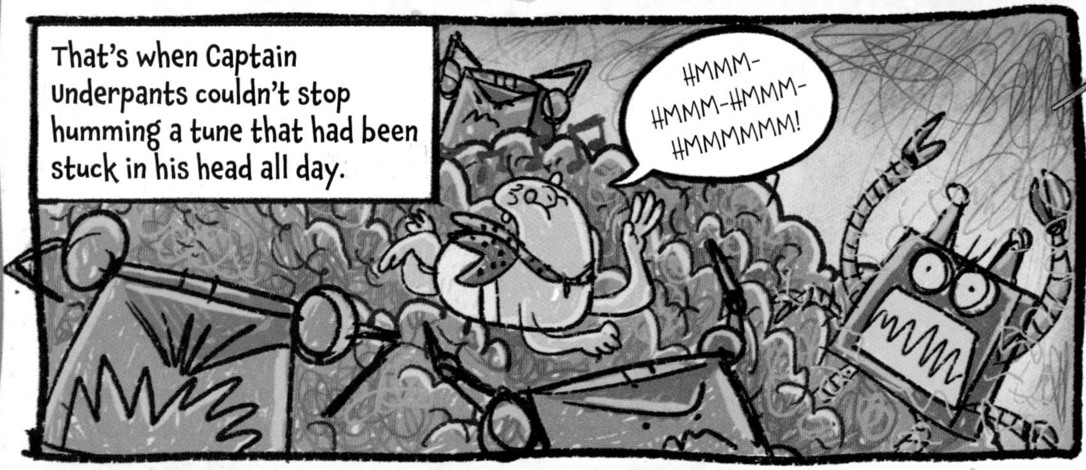
That's when Captain Underpants couldn't stop humming a tune that had been stuck in his head all day.
HMMM-HMMM-HMMM-HMMMMMM!

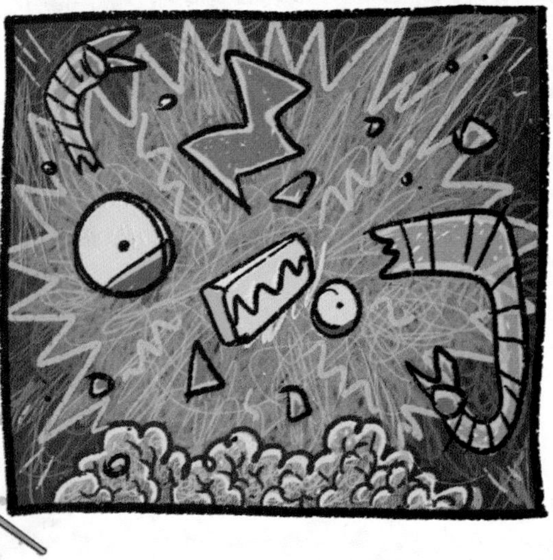

And the tune was so annoying it made Nanozero and all the other nanobots explode.

Then Captain Underpants stretched back to normal like a sweater. And the President of Earth was so happy he made Sledding Day a holiday. But not for schools.

The END!

THE EPIC TALES OF CAPTAIN UNDERPANTS

ALSO AVAILABLE:

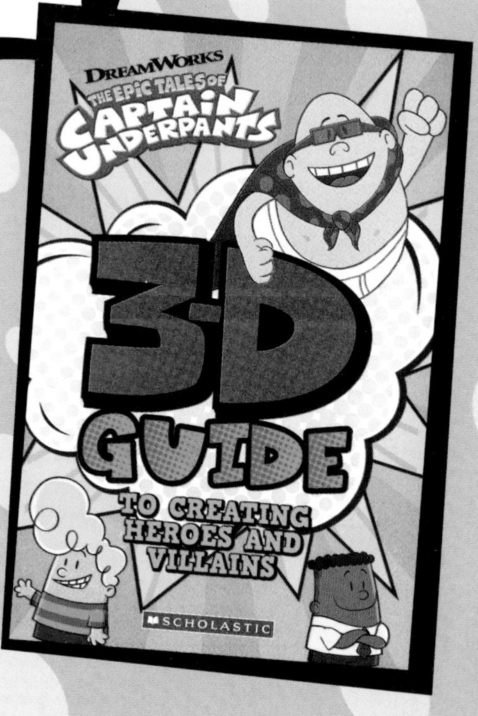
DREAMWORKS
THE EPIC TALES OF
CAPTAIN UNDERPANTS
3-D
GUIDE
TO CREATING HEROES AND VILLAINS
SCHOLASTIC

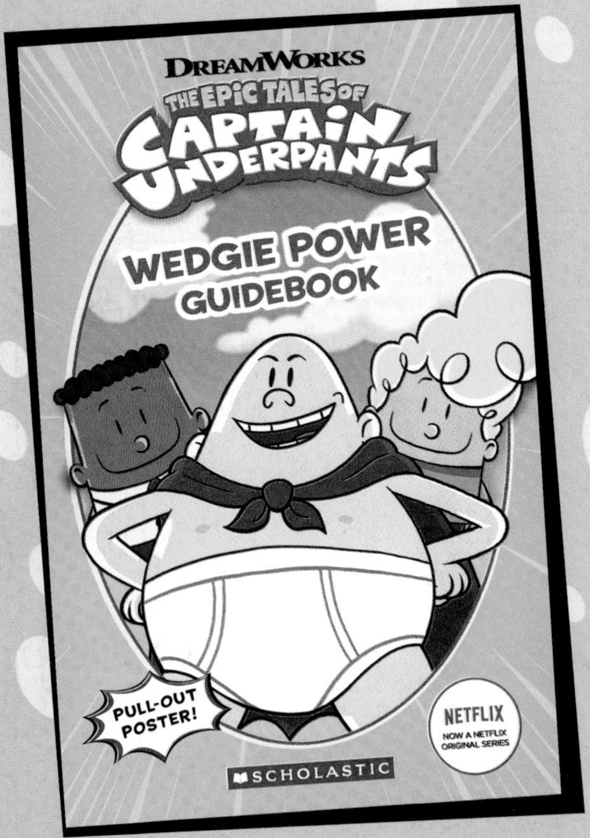
DREAMWORKS
THE EPIC TALES OF
CAPTAIN UNDERPANTS
WEDGIE POWER GUIDEBOOK
PULL-OUT POSTER!
NETFLIX
NOW A NETFLIX ORIGINAL SERIES
SCHOLASTIC